The Last Seminarian

Revised and Edited - Second Edition

By
RM DAmato

Forget Jesus,
The stars died so you could be here today.
– Lawrence Kraus

If there were no God, it would have been necessary
to invent him.
– Voltaire

The universe is change; our life is what our thoughts
make it.
– Marcus Aurelius

PART I

When the visitors first found the blue planet, they doubted its viability as a second home. Time ran out. Soon their own home would be pulled into the great, churning, black hole that fed off the galaxy with suicidal appetite. There was no turning back to Cygnus. Scores of families survived the epic journey among the thousands of people who initially crossed hundreds of light-years to find what the common traveler called the "blue speck." After many attempts to contact the blue planet as it orbited a mediocre star in absolute silence, the alien astrophysicists had given up.

Chapter 1

All in all is all we are
– Nirvana, "All Apologies"

Rico sat in front of his monitor and waited. He waited for lunch. One more hour remained. It was not that he had to wait for someone to serve him. Even though he was 90 years old, he still made his own lunch. It was part of the ritual every day to wait for the precise time to do each task. His life had been reduced to one redundant routine after another. Routines anchored his sanity. Most of the time his tasks had become vile but he needed to stay focused on his schedule. The schedule carried him from the time he turned 80 into his nonagenarian decade. Rico thought it was all bullshit.

A long life, so far, was the result of exterminating his cigarettes at 15 and picking up a bottle of wine at 80. It also helped that the newly available medication extended his life and reduced the carcinogenic poisons he had been exposed to for almost a century. He firmly believed, without proof, that sex helped, too. For a while, he moved into a retirement community where the males were spread thin, providing him the lifestyle of a sole rooster in a large, aging, and eggless chicken coop. After a long and blissful debauchery, the fun ended when his physician discontinued his erectile dysfunction medication. The drug did not turn out to be the Fountain of Youth, but Ponce de Leon would have heartily approved of its usage.

The real Fountain of Youth in St. Augustine, Florida, was a well of sulfur water that gave tourists diarrhea. He wished the same fate since he suffered from constipation. A medical order to terminate his sexual adventures came from his physician daughter, Veronica, who worked at the Centers for Disease Control in Washington, D.C. She explained that the erectile dysfunction drug interfered with some other medications he took to keep his kidneys alive and filtering the waste that was slowly killing his body. What good medical science gave him had soon been taken away.

Added to his sudden loss of a chemical libido, Rico blamed his daughter for his constipation, too. The experience depressed him no end, leaving him wondering what was the point of going on. From the perspective of Rico's existential angst, his only escape, the Retirement

Home's lonely senior women, had been brutally removed from his life. Veronica forced him out of the chicken coop. So he moved into his daughter's vacation home, under her medical orders, and received daily visitations from a nurse who was young enough to be his great-granddaughter and who, strangely and annoyingly, also reminded him of his long-deceased wife.

Occasionally, the nurse's mother followed up with a visitation as a cleaning lady and Rico found the will to sacrifice his health and devour 20 mg of contraband erectile dysfunction drug. 'If there is a will there is an erection!' he thought. Why she decided to have sex with a chemically virile 90-year-old was easy to understand. In an economically imploding America, cash did the walk and the talk. His lover never let on she was there for the cash, and Rico allowed her to pretend with false virtue and protestations until she quickly finished him off. In the end, she gratefully took the money and he felt good about the whole encounter, quite literally. Best of all, with the drug his constipation did not return. Despite his daughter's prudish admonitions and the results of weekly medical tests, the drug did not seem to interfere with his kidneys' function. In fact, he felt more energetic.

Researching his medication on the Internet and its interactions with other medicines, Rico uncovered what he had long suspected. Veronica deceived him about the drug. He lied to himself that he had wanted to be fooled so that he would not be too angry with his daughter. Of course, he was not surprised. He had played the same deception game with Veronica since she was a child. He told her once, when she was a young pre-teenager, that chocolate contained a certain amount of roasted cockroaches that fell into the tumbler during the fermentation process. The girl believed the story until she entered college. Since then, Veronica always reminded her father of how his cruel lie had denied her of the pleasure of eating chocolate for nearly a decade. He then reminded her that abstaining from the consumption of chocolate had reduced her acne and so-called baby fat. Despite her efforts, she could not rid herself of the pimply plaque.

Rico was sure that she knew about his stash of erectile dysfunction medicine and that she ignored it. He lied, and it failed to convince her. She lied about the negative interactions of drugs, and that failed too. Both of them pretended, and a tolerant stalemate existed. This polite denial of passive-aggressive behavior, while secretly derailing the other person's efforts to circumvent any prohibitions, was one of the reasons why Veronica was divorced and he was not a grandfather. Veronica's behavior drove her last three-month husband to divorce court. At the moment, she was courting her fifth husband despite the fact that she had aged beyond childbearing years and would not ever accept the option of an *ex vivo* pregnancy. On a personal level, Veronica was still like her mother and would not live an ascetic life like her father. Unlike others in society, Rico opted to live a personally countercultural existence of self-denial. It sprang from his adolescent conditioning in a subculture long gone.

"Another regret," thought Rico, bemoaning his lack of any extended progeny.

Feeling his stomach growl, Rico looked up at the digital display on his monitor which told him it would soon be lunchtime. Lately the news reports focused on private satellite launches, virtual reality advances and the upcoming presidential elections. He cared little about anything but his personal issues, such as lunch.

"It comes with age," he told himself. After lunch, he would have his weekly sexual escapade, an important scheduled event. The nurse's mother arrived in the afternoon, usually on time. Rico thought it was his right to enjoy the delights of the flesh before it eventually fell off his bones. His kidneys could stand or collapse in the process, for all he really cared. Thinking about his date, he swallowed his dose of enhancements and turned his attention to the monitor before him, tilted at a 25-degree angle towards his comfortable faux-leather chair.

He watched the continuing special on the presidential election as he sat down. The news broadcast, if it could be called news, continued to drone on with its political pundits' endless debates. Last year one of the slighted pundits brought a Taser and attacked his opponent, until security returned the favor with its own vicious form of cattle prod. The violence temporarily improved the show's rating, since most critics thought the show had been too high-brow before the fight. The recent violent exchange first appealed to Rico but soon after disappointed him for the program had lost its objectivity. Again he made a miscalculation. No news organization could achieve nor maintain any objectivity. Rico had long discovered that he needed to watch at least five stations to find the half-truth.

On the Internet it was not worth the effort, for the two major media outlets had long ago blurred out any differences between them. With his body-enhanced remote, Rico placed the settings at automatic self-direction, and the monitor adjusted itself to his posture as he slowly stood up. Walking was not too difficult yet, but the initial push to stand up took more effort each year. The monitor tilted back and forth, reading and calculating Rico's position, and then a hidden arm moved it to the right where the lunch counter sat at a 45-degree angle next to his other lounge chair. He liked eating while standing up. It gave him a strange feeling of defiance against aging. Rico felt confident. An infrared detector sensed his body heat and positioned the monitor in direct view of his eyesight. When he reached the counter, an organically processed sandwich and cup of vegetable soup appeared through a small open door on top of the counter. The temperature of the soup met his expectation of not being too hot nor too cold.

"Goldilocks would have approved," Rico mused.

Bringing the spoon to his mouth, he wondered if the taste of salt in his soup had diminished over the years due to the gustatory decline of his taste buds or his daughter's manipulation of the food processor's ingredient calibrator. He knew it was probably the latter. Then it happened once again—he had mentally conjured up Veronica on the monitor. As he took a second slurp from his spoon full of vegetable soup, with even more vegetable bits, a journalist suddenly ended the inane debate over individual carbon excise taxes and switched to the global threat of a new plague. Veronica's face appeared on the monitor, projected through a government computer cam that gave her an almost oblong appearance. Seeing her, Rico lost his appetite, knowing how she loathed speaking in public about such issues.

Veronica's face appeared almost pale, and her green eyes looked dull. Her imitation salt-and-pepper hair had been pulled back into a bun, and a hygienic blue net wrapped itself over her crown. She stared directly into the camera, expressing a passionate agenda of conviction that promised to take no prisoners. Rico had first seen that expression when she was three years old and he told her that a trip to the zoo been cancelled. Anyone on the receiving end of her disappointment or anger did not fare well. Her fifty years of mercurial anger cost her three jobs, four husbands, and thousands of dollars' worth of therapy. Focusing on the monitor again, Rico could almost read his daughter's thoughts. Veronica had been interrupted in her research and ordered to give this interview. He almost felt sorry for the journalist. Then the feelings of condolence quickly faded as Rico remembered that this particular journalist had upset him too more than once in the past.

Remembering that incident, he hoped that Veronica would be in a truly foul mood. But he also noticed that her eyes seemed to gloss over with a small hint of moisture. Never seeing Veronica in such an extremely turbulent emotional state, Rico had misgivings and trepidation. He suddenly lost his appetite and decided to walk back to his chair. Unfortunately, the monitor remained motionless and the motion driver had jammed up. Failing to move it with his remote, he reached up and pushed it. It still did not budge. So Rico angrily returned to the counter. Picking up his bowl of soup, he threw it at the monitor. A sharp clang ricocheted against the monitor's frame and reverberated across the semi-acoustic room as the polycarbonate bowl fell to the floor with a hollow, oscillating clang. Rico stepped on the bowl to stop the reverberating noise.

Looking up, he saw that the bowl's contents had splattered across the room, sending bits of soup all over the screen. Yellow droplets of soup fell like long, viscous tears. Immediately he regretted the shot until he saw how the dripping soup vandalized his least-favorite journalist's face. So instead he congratulated himself on his old-age marksmanship. The soup's liquid vegetable left an opaque glaze over the screen opposite Veronica's image. He then realized he would have to clean it before his paramour did. The extra chore could cost him more than a little money.

"I don't need the hassle," Rico concluded.

Promising himself to eliminate the inevitable recriminations from his cleaning lady, Rico watched Veronica, who had been answering some questions. He hadn't been listening until now. Rico's attention focused on Veronica's expression as he noticed that she seemed to have difficulty finding the right words to say.

The despised reporter, a middle-aged man in his sixties, wearing a cluster of small, multi-colored jewelry in his eyebrows, twitched his mouth from side to side, which moved his mustache from the right to the left and back again like some old, swaggering Keystone cop.

"So you are saying that we have a real crisis?" the reporter pressed his line of questioning.

"Yes," Veronica muttered. "This nation-state and the planet are facing a crisis. My colleagues and I are meeting with U.N. President Morales in the next hour to discuss our options."

"And the American president?" the reported countered incredulously. "Does our government have any say?"

"It has escalated to a new level," Veronica warned. "We do not know what we are dealing with. The president will be in conversation via satellite."

The reporter let out a frustrated sigh that did not affect the adhesive stiffness of his black, dyed mustache. Rico then noticed that his bleached blond hair emitted an eerie visual glow from behind the yellow, drying soup on the monitor. The wavelengths of color shifted from a deep mustard yellow to the color of a bright sunflower. Rico regretted that the monitor needed to be cleaned. What a shame!

"So," the reporter spoke in an almost condescending tone. "Let me summarize. One day…"

"No!" Veronica's shouted opposition interrupted him. The poll meter at the bottom of the screen spiked up. The audience loved confrontations. "Shut up and listen."

"Good thing the audio condenser was working," Rico thought, taking a bite from his sandwich. He wanted to laugh at Veronica's impassioned interruption but he stopped himself just before choking. Although her outburst amused him, he became more concerned, not recently having seen her as intense as the time when he had forgotten to pay her prom fee in high school.

"This isn't a normal virus!" she warned with a wide gesticulating swing of her arms. She unintentionally rapped the monitor cam hard, knocking it to the side. Instantly she righted it. "You have to understand."

Rico watched and began to whistle out loud. He knew she was in a rage but he felt his anger also climb, knowing that the reporter had baited his daughter. Veronica's reputation for passionate outbursts provided the news broadcast an excellent opportunity for hours of entertainment. She walked into a trap. As always, her feelings had suppressed her common sense.

"Go ahead," the reporter courted her with a sarcastic grin. "Explain it, Doctor."

His calm invitation masked the excitement of having a government research scientist lose her composure and maybe have a breakdown during the midday broadcast doldrums. The reporter woke up that morning worrying about how boring this interview would be and how it would continue to hamper his career. He doubted the staff and editorial board who told him about Veronica's rumored bad temper. Now, he possessed the old definition of a news scoop. Not only was there a potential viral threat, which he doubted since the agency had been actively lobbying for more funds for weeks, but he had something better than a mega-death wrestling match. Looking at the ratings indicator, he silently cheered as the audience numbers continued to climb. The public loved watching confrontations and texted their friends to join.

"Okay," Veronica took a deep breath and stared intently into the cam. "In Egypt, archeologists found a tomb in the deep caverns of the Valley of Death. This necropolis housed the artisans and engineers of the old civilization. In one area, many tombs were different."

"The report said 'sealed differently,'" the reporter interrupted.

"Let me finish," Veronica demanded. The reporter tried hard to suppress his grin. "These tombs were isolated far from the rest. They had a special waxy compound added to the cracks in the sarcophagus. Whoever sealed it meant to keep something out."

"And that something is the Mummy's Virus?" the reporter finished her thoughts. He suddenly realized that he had coined a new phrase and reminded himself to immediately copyright it before another rival stole it. "It's kind of like a Halloween story?"

"Why do you do that?" Veronica snapped harshly. The reporter could not hold back his large grin. "It's *not* humorous!" she lectured him but the reporter's smile barely diminished. "As I explained earlier, archeologists unsuspectingly released a virus when they broke the seal. The disease killed thousands in Egypt and went dormant in the past. This disease explains why there are gaps in the hieroglyphics of the period. Scores of recorded decades are missing. We have no immunity to this new contamination. When we analyzed those currently infected, we continued our investigation and trailed the illness back to the archeological site that is now quarantined. Now the general public has also been exposed to the virus before we could intervene. Calculating the rate of its progress, we have the potential of an international epidemic."

Rico then saw the three-dimensional graph charting the progress of the disease. At this very moment, he had doubts whether it had been a good idea to have mortgaged his old home to pay for Veronica's medical school tuition. His daughter will be the cause of panic on the street and doomsday gurus preaching apocalyptic nightmares. Despite his regret, the disease would have still remained a threat, with or without his daughter's input. He just wished Veronica was not now in the middle of the turmoil.

"Soon," Veronica continued, "we will all be infected. It will seriously impact our economy." Veronica paused to catch her breath and then anticipated the next question. "The symptoms are similar to the flu magnified one hundred times."

"So," the reporter responded flippantly, "do we all panic?" He then smiled sarcastically. Veronica glared at him, seemingly wanting to hit him. Suddenly the reporter winced from a shout going off into his earpiece. Upon receiving a cacophonous castigation, he immediately changed his tone and expression. "Seriously, what can our citizens do to protect themselves?"

"Son of a bitch," Rico muttered, regretting that he did not have another bowl of soup to throw at the monitor.

"The government will issue an advisory and…" Veronica's voice continued to transmit without any sound. The camera then switched to the reporter who seemed to be listening to additional instructions from his earpiece.

"Sorry, Doctor," the reporter apologized and the screen changed to an austere blue room displaying several national flags in the background. A mahogany podium with the Presidential Seal stood alone in the room. A large team of reporters flanked the room and the Secret Service kept them far away from the podium. "We are expecting an emergency statement from the White House. The president will soon speak to the nation about the virus, and our sources say…"

"Fuck you!" Rico shouted at the reporter and turned off the monitor. "And fuck the fucking mummies."

Moving himself away from the monitor, Rico had completely forgotten about his upcoming afternoon tryst and instead thought about his daughter's state of mind. He knew she would be enraged and he needed to call her. After stumbling through the kitchen area, he spotted the phone and recognized the flashing green light, immediately grasping its meaning. Veronica had left him a text message telling her father she would call him later.

"Stand by?" Rico sarcastically repeated to himself. He didn't want to hear the president since he expected his daughter to fill him in with the behind-the-scenes information. Her take on medical stories covered more depth than 60 hours of satellite news broadcasts. "Now what do I do?"

Tossing his sandwich, Rico sat down in his chair. He felt deflated, very old, and totally useless. It finally hit him that he was a burden, especially a burden on his daughter. He knew he was dependent and could not take action anymore. Anyway, even if he could, how would he be able to help Veronica? Rico knew he did not even have the skills to help when he was younger. All of his life he had been a history professor at the local college. Now, he had no audience, nor anyone to share his ideas with. Rico had outlived most of his friends. All he could do was sit at home and wait for the women to arrive, like a latchkey child.

It had been a long time since he allowed himself to sit around and feel sorry for himself. Then, he quickly had come to the conclusion after retirement that he needed to make the best of the situation. He tried tutoring and community services but he often felt too weak or too bored to continue any reliable and consistent schedule. Often, his "afternoon girlfriend" would say he needed to go to church. Any sanctified suggestion invited an outburst of laughter and a sneer that would cost him a romantic rendezvous. She called him the Devil and left the house. He could not grovel to some unknown superior being that he felt did not exist. It was not reasonable to give up his independent thoughts and submit to a Bronze Age god who was a character in a religious text. These thoughts killed his good mood. He decided to call the two women he was expecting and cancel his appointments for the afternoon. The drying soup would have to wait until tomorrow to be cleaned up.

Rico felt like staying where he was and waiting for Veronica's call. So he picked up his phone and sent two text messages to cancel the appointments. No one responded so he sat down and waited. While he waited, his anger and anxiety diminished and he slowly fell asleep. He knew that his caretakers would still come to the house; both the promise of money and the implied legal obligations of their contract impelled them to visit Rico. His last thoughts before falling asleep were about his daughter. Nevertheless, his nap didn't last long. A long, high-pitched buzz boomed out of every electronic orifice and reverberated throughout the rooms of his home. It crisscrossed and echoed into Rico's deep consciousness, instinctively lifting him into an upright position like a doctor's old-fashioned knee-jerk reflex test.

Rico instantly clicked the monitor on and, trying to pull himself out of a deep nihilistic shock, he grasped the remote to turn off the buzzing noise. The sound remained and he continued to press the button, hoping that it would end the buzzing noise. But the noise increased. Realizing his efforts had become futile, Rico opened his eyes again and decided that one soup bowl had not been enough. This time he would use a frying pan or a crock pot against the monitor. Spaghetti and steamed meat would add a new flavor to the gustatory experience of watching a monitor and Internet broadcasts through the veil of chicken soup. Although he told himself to stand up, he could not move. His body remained frozen while his anger began to ferment. It spoke of an unconscious rebellion—a bad sign for Rico. For the last time, Rico decided that computers would be eliminated from his life. He would extract all electronic communication devices from the house and return to the only friendly and archaic form of communication: letter-writing. Then, as he began to feel life returning to his legs, another sound surprised him, pushing him back into his lounge chair.

"Rico," a scratchy voice called. "Are you there?"

Rico looked at the monitor but could not see a face. The voice, although it came out of the monitor's speaker, seemed to be emitted from every direction in the room. The whole room and all the electronic devices had been converted to speakers with the sole purpose of pushing him to the edge of dementia. He then feared that he was experiencing a psychotic episode that was symptomatic of dementia.

"Rico!" the voice jumped up a couple of decibels. "Answer! Time's running out."

"Is it you, God?" Rico scoffed. "Tell me, you motherfucker." He was convinced that he had lost his mind.

Suspecting the voice was further evidence of oncoming dementia, Rico placed two empty soup bowls over his ears and closed his eyes shut as he had done in kindergarten when Mrs. Lee told him to clean up his spilled paint. The juxtaposing of the spilled soup and childhood paint gave Rico some hope that his mind could be kept intact.

"Take the bowls off your ears," the voice boomed. "I don't have time. We have to talk soon. Don't be a jerk. I am not God."

"Obviously," Rico bitterly dismissed the assumption. "God would use a better word than *jerk*."

The unnamed voice had not been as offensive as Rico thought it had been. For some strange reason, it had a familiar and friendly ring to it. Yes, Rico had been called a *jerk* from time to time, but it never brought a smile to his face unless it had been spoken by an old, forgotten friend. The intonation of the words could only be uttered by one person.

"Bill?" Rico answered, hearing his muffled voice through the soup bowl. "What the hell?"

"Your memory is good," Rico's friend observed. "How are you doing, my friend?"

"Friends don't scare the shit out of each other!" Rico barked, holding up the soup bowls in defiance.

"Were you hoping the soup bowls would protect you from the big, bad wolf?" Bill taunted him. "Feel okay?"

"Yeah," Rico told him, holding the bowls in his lap.

For a long while, he thought all of his friends were dead. Now suddenly, one old friend had resurrected himself. Maybe his dementia had truly taken hold? If Bill lived, new challenges waited in the shadows of his decline.

Rico knew exactly whom he was dealing with. His friend Bill started several entrepreneurial software companies and had become a billionaire. They spoke on and off up to his fiftieth birthday. Then, Rico never spoke to him again. Relationships sometimes ended unexpectedly without any bad will. He had never asked his friend for money, although Bill arranged to have reunions for years at his mansion or on his yacht. Rico always felt that Bill had a reason to be secluded when he retreated from society, and he did not wish to bother him about his motivations. In fact, Bill did not *want* to be bothered. There remained an extremely private aspect to Bill's personality that did not allow anyone to enter. Rico wondered if any of his children or wives could penetrate that wall. Maybe they never did.

"Why can't I see your face but you can see me?" Rico challenged him. "Is there a virus in the system?"

"I have had some personal health glitches," Bill said apologetically, ignoring the question. "But you know my mind is always good."

"Yeah," Rico agreed and tried to stand up in a dignified manner. Bill never spoke of his health in the past and Rico did not wish to press the issue. From past experience, he knew Bill would soon tell him what he wanted to know. "You wired the whole fucking place and can see me from every angle. Pretty cool software, you son of a bitch!" Rico turned around in admiration, nodding his head up and down. "So you are still alive? How many more of us are still alive? I haven't talked to anyone in decades."

"Four only, including us," Bill stated. "I have all your records. Do you want to see some old friends?"

"Yeah," Rico answered without thinking. He felt suddenly invigorated like a child being invited to see a traveling circus. "When? A couple of weeks?"

"Much sooner," Bill spoke solemnly. "We are running out of time."

"Aren't we all?" Rico commented to himself. A feeling of resentment against Bill's imposition swelled. "By the way, I don't like the way you pry into my life. You sometimes really bother me, you know."

"Don't worry, Rico," Bill assured him. "Your daughter will approve."

"Shit!" Rico cursed angrily, looking to find the soup bowl he had laid down. He picked it up. "I thought so. Did you talk to her?"

"At least your paranoia is healthy," Bill joked, again dismissing Rico's question. "Why is your monitor screen so blurry?"

"Worried?" Rico taunted him. "About flying soup bowls."

"Oh," Bill tried to understand. "I see you are still easily riled. Must have been the news today?" Rico refused to respond, knowing that he alluded to his daughter's interview and the government announcements at the CDC. There was a long pause, and Rico fingered the bowl with his gnarled fingers. "Can you visit me this hour? I mean get way from your nurse without too much suspicion?"

"What else don't you know?" Rico complained. "Where?"

Rico agreed quickly, not because he feared his friend or felt obligated. Rico had been contacted at a vulnerable moment, and Bill provided an escape from the melee he'd been experiencing earlier. Nothing could surpass the entertainment and creativity Bill could provide. His nurse, as Bill called her, could definitely wait. Ironically, at that moment, his caretaker was trying to reach him on his cell phone. Rico ignored the flashing light.

"An associate will pick you up," Bill said. "Just be ready."

"You mean an employee?" Rico corrected his euphemism. For some reason, Rico felt as if he were Scrooge talking to his Marley. "Are you sending me the ghost of Christmas Past?"

"No," Bill gently corrected him. "An assistant. Very trustworthy young man."

"You trust people?" Rico chided him, continuing to ignore the flashing cell phone. He hoped it would be Veronica.

"I do trust you," Bill responded with a hint of humor. Rico understood the sarcasm and chuckled. "I have only four real friends."

"We're more like preserved friends in a pickle jar," Rico joked. "Okay. But what's the rush?"

"Like I said," Bill repeated, "we are running out of time. Leave all your traceable devices behind. Anything that can find you. Bye."

The communication terminated, and Rico noticed that the recent surge of electronic noise had vanished. His cell phone ceased to ring too. Rico wondered if Bill's electric show would spike his monthly bill. "Bill will get a bill," he laughed at his own stupid joke.

But then, Rico felt some dread from the invitation. Bill could be trusted to a point but his manners were always serious and forceful. Rico knew he had an agenda. Rico momentarily suppressed his skepticism as he looked at the text message and time on his phone. Surprisingly, the message had come from Bill and not Veronica or his nurse.

"The bastard gave me a half an hour!" he spoke to himself. Then he looked up at the monitor. "Next time I'll send more chicken soup his way."

After Bill ended the call, Rico left a message with his caretaker and texted his daughter with an excuse. He hoped that they would give him a couple of hours of freedom before they called the emergency Alzheimer's rescue center. Remembering Bill's recommendation, Rico left his electronic devices and his credit cards that contained a GPS chip at home . Nothing on him could be traceable as far as he knew. But he still carried his Taser and refused to go unprotected. He would have to ask Bill about the possibility of being traced with a Taser.

In exactly half an hour, the house buzzed to life again. Bill's assistant had used the same technology to tap into every electronic device to announce his employer's arrival. This time the sound came across in lower but consistent decibels. Rico had been ready for ten minutes, not needing to comb his nearly bald head and only having to brush his prosthetic teeth. He wore his favorite black sport jacket, white shirt and low brim hat. Looking in the mirror, he smiled, anticipating Bill's reaction when he saw how his clothes imitated their austere high school uniform. Then he walked to the door and opened it. Instantly the subtle, low-pitched buzzing stopped. Without greeting the assistant, Rico took the initiative to speak.

"So," Rico announced himself. "Let's go."

The man in front of him seemed to be in his early thirties, if you lived in the twentieth century, but Rico thought he could have been in his late fifties since much age modification had been available for a couple of decades. He had long hair, tied back, and a thin-line beard. His eyes were not visible. The chauffeur wore Internet scanners, which shielded his eyes and prevented anyone from eavesdropping from behind while he manipulated information through the Internet using his retina as a guide. A thin, barely visible wire left the end of the glasses frame and entered into the rear of his skull. Under his black tailored suit, muscles flexed and rippled, showing off their artificially enhanced sinews. Like others who bought enhancers, the chauffeur demonstrated the effects of a drug that reduced the appearance of age by about twenty years.

Unlike most people, Rico had rejected the artificial enhancers, which were mostly cosmetic. Many elders rejected them but it had recently become a social stigma for younger people to reject them. The only medical enhancements Rico accepted were the ones that made him mentally and physically vital and healthy so that he could enjoy his afternoon dalliances and his books. Most cosmetic enhancements did not dramatically extend life, and Rico only cared about the enhancements that improved the quality of his life. For his critics, Rico showed off his adroit physical condition, like falling down and doing a straddle, when people called him out for being old. The demonstration always made matters worse. They would call him a freak. A "Fuck off" from Rico usually sent them scampering away. Waving the Taser helped too.

"Good afternoon, sir," the chauffeur said in an almost falsetto voice. He stood his ground as Rico tried to push himself through the doorway. "You must leave all traceable devices behind."

"I did," Rico said proudly, deciding to wait. "You're the assistant?"

The chauffeur nodded and then pulled out a small, thin, black device and lightly touched the screen. A second later, a red light flashed and a small message appeared.

"No traceable implants. Amazing for a man of your status? You have a Taser? I'm sorry," the chauffeur spoke apologetically. "You must leave it behind, although it is a good idea to carry one."

"It's traceable?" Rico inquired. The chauffeur nodded. Rico nodded back and mentally scratched off one of his many questions for Bill.

Then he took out the Taser and put it on the counter.

"Let's go before I decide to order an implant."

"Sorry, sir," the chauffeur tried to explain himself. "It's common procedure."

"And what would you do if I had a subcutaneous GPS implant? Most old folks have them," Rico challenged him. "Cut it out?"

"No," the chauffeur responded in a matter-of-fact tone. "Disable it."

"Good to know," Rico said sarcastically, taking a look at his forearm. That's where GPS implants were usually located for seniors and children.

The chauffeur stepped aside and let Rico pass in front of him. Outside, the day seemed hazy and the streets appeared to be busier than usual. No pedestrians were visible, and in fact Rico had not seen a pedestrian for at least a decade. Everyone moved about in a vehicle and exercised in climate-controlled park arenas. Only the extremely impoverished ventured outside, and Rico's home was far from the challenged zones. The Earth's environment had greatly improved in the last 30 years yet the culture rejected the benefits of cleaner air. It was not popular to be out because of old fears concerning UV and carcinogenetic chemicals in the atmosphere.

The only observable objects were birds, stray animals, and surface vehicles called grounders. The grounders moved slowly in both directions as their lithium battery motors whined loudly. Years ago, the advent of the electric car caused too many unfortunate deaths since pedestrians and cyclists did not hear the vehicles. Artificial whining sounds had been added as a safety feature but they caused an unnecessary annoyance, especially to those with sensitive hearing. It reminded Rico of the same buzzing sound that had reverberated in his home less than an hour ago. As a consequence, these noises pushed people further indoors. Worst of all, the whining noise would be audible in the grounder too.

The chauffeur walked a little ahead of Rico who followed him around the corner of the house where an aerial hover sat parked. It was not a grounder. Only companies and the rich owned hovers since the cost was prohibitive. The only time an average person hired a hover was to call for a taxi or to rent one for important occasions like funerals, medical emergencies, or weddings, but hopefully not in that order. These "flying cars," the hovers, operated with the same privilege Lear jets once did in the past century. Less expensive but more practical than a Lear jet within short distances, hovers were guided by a GPS at 100 to 200 feet above the ground, moving at up to 150 miles an hour. The driver, who was a pseudo-pilot at best, only controlled the hover at lift-off and landing. Most of the flight followed a pre-programmed plan. Since the introduction of the hover, accidents in the air had become very rare.

As Rico and the chauffeur approached the hover, the gull-wing doors sensed their approach and opened automatically. Rico entered the passenger side and hooked on the safety belts. The chauffeur then entered and spoke some commands into the console, first providing a password code. A slight vibration told Rico that the hover was operational. Unlike the grounder, a whining sound did not follow the start-up. Taking the lift handle into his control, the hover slowly rose to a hundred feet and the lift handle went suddenly limp in the chauffeur's hand as the GPS satellite took control at 150 feet above the surface street.

"I like your car, Bill," Rico spoke out loud, hoping Bill was listening. He loved new modes of transportation, especially hovers. Two years ago, Rico even went so far as to suggest to his daughter that they purchase one. She hated flying so he still waited for her to reconsider. At his age, Rico would not be given a license. "Hello? Bill?"

No one answered. Although Bill did not respond, Rico believed he could still be listening. Further, he did not care to strike up a conversation with the chauffeur, now a pilot, knowing that Bill would have given the pilot strict instructions not to answer any questions about the purpose of the trip. Nevertheless, the pilot probably knew little to nothing about the meeting. Rico knew that Bill would tell him what he needed to know—but maybe not what he wanted to know.

The journey was shorter than expected, for Rico had been caught up in his thoughts as he watched the bustle of traffic below him. The traffic was thick and he felt pleased to be above the stressful confusion. He also thought about how wonderful it was that he had reached the end of his life and would not have to struggle further against the competition and demands of neo-modern society. The increase of technology in the last 70 years had given him and others more avenues for enjoyment and productivity. But the negative effect was that technology cost more money and bundled away quality time.

In the United States, technology recreated a social pyramid scheme where those on top reaped the wealth and the privileges while those on the bottom or in the middle believed that perseverance and personal dedication would push them up to the top. Financial success awaited all who tried. It was just out of reach for most citizens. The average citizen settled for imitation and cheap technology, which straddled him with the added debt of licensing and subscriptions. Rico harbored the belief that the smart ones were those who moved away from the delusion of meaningless competition for more toys. Again, he was glad he was off life's financially challenged game board where most people lived in a merry-go-round of slave wages and inescapable debt.

A strong surge of acceleration pushed the hover up, parallel with the shaft of an obsidian building. The dark, tinted windows of the building reflected the enormous maze and confusion of the city. In the refracted reflections of the glass, Rico saw hovers flying in stilted angles like excited gnats caught in a beam of light. A jolt from the hover returned Rico to the present moment as the chauffeur took control of the handle stick and briefly guided the hover over the top of a black tarmac roof. When the hover landed, another assistant, dressed in black and wearing the same dark, wired glasses, met them. He waited solemnly for the gull-wing door to open. Offering Rico his hand, he respectfully backed off when Rico waved him away. Rico took a careful look at the two assistants and could not discern any differences in their appearance. They seemed identical in size and shape.

The new assistant gestured for Rico to follow him. Looking back, Rico noticed that his chauffeur pilot remained in the hover, speaking into the console. When the new assistant led Rico to a red circle on the roof, a small tube-like apparatus rose through the roof. A circular door opened effortlessly and they entered. Once inside, the rotating, circular door encapsulated them in a dark, cylindrical carbon composite. This elevator made a soft descent in the dark obsidian monolith beneath them before a soft, white light illuminated the interior. Then the light gave way to three-dimensional images. A hologram created an illusion of floating through cumulus clouds.

"Twenty-five," the second assistant spoke calmly.

The elevator continued to descend before stopping. Slight jerky motions told Rico he was riding in a less-than-perfect elevator while experiencing some simulation sickness. Rico was also experiencing vertigo. Fortunately, the hologram changed its background to a prairie of golden wheat briskly dancing side-to-side in the breeze. At the same moment, the elevator made a lateral move and rolled forward for several long minutes before coming to a complete stop.

Rico had heard about cross-transversal elevators but he never expected to ride in one. The door slid away and the assistant gestured for Rico to step out. He did so and the circular door swiftly closed behind him, leaving him alone in a comfortable room. In front of Rico, a monitor, 15 feet wide, seemed to be suspended in the middle of the room without any attachments. The monitor looked like a prop used in a magic show. Around the monitor rested several different lounge sofas and chairs. On one side of the room stood a table with food and refreshments. A small icon in the corner of the room labeled the rest room's location.

If anyone asked how the room was decorated, Rico could not have said for sure. He was surrounded by a virtual wall where nature scenes and landmarks from around the world gracefully appeared and disappeared. When Rico first entered the room, he was watching the Grand Canyon as it moved around him in a 360-degree direction, recreating the experience of floating in air. This time he hung suspended over the middle of the giant chasm. Then the images changed to the giant waterfalls of Iguacu in Brazil. For a split second, Rico cringed as the waters broke over the falls, giving him the impression of experiencing a gargantuan deluge smashing over his body. Experiencing again a feeling of simulation sickness, Rico could not deny that the view was spectacular. He wondered if the real falls were as majestic as the simulated ones. Nevertheless, the view stunned his senses.

"You never went there?" Bill's voice suddenly spoke. His face was not visible on any monitor or in person. Rico looked around but he did not see his old friend, eliciting the same eerie effect that he had experienced at home. "The virtual experience is beyond magnificent. Have you ever thought about virtual vacations?"

"No," Rico retorted sarcastically. "I have a successful old friend who can send me there on a hover. Right?"

The waterfall continued to spray over the cliff and crash on the rock below. Then the scene changed to a coral reef in the south Pacific. A multitude of fish, crustaceans, eels, mollusks, and sharks moved in the synchronized dance of life and death, evading and maintaining their existence against other life and all the lifeless threats from the sea. Rico often thought, when he privately waxed philosophical, how life was the inanimate world's only temporary escape from its empty existence. Eventually it faced extinction and an absurd return to its original status of simple molecules and atoms. The existence of life on Earth gave the proverbial middle finger to the rest of the universe.

"Yes," Bill agreed seriously. "But any person with resources can do that."

Rico waited for the rest of his explanation, remembering how Bill liked to use dramatic pauses.

"I can share something unique," Bill revealed.

"And I am supposed to say, 'Oh, goody!'?" Rico asked dryly. He was tired of the dog-and-pony show around him.

The scene of the coral reefs shifted to a hyper plane's view of space on the edge of the Earth's atmosphere. A thin purple line divided the realm of oxygen and nitrogen from infinite vacuum. Rico watched with awe, trying to imagine what Bill had in mind with this effect. He always hoped to travel to space, in fact it had been a life-long dream. But he still did not wish to massage Bill's ego. The less he said the more Bill would divulge. Rico remembered mentally fencing with Bill as a young man and he knew answers would come as rhetorical questions or half-truths at best. In the end, Bill would always win the intellectual argument.

"Where are you, Bill? Why are you hiding?" Rico questioned. He then waited a minute, watching the Earth slowly rotate away from the hyper plane's orbital position. "Are you out of town? Are you scared?"

"I can't come to you," Bill stated bluntly, expressing his annoyance at Rico's taunt. "I can't come to you but you can come to me. I called you here because I…died recently."

At that moment, the monitor's scene changed to Hawaii's Kilauea volcano during a violent eruption. Lava spewed out and flowed down its side against a black and eerie night background.

"Okay," Rico paused, trying to find some hidden message in his friend's admission. He believed that the word *dead* had a special or hidden meaning. Dead was not dead, obviously. He believed that his friend was using a metaphor. "This is Halloween…a trick or treat, right? Or you're the second person who has claimed to have been resurrected from the dead."

At that moment, Rico's fingers tingled with anxiety and he wished he had the soup bowls in his hands. His friend's monitor was in serious need of some hot chicken broth. Although Bill always enjoyed a friendly repartee, Rico hated playing word games.

"I am dead and the dead are now speaking to you," Bill's voice pitched up.

"And when will you give me the tablet, oh Lord?" Rico continued to taunt him. "I don't see any burning bush."

Bill waited a long while before answering and the same images continued to play on the panoramic monitor. "My mind is in the computer," Bill explained. "I was dying from cancer and I had it transferred before I expired."

Rico wanted say "Bullshit" but became distracted by the changing imagery. Watching the scenery change to a stark Sahara knoll of undulating sand crisscrossing in ripples, Rico sighed in frustration and pulled his hat off, quietly wringing it in his hands.

"You don't believe me?" Bill continued. "I understand. But you have to know something. I can't stay like this for long. My memories will soon deteriorate and I don't have a body to return to."

Suddenly, a tropical hurricane lashed a shoreline on the monitor screen and Rico began to smile to himself. The irony of the situation and its correlating images were becoming ironically apparent, predictable, and pedantic. "Nice," Rico dismissed, tossing his hat at the monitor in lieu of the soup bowl.

"It's genuine," Bill assured him. "We don't have much time. We are dying again."

"We?" Rico questioned further. "I am fine and I have my doubts about all this talk about…living in a machine."

He thought about the disembodying experience of entering into the silicon flash drives and organic prism of a computer system and its monitors. It all repelled and fascinated him. Despite a small revulsion at the thought of joining Bill, Rico wished on a deep level that Bill could offer him a hyper-speed visit to the international space station—but not in a simulator.

"You said we? Who are we?" Rico continued to press.

"Another," Bill clarified.

"Are they all in there already? Who?" Rico demanded to know. Picking up his hat, Rico slapped it angrily against his thigh.

"Only one person," Bill confided. "Juan."

"Juan?" Rico repeated, recalling his old high school friend who suffered a coma after an automobile accident. "He's still conscious? I remember him being a vegetable."

"Yes," Bill admitted. "Inside he is alive. I am giving him the life he never had, albeit a virtual one. But he'll suffer from the same consequences as me. His body has been cremated already. That's why we must move along with my plans."

"Juan," Rico thought to himself. Their mutual friend drove off a Malibu cliff a couple of days before their graduation. The result was that they never had a formal graduation, only receiving their diplomas through a postal dispersal. The tragedy caused enough controversy to almost close his school. Rico tried to stop Juan, chasing him through the canyon when his car swerved off the road. They had all been drinking on the beach and Juan drank much more than the others.

The accident paralyzed Juan and put him in a coma. He became the living dead—trapped in his body for 70 years. Some advocated taking him off life support but his Catholic parents maintained their faith that their son would recover, giving God a chance to heal him. Eventually, he came off life support in a coma. Most doctors and therapists said that there was a possibility that Juan could still see, hear, and think. Rico never witnessed it, and over time he, like others, slowly stopped visiting their friend whose parents continued to wait for God's rescue. But Juan would never be paroled from the horror of his existence until Bill's technology inserted itself into his life. This bit of news sounded apocryphal but enticing.

"The transition to a virtual word must have been more than dramatic," thought Rico.

"And you expect me to take the same risk? And die in a machine!" Rico spoke accusingly. "I know I don't have much of a life left but it's a real life." The monitor screen changed to a view of the sequoia trees towering hundreds of feet above the Sierra Nevada ridgeline.

"You will be sent back with no problem," Bill assured him. "My doctors checked your medical records. You will be able to survive the transition. Rico, listen, you can still live out there for a decade or more. We have only nanoseconds in here, which will seem like a week to you. Give us a try. Please. It will be our final reunion. Maybe we can set things right? It's an opportunity."

"And maybe have a graduation?" Rico chided. "How nostalgically nice of you for working on my guilt. That's what you mean about setting things right? I am not responsible for Juan."

Bill did not answer. Bill, like all of their classmates, knew that Juan's accident had had a dramatic effect on Rico and Rico had blamed himself when he was young. But Bill never knew that Rico had come to terms with his guilt, deciding that Juan was his own agent of misery and destruction.

Rico continued to watch the giant trees as sunlight pierced the thick canopy and wavered on the pine needle floors below. A black bear approached one tree and investigated its surroundings. Soon cubs followed the mother to another location behind another tree. Slowly they disappeared under the forest's umber as if the deep shadows absorbed them into a nihilistic trench.

"And are there any other friends who will join us?" Rico asked anxiously, turning his attention away from the forest.

Rico did not wish to see Juan again but felt that Bill might be hiding a special reason he would not be privy to unless he agreed to Bill's terms. Instinctively, Rico thought the trip to the simulator might be a vicarious purge for old guilt and resentments. Memories of those feelings of guilt once again welled up as Rico turned his attention to the monitor. Studying the images of sequoias, he wondered how tall many of the surviving trees were that still existed, for they had once extended themselves in every direction for miles out in the woods of central California. The current surviving sequoias had been decimated by the global changes in weather patterns that brought parching draughts to the Pacific coast. Once, when Rico was a young boy, some of the fallen trees even served as tunnels for passing cars and homes for animals and hikers.

"Mike," Bill uttered. "I convinced him yesterday."

The mentioning of Mike shocked Rico. He had thought his classmate had died years ago. He once heard that he had terminal cancer. Why did Mike survive the cancer and not Bill? Few people actually died of cancer unless it had metastasized beyond medical intervention. Bill's explanations made him skeptical.

"He entered a Trappist Monastery and led a sequestered life. He wanted to be dead to the world after he retired from the diocese," Bill added.

"Same old shit," Rico mocked. "So my old classmate Mike will lecture me about spiritual bliss and repentance in the bowels of silicon chips and organic pixels. How wonderful! How ironic! Actually, it will be interesting to listen to his rationale for having a soul while floating in a memory chip. His explanation of how a god would permit the technological capture of his spiritual essence will be fascinating. This may be entertaining. Hey, how did you convince him?"

"I mentioned one word," Bill revealed.

"Juan," Rico understood. "You are a bastard. You pulled off the same trick. What if Juan had died? You knew we wouldn't go, didn't you?"

"Well?" Bill asked again. "What's your answer?"

"How can I refuse the party?" Rico agreed and opened his crinkled cap and placed it on his bald head. "You know it's awfully weird to have this mix of individuals from our past. We were all so different."

"You forget," Bill corrected him. "We were all the same too."

"Really," Rico doubted. "I just want my body back and not trapped in the machine. How long am I staying in the machine?'

"For an hour your time," Bill blurted. "But once you're inside, it will seem like five days."

"Five days," Rico repeated to himself. The monitor's scene changed once more to a brilliant sunset on some Caribbean beach with sailboats and palm trees in the background. "So, when do the games begin?"

"Tomorrow," Bill told him. "I want to tell you that you are doing me a personal favor. Thank you."

"Am I doing myself a favor, Bill?" Rico challenged him, remembering Juan's accident and the tragedy that he and his friends had experienced. Bill remained silent. "See you tomorrow. Time?"

"Be here at eight," Bill announced. "You'll have to sign some papers. We will put your body in suspension. I'll contact Veronica later when you are transferred back."

"Yeah," Rico considered the possibility. "She will appreciate it." Then he remembered the international health crisis. "What are you not telling me, Bill? Is this pandemic a part of the deal?"

"No," Bill countered. "It's all really about us only."

"And what do you expect to find out?" Rico continued to press.

"The final outcome? We will be able to create that," Bill told him. "This reunion will have open software parameters. Everything will be driven by our imaginations and feelings. We write the story in here. The conclusion…will be an open book. You'll see."

"And then you and Juan die?" Rico concluded. The setting sun on the monitors disappeared and went blank.

"We'll make our arrangements," Bill admitted reluctantly. "Maybe inside? It's something for us to talk about later. Okay?"

"Mike will have his objections. Spiritually speaking. You know that!" Rico reminded him. "I bet you didn't tell him."

"No. I didn't," Bill reluctantly admitted.

"No," Rico smiled mischievously, understanding the coming confrontations. "That will all be part of the fun, won't it? And all the other things you haven't told me or Juan either?"

"We'll do our best. I am sure of it," Bill said confidently. "You have to trust me for a change."

"I can trust," Rico misquoted an Old Russian adage, "but I won't be able to verify. Will I?"

"See you later, my old friend," Bill signed off abruptly.

His sudden disappearance struck Rico hard. He felt that Bill had dismissed him like an elementary school student without any regard for his feelings or thoughts. A slow eruption of anger swelled in his chest as Rico tried to push it away. But despite his effort, the anger broke over his consciousness.

"That's it?" Rico challenged Bill and a blank monitor. Only silence remained in the room. Rico took a look around the room, picked up an apple on a small table, and stood quietly in front of the monitor. He placed his hat on his head. "Hey! Fuck you, Bill! I hope I can kick your ass in a virtual world."

Bill did not respond and the lounge door to the elevator slid open. No one stood inside. Rico took a last look at the blank monitor before stepping into the elevator and biting into the apple. He finished it when the chute pushed up through the ceiling and opened on the roof. The trip in the elevator was very different. In fact, it was ordinary with plain dark panels and a simple key lock that opened to a secure control panel. A bright light shone through the polymer ceiling and Rico could see his reflection in the panel's reflective carbon surface. He looked at his sagging and aging body and wondered if Bill would replace it with a simulated young body. If Juan could interact with them, according to Bill, the possibilities would be endless and maybe intimidating or frightening.

Once outside, the same hover awaited him, and the chauffeur sat inside behind the handle stick. Before entering the hover, he took a final bite out of the apple and threw it onto the tarmac. The pilot did not move or express any disapproval at his littering. He then sat down, attached his safety harness, and watched the tarmac shrink away from underneath him. On the way home, Rico thought about Bill and what had just transpired. He played the words over and over in his head, trying to uncover some hidden message or clue.

Rico had never heard of or read about any institution or eminent person transporting a person's conscious to a machine. Bill told him about this impossible venture because Rico was too jealous to share it with anyone. Deep down, Rico wanted to know if he could meet his once-dead friend. He would not jeopardize telling anyone of the experiment and sabotaging a chance to interact with Juan. Only his friendship and trust compelled him to return to meet with Bill and his friends, who would try to make sense out of a tattered part of their youth. How many people would have that chance?

"Don't pay any attention to the man behind the curtain," Rico muttered, paraphrasing a line from his favorite childhood movie. Rico knew he would have to pay very close attention to Bill's antics and motivations. Tomorrow, he would pierce the mirror darkly and enter a virtual world, neither dead nor alive. Whether or not he resided in the computer for one real hour remained to be seen.

Chapter 2

Your wise men don't know how it feels to be thick as a brick.
– Ian Anderson, "Thick as a Brick"

It was early in the morning when Rico awoke. He showered and had breakfast. Then he sat in his lounge chair and watched the news. No mention was made of Veronica, but the news shifted further away from the presidential race and more attention focused on the growing epidemic. More evidence of the disease's progress increased overnight. Disgusted with the drama of the news and endless speculation, he turned off the monitor, finished his coffee, and stood up to pour another cup. Everything had been uneventful since Rico spoke to Bill. The previous evening was uneventful for him. When he arrived home, the house had been visited and cleaned. Chicken soup no longer smeared the monitor.

"What a shame," Rico thought out loud.

His cleaning lady and nurse appeared to ignore his message, and Rico wondered if they had tried to contact Veronica. When Rico checked his messages, it seemed as if they had not tried to contact him or Veronica. His intermittent lover just came and did her job. The chicken soup probably upset her to the point that she was glad that Rico was nowhere to be found.

"I guess our funds are up to date," Rico sarcastically commented to himself.

He returned to his chair and sat down with his second cup of coffee. Looking up at the dark monitor, Rico caught a glimpse of himself in its reflection. Inside he felt like the same person he had been as a young man. Despite his feelings, the reflection reminded him that he was an old man.

"What an old fool you are. I guess there's not another type of fool," he thought.

Rico's daughter sent a simple video message the day before: "Busy. Don't worry. All is under control." He reread the message and understood that she would remain incommunicado for a long while. They had agreed to use certain words to communicate important messages. "All is under control" meant "Don't call me. I'll call you!" Neither Rico nor anyone else could contact Veronica unless the government granted her leave or permission. Rico could still contact his daughter if he wanted to but he decided to let it go. If Bill told the truth, he would be back in a few hours and then he could talk to her. Otherwise, if Rico never returned, what would it matter? His daughter would have one less problem to deal with. She was busy saving the world. Rico seriously believed the world should not be saved.

He shook his head and turned on the monitor again to avoid seeing his reflection. This time he switched the channel to a nature program. Leaving Bill's company, Rico felt as if his life changed again. He suddenly was embarrassed by his feelings of self-importance as an object for a younger woman's love. After returning home, Rico felt that most of what had recently been important to him was not very important anymore. And it was not just his conversation with Bill that changed his perspective. It only confirmed what he always felt and knew but had denied to keep himself distracted. Happiness had been difficult for him.

The word "happy" had so many connotations but now he could not find one for himself. A feeling of worthlessness overcame him. When he felt this despondent, Rico had learned to divert his attention, but this time the sadness and embarrassment could not be easily dismissed. Discovering Juan's existence and his plight brought forward deeper roots of regret and fear. Bill wanted too much and Rico risked too much by going into the machine and socializing with nearly extinct twentieth-century men. The risk did not lie in the fact that he was transporting his mind into a machine. The very concept was still unbelievable.

What annoyed Rico was the fact that he had to confront a time in his life when foolishness made up the greater part of his personality and character. Worst of all, his immature behavior with the monitor and his caretaker told him that he still had not overcome a certain amount of his young foolishness. In the past, years after Juan crashed his car, the thought of youthful indulgence most comforted Rico as a young and justifiably foolish boy. But now he knew himself better. Juan's death was indirectly his fault, and he could have stopped the accident if he had intervened. Instead he laughed at Juan at the wrong time, and so he was actually was in the wrong.

All these years, he convinced himself of the lie that he was not responsible for Juan's debilitating accident. Everyone made him understand it was the priests' fault for not supervising them properly. Then he was told that Juan had made his own decision to drive recklessly back to the Valley. Rico knew the real truth that only he and Juan shared, a single ridiculing laugh operated like the proverbial butterfly wing that set off a chain of unpredictable and regretful events. But the truth would have to wait until he talked to Juan again, and Rico would have to face himself in the process. The journey to Bill's office would be like a prisoner's walk to the gallows— a walk Rico would dread more than death.

"If I wake up dead in the machine," Rico told himself with false hope, "then I don't have to do this, whatever it is." The chances of his waking up dead were good but not great. This grim conclusion caused him to sink deeper into his despondency. At the same moment, he noticed on the monitor that the nature show ironically covered the famous waterfalls of Brazil—the same falls he had seen earlier. So he quickly switched the channel to an old sitcom from the 2020s. The show's fake laugh track could not ease his mind as he played back the last moments before Juan took his car keys and drove off. A loud burst of laughter jolted him, for it coincided with a loud buzz. Rico recognized the disturbing electronic sound to be identical to the one Bill sent the day before.

"We're ready to go," Bill announced.

Rico did not respond but put down his coffee cup, stood, walked up to his daughter's digital portrait, and turned on the chronology cycle which displayed her growth from infancy to adulthood in a subtle progression. The playback created the illusion of seeing a child naturally mature.

"Bye little one," he said silently.

Rico's eyes began to moisten as he shuffled towards the door. He took one look back. He felt very old and defeated at that moment but he could not say no to himself and the others. He owed it to himself and his youth—a temporal youth that would be synthetically reincarnated in a lab directed by a mad scientist who was playing God. Rico wondered if Bill was mad, and he wondered if the others knew too. Maybe they were all mad. Maybe the virtual reality they would step into would induce a permanent madness in its participants.

"It will be fine," Bill reassured him, reading Rico's skeptical thoughts.

Rico ignored him. After the third buzz, Rico opened the door and stepped out without looking back. His escort was a different man who took the same path to the obsidian building. They rode the elevator down to another section. They did not exchange a word. A nurse and a man dressed in a conservative suit, a lawyer, met Rico, who sat and signed a list of legal forms that waived Bill's responsibility and the responsibility of the company. The last document bequeathed an amount of $500 million to him and his heirs after Rico returned to his body. The beneficence shocked him. He thought about his daughter and the fact that he had nothing to lose at this point in his life. Veronica would be taken care of. So he signed the forms.

Then, the medical staff cleaned and sterilized his body in a hyperbaric-type chamber before whisking him to another medical room, although it looked more like a room that housed computer servers. Rico remained in the chamber while doctors and technicians ran some scans. An IV had been inserted into his arm and he felt the calming effects of a mild sedative. Then, several technicians attached probes to his head and a device over his right eye. The instrument looked like a small scope. Over his head, with his exposed eye, Rico watched a thin, platinum-colored metal skin being slipped over his forehead. It adhered to his skin and Rico felt as if it had grafted itself and dissolved into his skin as it tightened firmly over his eyebrows.

"Sir," a female doctor spoke to him. "I'm Dr. Singh. We are ready."

Rico nodded and smiled faintly. He waited. A small pulsing light from the scope blinked slowly and then rapidly.

"See you soon, my friend," Bill promised in a distant, soothing tone.

Rico moved his head to see if Bill were there, but the technician gently pushed him back down.

"You will feel light-headed but will not be unconscious. Try to focus your mind on one thought or object. It will make the passage easier," she gently suggested, guiding him through the process. "We will begin soon."

The light continued to blink and Rico lost vision in his left eye. He could hear the doctors and technicians working and giving instructions but he could not understand any of their words. Slowly the voices and sounds began to distance themselves and Rico could only hear them faintly. He then heard nothing except a low whistle that reminded him of a dog whistle.

Rico remembered the doctor's instructions and tried to concentrate on an object. He thought about his first car and how good it felt when he drove it over the 100-mph mark and then tried to push it beyond 120 mph, pressing the accelerator, the dial on the speedometer inching forward like the staggered hand of an antique mechanical watch. When the dial reached the 110-mph mark, a loud wheezing sound pierced Rico's ears and the red blinking light turned blue. He felt his body being compressed down into a small funnel and his chest heaved, fighting for breath.

Panicking, Rico desperately gasped for air but he could not inhale. The increasing pressure was so strong that Rico felt as if his body were being squeezed into a long and narrow tube. There was no pain but Rico knew he was not breathing. He was awake but his body felt no life. Only a blue light flashed before him and wrapped itself around his consciousness. In an instant, the light stopped and Rico took a deep breath. His chest heaved. He opened his eyes on a green lawn facing the façade of his seminary high school. There were no instruments on his body, and he was dressed in the uniform of his school day—black trousers, black socks and shoes, and a white, starched shirt and black tie. Holding up his hands, Rico saw that he was a young man again. At least he appeared to be young, for inside he felt that the journey into the simulation had added another 90 years to his lifespan. Rising off the grass, Rico cautiously walked towards a building he had not seen in over half a century.

He had more spring in his step but his mind could not catch up to his young body, or perhaps fall back to his young body. Energy flowed through his body, and his mind addressed it skeptically as if it had suddenly been diagnosed with terminal cancer.

"But I am old, not young. It can't be." Rico felt intuitively that he would need time to learn to be young again but the luxury of time in the simulator would be limited. The grass felt real under his feet and he paused to touch it. It had the rough, prickly feeling of California grass that had been artificially irrigated through a summer of stinging heat and suffocatingly dry desert air. The school stood in the far northern county of Los Angeles, a one-hour drive to the Mojave Desert.

When Rico stood up, he noticed that the sky had a gray and brown haze that wrapped itself around the surrounding brown and gray mountains of the valley. Smog had been almost unknown for decades and its appearance and smell made his eyes water. He immediately hated it. Taking a breath of air was stifling and annoying. Any exercise in this environment would cause asthma-like symptoms. When he was younger, he often collapsed from the irritating smog after a track event, wheezing and coughing for long minutes. But his recollections were interrupted when a long line of slowly moving cars suddenly appeared and began to park in front of the building. The cars resembled models from the late 1960s and early 1970s. Some pumped white and gray smoke out of their tailpipes as they idled. The scene resembled a tailgate party without the party. Seeing that the sun was low in the sky, Rico surmised that it was early evening in late summer.

The architecture of the building imitated the eighteenth-century colonnaded building of the Catholic colonial mission next door. An adobe-type, three-story tower stood in the center-right of the building and a dark, bronze bell hung in the middle. Some light cracked through the space between the bell and the arch that supported it. In Rico's time, the bell never rang. After his second year at school, it was removed for unknown reasons during summer vacation, leaving a vacancy where it had once hung. Rico realized he was witnessing his very first day of high school after the Labor Day holiday. He froze for a moment and then slowly walked backward to the place where the cars suddenly appeared. Expecting them to vanish when he passed by, the cars did not leave the scene. Watching the cars for a moment, he saw that there were no students or parents inside them.

"I tripped the wire," he thought to himself. "Let's see the rest of the pageantry."

Feeling a little more confident about his body's ability to take some stress, he pushed his legs forward and was able to make quick strides across the lawn. A small circular driveway marked the area in front of the seminary's building. In the middle, the flagpole stood with the unfurled flags of the United States and the State of California. The U.S. flag had fifty stars and not 53 like the present banner. So Rico knew that Bill had set the date to 1972—his first day of high school. When he stepped onto the asphalt driveway, the cars allowed him to pass but they did not stop their hesitant movement. The effect was surrealistic. Then another action occurred. Young students and adults began to instantly appear and exit the cars.

The parents opened the trunks with their keys and pulled out suitcases as students either helped them or greeted passing friends and acquaintances. The freshmen usually stayed close to their parents, while the seniors simply parked their own cars in an asphalt lot farther behind the flagpole. Everyone interacted and responded with the typically familiar enthusiasm and dread of young adolescents returning to their first sequestered day in a place practically absent of women. Their uniforms gave them all a regimented appearance that masked their anxiety. Rico paused and watched and then moved cautiously again. The experience shocked him. It also scared him.

As he watched the parade of students moving en masse toward the seminary's arched glass doors, he realized that he remembered each of their names and the names of their parents. Every detail about each student could be recalled. After seventy-six years, he could do the impossible. He tried to remember and recall other facts and he did. He remembered everything about his first day, even his schedule for the next day of classes. The seminarians usually checked in on a Sunday night and slept the evening before, attending class the next day. But unlike the first day of school, no one spoke to him or greeted him. When he reached out to touch a student's shoulder, the student simply ignored Rico and continued as if he were a zombie. So Rico struck one of the students hard and the student continued to move nimbly to his prearranged destination, ignoring Rico's presence. Rico could not effect any change to the program.

"What's the point?" he asked out loud when he reached the red brick steps in front of the three archways.

"Do you know where we go first?" a student asked him.

Shocked, Rico turned around and saw his friend Chris. His shirt had never been bleached, displaying a light gray shade. His red hair was unkempt and he wore a hand-knit black tie. Chris smiled and waited for a moment. Rico simply stared at him.

"Thanks," he said and walked away as if Rico had given him an answer. Chris's greeting exactly replayed his meeting on the first day of school. Rico even remembered what he told him, although today he did not say a word.

"In the chapel," Rico repeated his past words as Chris walked far ahead through the arched doors. Then he turned around and watched his parents wave to him. A brown vinyl suitcase appeared at his feet and Rico waved foolishly back to his tearful mother and stoic father who entered a '62 Chevrolet Bellaire station wagon, slowly drove around the flagpole, and exited the area. He tried to call out to them but they continued to move away.

Not bothering to interact with his preprogrammed parents, he watched them drive away and then noticed that most of the other cars had also driven away. Most of the students who were loitering on the front steps had entered through the archway. He surprised himself by feeling nothing on seeing his parents' hologram. Then he felt a slow surge of anger and resentment, knowing that these strong feelings would have to be addressed later. His parents' decision to admit him to the school irritated him for decades. Turning his attention away from their diminishing car, Rico picked up the suitcase and thought about its contents and whether his adolescent or current possessions had been packed.

He entered the white alabaster entrance through the arched glass doors. Inside the building, the chapel stood directly in the middle. Two atriums flanked the chapel, and some students in the center of the left atrium stood next to a bronze copy of Michelangelo's *St. Peter Holding the Keys to Heaven*. Directly in front of Rico, an elaborate mosaic of the twelve apostles hung on the chapel's façade. Six of the apostles stood to the left and six on the right. They all had cold mosaic stones inlaid above their heads and all the figures were vibrantly decorated. Rico remembered the mosaics and still remained impressed with their fine craftsmanship.

He recognized another version of St. Peter who held his famous, or maybe infamous, keys. Next to St. Peter stood St. John, the only apostle who looked as if he could enter the school as a student. The other figures appeared to be either Social Security recipients or semi-retired trailer-park residents, heavily medicated with heavenly bliss. Rico noticed an effect that he had long forgotten. Watching the apostolic figures, their mosaic eyes created the illusion of side-to-side movement when the observer walked past them. Rico repeated his side-to-side walk several times, bumping into student holograms that simply moved around him, as the creepy mosaic eyes continued to follow him with a disapproving gaze.

"Good job," Rico said out loud to Bill, complimenting the re-creation of the most disturbing sight he had had to experience day in and day out during his secondary school years.

Between the mosaics stood the chapel's arched entrance. Rico looked inside. An elaborate sixteenth-century wooden altar carving dominated the chapel's apse. Some students were praying, while others practiced religious hymns on their guitars under the Stations of the Cross. Rico could see through the side glass walls into the other atriums. Studying the surroundings intently, he did not see any of his four classmates who had been transported into the simulator.

"What the fuck is going on?" he asked out loud, looking frustratedly around. "Bill! Do I have to play hide and seek?"

A student smacked him on the shoulder and Rico prepared himself for instant, oncoming pain. But he was not ninety years old anymore and the rap only felt like a light nudge.

"Rick," a student called him. "It's me. Ken."

"Where's Barbie?" Rico tried to joke with the hologram, who ignored his comment. Ken was a junior whom Rico met at one of the eighth-grade retreats held the previous school year.

"You made it."

"Yeah," Rico nodded in agreement. "After 77 years, dude."

Ken continued to smile and threw a light punch as a friendly gesture against Rico's right shoulder. Rico's body reacted slightly by jostling to the right and Ken chuckled. Ken appeared to be following a buried memory in Rico's deep consciousness and reacted accordingly to any comment Rico would make. Whatever Rico said would not matter. Still Rico could not remember the incident and how it had happened in the past. Bill had somehow tapped into his deeply repressed psyche.

"Do you know where you're staying?" Ken asked him

"No," Rico played along.

"I'll show you,' Ken responded gleefully. "Your name is posted outside the Dean of Student's office. Let's go see."

Ken turned to the right and walked with quick strides towards the dormitories. The hallway darkened when they entered. A dull yellow light dimly illuminated the musty hallway and threadbare brown carpets. Pits and chips in the walls' paint gave the room the appearance of an abandoned museum. Copies of Renaissance paintings and portraits of Biblical characters and saints dotted the walls. The Dean's light-oak laminated door was to the right, a sheet of paper with typed names taped to the wall beside it. The unaligned letters on the paper showed that the words were typed on an old mechanical typewriter by someone who was less than proficient as a typist. Typos appeared throughout the paper, while the names and locations were arranged in two columns.

"Here you are," Ken pointed to Rico's name.

Rico looked and remembered that he was assigned to the A dormitory where the freshmen slept.

"You're in 9C," Ken emphasized, moving his finger across to the next column. "That's the honors class. There are three levels. 9A is remedial. Congratulations."

Rico remembered his classmates in 9C who numbered fewer than 20. Most would graduate with him, including a few from the other two levels, and most would drop out of the school over the years.

"I'll show you," Ken motioned with his hands.

Rico followed him down the hallway and walked to the left. A large bustle of students streamed in and out of the hallway, hurriedly attending to chores and assigned destinations. After another turn to the right, Rico entered the sophomore dormitory. Twenty beds were aligned in two rows of ten. Similarly, ugly brown lights plastered the ceiling and weakly illuminated the yellowed linoleum floors below in a long streak of yellow haze. Despite the jaundice-like reflection on the floor, the lights revealed years of student scraping and sliding through the center aisle of the dormitory.

Large plywood closets flanked the beds, and at the end of the dormitory, chrome-plated plumbing and several white washbasins stood on thin metal columns against white-tiled walls. Mirrored medicine cabinets framed in stainless steel were set above the basins at eye level for the average student. Rico and Ken passed through the wash area and into the transept that connected four perpendicular dormitories. To the right, a door shielded the showers and to the left, across from the showers, were the sleeping quarters of the Dean of Students. They passed his room and entered the freshman dormitory. It resembled the sophomore dormitory but the beds faced north instead of south.

"This is fucking unbelievable." Rico stood amazed at the accurate re-creation of his dormitory. At the far end, students entered and exited through a door that led to a storage closet for their suitcases. A stairway to the left ascended to the junior and senior dormitories above. Beyond the storage area, the door led to another exit, which directed the students to the common swimming pool and basketball court.

"You can unpack and leave your suitcase in there," Ken pointed to the exit.

"Can you fuck yourself?" Rico asked him. The hologram's effervescent behavior was saccharine and Rico became annoyed at its naïve enthusiasm. Ken smiled gleefully and waited. "Were we so fucking stupid?"

"Hey," Ken finished his program. "We'll be meeting in the chapel after the bell rings. See you later. I've got to unpack too." Ken waved to him and left the dormitory. The other holograms routinely unpacked their suitcases. Rico recognized some, not others. He stared at them for a moment until their movements back and forth began to irritate him further as the holograms bumped into him. Noticing that one of the beds was empty, Rico assumed that it was his sleeping area. Overall, the dormitory had no privacy and the closets, built like vertical pine coffins from the Old West, created the illusion of some privacy. Rico dropped his bag on the bed and waited.

No one objected. He had forgotten how close he had slept to the exit door when he was a freshman. Looking around, Rico understood that Bill was giving him time to make the transition to this past world. He sat down on his bed, opened his suitcase, and looked inside. On top of his folded shirts and clothes, he noticed that his shirts, ties, and trousers were ironed in the same exact manner as his mother had done on Sunday afternoons before he left for school. Every detail was just as he remembered. It was amazing and eerie. Seeing his clothes and thinking of his parents caused Rico to feel some regret and sadness. But he also spied something else buried between his shirts.

There was a laminated blue folder without a title. Rico picked it up and opened the folder. Inside the folder was a sheet of paper printed on a modern computer form. Only a few lines were typed on the paper. The lines provided him instructions for the evening. He was to proceed to the Ceremony of Adoration in the chapel and then to walk alone to the cafeteria. There would be no holograms to accompany him to the cafeteria. The only time holograms were to speak to him was when he needed to receive instructions or when he diverged from any predetermined path. Once he arrived in the cafeteria, he would meet with Bill, who would provide further instructions.

Rico looked up. The holograms continued to behave as if they were living freshman on the first day of school. Mixed with their ranks were a few sophomores and juniors. At the end of the dormitory, the only senior student sat on the bed reading a prayer book. Rico remembered him as the dormitory monitor, Frank. He was often an absentee monitor during the school year and spent more of his time with the other seniors upstairs or escaping incognito to some outside rendezvous. The junior across from him, Fred, became the de facto monitor who would report any underclassman's misbehavior to the Dean for detention. As Rico remembered, Fred was seriously overweight and slept on his bedsheets in his favorite brown housecoat, wearing his threadbare black socks all the time. Often, Rico remembered Fred reading science fiction books and playing music on a phonograph hidden in the closet.

Radios and phonographs were prohibited but no one reported Fred's electronics to the Dean, for two reasons. The students enjoyed the distraction of having music and listening to Led Zeppelin, and they all feared Fred, who could be very vengeful, assisted by a band of incorrigible juniors. A set of muffin earphones attached to an extension wire that sat on his head. Fred blasted the music, which could be overheard by most of the students after dark. Rico was glad that the fat hologram ignored him, since he had little patience for any absurdity at this time. He placed his folder on top of the nightstand opposite the closet, and he began to put away his clothes. A feeling of loneliness instead of nostalgia overwhelmed him as he remembered how sad and isolated he felt during the first few weeks of being away from his family and alone among two hundred strangers.

Rico then took his suitcase and deposited it in the luggage closet. Outside the closet, some students opened the exit and others climbed or descended the stairway that ran alongside it. Looking through the exit, he saw several cliques of students walking around and conversing privately. Some sat on benches at the basketball court and joked around. When he returned, he noticed that his folder had disappeared. Since the holograms had no interest in a folder, Rico surmised that Bill or the computer would provide him with information through different avenues if need be. Once the program confirmed that the information had been transmitted, it terminated the source of the information. Noticing that he was wearing a watch, Rico saw that he had a half an hour before the bell would ring for Adoration. So he decided to stand up and explore the school to test the limits of his freedom.

Everyone from his first year to his last walked the dormitory's aisles and hallways. Rico recognized every student and friend. Remembering each person's name amazed him. Bill had done an excellent job probing his mind and the mind of others, in addition to researching the records. Everything he experienced felt real. His senses seemed to be fine-tuned and each sound, smell, and touch reverberated through his consciousness. Testing the program, Rico stopped to address some old acquaintances, but no one responded. The holograms continued to act as if he were invisible.

"Fucking unbelievable," he kept telling himself.

Leaving the dormitory, he wondered through the building first, passing the community telephone tucked into a closet with a wood-framed, bi-fold, glass door. Inside was an antique rotary pay phone that accepted dimes for local calls. Rico pulled back the door and lifted the receiver attached to a stainless-steel armored cord. There was no dial tone. When he looked up, he saw a sophomore waiting outside the phone booth.

"Are you done, dude?" the student demanded to know.

Carefully looking at the student, Rico saw a frustrated adolescent with a serious acne problem.

"Yeah," Rico said, opening the door.

The sophomore pushed his way through and quickly dropped a dime into the phone's slot and rapidly began to dial. Then he looked at Rico and pushed the bi-door closed, turning his back to him. At the same time, a couple of students stood next to Rico waiting to make the next call. Strangely, there were no calls really being made. Rico stepped away, watching students begin to stream through the school hallway. Next to the phone booth was a classroom. Rico looked through the window into the classroom and recognized it to be the Spiritual Director's religion class.

A large crucifix hung in the middle of the room, and the desks were aligned in rows to directly face the crucifix. Each desk was made of solid wood and steel with a storage compartment under the desk table. A small divider on top of the desktop had the circular depression carved into it for a long-forgotten inkwell. Across the room were two additional classrooms that were used for music and language instruction.

He walked to the next room, looking for one important artifact from his past. This action would test the computer's verisimilitude. Next to the music room, Rico peered into the Dean of Students' room where the social sciences were taught. Although the hallway light did not completely penetrate the room's darkness, Rico could see a stack of leather antique books bound from the seventeenth century.

"Unbelievable," he said out loud, hoping Bill would listen. Again, the holograms did not react. "Bill, you remember this shit too?"

Half-expecting Bill to react and waiting for his friend's omnipresent voice-over, he read the titles of the books. Each book had the words *Malleus Maleficarum* inscribed into its brittle leather spine.

"Witches' spells," Rico said to himself.

Rico remembered how fascinated he was with the books and how they contained spells and incantations in Latin. The priest once allowed him to peruse the pages of one volume when he completed his second year of Latin. The linen paper had been crisp and stiff to the touch. Opening the book, Rico remembered how the leather spine lightly cracked open. Although none of the material could be recalled, the books were an entertaining conversation-piece when the students sat in their social science classes. But the priest never told them why he had the collection in the first place, except for the fact that it was an example of purposeless superstitions.

"Fucking ironic," Rico spoke out loud. "The superstitious calling others superstitious."

His words were followed by the loud ringing of a mechanical bell above his head. A steel hammer rapidly struck the round, silver steel with violent force. The bell was a warning bell for Adoration. After the bell's echo subsided, Rico noticed that the priests were missing. Only students were present, which was very unusual on the first day of school. Most of the principal priests, such as the Rector and the Dean, greeted the parents and students on the entrance steps. Their absence violated some of the normal protocols.

"Let's go to chapel," a student spoke to Rico and happily moved in the opposite direction towards the chapel. The other holograms fell into place and moved like normal students who had not yet tired of common rituals.

Each student expressed a happy anxiety about the start of a new school year. Rico let the students pass him before following them around the corner to the chapel. When most had entered the building, he peered through the door and saw the golden monstrance that would house the Eucharist, or Body of Christ. It sat on top of a white-and gold-draped marble altar. Behind the altar stood a work of art. It was a seventeenth-century gilded, black walnut, Spanish Baroque *retablo*. It was on a gilded shelf raised above the altar to support ornaments, pictures, and statues. The center crucifix of the *retablo* was surrounded by saints, the Madonna and Child overhead. Four twisted columns carved from single walnut trees supported the central edifice. Clusters of grapes surrounded the walnut columns and stretched up to the top capital.

Rico remembered seeing families attend the first Adoration of the year. Tonight, only the seminarians stood in their assigned pews by class level. The freshmen stood in the back. A choir of boys began to sing Latin hymns in the loft and all the seminarians immediately genuflected. Normally, a priest removed the Eucharist from the gold and white tabernacle behind the altar and carried it in a container called the ciborium, which was placed in the monstrance. But nothing happened. The ceremony and prayers continued but there was no priest. Rico continued to curiously watch the ceremony, when a tap on his shoulder broke his concentration.

"Please go to the cafeteria," the voice of a seminarian told him.

Rico turned around but saw no one. He then walked to the right and left of the chapel and looked out into the two atriums but no one could be seen. As far as he could tell, all the holograms were still in the chapel.

"No one is in there, either," Rico concluded, realizing that all that he felt was a predetermined computer reminder.

A feeling of mounting frustration at Bill's program and its inexplicable behavior annoyed him to the point of anger. He did not like being manipulated, and Bill seemed to have egged him on to this point. Taking advantage of his simulated body's newfound youth, Rico leaped up and skipped forward in front of the arched entrance, kicking hard at the cross-bar handle of the glass door. The twin doors flew open and he took long, rapid strides to cross the asphalt path and parking lot in front of the chapel. To the right of the chapel stood the cafeteria, which seemed to have been built in a popular architectural style of the 1960s. The side of the cafeteria that faced the access road had a steel door that led to the priests' private dining area. Thin support pillars made of steel and painted brown functioned as frames for the glass walls that wrapped themselves around the rest of the cafeteria. All around the cafeteria, the glass windows created the effect of solely supporting an overhanging red terracotta roof. Only two sold stone walls stood opposite the main entrance glass doors that swung outward.

Rico peered inside the glass entrance and saw no one. He then took a walk around the cafeteria to the side of the priests' dining area and saw that the interior lights were turned on. He tried turning the knob, but the door did not open. He knocked and no one answered. Knowing someone was inside, and most likely it was Bill, Rico continued to circle the building to the rear where a line of trash bins stood beside the service door that received morning deliveries of food. Rico saw a 1975 maroon Chevrolet Monte Carlo parked next to the double steel service doors, which were open. The car had once belonged to the Rector and it seemed to be in excellent condition. The yellow light outside the building gave the car's light copper vinyl interior a translucent effect. Rico tried the Chevrolet's door but the car was locked. He then looked up and spied a familiar object.

Outside, on the other side of the doors, stood an aluminum cart with eight tray stacks containing various types of pastries. Seeing the pastries, Rico began to relax and momentarily forgot about his frustration with Bill. He instead examined the breakfast items, besides the oatmeal, that the students were served in the early hours after Morning Prayer. He remembered the aromatic scent of cinnamon bear claws, donuts, rolls, éclairs, and cakes. Looking through the selections, Rico found his favorite cream-filled éclair with chocolate icing. He took it from the tray and smelled it. It seemed real. Then, he tasted it to see if the simulation was as good as it appeared to be. Taking a bite of the éclair, he savored the chocolate and felt the warm vanilla pudding squeeze itself onto his palate. The éclair was exactly like the one he ate in his adolescent years. It melted in his mouth and smoothly slid down his throat. He devoured the éclair, almost choking on the last bite.

"Shit. It's good," Rico exclaimed. "How did he do it?"

"Lots of expensive programming," Bill's voice responded from behind.

Rico turned around and saw Bill as a young man in his school uniform standing in the doorway. He was slightly overweight and had an unkempt appearance. His hair was combed to the side like a caricature of Hitler, but his face beamed with the mischievous warmth of Howdy Doody. Replicating the past with absolute accuracy, Bill wore the typical oversized clothes and black loafer boots of his school years, a severe contrast to the tailored English suits and expensive Italian shoes of his late adulthood.

"Fucking amazing," Rico stammered. He grabbed another éclair and swallowed it almost whole. "Why the fuck not? I won't gain weight."

"You won't," Bill confirmed. "I thought you would like experiencing the old days when we raided the pantry early in the morning."

"Great," Rico agreed and licked his lips. "I miss those éclairs."

Turning around and pointing to the Monte Carlo, Rico spoke to Bill without looking at him.

"That had a nice effect when I saw it," Rico admitted openly. "I almost thought the old dude would step out and yell at me for being away from the chapel." Rico then turned around and looked at Bill. They burst out laughing and Bill grabbed a cinnamon bear claw and devoured it.

"I like this part of the program," Bill admitted before swallowing a glazed chocolate donut. "And the best part is we don't do detention."

They laughed again and Rico grabbed a glazed donut and then smacked his lips with delight. He looked at Bill whose hologram began to shred and go opaque for a split second.

"Is that what you were mentioning?" Rico questioned him about his deterioration.

"No," Bill corrected him. "We have some glitches since my deterioration is accelerating. So is Juan's. It's inevitable."

"Where is everyone, by the way?" Rico dismissed his cryptic inquiry. He did not wish to dampen the pleasure of the moment.

"Let's take a walk," Bill invited him.

Bill grabbed Rico's arm and guided him into the cafeteria. They walked through the kitchen filled with aluminum utensils, tables, and sinks. Stainless-steel refrigerators and freezers stood against the wall. Rico walked up to one and yanked on the padlock but it did not give way. Bill watched him and smiled.

"We figured out how to open it," Bill reminded him.

"Unscrew the hinges," Rico blurted. "That was the best steak dinner I ever had at three in the morning."

Rico laughed and Bill continued to smile at the memory of how the two of them and Juan had broken into the kitchen and served themselves a four-course meal, consuming the best food that was reserved for the priests on the campus.

"Who knew the Bishop would be visiting the Rector later? Poor devils. No steak to be found," Bill remembered fondly and chuckling. "Or rectum, as we called him."

"Yeah," Rico recalled, snickering at the old memory. "At least we only got work detention, thanks to Juan."

"One of us would have broken down anyway," Bill excused his old friend's temporary weakness under the Rector's inquisition. "The whole institution and school created so much fear and guilt that it would have strangled our consciences."

"Not mine," Rico declared defiantly, throwing the rest of his pastry into the bushes.

Bill reflectively watched him for a moment.

"Probably," Bill half-agreed. "You really operated on a different wavelength."

"They said worse about me," Rico recalled.

"A bad influence," Bill recalled.

They then looked at each other and laughed.

"Let's go," Bill invited him.

Rico followed Bill through the rest of the kitchen and into the side room, walking past the industrial dishwasher. At first, Rico thought they were going to the main cafeteria but then he knew where they would go instead. Bill opened a laminated wooden door and they entered the priests' dining room. The room was narrow, with a single dining table and six high wooden chairs on each side. The furniture looked like it had been carved and built centuries ago, imitating the Rococo period of Spain. Chairs with large armrests flanked the opposite ends of the table. Against one was a hutch holding various pieces of china. On the opposite side was a thin wooden service door. Directly across from Rico, a steel door led to the access road outside.

The room was decorated with various religious icons of the Virgin Mary and saints. A large portrait of Pope Paul VI hung next to the service door. Above the exit door hung a large sixteenth-century crucifix with a tortured Christ. The artist had spent an inordinate amount of time recreating, in the statue's features, the tortured misery of a dying man. In the corner, an older man, another hologram, suddenly appeared, wearing a tall paper chef's hat, and stood in the corner of the room. He was dressed in a traditional culinary white jacket and white cotton pants, holding a white cloth across his forearm. The old man was of Mexican descent and he had a dour expression. He was instantly recognizable by any ex-seminarian.

"Alphonse," Rico blurted out. He then looked at Bill. Everyone at the school despised his food for its bland taste and strange recipes. Although the cook was known to prepare the food with the highest attention to nutritional content, most adolescents would have preferred more fattening and tasty choices. "This is great but I hope we don't get any mystery meat."

"And no S.O.S," Bill assured him, referring to their most infamously favorite dish: Shit-on-a-shingle.

Rico laughed again remembering the staggered toasted slices of bread on a plate covered with shredded pork and gravy. In the center of the small dining room, a large five-course meal of steak, vegetables, salad, soup, and dessert awaited them.

"I am still hungry after eating all those pastries," Rico declared. "Part of the program?"

Bill nodded to Rico and motioned for him to sit. He sat at the head of the table with his back to the access road outside. Although Rico had some reservations and suspicions, he pushed them aside and welcomed his computer-generated appetite.

"It's great that you got Alfonse to serve us," Rico commented. "Kind of like poetic justice."

"I knew you would appreciate the gesture," Bill said, accepting the compliment. "Eat."

Rico cut into his steak after pouring some steak sauce on his plate. Dipping the piece of steak in the sauce, he ate it and savored each delicious moment before slowly swallowing it.

"Incredible!" Rico exclaimed while cutting another piece of steak. "Alfonse never cooked like this."

They both burst out laughing and Rico took another bite of his steak. The Alfonse hologram walked around the table and poured a dark merlot into Rico's goblet. After eating his second piece, Rico held up the goblet to toast Bill and then drank the wine. He let the wine wallow in his mouth before swallowing it.

"How do you make it taste so good?" Rico asked.

"Well," Bill began to explain. "it's really a normal steak, like the pastries. It's you that is different."

Bill paused, and Rico nodded for Bill to continue as he ate his third piece of steak.

"You are now young," Bill continued. "All your senses are working in their prime. Your old body with its failing senses is no longer in the way."

"But I feel kind of old," Rico added but then corrected himself. "I think I am old still. You understand?"

"You think like an old person," Bill clarified. "It's the years of experience that control your body's reactions. But I think you will have new experiences soon. They will cause conflicts between your body and mind."

"How's that?" Rico inquired, speaking through a mouthful of steak and potatoes.

"You will begin to enjoy your youth again," Bill pointed out. "It will cause a conflict and some stress maybe. Everyone is different. You will see."

"Okay," Rico accepted the facts. "But my mind is so clear. I can recall everything."

"I knew you would enjoy that part," Bill said proudly.

"So," Rico added. "are you fattening me up for the kill?"

Bill laughed and then his laughter suddenly stopped. The holograms of the room, Bill, Alfonse, and Rico began to dissipate and fragment. Rico felt extremely dizzy and disoriented. It seemed to go on for a long while before halting.

"What the fuck!" Rico shouted, losing his appetite.

Bill held up his hand to calm him.

"Don't worry," Bill assured him. "The program is uploading for tomorrow. You may feel these virtual seismic shifts occur. I have to sometimes tap into outside sources for memory boosts. There's nothing to worry about."

"Okay," Rico answered and pushed the food back. He began to feel a slight inebriation from the wine. "Tell me the game plan, Bill. Where does this all begin?"

Bill nodded solemnly and pushed his food in front of him. The hologram of Alfonse stood at attention and then slowly dissolved.

"Log on," Bill simply stated.

Rico looked at him and tried to make a connection.

"Log on," Bill repeated.

He then gave Rico his feral smile with his teeth half-showing through thinly stretched lips. Rico knew that the expression meant mischief.

"I don't get it," Rico admitted. "Computers? What the hell are you saying?"

Bill's smile melted into a pout.

"Let's try this," he spoke with forced patience. "*What hath God wrought? and Mr. Watson – Come here – I want to see you!* or *One small step for man, one giant leap for mankind.*"

"Famous words from Morse, Bell, and Armstrong," Rico concluded. "So?"

"So?" Bill mocked his question. His feral smile returned. "The telegraph, the telephone, and the moon landing were all technological turning points in the last two hundred years. Each man was prepared to say something for the occasion."

Bill waited.

"Log on," Rico repeated. "I'm lost."

"Okay," Bill continued patiently as if he were speaking to an incorrigible child. "The date was October 29, 1969. It happened at UCLA."

Rico smiled.

"You remember!" Bill's face lit up.

"The first transmission over the Internet," Rico slowly recalled. "Log on! Not too memorable?"

"No," Bill concurred. "But when Dr. Kleinrock sent the message to Stanford Research four hundred miles away—L-O—the computer crashed. On the second attempt, L-O-G-O-N was sent. It was such a bland message with true portents. Just think that Armstrong sent such a poetic message three months earlier on the moon. You can appreciate the cosmic irony, being a man of history and letters?"

"Okay," Rico understood. He was beginning to feel impatient. "I get the irony. We missed the boat and the Internet turned out to be anything but bland. It's the most dynamic communication device since the first printed book or the first letters. Where is this all going, Bill?"

"We have to write something memorable," Bill announced. "Not a line or group of rhetorical devices. We have to write a work of literature. Tell our story in virtual reality. This is the first time people have been able to live in a computer as sentient beings. We are making history, and we will tell a story."

"Shit," Rico exclaimed. "You didn't do this before?"

"No," Bill told him. "But I was thinking of starting with something better than 'Shit.' How about: 'Once Upon a Time'?"

"This is bizarre," Rico retorted. "I can't believe I am alive in a computer talking about composing an epigram for history. Are we going to sit down and compose it as a committee?"

"Nothing Marxist," Bill assured him. "You and our friends, including me, will just relive key moments in our lives. Moments that will stand out as archetypes for humanity. We will make a statement about our lives, one that will be remembered and emulated. Get it? Others will see that our lives didn't add up to *LOG ON* and *LOG OFF*. There's something more."

Rico remained speechless as he thought hard about Bill's words.

"Bill. Have you become some mystical digital megalomaniac?" Rico challenged him. "I don't buy this stuff."

"I am only telling you this," Bill confessed, showing his disappointment. "The others don't know. I thought you would grasp the challenge and beauty of it all."

"Let me explain myself," Rico began, pulling his ideas together. "I came here to see some friends. This virtual place never pleased me and doesn't exactly make me comfortable. I came to this specific school when I was very young and naïve. I arrived with expectations and wanted out the second year of my high-school enrollment. My parents, being from the old country, would never think of it. So I spent my last two years here in dread. I feel the dread and depression now. Seeing you is great, now that we're young again. But I know it's an illusion, and I am looking forward to seeing Juan again. Really. That's all."

Bill nodded and stared at Rico for a while. Alfonse became animated again and produced a chocolate ice cream sundae and placed it in front of Rico. Rico looked at the fudge on top of the ice cream and scooped some onto his finger, sucking it off with one quick swipe.

"Same stale ice cream," he pronounced. "What makes you think our lives will make a statement?"

"It will," Bill assured Rico, taking a bite of his ice cream with a spoon. "We all have diametrically different and opposing points of view, with the life experience to boot. There will be a dynamic exchange without the limits on time or other limiting factors. Everything here can accommodate you and your needs. Only some rare obstacles will hinder us. Like the memory surge earlier."

Rico finished the rest of his ice cream with a spoon, and Alfonse took the empty cup away. The hologram became inanimate again.

"I know how you feel about this place," Bill sympathized. "But after seventy-plus years? Why don't you put aside your anger and resentment for a little while?"

"What are we going to do? Come on, Bill," Rico demanded, leaning back in his chair. He swept his arms out. "This was made for posterity. Wasn't it?"

"Trust me, my friend," Bill pleaded. "You're here because it's necessary to all of us. Tomorrow, we all meet after morning prayers in the cafeteria." He observed Rico's apparent discomfort. "Of course, you don't have to go. When you go back to the dorm, the holograms will be turned off until tomorrow. At breakfast, I'll give you an orientation. It will make sense when we see each other. It's just that the other two won't know what I told you here."

"And did you give them other reasons I am not privy to?" Rico inquired.

Bill coughed and turned his eyes away.

"That's your business," Rico deferred. "But I won't go to morning prayers or night prayers or any other prayer service."

"Okay," Bill accepted. "I know that already, which is why I pulled you out of Adoration."

"Where are the other two?" he asked.

"Asleep in the other dorms," Bill revealed. "You can only see them on neutral ground."

"The cafeteria?" Rico concluded.

"Yes," Bill clarified. "and during programs that we agree to participate in." Rico opened his mouth to speak and Bill raised his hand. "Tomorrow, please."

"Why do we need to sleep?" Rico probed. "We're not in our bodies."

"Yes," Bill acquiesced to his point. "But you do. You did eat didn't you? Your body's needs are functioning in the machine because it keeps your mind healthy. After almost a century of biological rhythms, your brain needs to be exercised, rested, and nourished. Even if it is simulated, it's a psychological need and not a physical one. Eventually you could overcome the psychological need in here, if we had centuries at our disposal. That would be a great experiment."

"So it's a need but not a reality," Rico explained to himself. "That means we can overcome the final cerebral illusion."

"Yes," Bill approved with a feral smile. "But that will require time, effort, and sacrifice. We don't have time. My personal program is deteriorating."

"I'm sorry," Rico expressed his condolences and stood up to touch Bill's shoulder. He nodded and stood up too. "What about us?"

"The same will happen. But I've been in here for a long time. You two are safe for now as long as your body is alive outside the computer," Bill promised. "You'll be sent to your bodies. We don't have one."

"Juan's body is dead?" Rico said. The thought shocked him.

"He was dying anyway, like me," Bill explained. "We had no choice. You see, my friend, this is our last chance to relive our most formative years. I know how you feel about this place, and I appreciate it deeply. Please do it for me. You'll understand once we are under way. I think it will benefit you."

"Okay," Rico said. "Until I feel that it has gone too far. I don't know what *too far* will be but I'll know it when I see it."

"Always the skeptic," Bill smiled and blinked. "I'm tired. Let's go rest. Come straight to the cafeteria after you wake up."

"Thanks," Rico responded half-heartedly. "I don't think I can stand the Marshall's meditation."

They both laughed at the inside joke. The priest who presided over morning prayers was an old Kansan farm boy who often mixed western anecdotes with Biblical tales. His authoritarian tone earned him the nickname of the Marshall.

"Let's see," Rico tried to recall a quote. "May your horse never stumble, your spurs never rust, your guts never grumble, and your cinch never bust. Amen."

"And may your guts never pinch," Bill added, chiming in with his memory. "and your crops never fail. And may you eats lots of beans, but never go to hell. Amen. You son of a bitch."

Bill burst out laughing. Rico joined him and they both laughed for a long while. Alfonse watched in silence. Rico looked up and suddenly lost his glee. Bill looked up and stopped laughing too.

"All gone," Rico realized. "I love that old Cowboy Prayer."

"We'll have some laughs again," Bill assured him, tapping his shoulder. "For a little while, I hope."

"If you wanted to they were always here," Rico told him, pointing to his head.

"Remember. Don't knock it till you try it," Bill challenged him. "This is really different."

"If we don't like it, then what?" Rico pushed his point.

"I'll get into that too," Bill assured him.

Rico remained silent, knowing that the timing would be wrong. The computer hologram projected a weary Bill and Rico almost believed he looked tired. He thought that the program somehow tied into their emotional state and recreated facial expressions.

"Thanks for your first decent meal," Rico sarcastically saluted a stoic Alfonse.

Bill chuckled for a moment, and Rico waved goodbye to the hologram. Then, Bill escorted Rico through the kitchen and into the empty cafeteria where the bulk of the students had sat together. The walls were painted in light brown. The red terracotta tiles rose and descended in an uneven pattern, giving the observer the impression of a wave of red scales. Only the black support posts broke up the crenellation. Above the tiles, the white acoustic ceiling suffered the indignity of hundreds of toothpicks, adding more perforations to its surface. Rico paused and pointed to the ceiling.

"Does the ceiling in the study hallway still have the fist marks?" Rico asked referring to the seminarians' favorite habit of jumping up under the low ceiling and punching their knuckles into the soft material.

"The imprints are perfect," Bill said approvingly.

"I might like to add some more," Rico promised.

They both laughed some more and walked out of the cafeteria. Once outside, they looked over to the main building's entrance and saw no one. The lights were on but the place was abandoned.

"The program is on standby," Bill explained anticipating Rico's question.

Rico did not really give the students' absence any credulity but he did notice a phenomenon that caught his attention. The skyline above the faux bell tower shifted colors in a fluid motion. Green, red, and blue hues shifted like pixels embedded into chainmail. The sky and its three colors shifted from side to side and then moved in waves that almost seemed to break up the very fabric of the sky.

"More glitches?" Rico gently demanded, wanting to know the meaning of the strange phenomenon. "I never saw this shit in school, even when we had a bad smog alert day."

Bill did not respond. He studied the sky for a while and then continued walking towards the dormitory, not waiting for Rico.

"Memory glitches," he explained in a halfhearted voice. "Like before in the dining room. By tomorrow, all the memory will be upgraded. I'll contact my people. Don't worry. The show will go on."

Rico continued staring at the sky, which slowly morphed into a black clay-like appearance that stretched and oozed, as if it were being kneaded like dough. Feeling his sides and belly to see if his holographic body also morphed like the sky, he was satisfied that it had not. So he watched and skeptically shook his head before trotting up to catch Bill. Rico had forgotten that his body could respond with resilience and stamina. When he reached the brick entrance steps, Bill gestured for him to enter.

"You'll only be able to walk straight to your bed," Bill revealed. "I'm sorry but I have to conserve memory. You can explore more later."

"What's beyond the grounds?" Rico demanded to know. "Out beyond the gate entrance?"

"The real world," Bill told him. "Or the world you want to see. Bye."

Bill took Rico's right hand and affectionately tapped the top of it before entering the building, walking to the left, and passing the chapel. Rico waited for a moment and tried to follow. He was only able to reach the chapel before running into an opaque canvas wall. The three-dimensional world of the schools grounds could be seen but Bill's program prevented him from entering. It looked real, but when he touched it, the tactile experience felt like a silicon sheet. It would pulse and shift at his touch but would not let his hologram interface with it. Bill had walked into the surrealist environment and disappeared into its maze of canvas shapes and colors. All was real but not real.

Staring for a moment into the flux of colors and shapes, Rico turned around and thought about the irony of looking into a hologram's morphing canvas with one's hologram eyesight.

"Outrageous," he told himself in frustration.

Then, his eyes rested on the 12 Apostles whose gaze followed him on the same path he had taken when he entered the dorm earlier. The dim amber lights guided him through the vacant dorm, and he tested Bill's resolve when he tried to climb the center stairway to the dorm above him. Neither the center stairwell nor the stairwell at the end would allow him to ascend or enter another dormitory. In fact, when he tried to backtrack, he could not leave the dormitory except for a visit to the restroom. Rico wondered if his need to urinate actually occurred in the outside world where he had just wet himself. The possibility of wetting himself only added to his skepticism and doubts.

So he reluctantly returned to his bed and sat down, staring at the far doorway. Not bothering to change his clothes, he leaned back on his bed and lay down. The amber lights began to dim and finally turned off. A deep feeling of exhaustion drained Rico's body as if he had been given a powerful sedative. The feeling was not welcomed consciously but his hologram body easily embraced the descent into unconsciousness. Rico succumbed to the induced sleep and dreamed his dream-within-a-dream of his first genuine day in high school and his memories of anticipation, expectation, and wonderment. His dream turned into a Morpheus purgatory. He relived his detentions when he suffered from induced insomnia. Like the mythical Sisyphus, Rico and some incorrigible acquaintances were forced to play basketball after evening prayer until three in the morning. Then he listened to various priests and nuns and their repetitious reprimands under overhanging crucifixes. The words did not come from any specific person and seemed to be generic in nature. But they all threatened him with dire consequences in the next world, along with all its spiritual retribution. All night Rico kicked and twisted under the recurring torturous images. Beyond the words and the sound of bouncing basketballs, he could hear the dry Santa Ana winds racking the flagpole chain with hollow metallic clangs. Slowly the clanging chain washed out the sounds of words and human actions in his dreams.

Suddenly, a loud mechanical bell pushed Rico out of bed. He almost stumbled as he rose in his school uniform. Although he knew, for he barely recalled, that he was living in a hologram's body, he felt the need to clean up and change before walking to the cafeteria. Across from his bed, the early morning sunlight cracked through the tan-colored blinds and began to compete with the dim luminescence of the dormitory's amber lights. Rico walked through the empty, abandoned dorm holding a bundle of clothes under his arm. He entered an open gray shower stall where the students, like Adam and Eve, were never able to hide their nakedness. The plumbing in the stall lined the walls and divided themselves into two chrome handles for the hot and cold water. Moving both handles delicately to the left or right kept the water temperature in balance as it sprouted from an oversized, perforated chrome showerhead above him. He first brushed his teeth and then grabbed a bar of white soap from a tray that seemed to be chiseled into the gray marble wall. As he soaped himself, he self-consciously turned around to guard his privacy.

"This is crazy," Rico thought, laughing at the absurdity of his embarrassment.

Although he showered alone, he kept feeling awkward and embarrassed. Anyone could enter and see him showering in an open stall.

"Why in the hell did I bother?" he argued with himself, determined to end the bogus act of hygiene.

Then, for the first time in decades, a pulsing erection gripped Rico. He felt sexually famished and in need of a quick release. Visions of his lovers and their different sexual escapades crossed his mind. The feeling of hardness gripped him and he felt compelled to relieve himself in a desperate act. But he knew it was all in his mind. He didn't have a real body, only a virtual one. He finished quickly and toweled himself off before changing into a fresh set of clothes. Although he did not see anyone, he had a feeling that there were prying eyes in the shower room.

"Paranoia," he told himself.

When he stepped out of the shower room, students could be seen running about and preparing themselves for Morning Prayer. He walked back into the dormitory and put away his dirty clothes. Everyone ignored him but Rico felt relieved at not having one of Bill's angelic holograms escort him or direct him to his destination. Sitting on his bed, he waited for the holograms to depart before standing up and walking to the cafeteria. On the way out, he stopped to look at himself in the mirror. He looked deeply into his young face and he thought he could see the eyes of an old man, like the characters who peered into the mirror in *Dr. Heidegger's*

Experiment. Without notice, his appearance changed. In the blink of an instant, he was old again. Then he closed his eyes and opened them again to find a young man's reflection looking back at him.

"Like old Doctor's four guests," Rico recalled the classic story. "I hope my luck is better and the water doesn't run out."

Rico combed his hair back, enjoying the feeling of having hair and feeling its thickness in the bristles of his comb. As his brushed his hair, a sudden rush of nervous energy invaded his body. This morning, unlike the past evening, Rico began to enjoy his body. Life flowed through him and he felt energized and restless. He wanted to go out and discover what Bill had programmed in his holographic body. But his mind pulled him back into the present. Rico felt his youth surge again but the hologram and its effects could not erase the weary wisdom and tempered skepticism that clawed at his aged memories.

He felt a struggle between what he wanted and what he thought. It was a tempered compulsion that he could control for now. The conflict concerned him and he decided to bring it up to Bill in the cafeteria. Not knowing the depth of the computer's ability to tap into his deep subconscious, Rico feared that he would lose himself to his youth. It was a youth that had long dissipated into the past and was long forgotten. The current rush of juvenility resurrected itself. It also frightened him to the core of his identity.

"I'm a fucking pixilated zombie," Rico told his reflection.

A feeling of undirected energy and happiness swelled and lifted him up. Rico wanted to conquer the world and reach out for adventures with boundless energy. Leaving his reflection was not easy as he reluctantly pulled himself away and walked out of his dormitory. The effect of his youthful ascendancy came like a powerful rush of heroine through his system. As he walked through the first dormitory, Rico reminded himself of who he was and what he had made of his life. He felt like a drunk forcing himself to walk a straight line in front of a policeman who shined a bright light into his face. The emotions and energy overwhelmed him and he had to lean against the chapel wall as he reached the front entrance. Scraping his back against several of the Apostles, Rico let himself squat down on the cold tile floor. He looked up. The Apostle John gazed down with apocalyptic judgment at the unnatural adolescent crouching at his feet. Rico stared back at him and flipped up his middle finger.

"Cocksucker," he cursed the mosaic effigy of God's wrath. "I really don't need this shit, Bill."

A choking feeling gripped Rico's upper chest and he felt his heart pounding hard. The sound echoed in his ears and he held his hand up to his head, trying to squeeze out the noise and pressure. Through the pounding, he could hear the hypnotic repetition of the students' prayers as the exhausted holograms muttered to themselves the same meaningless religious orations of his youth. When he sat in the chapel decades ago, he had often let his mind drift back to sleep or tried to ignore the lustful impulses that swelled in his trousers. But now he could only feel the effects of his body mimicking a cardiac arrest. Rico told himself a heart attack was not possible but his simulated body said differently. As long, draining seconds passed, he could feel the pounding diminish, and his chest slowly relaxed.

Taking two long gasps of air, Rico's body began to respond to his thoughts and he lifted himself up and walked through the entrance doors on the way to the cafeteria. He still felt the same level of elation and energy but the previous overwhelming effect and its suffocating dominance seemed to have been diluted with calm control. Like an ex-smoker, Rico secretly craved the uncontrollable impulses that possessed him but he nevertheless welcomed a return to calm objectivity.

"This is bullshit!" Rico exclaimed loudly. "Fucking unbelievable! I am going to kick Bill's holographic ass."

Experiencing a reduced rush of exhilaration and anger, Rico dashed to the cafeteria. In his mind, he rehearsed the words and actions he would take once he encountered Bill. Within a score of seconds, he reached the cafeteria door and flung it open, holding his fists close to his sides. At the far end of the cafeteria where the supervising priests once ate on a raised platform, three young men sat and waited. Their backs were turned away from Rico. Facing Rico and directly opposite the three young men, under the large, hanging wooden crucifix, a lone, empty, armed chair rested on a raised platform overlooking the empty cafeteria space below it. It seemed to invite some imperial authority who once looked down upon a large pond of hungry adolescents.

"Bill!" Rico shouted. "Turn around, you bastard!"

One of the three young men turned around and he smiled at Rico, who stopped dead in his tracks. Frozen in shock, Rico stared at the hologram and felt his anger turn into regret and sadness.

"Hi," Juan greeted him. "I see you can still go off half-cocked."

Rico could not muster the words he felt for he did not expect to meet his long-lost school friend in the very time and place where they had spent their adolescent years together. Juan did not look like the paralyzed victim on a distant canyon road over seventy years ago. He looked young, happy, and alive. His green eyes glittered under his brown curly hair and his lips trembled.

"I am so sorry, my old friend," a voice spoke behind Rico.

Rico felt the icy shock melt away and he managed to slowly turn his head in time to see Bill walk by him and climb up to the platform. Rico then noticed that the other two had turned around. One of them was Mike, the Trappist monk. Mike sat tall and straight in his chair. He looked like he could stand at least a foot above the rest. If anyone had described Mike in high school, he would not physically describe him to be a pious young man. He was the antithesis of the stereotypical pale, anemic recluse. Instead, Mike looked like a Zuma Beach surfer with sandy bushy hair and a light sunburn. It had been known that Mike was suffering from the effects of a melanoma cancer that had spread to his vital organs, the result of spending too much time on California beaches as a young man. Mike had always had a strong passion for the outdoors.

The other person between Juan and Mike was an unknown guest. Rico could not place the face of the dark young man who seemed to be of Spanish descent. He had dark coal eyes, a small hooked nose and a very solemn expression under his long, straight hair and sideburns. He reminded Rico of the portrait of a Florentine contemplative in a Renaissance portrait.

"Your program had to be adjusted," Bill continued to explain. "I didn't think the full rush of youth could have been so overwhelming. Sorry about that."

"You have no idea," Rico muttered, thinking about who the mystery person was and when he could corner Bill alone for a good whipping. "I forgot how it was."

"Come up here and we'll begin after breakfast," Bill invited him, following Rico's line of sight. "I'll introduce our guest. You remember him. Don't you?"

Rico forced his legs to move and he watched the smiling face of Juan as he gestured his head towards the table. Mike nodded to him and turned around as had the guest. Bill sat at the end of the table and Juan pointed to Rico's chair directly opposite Bill's seating position. When Rico rose to the platform, Juan gleefully turned around and slapped Rico's thigh. The slap gladdened Rico and he finally smiled back at his old friend. Not being able to help himself, he bent forward and hugged Juan hard. They remained in a strong embrace for a long moment before separating. Both men then wiped their eyes with their napkins and remained silent but smiling.

"The Lord will bless you two," Mike declared. "Forgiveness is the highest Christian virtue. We need His blessings in this endeavor."

Rico did not want to listen to Mike. Seeing Mike felt momentarily good but he wished Bill could have foregone his presence. Juan was another matter—a deep one. He could only think about how much he had deeply missed his close adolescent friend. Seeing Juan again filled a void he had forgotten about for a long time. There would be challenges ahead so he tried to block out his anxiety. While he was lost in his thoughts, Alfonse's hologram placed a cup of coffee and a small creamer in front of Rico.

"You liked cream in your coffee," Bill recalled, smiling at Rico who continued to look down at his place setting.

"Bill," Mike interrupted. "This hologram of Alfonse is disrespectful. The man was a dignified cook, a Le Cordon Bleu chef."

When Rico heard Mike's last words, both he and Juan burst out laughing. Neither one had any serious respect for Mike in high school, believing he was a fanatical blowhard. Alfonse continued to serve the others coffee and tea according to his program and without any reaction to the outburst. Mike looked at both young men and expressed his disapproval by tilting his head slightly back before diverting his attention.

"You can't take the playground out of the boys," Mike declared, looking at the plate.

Rico half rose out of his seat to respond and Bill held up his hand. He then quietly sat down, relishing the thought that he would have a chance to knock Mike down before their programs were terminated.

"It would only be a virtual punch," Rico whispered to himself, showing everyone a less-than-benevolent wry smile.

Bill then stared disapprovingly at Rico.

"Bill," Mike interrupted. "Who is our guest? You never told me about him. Is he an ex-seminarian too? I don't recognize him."

Rico and Juan looked at the guest and then at Bill who took a long slurp of coffee before placing his cup down.

"Don't you recognize him?" he pointed to the hologram. At that moment, Alfonse appeared with a cart and extracted trays containing huevos rancheros and fried potatoes and served them. Bill waited for the hologram to finish. "He's our moderator. Juan and Rico should know."

"Interesting," Mike mused.

"Interesting?" Rico questioned.

Bill looked at Juan and then at Rico. Juan kept his eyes down, not wishing to look at Bill.

"Father Clement will explain his role," Bill added, pointing at the hologram of Father Clement who stood up and faced all of them. He then sat himself on the platform chair, peering quietly down on the four ex-seminarians.

"Clement," Rico repeated to himself out loud. "In his younger days I guess? I would have never thought he had a youth."

The joke struck Juan as being very humorous and both he and Rico again burst out laughing.

"Father C and Sister Big-Tits!" Juan shouted and cupped his hands on his chest, then extended his hands out. "Remember how he was caught leaving the convent early in the morning?"

"They got married later," Rico finished the rest of the scandalous story.

They again burst out laughing and Mike's face expressed dismay. Juan noticed his disapproval through his watering eyes.

"Mike," he addressed him. "You weren't there that year. He was our freshman religion teacher."

"You shouldn't mistreat the memory of a priest," Mike objected. "Even a fallen one."

"Bullshit," Rico retorted and held up his spoon in the position of his middle finger.

"Our moral ethics teacher," Bill sarcastically added, before Mike could initiate a rant against Rico. "He had a brilliant command of syllogistic logic and historical references."

Juan and Rico again laughed at the irony of the whole situation.

"He's also our judge and jury," Bill cryptically concluded. "We don't go back until he passes his verdict."

A gavel suddenly appeared in Father Clements's right hand.

"Un-fucking believable!" Rico cursed. "What verdict?"

Both young men fell immediately quiet and became somber and serious.

"I knew you were full of shit, Bill," Rico voiced his frustration. "You're going to start it now?"

"Nothing better than the present," Bill said in a cavalier tone, ignoring the accusation. "You'll live through the moments without preparation. So sit back and experience it all. I'll see you later."

Bill looked at Rico and gave him his infamous feral smile. Rico flipped him off and Juan pushed back his plate. Mike sighed out loud and made the sign of the cross.

"Shit!" Juan exclaimed.

Darkness cloaked their vision before they became unconscious.

Chapter 3

Jesus loves the little children,
All the children of the world.
Red and yellow, black and white,
They are precious in his sight.
Jesus loves the little children of the world.
– C. Herbert Woolston (1856-1927)

Rico waited for his father to pick him up before heading home. He waited on the curbside, holding his brown, tattered vinyl luggage, and watched for his father's Chevy station wagon to arrive with his two siblings sitting in the back bench seat. Like many other events before, the car arrived like a distant smudge in the smoggy afternoon haze from the oncoming traffic. Slowly, the smudge materialized into an apparition of a battered car. Inside, the occupants finally materialized after a long, watchful minute.

Like the car, their faces slowly became defined into recognizable shapes, displaying a contented mother and a grim, exhausted father. His siblings sat behind his parents and leaped up and down like two rubbery stick figures until they too acquired further shape and form. Soon Rico could see every detail of their features. His father parked several feet from the curb and he exited the car to open the hatch. After a quick hug, he took Rico's luggage and threw it into the back while Rico's brother opened the rear door.

When the hatch slammed shut, Rico's father gunned the engine and immediately accelerated into the traffic, leaving Rico behind. His parents were not aware of the mistake. He had a split second to close the rear door before the car mingled with the rush-hour traffic heading north. From the rear hatch, Rico watched his siblings wave and laugh as the car accelerated, reversing the visual Doppler Effect that had greeted Rico several minutes before. The well-defined appearance of his family car soon turned into an indistinct smudge that devoured the whole car and disappeared into the haze. Rico then abruptly awoke in the dark. He had experienced this dream every week since his first attendance at the seminary. Trying to calm his rapidly beating heart, he stared up in the dark for a long while.

After the mechanical bell clanged for the last time, the amber lights switched on and everyone in the dormitory slowly rolled out of bed. Although he subconsciously expected this moment to arrive, the bell and the lights upset him. He pushed the dream out of his mind. Rico had already been semi-awake for an hour before the bell rang and he thought about this very moment when he would have to rise out of his single, lopsided bed for the last time. It was his last complete day in high school. The actual experience could never be fully envisioned.

His long meditation on the subject had been washed away at the very moment the wake-up bell's clang reverberated through the dormitories. Looking beyond his immediate surroundings, he noticed a pall of sadness blanketing the space surrounding the rising graduates on this particular dawn, while elation could be heard coming from the dorms of lower-classmen below. The lower classmen had summer and a new school year to look forward to, but Rico and his senior classmates instead had a lifetime to look back on their high school experiences.

He would never again face the same level of assurance and predictability every September. Life would now become unpredictable in his mind even though it had always been unpredictable and dangerous. The element of stagnant routine had been removed. Commencement would be celebrated the following evening and his last school day on campus, today, would be spent in class and by the poolside. According to his secret plan that day, Rico and his friends were not only going to the poolside. But that extracurricular plan had to wait. Rico looked up at his friends and began to take stock of every item in the dormitory, committing them to memory for posterity. He became acutely aware of his every sense as he tried to maintain the memory of every experience on this last day of the seven-hundred and twenty days he and his classmates spent in a minor seminary. The final departure from his friends was more regretful than the departure from his school. Only one classmate was missing: Mike, who suffered from a debilitating flu in the infirmary and from the fact that no one liked him. Unlike Mike, Rico adamantly hated the school but loved his friends. There rested the dilemma, the paradox. Rico could not separate the school from his friends. Both were intertwined and inseparable. If he gave up one, he would have to lose the other.

"Last day! We're free, dude!" his classmate Chris called out.

"What?" Rico heard Chris but did not listen to his words.

Chris was a tall seventeen-year-old who dressed in the fashionable clothes of the disco period but still found a way to remain within the dress code. Superficially, he had an arrogant disposition, but his demeanor was always friendly towards his classmates. He father was wealthy and owned an aircraft parts company. Unlike the other students, who came from immigrant, working-class, Catholic families, Chris's family belonged to those blue-blooded Catholics who arrived long before the Irish, Poles, Mexicans, and Italians.

"Get up!" Chris shouted. "We have to go to our favorite penultimate breakfast. Stale pastries and concrete oatmeal."

A loud shout of laughter erupted in the dormitory.

"Shit. It's Thursday. I'm goin' to get constipation again!" another classmate, Louis, shouted. He walked up to Rico's footrest and raised his right leg. A loud fart blasted. "That should help get you up. *¡Chupa mis huevos!*"

A loud hoot filled the room and everyone laughed heartily. If Mike were present, he would openly disapprove of Louis's vulgarity.

Rico smiled tightly and held his breath as he walked to the sink. He then cleaned up and shaved. A bustle of young men ran in and out of the washroom with timed expertise. Within ten minutes he was ready to go to morning prayers. After four years of predictable routine, he still could not recall what had transpired in the last few minutes. Every effort to try to remember this last day was being overshadowed by his automatic responses to routine behavior.

"*Señors!*" Louis screamed on his way out of the dormitory, mocking the perennial admonition that would precede the Spiritual Director's rebuke.

Louis stopped for an instant to fart again before escaping outside. The ripple effect of the fart echoed through the dorm. The malodorous consequences would linger for a while. Louis' mischievous glee could be heard beyond the doorway.

"Here we go!" shouted Juan, Rico's best friend, as he ran past Rico on the way to the chapel.

Rico caught up with his friends and entered the chapel last. He sat in his assigned pew and pulled out his prayer book while Louis ascended to the altar's podium to read the Morning Prayer and meditation. He tried to walk with dignity but instead communicated a subdued mocking gait. Rico hoped Louis would let some air escape. Across from Rico sat the Spiritual Director, Father Kurtz. He looked disapprovingly at an animated Louis who immediately showed some fake contrition. No one believed Louis had any remorse, especially Kurtz, who stopped glaring at Louis and began glaring at the other smiling students who were genuflecting in their pews.

O Master and holy God, you are beyond our understanding: at your word, light came forth out of darkness. In your mercy, you gave us rest through night-long sleep, and raised us up to glorify your goodness…

Louis raised the pitch of his voice to mock the Director's whiny intonation when he read prayers or lectured. The students immediately caught on and began to giggle and smirk. A similar smirk grew on Louis's face as he continued to read the prayers.

O Lord, remember all your people; all those present who pray with us...pour down your great mercy...

Louis's voice pitched an octave higher and he added the small gesture of slowly and subtly placing his middle finger on his upper lip in the direction of his nostril. The gesture invited suppressed guffaws and chuckles throughout the pews. Kurtz responded angrily and nervously at the disruption although he did not grasp the fact that he was the target of Louis's derision.

...that in our confidence, we may extol your exalted and blessed Name, Father, Son, and Holy Spirit, always, now and forever. Amen.

"Amen," the congregation repeated with a long, whiny denouement that lampooned Father Kurtz. Some students exaggerated and boldly inserted their fingers into their nostrils with vehement emphasis. The ripple effect of their laughs could not be subdued, even when Kurtz rose out of his seat to stare them down.

During the whole escape, Rico watched Louis read the prayers, seeing him mouth the words but not listening to their meaning. Slowly, Rico drifted in a daydream. He could not believe that he would not have to genuflect in Morning Prayer for the rest of his life. These personally empty and meaningless rituals at school would end soon and he could soon behave as he wished without the imposition of an outside authority. When the morning prayers finally ended, everyone stood up. Most continued to laugh and to beam with mischievous intent. When he left the chapel, he caught a glimpse of Kurtz admonishing Louis in private near the podium. Rico just wished that Louis would end Kurtz's diatribe with a loud, wet fart. Outside the chapel, Juan waited for Rico.

"Do you think Louis will do it this time?" Juan asked.

Rico shook his head as they walked together to the cafeteria. The Dean of Students walked ahead of them as the other priests and clergy began to enter the staff's dining room.

"Are we going tonight?" Juan demanded to know.

"We have to," Rico confirmed. They both laughed. "I brought a lot of stuff."

"I can't believe you have all that shit in your car!" Juan almost shouted.

"Shut up, dude," Rico warned him. "Kurtz is behind us."

Juan looked over his shoulder to see Kurtz about fifty feet behind them. Kurtz looked warily at the two young men but the view of Louis jumping up and down behind the Director, gripping his crotch in a rotating motion, caused Juan to grab Rico's shoulder and laugh out loud. Kurtz then turned around, only to see a remorseful Louis walking solemnly to breakfast.

"*Caballeros!*" Kurtz called out to them in high-pitched voice.

The word *caballeros* usually anticipated a reprimand or a warning to the students. Rico and Juan understood it to be an order to stop and wait for Kurtz to catch up so he could harangue them. Rico wondered why Kurtz even bothered at this point in the game.

"*Caballeros*," Kurtz repeated offering them a grave expression. "Let's show our reverence today. It is the last day but we need to keep our dignity. The lower classmen all look up to you. And God looks down."

"Amen," Juan responded in a mocking tone.

Rico remained silent and nodded, and Kurtz returned his smile with forced composure. The priest then walked past them and they waited for Louis to catch up. When he did, he belched out a fart and whispered, "*Caballeros*."

"Louis got more gas reserve than the Middle East," Juan declared.

"Yes, *caballeros*," Rico answered and they trotted to catch up to the students who poured into the cafeteria.

When they reached their assigned tables, a brief prayer was said, while the students waited anxiously to consume the much-anticipated breakfast. Scrambled eggs, bacon, and sausages were served on large enough platters that freshman could even find enough food to enjoy. Rico sat at the head of the table with a junior, two sophomores, and two freshmen. Following tradition, Rico received all the food first but he generously let the lower classmen take their portions. Most of the time, the freshmen had to settle for the leftovers. Today, everyone was satiated. The special meal was rarely offered and no one bothered to talk except for some comments and small side jokes.

Immediately after the meal and another prayer, some of the seniors left their tables and congregated with the senior refectorian at the long table across from the priests' table. Kurtz gave the seniors a long, warning stare before leaving the refectory. Rico ignored the stare and sat across from the refectorian, Bobby, who had a reputation of being a strict disciplinarian in the refectory. Bobby was next to the tallest person in his class. He had a lanky figure, dark brown eyes, and wavy hair. Although his appearance seemed ordinary, outside of the refectory, everyone recognized him for his warm nature and wide, happy expression. Inside the refectory, where he ruled, he donned the mantle of the stern disciplinarian.

Despite having a rapport with Bobby, Rico almost doubted Bobby would grant him his request. Bobby was strongly single-minded but most of his classmates knew he was simple-minded, too. Rico thought the strict adherence to rules only compensated for his lack of creative thought. Bobby did not lack the ability to reason but he accepted authority blindly because it was easier and less messy than asking too many questions.

"Bobby," Rico smoothly called his name. Louis sat next to him and continued to munch on dry, overcooked bacon. "We need ice chests."

"I said I'd ask Kurtz," Bobby reminded him.

"And if he says no?" Rico retorted. "We won't have the cool drinks in the afternoon by the pool. What's the big deal? He'll figure out we can't have the soda out there without a cooler."

"*Caballeros*," Louis spat out, along with a piece of bacon.

Bobby sat silently and ate some more bacon from the large leftover plate collected from all the tables. Most of it would be thrown away and the seniors ate more even though they were full. The principle of living with a half-empty stomach for four years dictated their instincts to overindulge when excess food was available. They learned to hoard food, since the next meal could be scant. Rico understood this feeling and he often participated in the feast or famine syndrome. So he waited for Bobby to have his fill. Otherwise, the refectorian would not give him what he needed. Of course, Rico did not tell him his real need for the coolers. Bobby probably had his suspicions but Rico hoped he would not be inclined to ask any more questions. Today he avoided overeating. Rico was not hungry. He was driven with a purpose. So he continued to wait.

"Yeah, Rico," Bobby announced. Rico looked up at Juan who gave him a thumbs-up. "But don't take it into the dormitory. It's gotta be here tomorrow morning. Okay?"

"Yeah," Rico agreed. "We'll have fun at the pool. The kraut will bring the sodas."

Rico had referred to his friend, Steve, who was the senior in charge of the refreshments at the seminary. He had secured a free stock of Coca-Cola for the afternoon from Kurtz and the Rector, Monsignor O'Malley. His parents were immigrants from Holland and he did not like being called a German.

"Fuck you," Steve told everyone. "I'm Dutch."

"Yah, Yah," Rico would repeat after Steve's stock correction.

Unlike most stereotypical Dutch, Steve was short and dark but had deep blue eyes and a proclivity to drive cars with a lot of horsepower and torque. Steve had often driven Rico on the Ventura Freeway to and from his home in Camarillo, doing over 120 mph. He was one of the few students who owned a real modified sports car. It was a 1971 AMC Javelin, once belonging to a dealership that went out of business. In fact, many dealerships had been slowly dying for a long time since the first oil crisis. All of the seniors sitting together understood that their friendships were endangered too. After high school, few would be able to continue to maintain their amicable relationships.

Unlike Rico and Juan, Rico and Steve were never really very close, but both Rico and Steve shared similar attitudes of cynicism, skepticism, and derision for any institution, especially the one they occupied. It was not always so for Rico when he entered the seminary four years ago. On the first morning of his freshman year, he nervously attended Morning Prayers with pious regard and he walked to the cafeteria in quiet awe, reflecting on his relationship with God and his new vocation of becoming a priest. He was late to the cafeteria and had to stand by the entrance when prayers commenced.

After the morning blessing of the meal, Rico timidly sat down at his table after everyone else had already sat. The table contained the traditional company of two freshmen, two sophomores, a junior, and a senior. The junior at the table continued to pray, keeping his head bowed. The senior ignored everyone at the table and turned around to talk to another senior behind him. Rico soon found out that his name was Tom and he seemed to be too large for his chair. Later, Rico would learn that Tom weighed more than 250 pounds and stood over 6 feet 8 inches tall. Compared to the small, undernourished students, Tom was a behemoth. His classmates called him the Hulk and he soon taught Rico that charity never began at home, even at the seminary. When the first serving of breakfast arrived, a platter of six pastries was placed on the table. Tom grabbed three pastries and offered one to the junior. The other four boys had to share the only two remaining pastries. Both freshmen and sophomores split each one in half.

"Welcome to the jungle," Tom blurted out to the two freshmen at his table. "Do you have any questions?"

He immediately intimidated the freshmen, who shook their heads. Another waiter passed by their table and Tom reached out and stole two pastries.

"Go get more!" he ordered the annoyed waiter, who was a sophomore.

Rico felt a strong indignation but instinctively knew enough to realize he was alone in a strange environment with no friends or alliances. Unfortunately, his classmate Louis did not accept the quietly understood rules of seniority and submission at the seminary. The senior at the table or anywhere else had more authority and earned more respect than Jesus himself. Rico watched Louis begin to rant and thought that the junior who was praying earlier was making a plea to be spared a single pastry. God listened to him.

"*Cabrón*," Louis said with defiance to Tom. "I'm hungry."

"You won't enjoy it without teeth," Tom warned Louis.

He then growled at Louis as if he had discovered some dog feces under his shoe. Louis scowled back because he was naturally defiant. His defiance never left him but he later learned not to direct it openly against a senior. Rico felt lucky at being removed from the conflict. He saw that no one was eating the thick oatmeal that had been recently served after the platter of pastries, so he scooped a large amount onto his plate and swallowed it down with milk. The rest of the table momentarily ignored Tom and Louis to watch Rico swallow the glob of coagulating oats. Tom bellowed out a laugh.

"Hey, dude," he warned Rico. "That will plug you up later. First, it will give you a major stomach ache."

"Quiet," one of the priest admonished Tom from the head of the cafeteria.

Tom smiled and politely acknowledged the reprimand, mumbling a curse under his breath. The junior and sophomores snickered but Rico ignored them. He was starving and continued to eat the oatmeal everyone seemed to despise. Louis then wrenched two pastries from a passing waiter and shoved them into the folds of a linen napkin. No one saw him but Rico. The priest then stood up and dismissed everyone after a brief prayer. Rico sat down and watched Tom leave with a group of seniors. One of them looked back at Louis, who returned a wide grin. Unfortunately, the laugh would be on Louis. When the clique of seniors left the cafeteria, Louis looked around and saw only sophomores cleaning up. From his napkin, he extracted two large pastries.

"Eat," Louis offered him a bear claw. "They're a bunch of *cabrones*."

Rico took it and Louis devoured the remaining food.

"What class you got now?" Rico asked.

Louis finished his pastry before answering.

"I'm Louis," he told Rico, ignoring his question. "Don't let this *cabrón* get you. Gotta go."

"Later," Rico responded, watching Louis dash off and skip out of the cafeteria. He yelped out an unintelligible challenge in Spanish, which gave some sophomores pause to listen. Rico did not understand but the others who did understand the Mexican dialect laughed.

The sophomores were finishing up and one called out to Rico before he stepped out of the cafeteria.

"Soon it's your turn," an overweight sophomore reminded him after throwing a set of dirty plates into a bin.

Rico knew that freshmen would have to clean the cafeteria all year and that the sophomores served as waiters all year. For now, the sophomores cleaned up until the freshmen could make the transition in a week. He also knew that freshmen would to be obligated to clean the school on Wednesday afternoons, working with the janitors to vacuum, dust, and wash windows. Leaving the cafeteria, Rico began to feel distressed about attending his new school. A feeling of homesickness began to creep into his stomach. Loneliness just augmented the feeling and isolation began to produce anxiety.

At fourteen, Rico faced the wrath of upperclassmen, the neglect and demands of a religious staff, and the threat of the unknown. As he walked back to the dormitory, the weight of his anxiety dissipated in the wake of a new, terrifying anxiety, attending his first day of classes in a college preparatory school. He would soon walk into his first science class as dictated in his schedule folder. Twenty minutes remained before his first class began. So Rico walked back to the dorm to use the facilities and brush his teeth. While brushing his teeth in the open sink area, Rico saw Louis actively exchange insults in Spanish with other freshmen. Unlike Louis, Rico had talked to some of his classmates but he did not bond with anyone yet. When he cleaned up, the warning bell sounded and a fellow freshman tapped him on the shoulder.

"My name is Juan," he told him.

"Rico," he answered, grabbing his folder and notebook.

"Are you in 9C?" Juan asked.

"Yeah," Rico said, feeling awkward about carrying on a conversation. The whole experience of the cafeteria made him feel self-conscious and angry. He had told himself that he would stop by the chapel to offer a prayer before school began. But the anxiety he felt and the turmoil he experienced distracted him. Now he had to race to the lab, not knowing exactly where to go.

"You know where the lab is?" Rico inquired.

"Follow me," Juan assured him. "All my brothers go here. I got one in each grade. So they showed me around years ago. It's practically my second home."

Juan lightly slapped Rico's shoulder as a friendly gesture. His words slightly cheered up Rico until they passed the chapel. Students quickly scrambled out of the chapel to avoid being late to class.

"Hurry up, stupid," a tall, lanky senior with curly hair rushed past them, slapping Juan on the head as he went by.

"That's my brother, Nick," Juan said proudly, watching Nick sail by with two other seniors who soon caught up.

"That new kid in our class is going to get his ass kicked already," Juan referred to Louis. "Telling off Tom takes balls. I won't do it even if I got three brothers. He's an animal."

"Yeah," Rico agreed, thinking about Tom sitting on top of Louis and pounding his head on the sanctuary's marble tiles.

They did not speak again until they entered the library. The science class first met on a shortened schedule in the library where the other eleven freshmen sat around long rectangular tables waiting for a teacher. The teacher was a tall, thin priest with a balding head and wire-framed glasses. He was speaking to another priest who was almost a foot shorter and smoked a cigarette. As they spoke quietly, the science teacher kept subconsciously palming the side of his head above the ear and running his hand through his hair. Then he pulled off his glasses and examined them against the circular incandescent light above him. Satisfied with their condition, he placed his glasses upon his nose. The bell rang and the two priests finished their conversation.

The shorter priest, with a small beer belly and a red, cherubic face, dashed to the end of the library where two swinging doors led to the chemistry and biology laboratories in a distant recess, hidden from the school's main juncture. Turning around with a quick jerk, the science teacher approached the new freshmen as a junior unexpectedly plowed through the library, heading in the direction of the swinging doors. Rico watched the other boys laugh nervously at the junior. The science teacher took a quick glance, gave the departing junior a look of disapproval, and then turned his attention once again to the freshmen.

"Let us pray," the priest intoned.

All of the students stood up and said an "Our Father."

"I am Father Jones," the science teacher announced, producing a thin, plastic smile that quickly vanished. "First, this is not a sandbox."

Rico had taken out his pen and began to take notes while Father Jones spoke. The mention of a sandbox caused Rico to first look at Louis whose eyes expanded with enthusiastic humor. He took a quick look at his friend Juan who mouthed the word *later* and then smiled.

"We have very expensive equipment in my laboratory," Father Jones clarified, wiping his right palm against the side of his head. "It cost the school a large portion of the diocese funds. Most of the other equipment was donated by university and private foundations. Do you know we have a computer?"

The mention of a computer intrigued Rico but it seemed to generate a very serious interest in one particular student who sat across from him. He was a fat, nerdy boy who would soon be one of Rico's good friends. Bill suddenly raised his hand.

"Father," he spoke up without permission. "What kind of computer? Can we use it?"

Jones momentarily stared at Bill and then grimaced.

"The computer is in Denver," he clarified. "You will learn to write *BASIC* programming and then send the programming to Denver through a phone line. It's a teletype."

"Yeah," Bill responded eagerly. "I read about that. You can program it to do many types of calculations and it even…"

"I have an assignment for the computer," Jones interrupted Bill. "You will create a program for the computer to calculate the height of the electrical tower outside after you take its measurements. Carefully and accurately."

"You use a theodolite," Bill blurted proudly.

Father Jones took a deep breath and slowly exhaled. The other students also appeared to be agitated with Bill's outbursts.

"This is serious, Master," Jones tried to shut Bill down. "One minute of phone time with the computer costs two dollars. I must submit my financial requests to the Rector before the class transmits the program calculations this semester. It's expensive."

"But Father," Bill cut off the priest. "I need to know how to translate BASIC from a sheet so it can be sent into a phone line…"

Bill appeared excited, frustrated and completely oblivious to Father Jones's mounting exasperation. He tried to speak again but Jones raised his hand to silence him. Everyone in the class found Bill's overzealous reaction agitating and, in their minds, he became the instant butt of a new joke. Some of the students began to mock Bill's enthusiasm and others pretended to feed information into an imaginary machine, scornfully raising and dropping their fingers on imaginary typewriter keys.

Behind Jones's back an unidentified student, the once and future class clown, kept repetitively raising his hand and then hiding it in mock gesture before imitating the masturbatory behavior of stroking his hand up and down. The other students saw him and howled in laughter. Jones turned around to find only this conciliatory class clown, pretending to wait patiently for the rest of the lecture. Later he would be known as the official jester and nemesis of Father Jones' class. The howls diminished when Jones turned around to stare everyone down. Then he directly faced the jester with cool contempt.

"Your name?" Jones demanded from the jester, taking off his lenses, examining them, and then slamming them back onto the bridge of his nose.

"Uh," the student hesitated. "John Bates."

"Master Bates," Jones addressed him. "This isn't a sandbox."

Again the students howled in laughter at the innuendo while Bates maintained an expression of dismay and confusion. Rico chuckled out loud but it struck him as unusual that this very hallowed institution could harbor such sophomoric behavior from young men who were pursuing the priesthood.

"Enough," Jones demanded, wiping both sides of his balding skull. The students suddenly became silent and uneasy, except for Bates who seemed to relish the attention and commotion.

"You will be working on lab assignments in groups," Jones dismissed their voracious glee as a mild rainstorm. "All the assignments will be completed in two-week cycles and be kept in a notebook which will be graded each quarter."

Some students took notes and Rico looked over at Juan who smiled and shrugged. Bates looked at both of them and raised his middle finger when Jones looked away.

"Any misuse of the equipment will invite serious reprimands from the Rector," Jones added.

At that moment, the school bell rang, dismissing them for the next class. Jones expressed frustration at having forgotten about the shortened period. A second later, the swinging doors flew open and a score of juniors stormed through the library. Rico and Juan waited, watching the explosion of students mingle into a single-line mass of bodies rushing forward. The priest swayed stiffly in his place and watched the students depart. Ignoring those who dawdled, he walked over to the librarian's desk and pulled out a folder. Jones leafed through the folder and stopped, looking up at Rico and Juan.

"You'll be late," Jones reminded them, adjusting the lenses on the bridge of his nose.

Both students acknowledged the word of warning and collected their materials. Rico moved towards the exit door and as Juan followed he mockingly saluted an indignant and preoccupied Jones who had buried his attention in the folder's contents. Rico had learned already to follow Juan's lead which took him to his math class.

When they stepped into the hallway and ascended a small set of steps, they saw a middle-aged man with a slight paunch standing in the corner of the hallway. He wore a red-trimmed black cassock and a purple sash. His thin graying hair was combed back and his eyes protruded forward, peering through heavy black frames and thick glasses. Juan pulled Rico back and slowed him down. By the time they reached him, Rico and Juan walked cautiously by the Rector, Monsignor O'Malley.

"Monsignor," Juan greeted him.

The Rector blinked and hardly noticed the two students turning the corner.

"Hurry up, boys," he admonished them.

Rico and Juan respectfully passed the Rector who watched them for a moment and then shuffled towards the chapel. When Juan lost sight of the Rector, he turned to Rico.

"Stay out of his way," Juan warned him.

"No kidding," Rico said. "He looks scary."

"My brothers say he is an asshole," Juan noted. "He wants to get rid of all extracurricular activities."

"Like what?" Rico asked.

"All the sports," Juan explained. "Maybe more."

"Unbelievable," Rico responded, rehearsing in his mind activities he would never be able to enjoy. "More what?" The idea of the abstract word "more" troubled Rico.

"Fuck," Juan confirmed. "We're going to be late."

They reached their math class seconds before the bell rang. It was located on the west side of the seminary, directly behind the chapel. The math room belonged to a string of six rooms in the longest hallway in the school. Although incandescent light illuminated the hallway, most of the light in the hallway leaked through a series of Hopper windows that opened inward. As long as any student attended the school, no one could remember a time when a janitor opened the windows for ventilation. Rico and Juan entered the room and quickly found desks before the bell rang.

To their consternation, they had to sit next to Bates whose face beamed in anticipation of some performance. Rico looked around immediately and noticed an elderly priest standing behind the podium, perusing a red math textbook. He adjusted the wire-rimmed glasses that rested on his long thin nose. From where Rico sat, the priest looked deathly pale. Only his thin red lips showed any contrast against the pasty epidermis that loosely hung off his jawline.

"That's Mecum," Juan told Rico. "Ready to sleep?"

"What?" Rico asked and looked up when the bell rang.

"Stand up," Father Mecum commanded and began to say a *Hail Mary*.

The students stood up and followed the prayer after hastily doing the sign of the cross. As in every other room in the school, a lone, desolate crucifix hung above the teacher's desk. A black slate board hung below the crucifix behind the priest. His oak podium and desk, except for the math book, were bare. In fact, the room was Spartan. Green linoleum tiles offered the only contrast against an antique-white room. On the west side of the room, the windows looked out towards the cemetery grounds next to the seminary. Grated aluminum shutters decorated the windows with circular rings, which did not hide the fact that they served as security bars. Through the windows, the students witnessed a long line of mourners following a hearse. An abrasive voice pulled Rico's attention away from the gravesite.

"I'm Father Mecum. This class is an Algebra one course. Open your math books to Chapter one," he commanded in a brittle, low tone.

The students scrambled to open their desktops and pull out their math books. When Rico closed his desktop, he found two indentations where inkwells had once been used, black from the past ink that had been spilled and forgotten decades ago.

"Now I will read," Mecum began to drone in a monotone voice. "Algebra originates from the Arabic word *al-jabr*, and its origins can be traced to Indian mathematics in the eighth century. The mathematician…"

Mecum continued to speak and Rico's mind drifted off while Mecum's voice read the chapter aloud. Looking around, Rico observed how some of the students seriously followed the reading while others daydreamed. Bates took to drawing in his notebooks and Juan placed his head down and began to sleep. Rico wanted to wake him but his eyes wandered in the direction of the burial ceremony not fifty yards away.

Two pallbearers in military uniform extracted a large, gold and black coffin from the hearse. Another pallbearer paused to drape the coffin with a flag. Rico could not tell if it was built of wood or metal. A few extra soldiers appeared and Rico wondered if the deceased had recently arrived from Vietnam. Although the war was winding down, men still died there. Under a small canopy to the side of the hearse sat what appeared to be the young widow and two small children. A small group of family members flanked her in front of the open grave. On the other side of the grave a small group of observers and friends waited. A lone, elderly priest stood to the side of the grave with an altar boy holding up a crucifix on a staff. The priest held a small aspergillum, waiting to sprinkle holy water on the coffin as it passed by the grave. Rico watched the pallbearers carefully carry the coffin and place it on the supports above the open grave. The priest quickly circled the coffin, simultaneously spraying water on the draped coffin and attendants. The scene had an eerie surrealistic appearance, as Rico could not hear any prayers or cries coming from the gravesite. Despite the surreal effect, the ceremony moved with calculated steps and rehearsed motions.

Only Mecum's voice filled the void of silence. When Rico looked over at his classmates, more of them were asleep, including Bates, and in fact Juan had begun to snore. Mecum continued to read without looking up and never paused to catch his breath. The priest remained engrossed in the historical tale of mathematics. Nothing else mattered. Unexpectedly, the dismissal bell stopped Mecum's reading and shocked the sleeping students awake.

"Complete exercises 1 and 3 in the first chapter tonight," Mecum barked out with a dry throat. "Let us pray."

The students stood up and immediately followed the priest with a *Glory be to the Father* while the students from other classes streamed into the hallway to their next class. When they finished, Rico dashed out, taking a last look at the funeral in progress. No one moved at the gravesite as the priest was reading a prayer from the liturgical book he held in his hands. Once outside, a couple of students bumped into Rico and Juan.

"Mecum does the same shit every day," Juan told him. "Everyone fails his tests. Just do your homework and you'll get a C."

"We're going to P.E. now?" Rico remembered his schedule, trying to take his mind off the gravesite.

"We don't have to change today for P.E." Juan explained. "Next time we'll have only five minutes to change or the coach will make us run two miles."

The thought of running two miles sent a shiver through Rico. He once ran a mile in elementary school and collapsed from the strangling effect of the thick smog. The day had been an Alert 2 and the coach had ignored the city warning about refraining from outside activities. After running the mile,

Rico felt as if his lungs were being siphoned out of his chest cavity by some malevolent creature.

Without changing into his P.E. clothes, and scurrying through the obstacle courses of two dormitories with their staggered beds, Rico managed to reach the basketball court behind the sophomore dormitory. Six courts on a black asphalt paving faced each other in two rows of three. Beyond and behind the basketball courts, a dying field of grass served as a track and soccer arena. Two soccer posts stood opposite each other at each end of the field. From the basketball courts, Rico could make out the burnt track lines for a 440-yard track. The faint lines of white powder on the oval track dissipated under the dew in the early morning sun. Occasionally the line would disappear over dead patches of grass and then reappear several feet away.

Standing under the chain basketball hoop of the center court stood the P.E. coach. A defiant man, bearing his muscles proudly under his tight polo shirt and fitted shorts, he stood impatiently waiting for the freshmen to arrive. Holding a clipboard, he extended his right arm forward and swept it from side to side in front of himself.

"Sit in alphabetical order," he barked. "My name is Coach Krause."

"Santa he is not," Juan managed to whisper a warning to Rico.

Intimidated by the coach's powerful physique, every student instantly obeyed his command as he called out their names and pointed out their assigned positions on the asphalt. Since arriving, Rico had taken notice of the thirteen members in his class. Sitting outside allowed him to take an extended view of his classmates in the upper echelon of the freshmen class. There were nine members he did not know yet. They stayed in the background.

"As you know, or will know," the coach began. "St. Paul says the body is the temple of the Lord. We will treat our bodies as a temple in my class. You will all be dressed in your P.E. reversible shirts five minutes after the bell rings or you will earn my demerit."

Krause pointed to the box next to his feet. A large cardboard box contained the shirts and shorts that were to be distributed at the end of the period.

"You should find your size easily," he assumed, after making a quick estimation of each student's physique.

Pausing to stare at a particular student, the coach smiled and shook his head with benevolent castigation. The student was a light-skinned African-American who weighed a least three times as much as the average student in the class. His hair showed some premature balding where his scalp began. This student smiled widely but the smile contained no humor or kindness, only nervous fear. Since his name came last in the alphabet, he sat apart and farthest away from Krause.

"John Wilkins?" Krause asked, looking down at his clipboard. "You seem to have built a disproportionate mansion for yourself."

The allusion to John's weight set off an explosion of laughter, for the students were at the stage where humiliation and belittling statements artificially enhanced their self-confidence.

"Yes, Coach," John responded timidly.

"Don't worry," Krause assured him. "I came prepared for you."

He then reached into the box and began to search for shorts and a shirt that would accommodate John's large body. The delay inspired a greater round of laughter, which the coach seemed to subconsciously encourage.

"Here we go!" he exclaimed, pulling out a pair of extra-large shorts. "Let me know how they fit."

He opened up the wide shorts and did a mock double-take at their girth. The students howled in laughter as the coach threw the shorts to John. Bates seemed to bounce up and down on the asphalt as John timidly folded the shorts on his lap. His smile never left his face but his small, black pupils angrily darted out at his classmates.

"Thank you, Coach," John again said in a barely audible tone that masked his resentment.

Rico watched the repressed anger in John mount as his eyes squinted with a defiant stare. No one else seemed to care about the humiliation, although Krause seemed to be having some second thoughts about the whole episode. He walked over to John and clapped him on the shoulder with false camaraderie. With a sudden expression of chagrin, John's eyes softened and he then withdrew the shorts and shirt from view.

"Tomorrow," Krause bellowed. Everyone immediately went silent. "I will assess your physical condition. You will attempt to complete sit-ups, push-ups, and pull-ups, and run both a 100-yard dash and a mile. From there, you will rebuild the Lord's temple and glorify His majesty."

Krause looked around at the pudgy, soft, elitist students who nervously contemplated the torture events they would experience the next day.

"Let's stand up and pray," Krause ordered, not making the sign of the cross. Soon everyone would know he was not Catholic.

Every student immediately stood up and made a sign of the cross without instigation. John buried his head more deeply than any other student.

"Lord!" Krause shouted as if God wore a hearing aid. "Please lead these future ministers of the Word to a strong, clean, bill of health. May the purity of their bodies reflect the purity of their spirits. May their glowing good health be a lamp of Your light to the infidels and sinners. We ask you this in the name of Jesus."

"Amen," everyone answered.

Rico looked up and saw Bates imitate the length of John's shorts with extended arms. Fortunately, for Bates, the coach continued to bow his head, and Rico wondered how long his luck would hold out. Rico began to have doubts about the ease of being a priest among these misfits. The road seemed to be paved with buffoons.

"Dismissed!" Krause barked.

"He reminds me of Billy Graham on TV," Rico commented once he was safely away, but Juan did not respond.

With no prompting, all the students filed out in a straight line and marched into the dormitory on their way to their English class. Inside the dorm, Bates chided John.

"Hey John!" Bates shouted. "Are you sure you can fit inside those shorts? They seem small!"

The students laughed and John smiled widely, ignoring the insult. Jumping up and yelling like an Apache on the warpath, Bates whooped with glee.

"We're all fucked," Juan told Rico in an exasperated tone. "We're going to Father Davis's class."

"English class, right?" Rico could not grasp how an English class would be worse than the zealous Coach Krause.

"Just keep your mouth shut and your eyes down," Juan warned Rico. "And don't sleep. Ever!"

Bates continued to leap and shout like a crazed marauder. Rico had a feeling that Bates would soon be *persona non grata* at the school, probably giving Louis a reprieve.

"He's really fucked. This will be fun," Juan promised Rico. "My brother told me that Davis hates loudmouths."

The freshmen students bounced against walls and into other students on their way to their next class like loose billiard balls immediately after the break. Some students congregated into smaller groups and followed one path, while others moved along taking different paths. Short, staccato class periods that day contributed to the dilemma and confusion each student felt and intensified the nagging confusion most freshmen felt on the first day. Only the upper classmen managed to reach their classes with pedantic certitude and privilege. Rico and Juan avoided one small clique of seniors who acted like a rolling boulder in a fast-moving stream. Every other student smoothly moved around them. The freshmen backtracked their steps earlier in the morning and passed Mecum's room where juniors were filing reluctantly inside. Mecum stood stoically behind his podium as earlier, gravely examining the pages of his Algebra II textbook. Rico took a quick look through Mecum's open door and saw that the funeral had ended. The mourners and the hearse had departed.

"Don't be late," Juan urged and pulled Rico's shirtsleeve.

Rico obeyed automatically and trailed Juan into his English class two rooms south of Mecum's room. When he entered the room, he could see the same grated window as those that had been erected in his math class. Rico realized with disappointment that he could not get a clear view of the cemetery, since the faculty covered parking lot obscured some of the view. While all the others sat down, he stood near the window and tried to see where the mourners had gone, but he only captured brief glimpses of the tractors preparing to lower the coffin of the fallen soldier into his grave.

"Sit down!" Bates shouted, pointing at Rico's leaning figure. "Your parole officer won't get you out."

Some students laughed nervously, and when Rico turned around he saw that the only empty seats were in the back of the room with Bates and Juan. This time, Bill sat in front of Rico and wearily lay his head down, which gave Rico a clear view of what was ahead of him. Taking in the room, Rico noticed that it was decorated with literary aphorisms from distinguished writers like Milton, Chaucer, and Shakespeare. Sets of books lined the wall with perfect unity and their leather spines spoke with authority and respect. The spines showed no creases or wear. Sitting in front of the room, John's uncomfortably body squirmed in the small desk. Rico had not noticed his dilemma earlier but the sight of seeing John's lower torso bend outwards and extend itself in both directions, away from the seat, made him feel not only sympathetic but also nauseated. Since John sat in the front, Rico also noticed the student who sat next to John. He was dressed in a starched shirt and a black knit tie. His trousers were carefully pleated, and his hair was neatly combed back and parted on the right. The student seemed to take pride in his coiffed appearance. He stood out in the class for he was the only Asian student, appearing to be of Vietnamese or Filipino descent. The Asian student spoke to a student next to him who was shorter but also carefully dressed. Although his sartorial combination did not speak with the same monetary authority as the Asian student's clothes, the other student carried an air of self-importance and confidence. He was of Hispanic descent and had native features. He and the Asian student spoke quietly and laughed at some private joke without regard for anyone else in the room. Their conversation ended when the English teacher, a mature priest, tardily entered the room. Everyone immediately stood up as he placed a stack of blue-tinged dittoed papers on his desk.

"That's the seven pages," Juan warned in a careful whisper.

Rico wanted to ask him why seven pages and what was on the pages, but the teacher broke out into a prayer.

"*Oremus*," he said in Latin.

Everyone stood up in regimented fashion and began to say an *Our Father*. A pall of dread and fear gripped the class in anticipation of the next twenty minutes. A premonition of doom weighed over the students. When the prayer ended, the students sat down in quiet submissiveness and locked attention. Without knowing why, Rico experienced a nervous tremor in his body and a sudden need to use the restroom. His bladder screamed for attention but he suppressed the uncomfortable urge. Seeing Father Davis separate the stack of papers in his hand, Rico studied his features, which only heightened his trepidation. The priest smiled like a stereotypical mad scientist in a 1930s Universal B movie. His humor found its source in the creative mental and emotional torture and misery it would soon inflict on its naive victims. Father Davis's gruff appearance augured the dire consequences that awaited an incorrigible student in his class. His hair was snowy white, amplifying the slight pink color of his skin and his blisteringly blue eyes.

Although Davis had once been a handsome young man, he had lost his refined looks long ago in street brawls and in the boxing ring. The bridge of his nose bent in three different directions. In fact, ripples of cauliflower skin stretched across his ears as witness to the hours, days, and weeks spent on the receiving end of vicious pummeling. If Davis had not worn a Roman collar, anyone would have thought that he worked as bouncer in a third-rate dive out in Baker, California, where the lone gambler took his first or last drink on the way to or from Las Vegas.

"Hello, dollies," he greeted everyone, grimacing with ugly teeth.

Some of the students managed to mumble a "hello" or simply a nod. A burning sensation raced up Rico's esophagus and began to compete for attention against his twisted bladder. Bates misunderstood Davis's greeting as a genuinely gregarious gesture and he laughed at the reference to the Broadway play.

"Dolly," he repeated, gleefully bouncing up and down in his chair.

"What a sweetheart!" Davis called out.

Everyone smiled or laughed at Davis's apparent sentimentality but Juan became suddenly sullen and grave. Rico took his cue from Juan, sensing that Davis was leading them all into a trap. The priest's eyes mischievously darted from side to side and came to rest on Juan, who instinctively squirmed.

"So the last of the brood is here," Davis recognized him. "Tell them what I just said."

Juan shook his head, and Davis's eyes stopped smiling. His face melted into the shape of a dour, pocked English muffin.

"Okay," Davis accepted his plight with regret. "I will."

His dispassionate words and cold expression caused Bates to freeze up.

"Dolly is an asshole," Davis stated in a nonchalant tone. "Sweetheart is a fucker."

A silent shock of disbelief gripped the students like the sudden jolt of an earthquake.

71

"I am passing out the seven pages, dollies," he continued to torment the students. "You know about the seven pages?"

Davis looked directly at Juan, who acknowledged with a slight nod.

"My friend, Juan," Davis spoke disingenuously, "knows that the seven pages will be your Bible in this class. You will memorize every word on the pages."

Sitting in the back of the class, Rico had begun to receive the ditto sheets. They had been recently copied and the alcoholic aroma permeated the air. Some of the students smelled the paper and pretended to be intoxicated from the printing fluid's olfactory effect. Juan ignored the sheets, knowing their contents, while Bill studied them earnestly and with careful deliberation, as if he were parsing through a legal document. Once everyone had a moment to study the sheets, Bill raised his hand and all eyes watched him in disbelief. The unsaid counsel seemed to call for silence but Bill resisted the silent note of caution. Rico feared for him, remembering his encounter with Father Jones.

"Father Davis," Bill's interruption shattered the room. A small smile broke on Bates' face. "Do we have to memorize this by next class?"

"No, sweetheart," Davis berated him. A suppressed chuckle could be heard popping up in different locations of the classroom. "Memorize the definitions of a noun, adjective, and article only. I don't wish to tax your puny little freshman brains."

Davis stopped and took a quick assessment of the class's demeanor. The smiles melted away and nervous coughs supplanted the chuckles.

"I will call on you randomly," he added. "If you don't know the definition, you will write it out twenty-five times. I'll need a secretary. Any volunteers?"

Davis then looked at the front row, directly at the Asian and the Hispanic seminarians.

"What are your names?" he asked them.

"Tony," the Asian student said, in a controlled, suave manner.

"Tom," the Hispanic seminarian answered curtly.

"Tom will write down the names of those who don't know the definitions," Davis adjudicated. "You," He thumbed his hand at Tony. "You will alternate with Tom each week. If you make an error, you will write the others' detentions for them. Understand?"

Both seminarians nodded and Davis smiled viciously. When he walked to his desk in the corner of the room, they both looked at each other and rolled their eyes.

"Any questions, dollies?" Davis asked rhetorically.

No one dared to ask a question, except one student.

"Father, I think..." Bill began to raise a question but the short bell rang.

A mad dash out of the room followed the bell, and Juan motioned to Rico to leave. Bill never finished his question because Father Davis quickly abandoned the classroom, turning left towards the door that led to the chapel's sanctuary. Bill tried to follow but had enough sense to stop and change direction.

"What the hell happened this morning?" Rico asked himself and Juan simultaneously, trying to piece together the events of the day.

"Nothing I couldn't have already told you," Juan responded. "The next classes will be crazy too. We're going to the east side now."

"The east side?" Rico questioned, following Juan across the hallway and through the quad.

"It's where our religion and Latin classes are," Juan explained. "Look at your schedule. The classes are on the other side of the cafeteria."

Rico's head was in turmoil. The last four classes did not meet his expectations in the least. In fact, Rico felt numb. He had just left a class where a priest cursed at them. Earlier, the coach seemed to be more spiritual than his English teacher, a priest. His math teacher appeared to be disconnected from reality, and the science teacher cared more about his appearance and possessions than the students' achievements. Nothing fit the norm of a nurturing spiritual environment.

"The teachers are strange and crazy here," Rico blurted out.

Bates heard him and leaped in the air, laughing in a maniacal tone.

"*Loco*" he screamed and ran into a small crowd of freshmen walking across the cafeteria portico.

A large, black student pushed Bates to the side and he fell into the bushes. Everyone laughed and stopped to watch Bates, who was also laughing as he picked himself up and brushed the dead leaves off his trousers. Rico watched in disbelief and hoped that he could avoid sitting next to Bates in his Latin class. Of all the classes he attended in the morning, Rico looked forward to his Latin class. He had a secret interest in the language because one elementary school teacher, Sister Mary, had praised its value and usefulness in all subjects. Rico knew that Latin would assist him in learning medical terms. Medicine was his backup career if he changed his mind about the priesthood.

"Bates is going to get his ass kicked," Juan made the pronouncement.

"No kidding," Rico agreed. "He might get kicked out by the end of the day. Who knows?"

He then looked ahead to where Tony and Tom were walking. Both students were again sharing a private joke as they stepped over a small footbridge built over an open drain. Everyone moved in quick unison towards two long, rectangular, gray buildings. These east-side buildings contained classes for five hundred students and the architecture sharply contrasted with the Spanish colonial appearance of the main building. The course, fluted facades resembled granite cliffs, and the buildings' tinted windows projected an ominous chill. These building techniques created an appearance of solid security and permanence. But they had an ill effect on some people, like Rico.

"Here?" Rico questioned Juan, pointing at the building. "Why?'

"My brothers told me only our class is using the building," Juan boasted proudly. "It was built ten years ago but the enrollment fell so far that now they only use it for us. There are empty dorms on the other side. They have nice metal lockers. Not the crappy wooden ones we have."

Rico's classmates ascended several small concrete steps. At the top, the aroma of nearby orange groves greeted them. Several beds of flowers, especially jasmines, separated the sidewalk of the portico and the parking lot to the right of the building. They slowly navigated their way through an open portico, reading the small classroom numbers engraved on brass plaques above the doors. John reached the Latin class first and carefully opened the door outward. The rest of the students assembled behind him and cautiously entered the room, sitting down at the first available desks.

Seeing the room delighted Rico. Posters of ancient Rome and its monuments decorated the wall. Plaster busts of Julius Caesar, Pompey, and Marcus Aurelius rested on five-foot, white marble pedestals. Unlike in the other classrooms Rico had attended all morning, education and culture saturated the room. His eyes wandered across the posters on the wall that described major works of Latin literature, like Virgil's *Aeneid* and Ovid's *Metamorphosis*, until they fell upon an elderly priest sitting behind a desk next to the bust of Marcus Aurelius. He wore thick, square glasses and his thinning hair revealed his pink scalp beneath. Light blue lines of veins crisscrossed his face and formed a rooted network across his bumpy bone structure. From a distance of twenty feet, the priest's face seemed to have been chiseled from marble. With a wooden grin, the elderly priest sat with an open mouth, reminding Rico of a pirate's death grin while he dangled in a gibbet, slowly rotting away in the tempest-tossed air. Two large oblong earplugs, clasped behind each of the priest's earlobes, appeared like aviators' earphones.

"*Salve, domini,*" the elderly priest greeted them, standing up.

Rico prided himself on knowing the meaning of the priest's respectful salutation. He then looked down at his desk and read the word "dipshit" engraved into the hardwood desktop. Juan tapped him on the back and pointed to Bates nearby.

"This will be good," he said.

Bates sat like a loaded catapult, waiting for the right moment to launch into his erratic behavior.

"*Oremus,*" the priest commanded them to pray, and everyone stood up.

Yellowish wires fell from his earplugs and traced themselves into a leather-covered box that hung at the bottom of a black shoulder strap. He adjusted a knob on the black box before proceeding with the *Our Father* in Latin. No one could follow the prayer except for Rico and Juan.

"Pater noster, qui es in cælis, sanctificetur nomen tuum; adveniat regnum tuum; fiat voluntas tua, sicut in caelo et in terra. Panem nostrum cotidianum da nobis hodie, et dimitte nobis debita nostra, sicut et nos dimittimus debitoribus nostris; et ne nos inducas in tentationem sed libera nos a malo. Amen."

The priest had failed to introduce himself, and Rico privately gave him the only name he had available, "dipshit." The priest then walked to the front of the class and peered at the students over his glasses, emitting a low, grumbling sound that seemed to escape from his bowels.

"Eh," he muttered.

"Holy shit," Bates said gleefully.

"Ambulare," the priest commanded himself and walked in a straight line in front of the classroom before stopping.

"Reduco," he then announced and reversed his steps, walking a straight line back to his desk.

"Sedeat," he finished, returning to his chair and sitting down.

With his lips hardly moving, the priest's voice projected itself through his gapping grin and it rang hollow in the room. Before asking the priest to identify himself, Rico noticed that his name had been written on the green slate board. *Pater Pit* had been scribbled above the date. In his excitement, Bill failed to read the board and asked his question before Father Pit saw his hand.

"What's your name, Father?" he shouted, making an unconscious allowance for the priest's hearing aid.

Several students laughed and Father Pit adjusted the knob on his box again.

"Eh?" he responded, with an inarticulate groan.

"Your name, Father?" Bill raised the volume in his voice.

"Eh?" he groaned again and slowly shifted his body to point his hearing aid in Bill's direction.

Bates burst out laughing but managed to have enough sense to muffle his mouth.

"Dipshit," Rico read the graffiti on his desk again. "Dipshit."

Bates then began to howl into the palms of his hands.

"Let's practice again," Father Pit resumed the instruction, not comprehending Bill's question.

Rico heard some more muffled laughter but the majority seemed to be stunned. One new student sat in front of Rico. He had close-cropped hair and a dark complexion, looking more Arabic than Hispanic. As Father Pit walked back and forth repeating four Latin verbs, the student, Virgil, mockingly moved his head in timed sequence. He then abruptly turned around and looked at Rico, Bates, and Juan with an expression of amazement, opening his mouth wide and holding his hands up to his ears. At the same moment, Virgil mechanically shifted his eyes from the left to right like a metronome.

"*Domine*," Father Pit uttered in response.

Virgil turned around in contrite fashion and Pit tilted his head back, trying to find a better view through his trifocal glasses.

"Tonight," he ordered everyone, "read the first chapter of the *Primus*."

Juan looked under his desktop and found the books. The other students took his lead and they began to leaf through the pages. Rico counted seven pages of elementary Latin, with a list of new vocabulary words. Again, Bill raised his hand but the bell dismissed them.

"*Oremus*," Father Pit began the closing prayer.

"*In nomine Patris, et Filii, et Spiritus Sancti. Amen.*"

He then made the sign of the cross and the students blessed themselves.

"*Vale*," Father Pit dismissed everyone.

"We're going next door," Juan spoke almost into Rico's ear.

The class rushed through the doors, and Rico left last. Father Pit returned to his chair and began to fiddle with the knobs on his hearing device. Above him, the emperor's bust gazed austerely. Next to the bust hung the American flag, and a small crucifix in the room seemed to represent more the *Boni* of ancient Rome than it did of Jesus Christ. The objects appeared strangely incongruous together. Deep inside, Rico's subconscious told him that the rest of the school would offer more confusion. Juan noticed his delay and tugged his arm. Rico mindlessly followed Juan into the next room and again sat with him in the back rows.

When he entered his religion class, the dissimilarity between the Latin classroom and his religion class revealed an enormous historical paradigm shift from ancient Rome to the medieval epoch. Rico's religion classroom looked like the poster child or propaganda tool of the Spanish Inquisition. Spanish, Italian medieval, and Renaissance chiaroscuro prints from the Baroque and Rococo periods displayed the sufferings and executions of Christ, his disciples, and the most revered saints in the Catholic faith.

A particular print caught Rico's immediate attention. It hung on the left side of the class depicting Mantegna's *Saint Sebastian*. Rico stared up at the saint, who was tied to a white marble column and painfully enduring the long, bloodletting torture of martyrdom, while a witness below the column scornfully smirked at some unseen observer. Above the observer, Sebastian's rolling eyes pled to God as he suffered from a score of darts that vividly pierced almost every area of his lower torso. Saint Sebastian's martyrdom manifested the very heart and soul of medieval Catholicism and overshadowed the other cruel representations of martyrdom on the wall. As Rico tried to reconcile the artist's portrayal of Sebastian and God's desire to have him suffer, he felt a sharp thump on his shoulder. The sting of a wooden pointer had a delayed effect and the pain slowly escalated before a second strike caused him to wince violently.

"*Sientate!*" a diminutive Father Clement shouted. He had appeared out of nowhere.

Rico turned around and saw a short, Spanish priest, with a shadow mustache and dark-rimmed glasses, smiling behind a raised wooden pointer. He whirled the pointer and directed Rico to take a seat. Rico rubbed his shoulder and meekly sat down, stupefied that a priest would strike him without warning.

"Ju will follow my instructions when ju enter class," he barked in a shrill voice.

Father Clement walked bowlegged to his desk, which was centered directly in front of the whole class. A transparent, plastic piggy bank, in the shape of an elongated boar, sat contented on his desk. Clement approached the pig and tapped it with his pointer, continuing to smile. Displaying his gold-filled teeth, Clement lifted himself on his toes and peered down at the students.

"This is my portico," he explained. "I wish to see my *madre* in Spain in the summer. She is an Espanish woman of devout loyalty to God. When I give you detention, you will pay the *cerdo* in centavos. *¡Pagame!*"

Clement shouted "*pagame*" again and slammed the desktop with his pointer. It snapped back like a rapier in a fencing duel.

"My class is a religious class," he continued. "I will teach you the Bible and we will begin with Genesis. Let us begin. Who wrote Genesis?"

Two students confidently raised their hands and one unconsciously shook his curly brown hair. Unlike the other students in the class, the student seemed a little disheveled. His clothes seemed used, making his white shirt appear slightly yellowed. The other student had deep red hair and brown eyes. Next to the first student, the other appeared to have slept in his clothes. He tilted his head slightly to the left. Clement curiously looked at both of them and gave the curly-brown-haired student a warm, welcoming smile.

"Ju *hermano* was in my class last year," Clement observed. "Ju have the same face. Mike?"

"I'm Paul," the student corrected him. "My brother is a junior."

"My name is Henry," the red-haired student identified himself.

"Moses wrote Genesis, Father?" Paul answered the original question.

"We think it was Moses," Clement began to explain, looking at all the students for a moment. "That is one idea but Catholic scholars have many theories. The church also relies on tradition and not the Bible like the Protestant heretics…"

Rico stopped listening to Clement and his mind began to drift away as his eyes locked on another poster. A copy of an image from Gustave Dore's illustration of the French 1885 edition of Dante's *Divine Comedy* hung in a frame opposite the painting of *Saint Sebastian*. Although Rico was not aware of the literary allusion in the illustration, the image both repelled and fascinated him. The scene depicted Mohammed as one of the "Sowers of Discord" in the 19th chapter of the *Inferno's* 28th Canto, where God punishes those whom He condemned with wicked mutilations. Dante and his mentor Virgil stand on a rock looking down at a condemned soul who shows his entrails to the two robed men above him. Behind the suffering Mohammed, one of the devils strikes another condemned soul with a long sword, splitting the victim's back down the middle. Rico became slowly absorbed into the scenery and vicariously imagined the devil striking at his torso and spilling his guts out in front of him. Over and over again the scene played itself out in his mind. Then, a sudden pang of pain snapped across his shoulder.

"*Pagame cinco centavos!*" a voice pounded Rico's head from the periphery of his consciousness. The shout bothered him more than the sting of the pointer. In the next moment, Clement's pointer slammed down on his desk, missing his hand by millimeters. "*Pagame!* No daydreaming in my class!"

Rico looked up and Clement held up five fingers. Rico unconsciously dug into one pocket and produced a stained nickel, handing it meekly to Clement. The priest examined the nickel to be sure of its authenticity and gleefully deposited it into the piggy bank.

"*Mi madre* will thank you," Clement happily promised. "What's your name?"

"Rico," he answered, in a daze as pain from the two strikes on his shoulder bore deeply into his skin.

"Transgressions will be met with just punishment. 'Thus says the Lord,'" Clement droned, looking at the same scene from Dante's *Inferno*. "With just punishment," he repeated.

Rico turned his head and also looked at the "Sowers of Discord" as it gradually began to twist and dissolve into a dense transparency. The religion class and his classmates dissolved except for Clement. The cool, distant arbitrator in the cafeteria replaced the mercurial, cruel, religion teacher. Again, Clement peered down steadily at Rico with brooding eyes.

Phase 1

Rico found himself in the cafeteria with his four young-looking classmates. The experience of leaving one virtual world and entering another, as if each world represented reality, caused Rico momentarily feelings of disorientation. Then, he realized that one of his classes had been omitted from the regenerated program.

"He missed Hardy's class," Rico managed to stammer, pushing against the halting imposition of the transfer. "That history class was my favorite. The priest was a kind man. A real teacher."

"I liked the old guy," Juan chimed in. "His class was really enjoyable. We all looked forward to it."

"I heard about him," Mike remembered in high school. "Too bad. I would have liked to witness a good man's vocation in action."

"Hardy," Bill began to make an assumption, "apparently had no vital purpose in the program you experienced, Rico. Maybe?"

Moving within one program into another program caused Rico to experience a lapse between thought and action. He looked at Bill and then at Clement, but he could not generate the energy to speak again.

"Ask him," Bill pointed to Father Clement's hologram.

Rico did not have to ask. He had the answer. Impassively glaring at Rico, Father Clement sat with crossed arms, holding the gavel over his forearm. Rico watched Clement, instinctively touching his shoulder where the pointer had struck. After all the years that had transpired, the memory of this corporal punishment had remained most tangible. Seeing Clements's unmoving posture, Rico felt his anger well up at his parents for they had threatened him with further punishment if Clement ever struck him again. The injustices at home and at the school released long-suppressed feelings of resentment. His first day at the seminary resurrected every reason he had for his bitterness. Hardy never even had a positive effect on the eventful day.

"He's recording the events and your reactions," Bill interrupted Rico's thoughts. "We all saw it."

"What?" Rico spoke from a daze. He felt his speech slowly returning. "I saw it too. I think."

Realizing that his three friends had witnessed a private experience, Rico felt slightly embarrassed and irritated.

"You did," Bill clarified. He picked up a donut and placed it in front of Rico. "No calories."

Rico looked at the donut and then distrustfully stared at Bill.

"You mean I…we…were both in and out of the storyline?" Rico tried to wrap his mind around the paradox. "Simultaneous subjective and objective perspective?"

"Exactly," Bill confirmed. "We all see it the same way so we can have a vicarious discussion. How can we discuss our experiences without knowing them intimately? This process eliminates the need to have to explain the experience. Do you understand?"

"Too well," Rico responded in a sardonic tone. "What do you get out of this?"

"What do *we* get out of this," Bill corrected him. "Let's see."

"But Clement, of all people," Rico pointed at the still hologram. "I still don't understand his position."

"He represents all of the philosophers and psychologists that have ever existed," Bill spoke proudly, raising himself up in his seat. "I wanted an objective voice to observe and give us its feedback. No person but Clement can. He has no feelings."

"All from history?" Rico questioned. "Every belief, religion, political leaning or lack thereof?"

"The computer needed access to every value we had as a human species," Bill finished his explanation. "How else could it make a well-rounded and sound judgment?"

"Could you have picked a better character?" Rico rebuked him, rubbing his shoulder.

"Not Torquemada," Juan also objected.

Rico chuckled and Mike looked incredulously at both classmates.

"Maybe," Bill conceded, but he instantly dismissed the thought. "But that's academic. Clement always gave me the impression of being a true Inquisition judge."

"But to what purpose?" Rico demanded for the second time.

Bill stared at Rico and thought quietly before he answered.

"To find the answers to some of the unanswered questions we still have," he admitted. "The computer will search for our hidden questions or needs. I programmed it with open algorithms. It has open parameters. That's the adventure. Exciting, right?"

Rico looked up at Clement and realized that the computer was at that very moment using their conversations to make an assessment. Its silence spoke volumes, for the computer needed more information before it would offer an opinion or respond to a question.

"This is immoral," Mike added unequivocally. "I am uncomfortable with witnessing the private thoughts and experiences of anyone here. Even myself. All such thoughts and feelings should be privately exchanged with a confessor or God."

"I think he's right," Rico sadly agreed with him. "It's unethical. But I wouldn't add God or a confessor to the mix."

Mike prepared himself to respond to Rico's disagreement but Juan interrupted him.

"Then why did you agree to be here?" Juan challenged Mike.

"Let's try this," Rico offered a solution, interrupting both of his friends. "Clement. State your purpose."

Father Clement remained immobile.

"It's sacrilegious to be judged by a computer," Mike finally spoke. He began to nervously fidget in his chair. "It can't replace my conscience. My relationship with the Creator is sacred. The computer can't replace the spiritual aspiration and comfort a human soul needs."

"*Créador*," Clement repeated.

Every stopped speaking and stared at the hologram.

"This is all silly," Rico mused out loud. "The philosopher-king hologram conversing with other holograms? Are we now any more real than he is?"

"Good question," Bill chimed in.

"We all want to live a little bit more," Juan admitted, fearing that Rico and Mike may have second thoughts about the whole process. "No matter how. I'm here for a chance. My life was cut short. This computer is doing more for me than any god did for me all my years in a coma. So fuck you, Mike. Don't judge me. You can't imagine the hell it's been and how much I missed out."

Rico diverted his sympathetic eyes from Juan and looked to Bill to plead for a resolution. Bill diverted his attention and then motioned towards Mike who could not contain his need to speak.

"We have a soul," Mike explained with extended hands, as if he were prepared to give a homily. "This computer and our facsimile is an abomination. Only our souls matter! Only God can judge."

"Then why did you come here?" Juan asked again. "If this is an abomination, why did you agree to sin with us? You didn't walk into a whorehouse to fuck and say it's a sin at the same time? Did you?"

Mike dropped his hand and quietly sulked, refusing to admit his personal reasons for participating in a pagan ritual.

"I think Clement will trump you," Rico scoffed at Mike's refusal to divulge his motivations. "If you were in his class, he would tell you to '*Pagame*.'"

Laughing mockingly, Rico lifted his arm and pretended to strike down on Mike's shoulder with a pointer.

Juan also laughed and repeated the motion until a voice paralyzed his swiping motion.

"*Pagame!*" Clement repeated, pointing to Mike.

Greatly offended and incensed, Mike half stood up to object to the mocking gestures against him, but the instant he began to push his chair back to stand up, and before he could complete his action, his hologram dissolved. In the same instant, the cafeteria slowly dissolved away and a large public arena replaced it. Thousands of adolescents cheered, standing in front of a Catholic liturgical service. It was 1975.

Chapter 4

Minus solus, quam quum solus esset.
– Cicero

Mike found himself in a large yellow bus moving across the Golden State Freeway, heading for Anaheim. Fifty sophomores and juniors occupied the bus and carried on loud conversations among themselves across the aisle and seats. Some of the students, whom no one would have thought were seminarians, discussed girls and the potential of meeting girls at the convention. Unlike the rest of the juniors, Mike did not muscle his way to the rear of the bus and instead sat down in the front with John. And, unlike the other seminarians on the bus, Mike entered the seminary his sophomore year, making him an outsider. Others ostracized him not because of his late arrival as a classmate, which, in most cases, provided a valid reason for adolescents to distance themselves from each other. Rather, Mike did not fit in because he devoutly believed in God. Generally, all of the seminarians fit into a bell curve of belief and some were agnostics, bordering on atheism.

Among all the *true* believers in the class, Mike's faith was unwavering. The church was infallible and his teachers were near-infallible. According to Mike and his perspective on his newly adopted school, only the truly devout students ought to attend the seminary, eliminating at least ninety-five percent of his classmates. Discussions about sex and pot on a field trip to a religious convention tortured Mike's very sense of propriety. John sat attentively next to Mike, whom he felt was his brother in Christ. As for Mike, he felt that his bi-racial friend lacked some maturity and was overly self-conscious, but he gladly accepted John's company over that of the philistines who accompanied them on the trip. Although repelled by John's sweaty, flabby body, Mike charitably ignored the corpulent girth that stretched into his seating area.

"I wish these people would grow up," Mike commented. "Why do they go to a seminary and think about having sex with girls and smoking pot?"

John smiled as his body flinched. The mentioning of sex and drugs caused him to become uncomfortable. During his freshman year, the seniors had told him that he would be castrated when he took his priestly vows. According to the seniors, the general public did not know but God demanded castration for all priests to better serve the Lord. The seniors then added that the castration must be done without anesthesia since it did not exist in the Bible. For a long time, John believed the lie until he broke down and told his Spiritual Director. Night after night and day after day, John suffered from the knowledge that he would have to sacrifice his genitals for his love of God. He told himself that he was reliving the experience of Abraham preparing to sacrifice his son to God. *Maybe God would grant him a reprieve and he would be spared like Isaac? Why was God so cruel?* Then, to his relief, he found out the truth of the cruel joke. Afterward, the experience caused John to feel an aversion to any sexual reference.

"Yes," John agreed meekly. "They always talk about that stuff."

He then looked down and repressed some impure thoughts that began to well up. Mike recognized his discomfort and changed the subject.

"Did you go to the Youth Day before?" Mike asked, hoping John would open up.

Mike's expectations for the Youth Fair mounted as he fantasized about the possibility that the convention would attract true believers.

"Yes," John admitted. "I like going every year."

"What's it like?" Mike pressed.

"Did you sign up for the courses?" John tried to answer the question.

John felt uncomfortable about the questioning because it required him to express his feelings. He never wanted to tell anyone about his feelings, since all teenage boys ended up talking about sex.

"Yes," Mike answered curtly. A small swell of frustration crept up. "I mean the whole event. How did it all work out? What did you like or dislike?"

"Oh," John felt a sense of relief. "It was nice. Really nice."

"Nice," Mike repeated wanting more. "Just nice? Go ahead, John. What did you like about it?"

"I," John began nervously. "I liked the Mass. They had nice music."

"Music," Mike responded positively to the word. "I play the organ. What kind of music?"

"Oh," John thought hard. "I think it was Hurd and Canedo's music. The same stuff we hear in school."

"Really?" Mike listened incredulously. "I miss the sacred music. The type of music published out of the Academy of Santa Cecilia. You like Gregorian chants?"

"They're okay," John feebly admitted. He felt nervous for he knew very little about music but was afraid to admit it. The subject began to irk him like the subject of sex. "I...just...like good music."

"OK," Mike tried to change the subject. "So is the Mass different from the one at school?"

"Yes," John answered reluctantly. He knew he was not making a good impression on Mike but he wanted to be his friend. "They do a performance on the stage. Last year, some high school students performed the gospel on the stage in pantomime when the priest read the scripture. It was pretty cool." He paused and tried to recall the memory. "They played music too."

"A play?" Mike asked in disbelief. "Why is everything becoming so different, John?"

John shrugged, since the question demanded him to take a stand. He felt better when his parents or his teachers told him what to believe. Life was easier without any challenges.

"I don't know," John admitted nervously.

"My parents wanted me to go to a Jesuit school but I told them they were too liberal," Mike explained his disdain for current church politics. "All the orders are too liberal. The secular priests seem to be a little moderate. Did you guys ever have a Latin mass in these three years?"

"Yes," John admitted, feeling unsure about Mike's intentions. "When we took Latin last year. Now we have Spanish Masses as you know."

"I wish I could have gone to a Latin Mass," Mike mourned. "No churches in this diocese have Latin Masses. We should go back to the Tridentine Mass. Don't you think?"

"What?" John asked, confused. He suddenly wanted to end the conversation.

"Never mind," Mike dismissed the entire conversation, realizing John's ignorance of church liturgical history.

He smiled politely and turned to the window to gaze out. Watching the bus turn into the convention's parking lot, Mike began to have doubts about any chance of experiencing something special with the Lord. Instinctively, he knew that the convention would be filled with hormone-driven adolescents, desecrating the sacred event with their base pursuits while adults permitted the Mass to be polluted with secular folk music. The problem Mike faced was that he really wanted to serve God. He had a calling but God never talked to him. He wanted an answer from God. Mike sought for a divine resolution for his need. A fulfillment was needed from God, and he waited desperately.

Too much of the world filtered into Mike's search and he had little hope he could find God in the convention center. Despite his doubts, Mike obeyed his Spiritual Director who told him that God sometimes appears and answers our prayers where we least expect to find Him. In this convention center, Mike feared he was falling farther away from God. To make matters worse, his neutrality towards sex gave others the impression he was a homosexual. Despite what everyone thought about him, Mike loved women, but he fell in love with God first. The moment was unforgettable in middle school when he attended a Mass and watched the priest walk down the aisle during the opening hymn. An altar boy bearing a crucifix and a lecturer holding a Bible preceded a serene ceremonially garbed man who beamed with goodness and love. Mike noticed that other Catholics admired the priest for bringing them closer to God, enjoying the fruits of his relationship with the Lord. Mike wanted to be like the priest and to be wanted by God's people. He needed to have God want him first before he could fulfill his dream. Over time, the exhilaration melted and the dream became void but, like unrequited love, Mike held up his torch and waited for his God to claim him as His own.

"All out!" the bus driver shouted.

"Oh, man!" Bates shouted. "Check out those foxes, dude."

"Check out the tits on that one!" Juan called out.

Several boys slapped John on the shoulder and he nodded to them, forcing a congenial smile. A part of him wanted to joyfully go with his incorrigible classmates, but his self-consciousness about his weight prevented him from joining in the pagan celebration. John remained seated out of some false loyalty to Mike.

'What girl would like me?' John told himself.

A jumble of orgasmic shouting and whistling accompanied the stomping rush of thirty pairs of adolescent feet racing to the exit. The bus driver had enough sense to remain seated, as did Mike and John. Mike mourned this moment, not because he did not find girls attractive, but because he felt embarrassed at his classmates' behavior. The driver tried to make eye contact with Mike since only he and John remained seated on the bus. Averting his eyes from the driver, he peered out the window to try to see where God could be found in a sea of immature adolescents.

"Son," the driver tapped him on the shoulder. "You gotta get off."

John tugged at Mike's shirtsleeve.

"Let's go, Mike," John nervously pleaded.

Mike sighed and stood up, dreading what lay ahead. When he stepped off the bus, a crowd of students was pouring off the other busses from every region in the county. Mike lost sight of his classmates immediately. Within a few minutes, the seminarians dissipated into the bulging crowd like ants entering a large colony mound. Before Mike, the crowds contracted and expanded like a bubbling bowl of thick polenta. Great clumps of teenagers moved haphazardly in circular motions, defying the laws of physics, before dissolving into another nondescript mass of students. Seen from above, the jostling, laughing, and buoyant students seemed to respond to an indeterminate outside force that pressed in upon them from the periphery. While pushing out from the center, they moved in sweeping undulations, edging closer to the convention doors.

Mike and John again held back, waiting for the crowds to begin forming a line as they pushed towards the convention doors. Most of the students coagulated against the doors. Suddenly, several snapping sounds silenced the awaiting crowd. Mike could see the door being pushed open against an unseen resistance as it staggered slightly open before closing again. The action repeated itself until the doors completely swung open. In a minute, the crowd swayed and moved forward, transforming into a wedge and then slowly thinning out. Along the edges of the wedge, the adolescents collapsed into the center and a rapid steam of students poured through the doors like sand in an hourglass.

Mike and John followed the movement until they, like the last grains of sand in an hourglass, trickled through the doors into a circular foyer that revealed shadowed, unhinged openings into the convention center. As Mike looked around, the students dispersed and entered the dim convention center. The students walked rapidly to their unassigned seats and tried to find welcoming friends or acquaintances. Through the shadows, Mike watched some of the more mature and mischievous students sit in the upper chambers and slink into the darkness like resting bats. The openly gregarious and innocent students sat in the lower chamber, clamoring together as if they were attending a rock concert.

"What do we do first?" John inquired, without looking at Mike.

Mike was too proud to admit that he left his schedule on the bus, although he took the time to memorize the workshop assignments.

"Listen," Mike answered half-consciously. He wanted to sit in the upper chambers but decided against mingling with smoking, lecherous students. "Let's go there in the middle."

He pointed to a lit area close to the center stage but not next to the stage. The seating positions gave Mike and John some perspective to look down on the event without having to strain to see the participants' facial features. John studied the area for a moment.

"There are a lot of girls here," John observed.

Mike understood the meaning of his words well.

"They won't bite," Mike tried to allay his fear. "Some might even be thinking about being nuns." Mike half-joked, hoping to make John smile. "You may have something in common with them."

"Really?" John responded happily, missing the intended humor.

The idea of real teenage girls thinking about a vocation in the Church never occurred to John. He felt it was impossible but the presence of young nuns in the cafeteria contradicted his doubts. He then had a very different idea for the first time.

"It's too bad we can't marry," he commented out loud.

"Priests marrying nuns?" Mike pondered skeptically. "What's the point? It would be a spiritual distraction. It's a sin in the eyes of the Church."

"A marriage like that could solve the vocation crisis," speculated John.

"Of course," Mike scoffed. "And their teens could all be pre-enrolled in seminaries and convents. Like us. Can you imagine?"

Mike laughed to himself as if his absurd joke would entertain the whole Catholic world.

John thought about the possibility of being a married priest. It was distantly intriguing. Seeing the girls around him, he began to believe there was some merit to the idea.

"Didn't God say that it wasn't good for man to be alone?" John thought privately, even if he would not dare tell anyone in the seminary how he felt.

Ignoring John, Mike walked towards two empty seats directly facing the stage. He looked around and noticed that all of the surrounding students seemed to have made a commitment to Youth Day as true devotees. Some said the Rosary in small cliques, while others spoke about the upcoming events and presenters. Mike could not find any of the typical upper-chamber hypocrites who attended these events to escape the restrictions of home and school. For any of the students, not including the seminarians who would return in the late afternoon, these immediate Catholic students would attend the events for three days and stay at a nearby hotel. Ironically, they appeared to be more devout and loyal than the seminarians who professed their vocation each day in the chapel. Without asking John for his opinion, Mike obliviously sat down among a contingent of adolescent girls wearing plaid uniforms.

"This might be rewarding after all," Mike concluded. Deep down, Mike suddenly felt uneasy sitting among the girls but the thought of finding some connection with God thrilled him more. After he listened to nearby girls, who conversed about the presenter and their schedule for the next three days, Mike had mixed feelings about any chance that these adolescent girls in modern America could truly find God. The odds were probably against them.

"I am going to Father Tim's workshop," one girl announced gleefully.

"Really?" a friend responded disappointedly. "I had to accept my second choice. The workshop was closed."

"Oh, he's so hip!" another girl exclaimed.

"It's a shame he's a priest. What a waste," a girl bemoaned.

"Yeah," all agreeably chimed in together.

John felt very nervous about eavesdropping on their conversation. He could not believe his ears. Girls his age were not supposed to have any sexual desires, especially such feelings for a priest. Looking sideways to his right, John caught a glimpse of the girl who thought the priest's celibacy was a waste. Although she seemed a little overweight, she had soft brown hair, pulled up in a bun, and green eyes with long eyelashes. Her nose was small and round and sat like a button above her slightly thick rouged lips. She turned her head in John's direction and he quickly averted his eyes.

"Hey," the girl called to John. "What school are you from?"

John heard her but he made himself believe she was calling someone else.

"Hey," she reached over and tapped him on the shoulder. "What school? You're wearing a white shirt and black tie!"

John sheepishly looked to his right and tried to smile, feeling a muscle in his cheek twitch uncontrollably. He felt as if he were caught in a time warp or horrible nightmare where the dream victim tries to run and scream but cannot move despite all of his efforts.

"The minor seminary," Mike announce proudly. "I'm Mike and this is John."

"Hi," John heard himself squeak.

She smiled widely and extended her hand. The other girls giggled and pointed to both Mike and John. Another girl motioned to a female acquaintance one row above her while some of the girls leaned into each other and spoke with their hands cupped over their mouths.

"Now they all know we are in the seminary," John mourned to himself.

"My name is Elizabeth," the girl shook John's hand with strong conviction. "Call me Liz."

"John," he repeated his name and remained dumfounded.

She held his hand for a long moment before John slid it away.

"You don't talk to girls much?" Liz reasonably speculated, giving John a perplexed expression. Then she warmly smiled at him again. "That's OK. I was thinking about being a nun, for a while. How long have you been in the seminary?"

Liz's vivacious and affable attitude tied John up in a knot. He both wanted to embrace her while at the same time retreat under a rock. He could not find the ability to express his pleasure at meeting such a delightful person whom he instantly liked. At the same moment, he felt the pang of guilt for wanting to befriend a girl.

"Can't you talk?" Liz asked with a smile. "I don't bite."

A small group of nearby girls overheard Liz and began to laugh. John felt mortified and searched for some words to say.

"I'm sorry," he told her. "Are there any in L.A.?"

"Any what?" Liz asked impatiently.

"Convents?" John almost stuttered.

Several girls could be heard giggling. Mike was forced to take his eyes off the stage and look disapprovingly at John, who purposely ignored him.

"I mean," John waffled. "You said you thought about convents. Right?"

"Yeah," Liz admitted, relaxing her guard. "But it was talk. One of those moments when something grips you and you want to be that something. I've done that a dozen times. Didn't you ever have such an experience?"

John thought about her words but he could not think about wanting to be anything else but a priest until he met Liz. He began to fantasize about being a married priest so he could eliminate the sin of sex without sacrificing his vocation.

"No," John explained. "I always wanted to be a priest, I guess."

"Cool!" Liz exclaimed with false approval. "Are you taking workshops all weekend?"

"No," Mike interrupted unexpectedly. "We are going back to the seminary this afternoon."

Mike's last words aggravated John and pushed him to the point of embarrassment, since he felt he was making some inroads into courting Liz's favor. According to John's paranoiac fear, a time limit would just exacerbate an already difficult and short interlude with a girl he found attractive. John looked at Liz and thought about what she would look like under her clothes. As if Liz could understand John's thoughts, she smiled coyly and blushed slightly at John's appraising eyes. He caught her blush and blushed in return.

"We have all day still," he tried to assure her and himself.

"Maybe we are taking the same workshops," Liz added, moving slightly towards John. "Let's look at our schedule."

John could suddenly feel her warmth and smell her perfume, which wafted through the air around him. With slow-motion clumsiness, John pulled out his schedule and tried to fold it open to the right page. Not taking his eyes off her blouse, he watched the curvature of her breasts rise and fall as she adjusted her seating position to turn towards him. Liz then impatiently took the schedule out of John's hands and folded the papers over, comparing the events line by line like an auditor reviewing the client's accounting books.

"Well," Liz said disappointedly. "We don't have the same workshops. But we have the same lunchtime. That's cool. We can talk about our workshops and the seminary."

In the background, John could hear some girls giggle but he ignored them, losing himself in Liz's eyes. Everyone, except for Liz, melted into the background until Mike tapped John's shoulder.

"We're beginning," Mike spoke enthusiastically and pointed out the arrival of the speaker and a band onto the stage.

A priest walked out and greeted the audience. He spoke about the goals and aspirations he and the religious congress had for the next three days. Then, he introduced a Vietnamese teenage girl, a refugee from Saigon after its fall earlier in the year. The teenager related her experience of escaping from the Viet Cong after spending weeks in a reorientation camp. She and her family were smuggled out of Vietnam on an overloaded ship that leaked heavily as it wallowed across the Pacific Ocean. The refugees were starving and almost drowned before a U.S Navy ship rescued them, transporting them to Hawaii. The teenager emphasized the comforting refuge of her faith throughout the long, arduous odyssey from the Viet Cong camp to Hawaii.

"Hi. My name is Trinh. My family were all Catholics," she told the enraptured audience, who listened compassionately to her misadventure and suffering. "Many were raped and tortured in the camp and many died in the ocean. Many died because they refused to give up their faith. They were martyrs like those who died in the Coliseum hundreds of years ago. But we prayed to Jesus who saved us from the atheist Communists. The church gave us a home in Vietnam and in America. Wherever we go, the church is our home. Jesus loves us through the church, and I ask you to pray for the faithful who suffer in Vietnam for Jesus. They are now being seriously persecuted by the Communist people who don't believe in God."

Mike and John continued to listen as some of the girls expressed their discomfort upon hearing the tragic tale. The girls winced as the rapes were described and all of them had moist eyes when Trinh finished her story.

"Please stand up," the speaker asked. "Raise your hands up and let us sing out our joy to the Lord who loves us and His Church."

Everyone stood up as the priest began to sing and the band began to play a popular Bob Hurd folksong. The audience chimed in with a loud *Alleluia* and everyone spontaneously took their neighbors' hands and held up their arms, swaying gently from side to side. John happily took Liz's hand and Mike made a strong effort, reluctantly taking another girl's hand and allowing himself to participate in the sentimental ceremony. Liz tightly gripped John's hand and often exchanged coy, warm smiles with him. Her smiles overwhelmed and excited John and he felt a close union with God through Liz's smile and touch. John realized that God acted through her femininity and touched his soul with divine love.

"I love you," Liz seemed to say as she sang her song of praise to Jesus.

John's eyes darted from the stage to her face and he beamed a wide smile, slightly blushing as the chorus of students continued to sway. Mike looked at his friend and began to fear that Liz would take him down the proverbial primrose path. Too many seminarians, in Mike's estimation, lost their vocation with an innocent flirtation in church. According to Mike and the stern priests who counseled him, sharing God's love with a girl in the liturgy would soon lead the seminarian to the sacramental bed, but not always a holy one.

"John," Mike tried to knock him out of his trance. "John."

John barely heard Mike but his chastising tone reached his consciousness before he heard his name being called.

"John!" Mike almost shouted, feeling his voice becoming hoarse.

John finally heard his friend and looked in his disapproving eyes.

"What?" he challenged Mike's almost managerial manner.

Mike, taken aback, stared for a second and then looked away just as the song ended. Everyone slowly dropped their arms and let go of their neighbors' hands, except for John who momentarily snatched a few more seconds holding Liz's hand.

Liz reciprocated happily until one of her supervisors called to her.

"Liz," a nondescript female shouted. "We gotta go to the workshop."

Liz turned her head and caught sight of someone who had the ability to emotionally inject liquid nitrogen into any Catholic teenage girl's veins.

"Come along, Mistress Elizabeth," a mature woman's voice called out.

John automatically obeyed the voice and turned his head at the same time Liz saw her teacher, a nun, approach them. She wore a blue dress, and the habit of her order had the effect of augmenting the stern, calculating glare she directed at the couple.

"We must move along," the nun gave John a stinging smile that sent a subtle, nonverbal threat directly at him. "Where do you go to school?"

"Uh?" John stammered as if he had been abruptly thrown into a cold bath. "Uh.. sister...uh...the minor..."

"Seminary," the nun concluded. "I know Monsignor O'Malley. He's a very good religious man."

The additional implied threat sank deeper into John's psyche, for no seminarian thought the Monsignor was a *good* man. Most of the seminarians believed that the Monsignor was the wrath of God on Earth and John dreaded the thought of receiving a reprimand from the Rector, especially since the Monsignor told the seminarians to behave with the girls. No one listened, but John never expected that the admonition would now apply to him. For the first time in his life, John felt the conflicting surge of joy at rebelling against an authority.

"Yes, Sister," John responded politely as he looked upon the incarnation of the Antichrist.

The nun motioned for the girls to continue on to their workshops and she gave John another disapproving smile. When the nun turned around, John caught Liz mouthing the word "Later," giving John a surge of hope. Liz quickly turned around after the nun shooed her along. John watched her dash off with the nun, shadowing all the girls from behind until they faded into the escaping crowds that melted through the exit doors.

Standing alone in the stands, John dropped back into his seat and realized he had a crush. He could not believe that he had fallen in love with a strange girl. His feelings sent him into a tailspin, for he still wanted to be a priest, but less so at the moment. He simmered alone in his seat in blistering emotional turmoil until he realized that Mike was missing. A feeling of brief panic overwhelmed him and washed away the turmoil about his romantic dalliance and his desire to serve God. The convention center was practically empty at that point. Not only did he fear losing Liz by the end of the day when he had to return to the seminary, but he felt he would lose his only friend if he continued to pursue Liz after they returned to campus.

Another thought and emotion struck John. In the seminary, John would have almost no contact with Liz after lunch that day. Only a letter and an intermittent phone call would be available. Again, John felt that God had abandoned him and torched his desires. His joy rose rapidly, only to be shot down in despair. All of his options pointed to defeat unless he left the seminary and attended Liz's school. But where was her school? Los Angeles was a huge county. The complexity of the situation bore down on him further as all solutions evaporated. Trying to stand up, he fell back into his seat in despair and confusion.

John continued to sit and brood until lunch. For the next two hours, he sat alone and turned his dilemma over and over in his mind. No resolutions could be found. A few of the janitors asked him if he felt okay, but John politely responded with a "Yes" and continued to brood. When one of the janitors passed by, John asked for directions to the restroom. Standing up, he suddenly faced Mike who looked pleasantly happy even though John had not attended a single workshop.

"John," Mike announced. "My workshop was amazing. The Brother spoke with such fervent knowledge about the scriptures and his calling to religious life. I really felt I could identify with him. I am sorry you missed it. I saw Father and he asked for you. I told him you were sick."

"Thanks," John responded glumly, standing up.

He walked with Mike towards the restroom, not fully grasping the fact that Mike had violated one of his principles about lying.

"Why did you lie?" John asked.

"I didn't," Mike defended himself. "Your soul is sick."

"Right," John tried to understand the spiritual allusion but he couldn't. "I am kind of sick, I guess."

"You have to put the girl behind you," Mike tried to encourage his friend. He could see that Liz could seriously damage or destroy John's vocation. "You can't see her if you go back to school. You know that?"

"Yeah," John reluctantly agreed. "But I have to see her now. I feel it."

"Are you having doubts about your vocation?" Mike pursued.

John stopped and looked directly at Mike with moist eyes. Several tears began to fall and John rapidly wiped them with his sleeve. He sniffled before speaking.

"Why can't we have both?' John demanded to know through a choking voice. "Why does God give us these feelings and then tell us we can't enjoy them or have them? It's some kind of joke. I don't get it. Is God this cruel? I am afraid to think about it, Mike. Our God must be crazy and mean. He hurts us."

"It's the Devil," Mike responded with aplomb. "That's all there is to it. God has nothing to do with it. You are being tempted."

"Okay," John tried to be reasonably agreeable. At that very moment, he realized that any semblance of friendship had ended between them. Mike would take one path and John would have to go in another direction until he found a satisfying answer for his conflict. "It'll just be nice during lunch when I see her."

"I'll go to the restroom later," Mike changed his mind.

He decided to leave John alone with the girl, for his friend would be unreasonable until they returned to the security and shelter of the seminary. In time, Mike felt that the reassurance of the seminary's spiritual life would resurrect his friend's vocation. He even entertained the idea of discussing the issue with his Spiritual Director.

"I'll see you maybe in the afternoon or on the bus. Maybe it will be better then?" Mike tried to sound reassuring.

"Thanks," John answered, continuing to walk to the restroom.

He felt alone and abandoned but strangely buoyed with new confidence. Seeing a few seminarians on the way, they greeted each other and continued walking with their clique. A few of the seminarians walked sheepishly with a girl or a small group of girls, trying not to seem too seriously involved at the moment. The cafeteria was a short distance away from the restroom. John pushed himself forward, afraid of what he would find. His heart pounded with anticipation. Once in the cafeteria, he picked up a lunch tray and tried to appear normal. Once again, he avoided the seminarians and ate alone with a mixed group of Catholic high school students. Mike saw him and ignored him. John also pretended to ignore his presence. Mike understood and felt sorry for his friend when he walked away.

The anticipation caused his heart to pound harder and he began to sweat. Unlike at other times, John ate his lunch with meager bites and looked around, but Liz was not available. Then, John made a concerted effort to try to locate someone from her school who wore the same uniform. With desperate effort, he rose from the table and threw away his lunch and walked in circles through the cafeteria. Thinking that he might be mistaken, John walked outside the cafeteria and then raced back inside the cafeteria in case she might have entered. She could not be found. A long desperate hour passed with John moving fearfully in every direction until he collapsed in a chair, his eyes darting about the room. Slowly the students began to disperse from the cafeteria for the afternoon workshops, leaving John sitting alone. Liz never showed up and John sadly gave up, feeling that God had punished him for his infidelity. He felt condemned and defeated. Reluctantly, he stood up and returned to the bus where the driver sat inside reading the newspaper.

"It's already over, dude?" the driver asked, looking at his watch and thinking he had lost track of time.

The convention still had two hour remaining.

"No. I don't feel good. Can I just sit here?" John asked and walked to the back of the bus, not waiting for the driver to respond.

The driver did not respond and he let the strange, overweight seminarian walk to the back of the bus before returning to his newspaper. In a few moments, he spoke again to John.

"I'm going for a smoke and lunch," he announced to John, leaving the seminarian alone in the bus. "Catch you later."

John watched the bus driver leave and began quietly weeping until he slowly fell asleep across the rear bench seat. No one bothered to wake him up that long, lonely afternoon.

Phase 2

Clement sat immobile in his seat as Mike's hologram returned to the cafeteria. Momentarily feeling caught between two realities, Mike gripped the table in front of him and let the seeping new reality adjust and come into focus. He looked at Clement and tried to speak, but no words would come out. Then he looked around and saw the three other men also trying to adjust in the phase transition from one virtual world to another. With slow effort, Mike could feel his vocal cords begin to utter sounds and then phonemes. A few jumbled and mumbled words escaped his lips before the phase transition evaporated. A strong physical tug yanked him into the present, virtual world and out of the bus area with a depressed, sleeping John.

"That wasn't fair," Mike protested.

"Shit!" Juan exclaimed in disbelief. "I thought he was gay."

"Obviously not," Mike commented and turned to Bill. "That had more to do with John than me. How would the computer or Clement know? It was a separate experience."

"Was it?" Bill rhetorically challenged him. "Ask Clement."

Mike looked at Clement, expressing his defiance, but he then lowered his head in frustration.

"I now remember he told me months later," Mike recalled. "It was long ago. I forgot. But how did the computer retrieve it?"

"The computer is able to tap our deep memories," Bill explained further. It scans the engrams and draws a path to find the modality of each person's memories. Basically, it makes imprints of forgotten storage if you can say it that way. Language falls short, you know."

"But the event had nothing really to say about Mike," Rico added.

"Really?" Bill questioned sarcastically.

"Poor fuck," Juan concluded about John. "He didn't have too much going for himself."

"He left that year," Rico reminded Juan, preparing to mock John. "The darling of the faculty. I guess you replaced him as the special child, Mike?"

Mike ignored Rico's sarcasm and continued to review the experience in his mind.

"I don't understand," Mike continued.

"What?" Juan demanded to know.

"How it all had to do with me?" Mike clarified.

Clement suddenly appeared animated as he turned his attention towards Mike.

"Your vocation," Clement announced in a deep, Spanish-accented tone.

"Vocation?" Mike questioned. "Oh…I see."

"Yes," Clement spoke in a paternalistic tone.

"John's experience was the antithesis of your own," Bill interpreted the avatar's answer. "Maybe it reinforced your spiritual experience and the conclusions you came to at the convention."

"It did, I guess," Mike paused to review his memories. "You see, I felt that God had distanced himself from me, and the workshops brought me closer. At least, they carried me to the next step on my way to the priesthood."

"The workshops?" Clement questioned.

"No," Mike agreed, forgetting he was conversing with a computer. "It was John. It was his pitiful state to fall for such a girl. Seeing her for a short while caused him to lose his vocation. He gave up on his calling and fell into the misery of unrequited love. All for a girl."

"That's when you defined yourself?" Bill prodded him.

"Yes," Mike conceded. "I despised his wallowing self-pity. I promised myself never to fall into those temptations and to be so weak and emotionally malleable."

"Yeah, I agree," Rico blurted out viciously. "You are now the master of compassion and humanity."

Rico laughed out loud, while Bill remained quiet and still. Clement continued to appear interested and involved.

"I bet you tell poor sinners in the confessional to whip themselves and wear a hairshirt?" Rico continued to poke fun at him. "You are a fucking asshole. You could have helped John."

"I tried, but the girl did it to him," Mike spoke condescendingly. "But he was a nebbish, a weak-willed, timid fool. I didn't want to have anything to do with such a character. I didn't want it to taint my character and make me doubt my vocation. No doubts would touch me."

"A real humanitarian," Rico sarcastically commented. "Jerk."

"Then John felt abandoned and retreated further," Clement concluded. "Isolated and alone, he felt left out of the seminary. With no vocation and an aching heart, he felt God had abandoned him. He had no vocation. Your God does a real good job at helping his believers, don't you think?"

"He does for those who hold on to their faith," Mike summarized in a cool, objective voice. "God only helps those who reach out to him. John never took my advice and sought his help."

"You are a real jerk," Rico repeated.

"Your insults aren't helping," Mike retorted. "They don't fit into the reality of who our God is. He doesn't allow the tepid to enter his kingdom. Our faith must be strong and unflinching. Soon you will face Him. We all will. How will you justify yourself in his presence? What will you tell Him when He asks for an account of your actions in this life . . . whether it's real or in a computer?"

"If I weren't in a computer program, I would vomit all over you," Rico told him. "Maybe I should try?"

Juan laughed and slapped the table. As Juan continued to laugh, Clement reverted to his immobile stature. Seeing Clement's sudden immobility, Rico pushed the avatar, but Clement remained unmoved and stoic.

"You were always a skeptic," Mike reminded Rico. "You would be blasphemous in His presence at the Mass. I don't see why you attended the seminary and lasted until graduation. Rico, you always made a mockery of your faith."

Rico prepared himself to answer but Juan interrupted him.

"I kind of liked John," Juan added. "He had a funny side."

After pausing to reflect, Rico nodded in agreement.

"So Bill," Rico turned away from Mike. He wanted to debate his old classmate but decided that another question took precedence in his mind. "How long do I have to continue to listen to this self-righteous piece of shit?"

"I know you never liked Mike," Bill understood, showing sympathy for Rico's objection. "But we are all that are left."

"Left to do what?" Rico shouted. "Juan and I understand each other and are friends. Mike always remained aloof. He never fit in. I never knew him at all. He only stayed in the chapel and was always in the background of our activities."

Mike had ignored Rico and turned his head away to face the large crucifix. He then began a quiet, private prayer.

"It's great that you brought him here and gave him a second chance," Rico spoke to Bill, trying to ignore Mike's defiant prayers. "But why can't we just hang out and have fun, Bill?"

"Time," Clement spoke in a monolithic tone without moving or showing any expression.

"Time?" Rico questioned, looking at Bill for an explanation.

"We have little time," Bill reminded them. "This program serves a purpose. Maybe another time we can have more fun?"

Bill gave Rico a simple smile. Rico understood Bill's gesture as a request to acquiesce to the situation. Rico nodded and reluctantly agreed.

"We need to come to grips with our lives," Bill added. "Clement will continue to probe and find the events, which will help us. Are we willing to go on? Remember, I won't force this all on you. You can leave."

They all looked at each other silently.

"I think this will serve as a confessional," Mike surmised when he took his eyes off the crucifix. "I can see how this can serve as a penance."

"Why does everything have religious implications for you?" Rico queried. "God never gave us this ability to communicate and relive our lives in a virtual world. Bill did that. Why can't you take it as it is?"

Everyone looked over at Bill, who remained as fixed and immobile as Clement.

"That's the point," Mike explained. "Heaven will be the ultimate virtual reality. This is all a precursor. I am pleased with the prospect and experience. The more I reflect on this experience, the more I can see a glimpse of my judgment. I welcome the chance."

"You always find any method to twist facts and evidence for your own preconceived beliefs that have no basis in demonstrable facts," Rico disagreed. "And you're also an asshole."

"Why do you always dilute your points of argument with disrespect and insults?" Mike fired back in a distressed tone. "You think your curses will convince me or change my mind? I can't be swayed by insults like the victim of an elementary school bully."

"Or high school," Juan added. "You know…I've been unconscious for years and some things never change. You're still stuck up, dude."

Rico laughed, to Mike's consternation.

"The more things change, the more they remain the same," Bill mused. "I forget who said that."

"Who said that?" Juan speculated. "Aristotle?"

"It's from Ecclesiastes," Mike corrected him.

"No," Rico could not recall exactly. "I don't remember reading it in the Bible."

"Alfonse Karr," Clement corrected everyone as he once again became animated. A mischievous grin appeared on Clement's face as he directed his attention to Juan. "Let's begin again."

The room melted away and Juan found himself in an afternoon study hall with one hundred twenty freshmen and sophomores.

Chapter 5

Don't try to change me or rearrange me
To satisfy the selfishness in you
I'm not a piece of clay to mold to your moves each day
And I'm not a pawn to be told how to move
I'm sorry I ain't the fool you thought would play by your rules
A to-each-his-own philosophy
– P.F. Sloan, The Turtles

A large rectangular room severed by a removable partition served as a study hall for the sixty-odd freshman and sophomores who studied for a class period at the end of the school day. Entering through two small, faded, chipped, laminated doors, the student walked into a warehouse-sized auditorium with fifteen-foot tan walls. On top of the western wall, open transept windows supplemented the anemic yellow glow of the outdated incandescent lights that hung six feet from the ceiling. The bulbs hung in circular, white-aluminum containers with radiating aluminum flat-circle extensions that gave any observer the impression of witnessing a swarm of descending UFOs.

Two groups of thirty desks faced a raised wooden platform that supported a table and oak swivel chair under a six-foot wooden crucifix. Jesus' miserable tortured figure resembled some of the students in their pondering efforts to master Latin and algebra before taking a despised examination the next day. A small reprieve awaited them in forty-five minutes when the schedule allowed them to attend recreation. A retired Brother, wearing a black traditional cassock, sat obliviously at the table, trying to ignore the occasional flux of conversation and laughter that echoed through the room. Normally the Brother would need to reprimand the students to be silent, but today his inebriation squelched his usual cantankerous behavior and actually lifted him a little out of his depression. He read his latest bestseller with absorbed interest, only occasionally lifting his eyes to check the clock above the far-right entrance door.

Juan, like all the other freshmen, sat with the first group closest to the Brother. Next to his seat, Bates's assigned desk was empty. Earlier in the day, Father Davis had caught Bates misusing the school's computer teletype to print out his one thousand detention sentences, at a cost of several hundred dollars. Davis awarded Bates the "Dolly" prize and turned him in to the Rector. where he remained sequestered most of the day. His fate was unknown but Juan knew that Bates would resurface with little wear and tear for the experience. His attempt to copy the detention sentences using a simple language loop in the Basic DOS program was ingenious. But he had unfortunately printed the detentions on expensive perforated onionskin paper. The perforated dot-matrix paper had given Bates away. Maybe Bates would invent the first computer virus?

"Please be silent," the Brother mumbled, shocking Juan out of his daydream.

Some of the sophomores erupted with muffled laughs over an inside joke in the back of the study hall. The Brother should have ignored it but the echo effect of the study hall caused him to lose his place in the middle of the page. Although the alcohol helped to calm him, it had the unfortunate effect of blurring the lines of text. After Christmas, Juan had overheard the Brother thanking a student for the fifth of Jack Daniels. Juan suspected that the Brother had a few similar bottles stashed away since *Navidad*.

From where he sat, he could smell the alcohol that occasionally wafted in his direction. Juan looked up to see Rico mockingly tilting his nose up and they both laughed. From behind Rico, Juan could see through the windows of the laminated door where he saw his brothers, with two upper classmen, walking quickly and stealthily past the study hall. The Brother had not noticed and, even if he had, they would have not received a detention. All the juniors and seniors were assigned to the study rooms across from the huge study hall. Seeing his brother and his classmates dash past the study hall, Juan felt the urge to join them. He stood up and approached the Brother's desk, slamming into an invisible wall of alcoholic odor.

"Brother," Juan spoke in a determined voice. "Brother?"

The Brother slowly looked up at Juan with bloodshot eyes. His facial muscles seemed to droop in a counter direction, giving him the expression of an abandoned hound dog.

"I need to use the restroom," Juan spoke bluntly.

Without visually acknowledging Juan's presence, the Brother returned to his book and motioned a simple nod of agreement. Juan quickly looked behind him and saw that most of the students appeared disinterested too, except for Rico who mouthed some inaudible and unintelligible words. Ignoring his friend, Juan took advantage of the Brother's intoxicated state of mind and dashed out of the study hall, shaking his head with a decisive "No" at Rico. Juan knew that his brothers and their friends would not tolerate anyone joining them, not even his best friend, Rico.

Since they were upperclassmen, Juan felt privileged to follow them to their secret meeting place. Although he knew the path to their hiding spot, Juan had not personally been there. Next to the study hall, the hallway ended on the west side thirty feet from the entrance door. Seeing no students or priests, Juan descended a small flight of concrete steps and walked parallel to the wall, right behind the Brother's desk. The narrow concrete walk soon reached an arched entrance to the right that led to the Old Mission area. On the left side of the mission stood the convent. At this time in the late afternoon, every nun attended to her prayers in the chapel and they would not leave the convent for another hour, when dinner preparations were in order.

Juan took a careful assessment of the area before passing through the imitation terra cotta archway and entering the Old Mission grounds. A large brick-and-terracotta circular fountain, built like a layer-cake, occupied the center of a large plaza. Several old colonial buildings stood in front and to the sides of the fountain. In the eighteenth and nineteenth centuries, many of the buildings served as craft centers for leather works, carpentry, sod bricks, and blacksmithing. The buildings also provided a school where the Native Americans received training in animal husbandry and farming when their Spanish lords excused them from their servile tasks. Directly in front of the fountain, a long, rectangular, brown building contained the old colonial administration building.

Outside the administrative center, a large array of serial arches decorated the façade that draped the long colonnade housing the dining area. Inside, the missionary Franciscan priests oversaw the Old Mission's operation for the Church and the King of Spain over twelve thousand miles away. During the eighteenth century, the Old Mission served as the only oasis of western civilization in a sixty-mile area. Today, it represented a reminder of how one dominant, corrupt, foreign civilization attempted to bring its myopic and delusionary religious salvation to Native Americans on the far side of the known world.

Juan took trepid steps through the plaza and into the Old Mission church. He passed through two tall, arched, oak doors and, instead of entering a sun-soaked church, small streaks of sunlight illuminated the interior from the doors and windows opposite the main entrance. Recently, the carpenters had finished installing a new roof and ceiling, after the Sylmar earthquake in 1971 had caused the interior structure to collapse. The restoration process had continued for the last two years. Most of the artifacts, benches, and confessionals had been stored in the seminary basement, so that when Juan entered he saw only the bare walls that had been recently erected.

The original church could not be completely restored, so the State of California and the Church decided to build a replica that would withstand any future seismic events. Several steel grids lay across an unfinished concrete foundation, and Juan carefully manipulated himself through the construction equipment and supplies that haphazardly littered the floor. Directly opposite the entrance door, a smaller door led to the original cemetery grounds where the first Native American converts and priests had been buried since the 1780s. Juan walked through the makeshift opening and almost stumbled over the site of an archeological dig. Although no one attended to the site, archeologists had dug stratified plots in geometric order through the middle of the cemetery. Staring at the site, Juan could see places where layers of Native Americans were interred in fragile, wooden coffins and laid on top of each other. The site's topsoil was dark but it slowly changed color in the depths below to a lighter gray and tan shade where water never completely filtered through the arid land.

The hot California sun would sometimes mummify the corpses that escaped any of the brief, seasonal rains, which could seep into the crevices below the surface. Small ladders descended down into the pits and, at the bottom of one pit, Juan could see some archeological tools. At the precipice of one of the pits, Juan saw several bones protruding from the layered soil. One lone, extended forearm, from an opposite grave, pierced the surrounding, empty space of the pit. It was sheathed with a leathery brown skin that clung tightly to the bones underneath.

"Hey," a muffled voice warned him. "Get the fuck away. They can see you there."

Juan followed the direction of the voice and looked to his right where he could see his brother's head emerge from some gravestones stacked near the chapel's erect wall. From the seminary grounds, they would be unseen except for Juan himself. He grudgingly tore himself from the plot for it unnaturally attracted his attention. While looking at the bones and the hand, Juan could feel as if they were beckoning him from the grave. Feeling an affinity for the dead, he somehow felt he belonged to those forgotten peons from centuries ago. A numb but almost gratifying coldness gripped him as he scrambled to hide behind the gravestones.

When he reached his brother and his friends, he smelled the marijuana smoke rising from joints that were stuck between improvised roach clips made from bent and twisted paper clips. His brother sat to the far side behind a gravestone that had a primitive crucifix carved into its granite façade, along with an obscured name that had almost completely faded. A vandalized facsimile of Jesus hung on the crucifix, almost resembling some long-forgotten Aztec god. Looking around, he saw that some of the other gravestones had been chipped or cracked from years of erosion and earthquake tremors. The names of the interred gave them a pall of an identity. In life, they were unknown but in death they piqued the interest of archeologists and church archivists.

"Here," one of his brother's friends offered Juan the roach.

His name was Paul and he had an acne-riddled face. Among all the seniors, he was the most withdrawn but Juan had heard he was the most unpredictable and rowdy, too. Juan waved off the roach.

"Dude," Juan's brother called him out. "You know why we're here?"

Juan had smoked pot a couple of times before but he did not feel like smoking it at the moment.

"Why did you come?" his brother demanded, feeling annoyed at having to justify Juan's presence in front of his friends. Only bloodlines allowed Juan into this secret circle of malcontent, unholy seminarians.

Next to Paul, a senior, Tim, lay on his backside. He was unlike the others who squatted low against the pit's walls. Tim was unusually thin and rumors spoke of his serious addiction to harder drugs. Juan's brother told him that Tim was a borderline junkie and the seminary kept him off the hard drugs when he was away from home. Juan's brother often took him to the gravesite to help him get through the day.

"Maybe he'll just end up a pothead," Juan's brother philosophized one day.

Snatching the roach away from Paul, Tim took a long, deep drag. Juan looked at him and saw that his fingers were deeply stained brown from the nicotine of his cigarettes and the residue of his pot. He then took several long drags from the roach and held the smoke for a long time before slowly exhaling.

"Fuck, man," Paul cursed in aggravation. "You'll smoke up the little shit we have. Then, you'll send up more smoke signals so the sheriff can see us. Like some fucking Indians."

"The only fucking Indians are dead here," Juan's brother joked.

Paul yelped out a laugh and then gulped it back down his throat.

"Fuck," Tim spoke from a distant, hazy mind. "He's probably butt-fucking some freshman. The faggot!"

Juan's brother and Paul laughed but the thought almost disturbed Juan. His brother noticed.

"Don't worry," Juan's brother told him. "He likes them young and Mexican."

"I don't know," Tim disagreed. "He checked you out during morning prayers."

Tim chuckled at his own joke, which made Juan blush. His brother slapped Juan as if to tell him to ignore the joke.

"Black is better, I heard the dude say," Paul added in a bemused tone.

They all laughed with contorted giggles that made their slow inebriation more apparent.

"You're shittin' me?" Juan protested.

"Maybe," Tim slurred.

They all laughed again and Juan pretended to nervously join in the private joke.

"They're all faggots," Paul concluded. "Every one of those fucking priests. Some of this pot could help them horny bastards. Except they couldn't handle more sins on their conscience."

"We shouldn't have come here," Tim seriously concluded. "That's why I smoke. It's better than being a butt fucker."

Although they had all attended Catholic elementary schools, each boy privately felt that he had somehow been coerced or deceived into attending the seminary.

"You know," Juan's brother said in shrill, mocking voice. "all our moms want us to have a good education."

"In the fine art of butt fucking," Tim repeated acerbically.

Tim and Paul chuckled again before Juan's brother took away the roach and finished inhaling the last portion of the joint. Juan dropped his head and avoided his brother's gaze, knowing that his working-class parents had sacrificed themselves financially to send them to the seminary, believing that they would receive a superior education. Like Catholics a generation before, most working-class parents felt that the Catholic Church and its educational system provided the only educational opportunity for immigrants and the working poor. Any education offered not only an opportunity but also hope for a worthwhile future.

The seminary was an elite institution in the immigrants' eyes, and it gave their children a special window of opportunity into the elite world of the ecclesiastics. Juan began to have doubts about his parents' estimations of the seminary's erudite classical education, in light of his and his brothers' experiences. He kept his opinion to himself and had not voiced it to his family who would regard him as a fool and ingrate, since he was the youngest and most inexperienced with life. Juan ignored his family's phantom admonishments and turned his attention towards the gravesite, trying to count more of the buried peons. Tim and Paul's eyes followed his gaze.

"Shit," Paul exclaimed. "Look at all those dead fucking Indians."

"Better being here than there," Juan's brother concluded.

"How many do you think are there?" Tim asked.

"Could be hundreds," Paul surmised. "The priests and Brothers were buried in the church."

"Hey," Tim raised himself up in a half-stupor. "I've got an idea."

He spoke to Juan's brother and pointed to Juan.

"Why doesn't your brother go get us a souvenir?" Tim proposed. "It could be our class mascot. We don't have a secret mascot yet."

"What?" Paul asked, looking at the rubble and graves strewn about the place.

"It's bullshit. And we don't need more religious stuff," Juan's brother dismissed the idea.

"Oh," Paul came to a sudden epiphany. He raised himself up on his haunches and pointed to Juan. "I know what he can get."

Paul and Tim looked at each other and smiled. Then they let out a loud guffaw and fell back against the gravestone with a ripping laugh. Keeping their uproar concealed was a hard task but they managed to quickly squelch their laughter into their shirtsleeves. Juan's brother understood their allusion and he smiled disagreeably, shaking his head. Tim looked up at him and tried to mouth some words. Paul instead interrupted his thoughts.

"Look," Paul reasoned. "This will make your brother the coolest dude in our class and in the school. He can take it as a sort of legend when we graduate. Don't you see? It's his initiation. He can skip *Gaudeamus*."

"Yeah," Tim added. "Unless your brother is chickenshit?"

Juan listened intently, knowing what they were alluding to but trying to deny any understanding of their meaning. He looked at his brother and silently pleaded "No." His brother instead shook his head and looked nervously away, unwilling to make eye contact with Juan. In the current situation, Juan's brother owed his allegiance to his classmates instead of his family. It was an unwritten code at the seminary and one that Juan would very soon learn to adopt as his own. Besides, Juan's brother could not help Juan out of the situation or he would suffer the consequences of being ostracized from the class. With only a few months to go until graduation, and with two younger brothers in the seminary, he could not afford to show any compassion, even if Juan would be hurt or punished for his deed.

"That's cold," Juan's brother tried to object.

"No," Paul contradicted. "It's cool. It's the best. If we weren't here, we would never think about it."

Paul turned to Tim who gave him some "skin." Juan watched them both and felt a deep sense of dread. He wished he had never followed his brother here.

"What does he get?" Paul questioned.

"Let's make it a point system," Tim blurted out.

Paul and Juan's brother looked skeptically at each other. Juan immediately felt like vomiting.

"A finger is a point," Tim explained. "A leg bone is two points. A skull is the jackpot."

"Bring a skull," Paul demanded.

Juan silently pleaded with his brother, who again diverted his eyes.

"Bring something," Juan's brother ended the debate.

He then looked around and stood up after assuring himself that no one was visible from afar.

"Where the fuck is everyone?" Paul speculated.

"Probably fucking someone up the ass," Tim quipped.

"Or smoking weed," Paul added, holding up a newly rolled joint.

They laughed and Juan's brother gave an apologetic glance to Juan before strutting stealthily away from the gravestone. Paul slapped Juan on the back before scurrying away.

"If you bring a skull," Tim promised. "I'll get you some good shit. Like Maui-Wowy!"

He quickly caught up with Paul, only to trip over some debris. Tim scrambled across the ground like a cripple falling out of his wheelchair and desperately trying to escape some unseen pursuer. Almost rolling over into one of the pits, Tim lifted himself up and moved jauntily through the construction doors and out of view. Motionless, Juan watched the transpiring events, thinking about how cold-blooded his brother had become. This quest bedeviled Juan. The dead had always frightened him.

He half-believed that his brother and classmates were playing a joke and he would just have to return to the dorm begging and crying for a reprieve. His mendicant behavior would earn him a vocal castigation and a hounding humiliation, which he would accept if he were like any other freshman. But he was not any other freshman. If he did not return from the pit with a trophy, his brother would suffer the true humiliation, and his other brother would never let him live it down for the rest of his life.

"Goddamn it!" Juan shouted to himself, half-hoping a passing priest would hear him and call him out for a detention. "Fuck!"

Juan still took a careful look around for a wayward priest or religious Brother. Seeing no one, Juan reluctantly scurried like an escaped prisoner, letting his belly scrape against the dirt and debris of the archeological site. He paused for a while to look into the pit, trying to lay his eyes on any quick trophy so that he could snatch it up and run away. Several bones protruded through thick layers of sediment, and Juan tried to reach down and pull them out of the soil. But their proximity was an illusion.

"Shit," he grumbled, realizing that he would have to descend into the pit.

Moving like a mechanical snake, Juan proceeded with staccato grace and then rolled into the pit after some gravel gave way to his weight. He fell directly into the four-foot pit and landed with a loud thud, sending a chalky mist of fine, powdered bones and sediment into the air. From a short distance, an observer would have thought that someone had dumped a load of baby powder into the hole. Juan coughed slightly and tried to shield his eyes from the powdery mist. As the mist began to clear, he glanced at his caked trousers.

"Shit," he cursed, slapping at the barely noticeable black material.

In an instant, his actions caused more white powder to rise and cling to any surface it made contact with in the pit. When he realized the futility of his actions, Juan miserably recalled the very reason he had fallen into the pit. A feeling of nausea had to be pushed down his gullet as he continued to wave away the misty chalk and began to desperately search for anything he could steal and scamper away with to the dormitory. As the mist cleared, he could discern more detail hidden in the layers.

The last two centuries and the weight of numerous buried bodies had compressed the dead into thick layers like trapped fossilized dinosaurs. The process of fossilization had begun and would reach its perfection in a few million years. Juan needed to obtain a bone from the upper layers where the sediment was soft and malleable. He tried to find some object to help him dig for a bone. Standing up, he began to search and found an iron rod used to support the cinderblocks. The rusty rod bent slightly in his grip as he tested its tensile strength against a protruding stone. Then he walked back to his original spot and began to chip with dread in the upper layers of the pit. Without paying attention to his actions, he broke several artifacts and bone fragments, which crumpled to the bottom of the pit. Juan's crude and frantic efforts created a crevice on the side of the pit that cracked in both vertical and horizontal directions. The zigzagging crack resembled the tectonic faults of California's subterranean abyss. Reaching into the crevice, Juan scraped his fingers on the stones and debris and peeled away a chunk of the top layer, exposing a malformed and compressed skull. He wedged it away, trying not to think about his actions, until the skull broke free. The right side of the skull remained behind with the compressed debris as he managed to peel off the left side of the skull from its entombment. The brownish gray skull appeared to have been split in half as if someone had taken a sharp hatchet and cleaved it.

"Fuck," a familiar voice cursed above him. "You fucking did it!"

Juan looked up. The glare of the afternoon sun distorted his view of Paul standing over the pit. His brother stood behind him, and Tim leaned over the pit and stared down as if he had lost some object.

"Shit it's dusty in there," Tim observed.

"Give it," Paul demanded.

He snatched the hacked skull from Juan's grasp and held it up for study.

"Damn," Paul cursed, turning the malformed half-skull in his hands. "Did you fucking cut it in half? Where's the rest?"

Juan ignored his question and raised his hand to his brother who reached over the pit and pulled him up.

"It's in the pit," Tim pointed out, still looking down into the pit. "You can see it over there."

"No fuck," Paul spoke in disbelief. "Why don't you go get the rest?"

"Fuck yourself," Juan told him as he stumbled out of the pit. "You guys were fucking around just waiting to see if I was chickenshit.

Tim giggled like a girl and Juan's brother half-heartedly tried to brush some of the sediment out of Juan's shirt. A small layer of white dust hung in the air around them.

"Yeah," Paul admitted. He examined the skull again. "But you gotta go back in and get the rest.

"No way, Jose," Juan finished stamping out the dust on his shoes.

"Yes, way," Paul challenged him.

Tim stared at Paul to see what would happen next, and Juan's brother moved between Paul and Juan.

"Hey," Juan's brother said in his defense. "He got something. That's good enough. No one else got anything else. Why don't you go in and get the other half?"

"No," Paul rejected the compromise. He then threw Juan's half-skull in the pit. "Go get them both yourself."

Juan moved away from his brother and tried to pass by Paul.

"Fuck you," Juan told him.

At that moment, Paul grabbed Juan and pushed him hard. He stumbled back and kept his ground. Paul then made a dash towards Juan, who remained inert.

"You better get in there," Paul continued to demand. "You faggot. I know what you are!"

As Paul approached Juan, he tightened his grip, preparing to strike the freshman in the face.

"You've got one more chance, faggot," Paul warned him and made a violent move. "Jump down and get it. You know how to bend down, don't you?"

Tim laughed at the allusion and Paul joined in.

Juan's brother seemed to watch the whole event in disbelief that one of his classmates would try to bully his own brother. When he saw Paul take the last step to push Juan into the pit, he made an unconscious decision to intervene. But it was too late. Juan timed his movement and lifted his knee directly into Paul's path, making swift and hard contact with his testicles.

"Ah. Damn you!" Paul screamed as he slowly sank down and crumpled on the ground.

"Fuck you!" Juan screamed again and ran into the Old Mission chapel.

No one followed him but he could hear cursing, recriminations, laughter, and threats. He immediately passed through the plaza and backtracked his steps from the seminary. The sound of his brother and his friends faded slowly until he could only hear the thumping of his heart in his chest. Taking several deep breaths, Juan stopped in front of the study hall door to catch his breath. His chest heaved and he shook almost uncontrollably as he leaned on the doorframe.

"You did good," Juan's brother grabbed his shoulder and spun him around. "Don't worry. Paul won't bother you. Everyone knows he's an asshole."

"So are you," Juan whispered, opening the door. "What did you tell him? You really fucked things up."

"Sorry," his brother made a poor attempt to apologize.

Juan stumbled into the hallway and made his way back to the dorm. In the distance, he could hear the students exiting the building for their two-hour recreation. On the way to the dorm, he passed one of the elderly janitors who made eye contact but did not seem to find Juan's rumpled clothes and whitened appearance to be unusual. He managed to avoid any of the staff members or priests and was half undressed before reaching his bed. Taking his clothes completely off and wrapping a towel around himself, Juan stuffed his soiled clothes in a duffle bag and scampered into the shower room. The pit's dust and grime seemed to have coated his skin with a penetrating sheet.

Jumping into a shower stall, Juan turned on the water and adjusted the heat to a barely tolerable level, letting the water rush over his body. He then frantically scrubbed his body until his skin turned red from both his aggressive motions and the scalding water. Obsessively continuing to scrub himself, Juan stood in the stall for half an hour. The water heater emptied itself but he remained in the shower as the water turned into a tepid cascade. Exhausted, he collapsed in the corner of the shower's faux marble walls and leaned his head back against one side. The showerhead continued to spray water over his body and directly into his face. Despite removing the dust and grime, Juan sensed that his efforts had been ineffective. The dust of death never seemed to evaporate or slide off his skin. In his mind, it permanently adhered to his skin like a second epidermis, suffocating the life out of his body. Juan remained in the shower stall throughout the recreation period as the water turned stony cold and his body grew chilled.

Phase 3

When Rico became conscious of his surroundings in the cafeteria, he saw Juan slumped at the table with his head buried in his arms. He looked up to see Clement, who remained immobile. Then, Rico shot a glance at an uneasy Mike and embarrassed Bill.

"This is going to be tough," Rico told Bill. "Let's end it."

"Let's end it," Mike chimed in, surprising Rico.

"Is this the beginning of a new friendship, Mike?" Rico joked.

Mike ignored the comment and reached out to pat Juan on the shoulder. "This is going to cost us too much. We have a long, painful road if this continues."

"You all agreed to this," Bill reminded them. "But I have to have a consensus."

"No," Juan muttered.

Everyone turned to look at Juan, and Clement slightly nodded his head.

"We will go," Juan insisted as he lifted his head. His reddened eyes glared at them. "I won't end this chance to live again. Soon I'll be permanently dead. I need to do this."

"What the fuck are we doing?" Rico demanded. "Since this all started, all I see is that we are reliving moments the computer hand-picks for some nefarious reason. Moments that are important to *it*!" Rico pointed to the now stoic Clement. "For some unknown algorithmic reason! What's the point of all this?"

"I need it," Juan cut off Rico's stream-of-consciousness. "You can go back. The program will continue with me and Bill alone."

"No," Bill corrected him. "It needs all of you to work. The parameters are set. So if you go Rico, your friend Juan and I will have to face our demise."

"Demise?" Rico questioned. "We are all facing our demise. We're old and civilization is crumbling outside. You've heard of an impending epidemic? Who knows in here how far the epidemic has gone?"

"I will support Juan if he continues," Mike changed his mind. "It's basic charity."

Mike stood up and briefly hugged Juan, who did not repel his offer of friendship.

"There's too much here to revisit," Mike added. "We need to face ourselves and evaluate our childhood. It all made us who we are."

"This is fucking useless," Rico disagreed.

"You're out-voted," Bill pointed out.

"I would like to know what the agenda is," Rico continued to pursue his objection. He stood up and pointed to Clement. "This machine is nit-picking moments from our freshman year."

"Obviously," Mike answered. "Why are we here, Father Clement?"

"Father?" Rico challenged the legitimacy of the title. "A holy computer?"

"Clement," Bill interrupted. Clement remained immobile. "The computer…is correlating related events. Let's play out one more person and see."

"How do you know?" Rico probed further. "Are you plugged in?"

"Yes," Bill admitted. "I need my experience."

"Can you pick a specific event for yourself?" Rico continued to push.

"No," Bill vacillated. "I only programmed the parameters of our experiences. The computer and your subconscious select the specific events from a widely divergent array of experiences. I think I explained it already. There are tens of thousands of experiences to choose from in that one school year. Let's finish with my event and we can talk later."

"I want to go on," Juan added to Bill's voice. "I want to know more. The skull wasn't what bothered me."

He turned to Rico with an apologetic expression, and Rico, embarrassed, looked away from his friend and at Mike.

"Let's see what the next story tells us," Mike implored Rico. "One more? What harm is it at this point? Then we can compare notes, to use an old phrase."

Rico remained unmoved, which Bill interpreted as consent.

"Commencing," Clement authorized a new episode. "Questions are forthcoming."

"Bill, Clement had a Spanish accent," Rico quipped.

"This isn't Clement, as you know," Bill retorted, missing the implied sarcasm.

"Fucking unbelievable!" Rico managed to eject before disintegrating into a new hologram program.

Chapter 6

Smart lad, to slip betimes away
From fields where glory does not stay,
And early though the laurel grows
It withers quicker than the rose.
– A.E. Housman, "To An Athlete Dying Young"

Rico remembered his eighth-grade varsity basketball season when his school almost won the state championship. His small, Catholic school had challenged and beaten most of the city's larger public schools and the state's champion junior high school team. Throughout the season, Rico played on the second-string team until he stepped in as a substitute and scored a three-point shot and a couple of hard-press lay-ups. The coach began to take him seriously, but he still never started and never played in the last game when his team had been soundly beaten in Sacramento. Entering the seminary, he aspired to play on the high school varsity team. Even though the rest of Rico's family was of average height, he benefited from the good fortune of early puberty, which gave him an early height advantage.

Rico knew this advantage would be short-lived within the next year. Playing the forward position would be unavailable and he would need to improve his shooting ability if he wished to start in a guard position. The prospect of remaining on the second string team in high school was unacceptable. Unfortunately, he had to wait until the basketball season began in November. So Rico wanted to find another outlet for his energy. He decided to try out for the junior varsity football team. Coach Krause made the suggestion to play football one day when Rico had to run the hundred-yard dash in a P.E. class.

"Let's see if you prima donnas can make any speed," Krause mocked his students.

The coach lined up the students in Rico's freshmen class, four abreast at the starter's line of the 100-yard dash track. Unlike most modern high schools, the seminary's racetrack lacked the red clay surface and the white chalk outline of a real 440-yard track field. Although the grassy area could easily contain two track fields, the Rector decided to use weed killer to burn the demarcation lines into the track field.

"Line up!" Krause shouted. "Watch me."

Krause walked to the starter's line, placed his open palms on the dead-grass line, and lifted his fingers up as he knelt.

"Lift yourself up when I say 'Mark!'" Krause explained. He raised himself up halfway and extended his left leg back while bending his right leg forward for the leverage to push out. "You then take off as fast as you can when I say 'Go!'"

Krause stood up and repeated the action.

"Mark and Go!" he shouted and leaped up and ran a quick ten yards before stopping. "Now begin."

Bill, Bates, and Tony moved towards the starter's line. Rico, who stood next to John, made a motion toward the starter's line. John tried to move away from his classmates, trying to avoid being the first to start, until Krause noticed.

"John," Krause called out to him. "Put those shorts to good use. Get up there."

Everyone stopped to stare at John, knowing that the coming sprint would be a fiasco. John hesitated and looked desperately around for support or escape.

"No one's going to help you," Krause clarified the reality of the situation.

Taking his clipboard and raising it, he walked up to John and held it up at shoulder height to escort John to the line. John obeyed but his body moved reluctantly. He hesitated when he reached the starter's line.

"Ah," Bates laughed from the starter's line.

Then, everyone burst out laughing and Krause took his position at the sidelines, smiling at the upcoming absurdity. John clumsily dropped to his knees and struggled to balance his legs, failing to raise his right knee or extend his left leg. He wobbled unsteadily and his classmates' laughing turned into snickering.

"Mark," Krause shouted, holding up a stopwatch. All the runners raised themselves but John fell back and slumped on the grass. Krause mockingly smiled at his failed effort and Bates laughed again. "Go!"

Bates took off first and Tom followed right behind him. Bill soon fell behind both boys but he never lost more than five yards. John almost immediately fell behind. His body jiggled and shuffled as his legs failed to make the proper lifting and pushing motions needed to gain speed. He huffed and sweated immediately. As he rumbled up to the thirty-yard line, the others had reached the eighty-yard line, with Bates still ahead of the crowd. Like a slow-motion film, John came to a halt and his belt descended in a circular motion towards his crotch, allowing his belly to fold out over his nearly invisible waistline. John then suddenly leaned over to vomit on the sidelines. The retching sound caused Bill and Tony to stop and look, but Bates continued to leap ahead and cheer himself to the finishing line.

"Yay!" Bates shouted.

"Good job," Krause congratulated him. "You made good time. 11.2 seconds on grass is real good."

Bates raised his arms up and danced around. Most students diverted their attention from Bates and focused on John's struggle to breathe. Rico walked up to John but felt a strong hand push him aside before he reached his classmate.

"Out of the way," Krause told Rico as he used his clipboard to wave everyone off. "Stand back."

John had fallen to his knees. Vomit strung itself out in a long, viscous line from his mouth to the grass. Remaining still for a moment, John began having a coughing fit until a cacophony of oscillating belches rumbled from deep inside.

"Get up and walk it off," Krause ordered. "Take him to the infirmary."

He placed his clipboard arm under John and stabbed him in the side.

"Get up," he repeated the order.

Krause's face reddened and he continued to push the clipboard into John's side until Mike and Bill approached from the other side and tried to yank up their friend.

"I won," Bates shouted, jumping up and down in front of John who had now stood up.

John leaned forward a bit as Bill and Mike began to escort him towards the infirmary.

"Hey, Bates! Mind if I interrupt your moment of triumph?" Krause sarcastically called him out. "Since you're so fast, why don't you run ahead and tell the people in the office what happened?"

Bates stopped leaping up and down and remained still, slightly slumping at the news as if a large sack of meal had been placed on his shoulders.

"What, Coach?" Bates demanded clarification.

"You heard me!" Krause shouted. "Move!'

Bate tried to object but shuffled reluctantly behind John who began to walk under his own volition while Bill and Mike compassionately steadied him with their grip. A few moments later, the students could see Bates sprint ahead and reach the office within a minute.

"Run, Bates!" a group of students mocked him.

"Next!" Krause ordered the other four students to line up.

Rico walked to the starter's line, and Juan joined him along with two other students. The other students were practically strangers to Rico although he occasionally exchanged some words with them in passing or in the classroom. The whole freshmen class had been divided into three academic levels, and each class isolated itself from the others. For the most part, Rico, like the other students, remained in his clique and never took the time to become familiar with Bobby or Louis. Bobby stood a couple of inches taller than Rico and had long limbs that seemed to stretch out like spacers on a car's wheels. The other student, Louis, was built like a compact horse. He had a dark complexion that did not hide his hard, compact muscles that tensed in preparation for the race. Bobby looked a little nervous but Louis seemed to relish the challenge. In the next couple of years, Rico would know them better and it would begin with the race. As for Juan, Rico already accepted him as a friend. Juan's eyes darted back and forth and his body language expressed his impending defeat.

"I hate racing," Juan admitted.

"I think I'll hate it too," Rico responded, motioning to Bobby and Louis.

"Line up!" Krause ordered.

Rico took his position and looked up to see that John had reached the office. A staff member came out to escort him inside. He felt sorry for John for a quick moment before Krause shocked him back into the present moment.

"Mark!" Krause shouted.

Rico dropped to his knees and placed his hands on the starter's line. His eyes caught Krause's right hand gripping the stopwatch. He then instantly focused on the finish line ahead, feeling his heart pounding in his chest.

"Go!" Krause ordered and brought his stopwatch hand down in a half-circular motion.

Rico felt himself being lifted up and ejected off the starter's line and into the air. Feeling a sense of weightlessness, Rico landed on his strong leg and pushed off on it like a catapult off a carrier deck. With quick, synchronized movements, his legs pumped up and down in rapid motion and his chest heaved as it forced more oxygen down into his lungs. The sound of his rapid breathing overwhelmed the pounding of his heart. Rico felt as if his legs had taken on a purpose and life of their own as his feet ground into the grass and continued pushing forward. As he saw the approaching finish line, he thought he could hear the ticking of the Swiss stopwatch counting down the last microseconds that slipped through the vortex of space and time before him. With concentrated effort, Rico lifted his left foot up and leaped over the finish line. He continued to run and slowly turned around to notice that the other runners had barely reached the line several seconds behind him.

"Great," Krause congratulated him from behind.

Rico had lost his bearings and only noticed Krause approaching him with the stopwatch in his hand. He held out the watch. The second demarcations on its face blurred under the strain of the race.

"You did that?" Krause demanded to know waving the watch up and down. "That's 9.9 seconds! On a real track with some training, you could compete and win at the city meets. Maybe even beat those spearchuckers!"

Rico wanted to laugh, but the tone Krause gave to the derogatory name made it seem more threatening and offensive than if it had been said by a classmate.

"What?" Rico asked, wishing that Krause would clarify the numbers. "What does that mean?"

"It means that you are a natural sprinter," Krause explained gleefully, appraising Rico's potential like a farmer looking to buy a heifer at the state fair. "You can also run the football by everyone if you have quick feet. Not everyone with fast feet has quick feet."

"I wanted to play basketball," Rico argued with himself out loud.

Krause thought that Rico had challenged his estimation.

"You are almost as tall as you're going to get," Krause warned him and dropped his smile, stashing the stopwatch in his pocket. "You better put your energies where you can use them. We begin practice tomorrow."

At the same moment Krause finished speaking, Bates, exhausted, returned from the office and slowly jogged over to the coach.

"How fast did he go?" Bates asked.

"9.9 seconds," Juan told him.

Bates stopped moving and stared at Rico.

"Damn, that's fast," Bates admitted. "I wanted to be the school sprinter."

"You better take a lesson from him," Krause advised and moved back to the starter's line. "Next bunch, line up!"

The remaining boys reluctantly drifted to the starter's line and a couple of students tapped Rico on the shoulder. Rico walked back to the starter's line behind Bates who looked severely grieved by the loss.

"How's John?" Rico tried to start a conversation.

Bates stopped and turned around to face Rico.

"That lard-ass will live," Bates responded annoyingly. "You can't have done a 9.9?"

"I want to play basketball," Rico half explained and apologized. "What the hell do I know about stopwatches?"

Bates shook his head and continued to speak with more conviction.

"You know how fast that is for this track?" Bates tried to drive the point home. "It would take me forever to shave 1.1 seconds from my time. Do you know what that means?"

"It means you and me can't both be sprinters," Rico concluded in frustration.

"Fuck you," Bates cursed and pushed aside Rico with his hand.

"Your mother," Rico countered and immediately felt the next shove turn into a flying fist.

The blow struck Rico's left cheek with little felt force since the race had increased his adrenalin. Bates's follow-up punch missed, and Rico returned the punch, which connected with Bates's chin. As Bates staggered back, Rico struck him again and again on the mouth. The cracking sound of teeth could be heard and blood trickled out of his mouth. A second later, Krause lifted Rico up by the shoulder and shoved him aside like a broken piece of corrugated cardboard. Rico fell to the ground and saw Krause rush towards Bates, who held his hand to his mouth as he began to mumble and whine. More blood dripped through the creases of his fingers and Bates's whine soon changed pitch and turned into a whimpering cry.

"My teeth," he groaned.

"Who started this?" Krause demanded, facing down the victor who struggled to get up.

"Bates," a chorus of voices spoke with intermittent unity. Everyone had his own reasons for despising the teenager.

Krause looked from side to side and searched all of the students' faces. Most of the students pointed to Bates who continued to whimper with pain. Krause then grabbed Rico and pushed him toward Bates, then took hold of Bates with his other hand.

"Come on," Krause spoke without expecting an answer. "You two come with me to see the Rector."

Krause shoved Rico ahead of him and continued to pull Bates along. He then withdrew a handkerchief and offered it to the wounded student.

"Cover your mouth," he told him. "Class dismissed."

Rico looked behind him to catch a glimpse of the students moving aimlessly about, trying to decide whether or not to follow Krause to the office.

"Get moving," Krause ordered both of them. He did not appear angry but only deeply annoyed at Rico. "You should have hit him only once. Now we might have a problem."

Rico shrugged and told himself that everyone had secretly supported his attack on Bates, who had earned the student body's loathing soon after the school year had begun. Unfortunately, the priests and his parents would not approve the mutilation of the class clown. As he continued towards the office, Bates's whimpering morphed into muffled curses.

"Buck up," Krause told Bates. "Stop being a girl."

Rico strangely felt like laughing as he heard Bates wheeze his frustration with a strong exhalation. The feeling seemed to possess him.

"You got some real trouble," Krause warned Rico when they reached the front steps of the school building. A small breeze picked up and the clanging chain rattled rhythmically against the steel pole. "But he struck you first."

"Right," Rico nodded, understanding Krause's implied recommendation.

Bates had first struck him and Rico responded in self-defense. Beside, Bates had a documented reputation for being a discipline problem since the first week of school, and Rico had not yet been reprimanded for any offense. The scales of seminary justice tilted in his favor but the unknown immediate future still weighed on Rico's mind and made him doubt that he would be cleared of any blame. They all walked through the glass doors and into the administration office.

"Sit here for the Monsignor," Krause commanded and tugged at Bates. "Let's go to the infirmary."

Rico looked at the elderly secretaries, who stared in dismay and shock as a bloodied Bates awkwardly tried to cover his swollen mouth.

"The boy needs to see a doctor," one old lady uttered.

"What happened?" another inquired.

"I…I," Rico began to explain.

At that moment, the door in the rear of the reception office opened and Monsignor O'Malley entered the area. He immediately appraised the situation and strutted straight towards Krause. Krause opened the door and took Bates with him. Holding the door open, he let the Monsignor step out ahead of him, ignoring Rico, and the Monsignor quickly entered into a conversation with Krause. Rico watched the Monsignor listen attentively to Krause's explanation of events. Krause spoke with quiet animation, gesticulating like a Shakespearean actor as to the cause and effects of the battle of the 100-yard dash. The Monsignor nodded intently at the coach's details and spoke a word or two to Bates. For one brief, chilling moment, the Monsignor peered at Rico and then immediately diverted his gaze. Then, Krause tugged Bates's arm again and walked him to the parking lot and to his car. The Monsignor paused and watched them leave momentarily before preparing to re-enter the waiting room. Seeing the old man's motions, Rico immediately turned away, hoping that the Monsignor would not make eye contact with him.

"How did that boy get hurt?" the first elderly woman demanded to know once more.

"Being stupid," Rico responded in a surly manner.

Before the secretary could respond, the Monsignor entered the office and walked past Rico, only to stop at his office door. He turned and glared straight at Rico. His eyes gripped Rico's attention with suppressed rage.

"Inside, now!" he bellowed.

The secretaries looked from side to side and expressed the same amount of unspoken sympathy and empathy as they had for Bates a few moments before. The Monsignor, not waiting for Rico, walked into his office as Rico plotted the longest walk of his life. Reaching the door became a heart-wrenching effort. When he arrived, Rico slowly tuned the doorknob and, making eye contact with the secretaries, he silently supplicated their prayers and sympathy before entering the office.

"It will be okay," the elderly woman assured him.

Sadly, for Rico, her assurances had the value of fool's gold. Entering the office carefully, Rico witnessed a potentate sitting behind a large oak desk, gripping a fountain pen poised over a document.

"Close the door behind you," the Monsignor demanded in a cold tone.

Rico reached unconsciously behind him and closed the door slowly, listening to the snap of the brass clicking against the doorframe. At the very moment he entered, his bladder began to twist with the need to urinate. He moved a few steps towards the desk and the Monsignor looked up from his glasses, peering over at him. His stare had a cold, reptilian feature that melted the heart and mind of every student who had the misfortune of standing in front of the Monsignor's desk. Rico had never heard of any student who stood in front of the desk on a congratulatory note.

"Son," the Monsignor spoke with a slight drawl. "I'll make this quick. Your behavior has been excellent up until today. I would normally suspend a student for what you did but you will be on detention for the month. The coach explained the circumstances, and Mr. Bates's behavior in the past has been...well, less than exemplary. Wanton violence does not excuse Christians and future priests."

The Monsignor paused to assess Rico's attention and response. Feeling satisfied, he continued.

"But you will talk to your Spiritual Director about how to funnel your emotions properly. The church cannot have its priests striking down their brethren with their fists. We must accept the Lord's pronouncement to turn the other cheek and forgive. Do you understand?"

"Yes," Rico muttered. "Thank you, Monsignor."

After expressing his gratitude, Rico wondered why he thanked the Monsignor for receiving a punishment for something he did not initiate. The Christian philosophy behind his religious education and the Monsignor's words had some objective value, but Rico's deep feelings told him that accepting a blow or injury without retaliation or at least defense was cowardice. His beliefs and feeling welled up in powerful contradiction.

"That's it," the Monsignor dismissed him, writing a note on small sheet of embossed stationery. "Hopefully Mr. Bates will have some teeth to chew his food. Give this to your teacher."

"Yes, Monsignor," Rico mumbled, feeling the need to rush out of the room immediately.

His bladder began to pound with pain and he desperately wanted to leave. At first, he moved reverently and cautiously backward until he turned and quickly opened the door. Stepping out with adroit determination, Rico closed the office door with a strong push that imperceptibly caused the doorframe to shudder. The secretaries looked up at him but remained silent as they continued to type with one eye on their documents and the other on Rico. He gave them a half-smile and walked silently out of the office and into the empty hallway. Waiting for Rico outside the office, the twelve apostles stared disapprovingly at him. He stared back and gave them the middle finger before turning around and heading for the nearest restroom.

Although he still wore his gym clothes, Rico left the restroom for his next class, which was in session. Most of the students were attending Father Davis's English class from hell. On the way to class, Rico struggled with the thought of finding an appropriate explanation for his parents. His parents might support him but he could never tell what their reaction would be under the present circumstances. In addition to having to do a month-long detention, Rico also resented the fact that he had to sit through Father Davis's class. He did not have the stamina for another humiliating bout with the most abrasive priest on campus. When he reached the door, Rico listened for a moment to determine the subject under discussion. Behind the door, Father Davis was counting off his fingers as an unlucky student struggled to give the definition of a part of speech. The student could not answer and Father Davis imposed his famous twenty-five. Then, Rico opened the door.

"Twenty-five times, Dolly!" he exclaimed.

The classroom erupted in jubilation like an old Roman mob in the Coliseum. Father Davis reenacted the old emperor's role of turning down his thumb. Taking the cacophony of cruelty as his cue to enter, Rico made a nonchalant entrance into the classroom, handing the Monsignor's note to Davis. When he entered, everyone instantly stopped laughing and stared at him.

"Welcome to our pugilist," Father Davis mocked him with a knowing smile after reading the note. He pointed out Rico's desk to him. "What's the definition of a conjunctive adverb?"

Rico wondered how Father Davis knew, but he suspected his obsequious classmates had described the drama of the racetrack.

"A conjunctive adverb," Rico began nervously, "is an adverb that indicates the relationship in meaning between two independent clauses."

Father Davis's smile melted and then slowly grew back with cool disdain. Rico looked over and saw that Juan had silently read the definition to himself as Rico recited it from his memory. Davis then raised his thumb up to Rico's success.

"Good job, sweetheart," he approved of the answer. "Sit down."

The classroom erupted simultaneously with a loud hoot and cheer. Suddenly, a deafening silence imploded the room when the galvanized pipes overhead rattled. Father Davis and the students looked up. Rico listened to the rattle and decide to sit down as his classmates began to converse in disjointed words and phrases. As the pipes continued to rattle, Father Davis smile stretched out with disdainful glee.

"Must be your mating call, sweetheart?" he mocked Rico.

Rico shook his head, embarrassed, and the class once more erupted into a wave of laughter. Rico smiled approvingly at the joke. He knew he had won a small battle in Davis's class despite the insult. Every freshman understood on a subconscious level that Davis would not let a student upstage him by successfully defining a difficult term. The real reason for everyone's exuberance was Davis's defeat and Bates's bloody face. His classmates despised them both, and Rico's victory earned him fifteen minutes of their adulation. The day would end on a victorious note for the weak as the meek and powerless took a symbolic stand against the obnoxious and cruel forces of the institution.

Days later, when the laurels of Rico's symbolic victory fell from his crest, Bates returned to school with blazing braces for all to see. He displayed them as his trophy of stupidity. Everyone showed his disdain and Bates taunted them both on and off the field. Despite the humiliation and chastisement, Rico earned Bates's respect. He went out of his way to befriend a suspicious Rico who kept his guard up in case Bates tried to reap his revenge. Unlike with Bates's infamous return, all the students welcomed John with open arms and gentle teasing. He invited feelings of pity, for most people knew he could not help his ineptitude and honest naiveté. Mike bolstered him on the field, and Krause now allowed John to move at his own pace without derision. In fact, Krause made it a habit to simply ignore John outright.

The next week, Krause used Rico's newfound ability to run the ball for the freshmen football team. During this transitional period, when Rico awaited the basketball season and kept in shape under Krause's tutelage, Rico served detention in the kitchen after each meal and spent his free time after the rosary hour helping the nuns prepare the meals for the next day. Although Rico lost some of his favorite activities and escapes during the few free moments allotted to the seminarians, he felt satisfied that his parents did not punish him nor did the staff hold any grudges against him. The battle with Bates placed upon him a mantle of respect. Even the gardeners joked with him in Spanish about the fight, which they had witnessed from the close shelter of the eucalyptus trees and tennis court garden. Day after day, Rico's experiences changed him. He ceased to be the same person who entered the seminary in September. Sometimes his ferocity when running the ball and the unrestrained elation he showed when he outran everyone who tried to tackle him, caused even his friend Juan to question his new focus.

"Cool down, buddy," Juan warned him gently at the goal line. "You're getting too fired up about this game."

"I am just getting started," Rico claimed, throwing the ball to Krause.

"Kickoff!" Krause shouted, giving the ball to Rico's team.

Without waiting for the other team to run down to the end of the field, the quarterback took the ball and kicked it down the field. It sailed up for thirty yards and then fell straight into the grass, tumbling over several times before a student scooped it up like a power shovel. Since they were playing flag football, a nearby opponent ripped off the flag before the runner could take two steps forward. Krause's whistle ripped through the air and the runner dropped the ball. The coach then picked up the ball and set it down on the 30-yard line.

"First down!" he shouted, whistling again.

Rico played defense and stayed a couple of yards behind the line as he watched the other team come out of their huddle. Krause blew his whistle and watched the center snap the ball to the quarterback. Everything then began to move in slow motion for Rico. The halfback ran past him and Rico jogged backward, making little effort to cover him. Then the quarterback fell back and looked in Rico's direction as his team rushers moved dangerously close. Releasing the ball with the accuracy of a bullet, the quarterback threw the football, which made a stinging move towards Rico's left side and into the direction of the waiting receiver. In a fraction of a second, Rico leaned to the left and snatched the football away from the receiver.

He cradled the interception in his arms and plowed forward towards his goal line. Although Rico could outrun most of the players on the field, his efforts failed against the converging numbers of opponents who gravitated in his direction. The other team mindlessly formed a pincher move that forced Rico to run towards the out-of-bounds area and along its chalky edge. Several opponents tried to snatch his flag but a slight twist of the hip allowed Rico to avoid their grasp. The goal post stood in front of him and he decided to make a touchdown. Then, from below his waist, he felt a tug and then another as some unseen student tore away the long vinyl flag from its raggedy Velcro holster. Ignoring the loss of his flag, Rico leaped ahead and a slight punch from behind knocked him off balance.

Another unseen person smashed into his back and he fell forward, sprawling face-down on the grass. The football skidded under his chest and both he and the ball came to a grass-stained halt on the chalky line.

Krause's whistle screamed in the background and Rico placed his right hand in front of himself. As he began to lift himself off the grass, the perpendicular position of his right wrist doomed him. A sudden and violent force moved his wrist forward and it slipped out of joint. Another student slammed onto Rico's back and two other students piled on top of his dislocated wrist. Rico painlessly felt the connection of wrist and forearm unnaturally melt away. He could not move as a group of students sat on him like sandbags.

"Get off!" Krause ordered, then repeated, along with several whistle blows.

Slowly, with stuttered effort, the opposing team players lifted themselves off Rico. Krause yanked the last tackler with impunity for he flew up and fell back on his side. Then, Krause bent down and looked at Rico's deformed wrist.

"That's the end of your football and basketball career this year," he judged callously. "Do you want me to pop it back in? It's dislocated."

Rico looked up at him in terror.

"No," Krause changed his mind. "Take him to the office."

Krause helped Rico up, and all the players stared in disbelief at how his wrist bent unnaturally backward. Although the injury looked horrible, Rico did not feel any pain. Krause turned Rico over to Bill who accompanied him quietly to the office. He escorted Rico holding up his elbow on the left side away from the injury. Rico cradled his arm, trying not to vibrate it unnecessarily. By the time they reached the office, the wrist began to throb.

"You okay?" Bill uttered his first words, noticing that Rico flinched when they ascended the steps.

"Yeah," Rico responded. "Second time, huh?"

"What?" Bill questioned. He then understood Rico's allusion. "John was worse, even if you look bad."

"Thanks," Rico sarcastically responded.

They entered the office and the Monsignor looked disapprovingly at Rico. In the office, the study-hall Brother sat behind a typewriter, preparing a pamphlet for a retreat. The Monsignor looked directly at him and tapped him on the shoulder. He then ordered the Brother to drive Rico to the emergency room across the way from the seminary. As in every other diocese in the United States, the Archdiocese built its churches, hospitals, and religious houses within the same square mile. The Brother kindly walked Rico to the school's old, rebuilt Chevy van that was used to transport students to events. Rico entered the passenger's seat with the Brother's careful guidance.

"Don't let that arm jiggle too much," he advised Rico with a tainted breath of alcohol. He then spoke to Bill. "You come too."

Bill looked at him skeptically before deciding to accept the invitation. He leaped into the back seat of the van as the Brother entered the driver's side and started the engine.

"We'll be there soon," the Brother assured Rico, noticing the look of pain in Rico's face.

Leaving the foot brake in place, the Brother accelerated the van and it jerked back and forth for a couple of seconds. The van's jerky motion sent an unexpected stream of pain up and down Rico's arm and through his wrist. He also noticed that his hand had begun to swell.

"Sorry. We should have gotten some ice," the Brother stopped the van and then released the foot brake to continue. "Don't worry. It won't be necessary. Pray to Our Lady for help."

Rico ignored the recommendation. The van moved across the service road and over several speed bumps. The first speed bump shot more pain through his arm as the van bounced up and down on its timeworn springs and struts.

"This car needs some work," the Brother felt compelled to utter an excuse. "It's always in the shop. In fact, it just came out of the shop."

Rico did not listen and Bill tried to force a smile.

"So how did it happen?" The Brother questioned, attempting to distract Rico as the Chevy continued to bounce over the second speed bump.

The second bump added more vibrating pain to the pulsating discomfort in Rico's wrist. The Brother waited for Rico to speak but Bill inserted himself into the conversation.

"He got tackled," Bill gave a curt response.

"Oh," the Brother mindlessly blurted out. "I broke my arm when I was very young in the play yard. I remember, I cried. But the best memory was the toy my father bought me. It was an airplane. I loved that plane."

"Do you fly?" Bill inquired naively.

"No," the Brother dismissed. "They don't pay for flying lessons in the seminary."

"Right," Bill nodded in agreement, wondering whether he had offended the Brother or had been told a joke.

He decided to smile instead and leaned forward to touch Rico's shoulder. Rico acknowledged his comfort with a grunt.

"We'll be there soon," the Brother drove almost recklessly down the street after leaving the last torturous speed bump behind.

He passed through a yellow light while making a right turn. The van leaned over hard as the van's shocks surrendered to the force of gravity. Rico had to catch himself with his good arm in order not to add further pain to his injury.

"Say an Our Father," the Brother suggested another prayer. "The Lord may hear your plight. Offer Him your pain as remittance for your sins."

Rico listened incredulously to the Brother. Rico wanted to pray for his safe arrival instead. He stopped himself from expressing an expletive. Morphine would be a better salve than prayer. The van soon approached the hospital emergency entrance and Rico gripped his arm, trying to avoid any contact with the metal dashboard as the van bounced into the driveway. He looked over at the Brother who seemed to be desperately hypnotizing himself with a feverish prayer. Bill again tapped Rico's shoulder as the van bounced over the hospital speed bump. Rico mumbled a curse. Another bolt of pain shot through his arm and his hand. His wrist continued to noticeably swell. The Brother stopped abruptly in front of the hospital entrance where two orderlies waited outside with cigarettes in their hands. They simultaneously took a drag from their cigarettes and waited. The Brother put the van into park and turned off the engine.

"You should go inside," he suggested to Rico, as if he needed to be encouraged.

Without waiting for him to respond, The Brother stepped out of the van and approached the orderlies who pointed to the glass sliding doors. They tapped a large, stainless steel button on the side of the door and it automatically opened. He walked into the hospital without looking back at the van.

"No," Rico whispered sarcastically to himself as he failed to open the door. "I'll wait here and suffer and pray like a good fucking seminarian."

Bill tapped him for the third time before exiting.

"I'll get it," he told Rico and jumped out of the van.

From the outside, Bill opened the door and held Rico by his good arm, allowing him to step down onto the van's high running board. The Brother did not return so they followed his direction and walked towards the entrance. One orderly finished his cigarette and tossed it on the sidewalk, crushing it underfoot while blowing a long trail of smoke out of his mouth and nostrils.

"What happened, dude?" he asked.

"Football," Bill answered for Rico.

"Shit," the orderly exclaimed. "Don't worry. They'll fix you up."

The other orderly waved his cigarette in agreement and leaned over again to push the stainless steel button for the two seminarians. Bill escorted Rico through the opening glass doors and into the emergency lobby. Rico saw the Brother speaking to a clerk behind a desk. A nurse approached Rico, holding a clipboard. She was a middle-aged woman with salt-and-pepper hair and she wore black-framed glasses. Looking above the frame of her glasses, she glanced down at her clipboard and then looked up at Rico. Motioning Bill to move away, she lifted Rico's injured arm at the elbow and made a quick diagnosis.

"You're the seminary boy?" she asked.

Rico nodded in agreement.

"Dislocated," she concluded factually as she continued to examine the wrist. "They heal quick but hurt a lot. You're lucky it wasn't a compound fracture. We'll take an X-ray."

The mentioning of pain sent a throbbing pulse through his wrist and Rico winced.

"Come with me," she commanded and allowed Bill to escort Rico.

Both students followed her into a room with two gurneys and an array of apparatus all along the walls. Thin linen curtains on a half-circular track separated one bed from the other and provided a minimal amount of privacy. The nurse pointed to the bed on the left and Rico carefully manipulated his body to sit on it.

"I am taking your temperature and blood pressure," the nurse explained. "The technician will be available soon to take you to the X-ray room."

She then began the tests and wrote the results on her clipboard. Bill began to move about and take a closer look at the instruments and apparatus.

"Miss," Bill called the nurse. "Are these the latest state-of-the-art?"

The nurse remained silent for a moment while she listened to the stethoscope resting on the inside of Rico's arm.

"Don't touch them," she warned Bill. "They've been sanitized recently. I'll be back."

The nurse finished writing her notes on the clipboard and dropped its contents into a tray next to the door before stepping out of the room. Rico looked up to see Bill studying the equipment. Far behind Bill, Rico could see the Brother completing some forms with the clerk. Another throb of pain jolted Rico upright, then sent him flat on his back. He carefully laid his injured wrist away from the gurney's hand guards and onto the clean cotton sheets. Pain vibrated through his wrist and arm. Rico counted the pulses as they ascended and dissipated and was able to keep time with the predictable throbs. He felt suddenly abandoned as his eyes began to moisten and the pain began to rise. Rico waited for relief as Bill immersed himself further in the surrounding technology. He forgot about Rico. The nurse did not return for a long while.

Phase 4

Rico became painfully conscious of his surroundings as his eyes locked with Father Clement's avatar that looked impassively at him and everyone at the table. Although the football accident had been a memory, Rico's eyes remained moistened as he remembered the past, phantom pain.

"This was supposed to be about Bill," Rico spoke directly to Clement. He stood up and directly faced Clement. "It was all about my injury."

Clement's eyes moved away from Rico and he lifted his head up.

"Ask Bill," Clement told Rico.

"Bill?" Rico inquired.

Bill sat immobilized on his chair and stared pensively at Clement for a moment. Rico thought that maybe Bill's avatar operated like Clement's hologram. He might only be a shell of the real person who had died long ago. No one could speak.

"I see," Bill finally said.

Clement nodded.

"I don't," Juan challenged.

"I am confused too," Mike added.

Bill raised his hands and stood up. He walked over to Rico, who began to rise, and placed his hand on Rico's shoulder, gently pushing him down into his chair.

"You see, my friend," Bill began to explain. "It *is* about me."

"Something happened to you that day," Mike intuitively understood. "And to Rico, too."

Bill and Mike made eye contact and Bill knowingly approved of Mike's insight.

"I can only speak for myself," Bill clarified. "I could guess about Rico…but not now."

"Go on," Juan pressed impatiently.

Juan stood up and walked away from the table, standing a few feet away from the avatar but directly in its line of sight. No one paid any attention to Juan except for Rico who vicariously sympathized with his friend's frustration and inner turmoil. But he also felt that Juan had caused some of his own misery and no one was at fault.

"You voted to keep this charade going," Rico thought, reminding himself of Juan's complicity.

"You see," Bill explained, speaking directly to Rico. "I decided to become a scientist that day. Seeing you in the hospital in that helpless position and in pain made me think about modern science's potential. I realized that the facilities were too primitive to do you any true justice even if they did fix your arm. Right?"

Rico nodded and held up his wrist.

"But at what cost and pain," Bill objected. "You took almost two full months to recover and you lost out on a season of sports. You couldn't play basketball? Right?"

Rico nodded in the affirmative. His aspirations to pursue any sport in college evaporated on the evening of his injury.

"And I remember you never played any of your beloved sports again?" Bill continued.

"I later ran track and cross country," Rico corrected him.

Bill shook his head in disagreement.

"But not your favorite," Bill corrected him.

"My interest in playing sports kind of deflated for me," Rico confessed.

"But the event was a catalyst for me," Bill clarified. "It was the beginning of everything that set me on my career. That is why we are all here, you see. The last show was for *my* benefit."

"Like Mike gaining his faith," Juan added.

"And Rico losing his to become a skeptic," Mike continued the train of thoughts.

"No, a realist," Rico added, causing Mike to express his pity at Rico's lack of faith.

"Believe me," Rico dismissed Mike's disappointment. "I am better off for it. I don't accept anything that is a fantasy."

"And I took my first step towards paralysis," Juan interrupted his classmates as they prepared to debate again.

Juan's comments caused a rush of guilt to seize Rico, and he stood up as if his emotions dominated his actions.

"Don't start, Juan," Rico pled.

Rico walked towards his friend who pushed him off when he reached him.

"I don't," Juan rejected his friend's compassion. "I am okay. I can deal with it."

Rico raised his hands in a show of surrender and then returned to the table. He wanted to talk to Juan about the tragic event that literally ended his life, imprisoning him in a human shell.

"Deal with it," Rico mocked, scoffing at Juan's sudden show of bulwark confidence. "I can't."

Juan looked away and stood up, taking several steps towards Bill to avoid making eye contact with Rico.

"You know about basic brain anatomy," Bill continued to explain as Rico sulkily sat down. "The left brain registers logic and language while the right brain focuses on art and abstractions."

"And the computer reads these differences in our brains and replicates it?" Rico speculated.

"Yes. Well," Bill began to explain further, expressing some irritation at Rico's interruption. "The algorithms in the computer scan your brains and locate memes. This is what is new about my computer. For a long time, virtual reality only replicated actions without purpose. I wanted to find purpose in our actions. Do you understand?"

"Memories?" Juan questioned returning to his chair.

"Mental virus?" Rico explained. "Memes! I remember reading something about those decades ago."

"Yes," Bill confirmed. "It's been known for decades."

"This is all sacrilegious," Mike objected, raising his voice. "You're rejecting the soul."

"Some may argue this meme *is* the soul," Bill countered. "So to speak."

"What is a meme, exactly?" Juan pressed.

"It is a fool's explanation," Mike interrupted.

"Of course," Rico challenged. "Psychologists use it to explain cult personalities and religions."

"Wait," Bill interrupted, stopping an escalating debate. "The computer searched our memories and looked for ideas…major life experiences that have a repeated effect."

"Consciously or subconsciously," Rico finished Bill's thoughts.

"Exactly," Bill agreed proudly. "Actually, the computer works backward…tracing major events and decisions before you were transported back to its common denominator."

"We are looking at what caused us to become who we are," Juan speculated as he returned to his chair.

"Not exactly," Bill corrected him. "But the kernels of those beginnings are in those stories."

"I don't agree that everything can be dissected to a specific moment," Mike broke in, rejecting the explanation. "We are too complex and spiritual for a computer to dissect and examine."

"The memes propagate and expand to dominate our behavior," Bill ignored Mike's rejection. "You are looking at a catalyst…a beginning for your life's meme."

"In the beginning," Rico quipped with a biblical allusion. "There was the meme."

"This blasphemy is going nowhere," Mike argued.

Before anyone could respond, the cafeteria began to shake violently, as if a real earthquake were rolling through the seminary grounds and surrounding city.

"Computer!" Bill shouted an order to the avatar. "Correct for instability."

The avatar stood up but remained silent.

"Computer!" Bill shouted his command again.

Clement remained silent and then spoke.

"Parameters are inconsistent," the avatar explained. "Trajectory has been corrected for errors. Normal processing will commence in 15 seconds."

The earthquake vanished as quickly as it had appeared.

"What the hell?" Juan asked jumping out of his seat and walking up to Bill, shouting in his face. "Are we going to die now in this machine?"

"No," Bill assured him confidently. "Not now. We won't die in this machine now. It isn't in the program."

Everyone at the moment looked at the avatar that had sat down. A cold, distant expression glazed over Clement's face, which gave his appearance a more alien and remote visage than the one he originally had.

"Trajectory?" Rico wondered out loud. "That means we are being thrown somewhere?"

"Yes," Bill reluctantly admitted. "This computer is in a transporter for security reasons."

The vibration and turmoil oscillated. When it halted, everyone fearfully looked at one another, except for Bill who approached Clement.

"Do we have stability?" Bill inquired.

"Making adjustments," Clement again responded.

"I am sorry," Bill apologized. "I have to make some corrections before we proceed with our little soirée."

"Are we safe?" Juan desperately wanted to know. "This is my only chance. I need the chance."

"We are safe," Bill assured him. "I am going to put the computer in recess mode. You will individually have some free time to explore the grounds and rest."

"Why rest?" Mike asked. "We are disembodied."

"But your minds need rest," Bill clarified. "It's primary for your health."

"How much time passed?" Rico asked.

"I'd guess a half hour," Bill ventured, "plus microseconds. I'll get you back before lunch."

Everyone nervously smiled at the joke, except for Juan.

"I'm hungry," Juan admitted. "But it's not real."

"I am hungry too," Mike agreed. "Strange."

"It's real in your mind," Bill corrected Juan. "The mind is everything. It maintains your humanity."

"I'll program lunch for everyone," Bill rushed out his words. "I must go."

"Wait!" Rico demanded as his surroundings began to dissolve and fade away.

A second later, Rico's classmates and Clement vanished. Bill isolated himself and the others. Each classmate experienced his own virtual reality like the first day of school. New characters and scenes replaced Rico's recent surroundings. The cafeteria then hosted seminarians from Rico's freshmen year. The students interacted without recognition of Rico's presence. Unlike the last manifestation of the cafeteria breakfast, Rico sat alone with the refectorian at the table at the far end of the student body. A sophomore brought him a bowl of clam chowder and several tuna sandwiches. Rico devoured the clam chowder and quickly took a bite of a sandwich.

"This is my favorite," Rico told the refectorian.

The refectorian did not respond, continuing to speak to the waiters and cleanup crew as if Rico did not exist.

"Good," Rico concluded. "I don't want to have my lunch disturbed."

As he finished the sandwiches, more were served to his table. Rico continued to eat until his virtual stomach rebelled. Then, another sophomore served him coffee and a dessert, a brownie with vanilla ice cream. Rico took a bite and savored a cheerful gustatory moment.

"Bill is really tapping into my brain now," Rico spoke out loud to see if any of the avatars would respond.

No one responded and the activities continued. A few moments later, several freshmen began removing the plates and utensils. The student body stood up to pray and the Rector dismissed them for their fifth-period class. Rico continued to nurse his coffee over the last bites of his dessert. As he swallowed his last bite, he reflected on his actions and the events of recent reminiscences. Suddenly, Rico realized that he needed to eat and sleep because those actions coexisted with the computer's maintenance program. Some unknown element implanted the thought. Sleeping and eating were symbolic representations of the computer running a maintenance check. Accepting the inescapable, Rico finished his coffee and made another astounding conclusion. Not only was the computer in maintenance mode, it might have experienced a virus. Bill actively operated and ran the computer from his mind and Clement represented the whole apparatus. Maybe a virus had infected the program, a possibility as likely as any physical disruption.

"Good conclusion," Bill spoke from behind.

Rico turned around and jumped out of his seat.

"You can read my fucking mind?" Rico demanded to know.

132

"Not exactly," Bill revealed. "But in a sense, yes. I wanted to talk to you."

"A virus infected the computer?" Rico asked him directly, somehow sensing the truth from Bill's mind.

"Yes," Bill told him. "You see, you can too. My competitors always try to access my system. This program will serve mankind's greatest psychological needs. But you made a wrong inference. We are still in motion."

"I see," Rico accepted Bill's explanation for the moment. "Where are we going?"

"Everywhere and nowhere," Bill provided a cagey answer. "Away from prying eyes."

"What do you want to talk about?" Rico asked impatiently. Bill's presence had an obvious purpose.

"Juan," Bill revealed. "You think he can take three more sessions?"

"Sessions?" Rico questioned, trying to define Bill's usage of the word.

"One for each school year," Bill impatiently articulated.

"Yeah. Maybe?" Rico understood, feeling embarrassed by his slow wit. "I don't know for sure. Who can say? You're going to follow the progress of his meme. Right?"

"His past addiction and life choices," Bill clarified. "He wants to see his life. To relive it! We talked about this being his last chance. But I don't know if it is good for him. I am a computer programmer and not a psychologist. Sometimes I have my doubts. So I need your input."

"Go ask Mike," Rico quipped. "He is plugged into God, the best psychologist."

"I did," Bill surprised Rico for he had thought Bill would speak to him first.

"And his answer?" Rico finished his question.

"Not satisfactory for me," Bill responded. "But basically…Mike says we should continue if Juan wants it. It would act like a confession."

"Like I'm surprised," Rico added. "But he might be right. You're waiting for my input before deciding?"

"Good question," Bill accepted. "Want to continue? Mike does."

"I don't know," Rico confessed. "This is really…difficult."

"Look," Bill pled. "This is more than memes. I really don't know where it will finally take us. We talked about it earlier. Why don't we give it more time…another round?"

"Okay. If Juan is up for it," Rico accepted. "Let's watch him and if it looks bad…call it off. What about it? Sound good?"

"Good," Bill concurred. "Go rest."

"You know," Rico interrupted him. "I can't believe we'll be back home before lunch."

"It's amazing how being in a computer changes the perspective of time. You can pass a lifetime here and it will be only hours and minutes outside. It makes time relative, like the experience of a dream," Bill philosophized.

"The stuff dreams are made of?" Rico misquoted.

"Are we that stuff?" Bill mused. "We'll have a lot to talk about later."

Rico agreed and patted him on the back. Bill turned away and began to fade out.

"Bill," Rico called for his attention. A feeling of deep fatigue began to overshadow Rico's consciousness. "I never told you how much I appreciated your being there in the hospital with me. I was a scared kid then."

"I should thank you," Bill disagreed as his visage melted into the surrounding scenes. "Going with you changed my life and gave us this unique possibility."

"You're welcome," Rico responded. "I guess."

"Hey," Rico continued as threads of Bill began to separate and melt away. "Can I be in touch with the outside world before lunch ends? It's my daughter I want to talk to."

"Later," Bill answered as if his voice crawled slowly out of a deep cavern.

Before Rico could think of a response, Bill's form finally dissolved into small, disorganized pixels. A veil of darkness descended on Rico and he rapidly fell into a deep sleep while the scenery gradually collapsed upon itself to the point of a small, dark pixel. Fleeting memories of flying soup bowls frayed into strands of gray shadows in the enveloping oblivion of virtual death.

PART II

The cities were empty and only the animals roamed the surface. Silence reigned. Everything remained as it was, but the slow erosion of time continued its irresistible progress. Soon, in geological time, nature reclaimed its dominance. The traveling aliens could not speak to anyone. No one greeted them. In orbit, silenced satellites predictably moved across predetermined, decaying trajectories until gravity welcomed them back home to a fiery extinction. But among the indistinguishable satellites, only one, in far geosynchronous orbit, played out the drama of the sentient lives that once lived below. The aliens listened to their disembodied echoes. They understood nothing.

Chapter 7

The times they are a-changin'
– Bob Dylan

Rico sat in a slouched position with his knees up against the pew's front stop, waiting for morning prayers to begin with the new Spiritual Director. Feet resting comfortably on the kneeler, he appraised his surroundings with some anticipation and dread on the first morning of his sophomore year. His freshman year had ended on a bittersweet note when a classmate ran into the study hall the Sunday before summer vacation.

"Hey, Rico, man!" Tony almost shouted, with a half-apprehensive, half-delighted smile. A companion stood behind him, with a physical appearance that confirmed Tony's next statement. "They are leaving."

"Leaving?" Rico turned the word over, searching for an explanation in their faces. No one had told him about any desire to leave the seminary.

"Who? Bates?" Rico joked, hoping that he was right.

"That asshole is going," Tony happily confirmed. "But the whole fucking, bunch of them are leaving too."

"Who the fuck 'bunch of them'?" Rico began to lose his patience.

"Tell him," the companion prodded Tony with a serious nudge against his shoulder.

Rico carefully studied Tony's face before the actual identity of the *bunch* entered his mind. It formed an almost terrifying image, along with the consequences it would inherit, wrapping itself like cellophane around his consciousness.

"You're shittin' me!" Rico demanded to be told. "The whole *bunch*?"

The word: *bunch* had lost its effect since the Christmas play when a skit satirized the seminary's faculty with an allegory about a rotting bunch of bananas being thrown out. Unfortunately, fiction had become stranger than reality. Recriminations dogged the seniors who had, for the most part, committed verbal atrocities on stage and crimes of bad taste without paying any serious penalty. But a public humiliation and lampoon in front of visiting dignitaries and parents crossed the proverbial Rubicon of seminary comportment.

Because of the seniors' social mortal sin, the word *bunch* hid itself in the black market of irretrievable words. No one feared using it in front of the staff but why would anyone invite their uninvited wrath? Despite the *verboten* status the word *bunch* had on the student body, no one dared to ask the obvious – why the skit had such traumatizing effects on the faculty as a whole. The answer and its coming effects could have been predictable. Tony's announcement changed the whole social and ecclesiastical paradigm that began to shift around Christmas. The *bunch* had been thrown out. A new, unknown regime would arrive and command.

"Fucking thrown out?" Rico begged for some confirmation.

"My pastor told my parents after Sunday mass," Tony proudly assured Rico, as if his parents held some grand, confidential post in the church's hierarchy.

"No shit?" Rico asked, incredulous.

Each boy remained silent for a few moments as the repercussions of the events began to set in.

"Know why?" Rico instinctively asked, not expecting an answer.

The church, as each seminarian had been acutely aware since the first day of school, secretly guarded its decisions with extreme prejudice as if God had commanded and approved each action.

"Yeah," Tony blurted out gravely.

The serious tone of his utterance caused the level of anxiety to rise. Looking around him, Rico saw that a small crowd of their classmates had eavesdropped and joined the conversation. No seniors presented themselves since they had graduated the weekend before. Although most of the interested students were freshmen, many others were sophomores and juniors.

"Well," Tony began to hedge. "I caught some of it. Let me piece it together." He paused for another moment, leaving everyone anxiously waiting for the explanation. "What I understand was that there was a big meeting with the Cardinal."

"The faculty?" Rico clarified.

"The Vincentians and the Superiors of the order," Tony continued. "The Cardinal basically told them that he was unhappy with the way the seminary was run. That they had lost control and the seminarians' spiritual health was in jeopardy. So he was replacing them with diocesan priests."

"Unhappy? Bullshit!" Rico rejected the Cardinal's conclusion. "They caught on."

Everyone instantly understood the implications of Rico's insight. Despite the seminarians' complaints about the strictness of the faculty, they all knew, deep down in their psyches, that they had had a very liberal and permissive faculty all year. Although the level of academics had been extraordinarily stellar, discipline had declined miserably throughout the school year and over the last four years, beginning sometime in the late '60s. Many inside the Church blamed Vatican II. Students could not ditch their classes but they were able to ditch their dormitories in the evening. Except for the few devout seminarians that guarded the purity of their vocations, most of the students took advantage of the lax atmosphere. Many students took jaunts in the evening to local pizza parlors and drive-in theaters when a car was available.

Those who owned a car would volunteer to drive their friends off campus under the veil of darkness. To avoid detection, the seven to eight students would put the car in neutral and silently push it off campus until the car sat on the boulevard. Driving off to their destination became routine. The seniors and juniors had the greatest advantage since they alone were allowed to possess cars. Adding to the defiance, many upper-classmen had clandestine encounters with females from the local Catholic high schools. Rico and his classmates had to settle with the local all-night pizza parlors and the inconvenience of jumping over a chain-link fence and avoiding a few mangy guard dogs through the orange and avocado fields on the north end of the campus. During one of these infamous escapes, the returning seniors proudly told the story of how they had caught Father Gomez exiting the convent at dawn and walking to the refectory. As they stealthily pushed their large '68 Impala up the service road, they saw Gomez close the convent door behind him. When the priest noticed them, he immediately went into a rage.

"What are you doing out of your dorms?" he demanded.

"What are *you* doing?" Juan's brother retorted.

Gomez smiled and ignored the question, continuing on his trek to the refectory.

"Yeah. The fuckers caught on," Tony confirmed.

"We're screwed next year," Rico concluded, along with the silent majority who stood behind him and listened.

Rico again looked up and watched the new Spiritual Director, a diocesan priest not belonging to any order, ascend the altar steps and walk to the podium. At first glance, Rico saw an imposing character who stood far above six feet, unlike the past fat, frumpy, short priests who occupied the classrooms, places of worship, and dormitories. Then, Rico's eyes latched onto his heavy-soled, black, almost orthopedic-type shoes. Instead of long flaring pant cuffs, the Director stepped out of fashion. Attending a seminary, or any secondary school, during the '70s, any student presupposed that clothes or shoes would reflect some of the finesse or glitz, at minimum some style, of the times. Instead of wearing matching colored socks, his too-short trousers revealed the contrasting color of white cotton socks that formed the stark space of a horizontal white stripe between the end of his black trousers and the edge of his shoe's leather. But the offense did not stop at his sartorial sin. It began to transform from a venal to a mortal offense.

While most students would not care too much about what a priest wore, since his choices were ecclesiastically restricted to black on black with a white collar, the effort, which was not a very subtle one, that the Spiritual Director took to look clownish reached the subconscious of even the least observant students. Despite the blurring effect of black on black clothes, the Spiritual Director wore baggy trousers and a tight-fitting shirt that emphasized a growing beer belly. Finally, to top off the disproportional attire, his square-shaped skull and closely cropped hair further opposed the beards, mustaches, and sideburns that most post-Vatican II priests wore to be *in touch* with their students.

Basically, the Spiritual Director was not cool. As a *square*, he had an agenda and everyone instantly and instinctively knew it. He paused to genuflect in front of the altar before turning around to face the congregation. With a pious expression, the Spiritual Director made the sign of the cross and Rico almost blurted out a laugh. A wide forehead rested above the Spiritual Director's disjointed gray eyes, which were set deeply into his lightly pock-marked face, making his forehead seem unusually prominent.

"He's a Frankenstein," a junior whispered at an almost audible level.

"More like Milton the Monster," another junior commented, alluding to children's cartoons that satirically characterized Frankenstein to be a good-natured yet goofy individual.

Rico did not hold out hope for an affable personality like the facetious TV monster.

"Let's call him Milty," the first junior announced and bequeathed the name to him.

The small circle of students surrounding Rico began to giggle quietly and the others smirked. Despite the unidentified disruption of muffled laughs on the Saint Joseph side of the chapel, the Spiritual Director's eyes rested on Rico who, alone among his classmates, slouched with open apathy and careless disdain. Everyone caught the Spiritual Director's disapproving stare, which gave him a menacing appearance. His scathing stare caused Rico to straighten up slightly. Although the stare lasted seconds, it felt like an eternity. When he returned to his missal, someone's whisper broke the chilling silence.

"Where's the torches and pitchforks?" an unidentified junior asked behind Rico.

Although no one openly laughed, a comedic surge of energy again spiked and gripped everyone within hearing distance.

"I am Father Siemens," the new Spiritual Director announced. "Let us pray."

On cue, everyone made the sign of the cross. The rest of the prayer passed in a blur of stiff boredom and humorous comments. Although Siemens appeared dedicated and pious, Rico felt that an air of hypocrisy or insecurity tickled his personality. The whole new faculty communicated a sense of innate incompetence that had never existed among the Vincentians and the token Jesuits the previous year. Except for Father Jones, every single priest had been replaced. Two nuns were added to the staff but they only taught the seniors and Rico had little or no interaction with them. They appeared to be transplanted Indian peons from Mexico who had been dressed in an overlay of several thick textures of medieval clothing. The nuns, very conservative and polite, exposed their dark, bean-shaped eyes in the center of a restricting cowl that only gave a glimpse of their salt-and-pepper hair beneath. Besides the nuns, Rico's new attention focused on two new teachers that day, although others would later become the focus of disdain, admiration, or criticism.

After morning prayers and breakfast, the first sophomore class awaited Rico and his classmates. Father Prada, another diocesan priest, taught the biology class. No one exactly mentioned the word *homosexual* when he first met the priest, but every seminarian instinctively understood, or believed to have understood, Father Prada's sexual inclinations. His reputation had preceded him in a closed, socially incestuous environment filled with hormone-raging adolescents.

"Hey," he welcomed them in a falsetto voice, wearing wide oval glasses that might have belonged to a 1950s sitcom female character.

He had a slightly oblong head, thin red hair and a bad complexion. The rest of his pink corpulent body had been stuffed into his baggy sacerdotal clothes, protruding on the side and in the front.

"Find your names," he commanded with a sneer.

When they first entered his lab, two deerskins, stretch out and nailed to a plywood board, stood on easels in the front of the class. Before the easels, on a lab table, two Petri dishes contained long, hairy specimens that had been dissected in the middle. Some walked by the Petri dishes while others looked for their names taped on various lab tables that had built-in Bunsen burners and sinks. Eventually every sophomore in Rico's small class found his name and stood at the lab table, entertaining similar speculation but not finding the courage to ask the questions he had in mind.

"Welcome," Prada spoke, standing in front of the outstretched deerskins.

He smiled at them with a happy, womanly smile and spoke through the incessant mastication of a glob of pink, hardened gum. Placing his hands on top of the lab table, he pushed his shoulders up and exhaled.

"Hey," he wheezed, momentarily halting the movement of his mouth.

Looking amusedly at one another with deliberate expressions of ridicule, the class smiled and giggled, waiting for some unexpected event. The next moment would not disappoint.

"So," Louis raised his hand and asked the question everyone had been thinking. "Father?" Prada acknowledged him with a nod. "What kind of animal part is that?"

"Well," Prada paused to chew his gum several more times. "deer skin. I am trying to make a jacket."

"Someone give it to you?" Louis pressed, since no one would believe a priest could hunt a deer or any other animal.

"No," Prada emphatically shook his head and beamed proudly. "I shot it with my thirty-ought-six."

The confession pleased most of the students for their confusion about Prada's sexual orientation had been replaced with the idea that the priest only demonstrated a little eccentricity.

"Father?" Juan continued to ask. Prada nodded and continued chewing pleasantly away. "What's in the cup?"

"Cup?" Prada wondered and stopped chewing for a second. "Oh, it's a Petri dish," he corrected Juan and smiled again. "I dissected two deer penises. Come and see"

Prada motioned the students to walk up to the two dishes and they responded slowly, shuffling forward with perverted curiosity and dread. Dissected deer penises would later, in both the immediate and distant future, invoke hoots of laughter and derision but, for the moment, the seminarians suffered through long moments of mind-shattering shock and awe. Who wouldn't want to see a dissected deer penis? Most of the students could not recognize the original shape of the penis but the sight of the dissection cause an involuntary sensation of pain in their loins.

Since the class periods were short, Prada then added some simple introductory statements and assigned homework readings before dismissing the students to their next class. Once they were a safe distance away from the classroom, Rico and his classmates exploded with laughter and derision.

"D-e-e-e-e-r penisisisisisisisis," they lisped.

But the bizarre and unusual did not end in Prada's class. English followed Biology, and the next teacher had served as a Marine master sergeant and medic in Vietnam. For the seminarians of Rico's day, the Vietnam War remained an ongoing point of contention despite the ascendancy of Watergate and Nixon's misdeeds. After leaving their Biology class, the students moved quickly through the lab hallway and library to the lockers outside the auditorium. Retrieving their English books in time to avoid being tardy to class, several students could be heard continuing to mock Prada and his proud specimen.

"Hey," one student exhaled loudly and began to imitate the sound of loud, obnoxious gum chewing. "Do you want to see a deer penis?"

"If you like this," another student followed. "I'll show you my penis. Hey."

All the students erupted into laughter and quickly stumbled into their English class where the master sergeant, Mr. Cabrera, waited for them to be seated. Besides teaching English that school year, Cabrera doubled as a Latin teacher. In fact, he functioned as one of the few accomplished Latin teachers who had actually humped it across the rice paddies of the Mekong Delta while reading Caesar's commentaries on Gaul. Balding and in his late twenties, he stood just under six feet tall. Despite his military background, he seemed to fit into the physical category of the other faculty members who fought the "battle of the bulge." Just looking at his greasy, corpulent physique, the student or observer would never have accepted him as an ex-Marine. The students took a quick appraisal of him only to return to the mental fixture of an effeminate priest joyfully displaying a dissected deer penis.

"You boys seem to be amused," Cabrera commented once the mechanical bell clanged and they all automatically sat down. "I guess you don't like deer meat."

Hearing his comment, the students became suddenly self-conscious and silent. They were stunned, not appreciating the possibility that their sarcasm had been communicated to Prada or to the new Rector. So they retreated into their conditioned behavior as a form of repentance. Since their freshmen year, the seminarians had learned to conform immediately to their seating arrangement and sat in alphabetical order without any prompting from the clergy or the faculty in general.

"Some things never change," Cabrera observed out loud, offering every student a wide, friendly smile. When he spoke, his body jiggled and complimented his upbeat attitude. "I am Mr. Cabrera. Let's get to know each other."

He waited, still smiling, and then stepped down from his raised desk, and walked to the front of the class.

"I was a seminarian like you in the '60s and I went to the major seminary after I graduated in '68," he continued to introduce himself. "Up until last year, everything had been the same."

He again paused and waited, understanding that his allusion to the new faculty had been resented and rejected.

"So," he spoke seriously. "I got drafted when I dropped out of St. James and the Marines put me in the Medical Corps. I thought about medicine as a career. You know what they tell you when you go out to the paddies as a medic?"

Everyone looked at one another and shook their heads.

"Take the caduceus off," he explained. "The gooks shoot medics first."

He again waited for the dramatic effect to sink in. It did not.

"You don't get it," his smile melted slightly in disappointment. "In 'Nam, they kill the medics first. Without medics, the soldiers bleed and die faster. This ties everyone up and causes more chaos in a chaotic situation. A bunch of bastards they are."

Rico looked at Juan and his other friends who shrugged and wondered why the new teacher spent so much time talking about the war. Everyone had some curiosity about the war, but Cabrera's bipolar behavior dissuaded the students from asking any questions. When he spoke, he would often smile and then suddenly grimace as if someone had shouted an insulting epithet into his ear. Looking a little beyond Juan, Rico noticed that Bates had become a little edgy. As always, Bates's behavior and reactions to any situation would be unpredictable. But for the first time in several months, Rico's attention caught Bates's next move, which would be the catalyst for his expulsion. With calculated stealth, Bates edged the large literature textbook closer to the desk's precipice. It then fell to the floor. For some unknown reason, Rico watched the pending cataclysm in slow motion. Unlike other moments in slow motion, Rico observed finite segments in the passage of time that delivered seconds in fractions, and an abrupt conclusion, which compressed fractions into a swift explosion of activity. A loud crash reverberated through the room and echoed in and out of Rico's consciousness, cutting the room in half.

"Incoming!" Cabrera screamed, diving under the open desk area in front of the class.

Everyone watched with fascination as he cringed under the desk and shivered intensively. All the students stared in disbelief. Some wondered if Cabrera was playing a prank on the class, and others thought he might be having a heart attack.

"Incoming!" Bates shouted and stood up, mocking Cabrera with a diving motion under his desk.

Bates' actions won everyone's disapproval as they witnessed Cabrera's next move. He slowly unfolded himself and pulled his body out from under the desk like a curious hermit crab. Showing the dexterity of a gymnast, Cabrera seemed to defy the laws of neuromuscular movement as he pushed himself forward and leaped up on the desk with one continuous motion. He then pointed down at a surprised Bates who looked up at his teacher from the frail shelter of his plywood desk.

"You-are-going-to-die-you-mother-fucker!" Cabrera cursed at him with controlled, clearly enunciated words.

The last word "fucker," set the slow-motion clock off again in Rico's head as he observed one of the most maddening moments in his adolescent life. Cabrera bounced into the center of the room, raging mad and apparently determined to wreak retribution, whether physical or emotional, on Bates. As he lunged forward, his body seemed to stretch out against gravity. From Rico's perspective, Cabrera moved in stilted phases towards his target. On the receiving end of Cabrera's wrath, Bates remained frozen in place for long moments until Cabrera reached the first desk in his row. Then, with equal reaction to Cabrera's every action, Bates slid away with perfect timing, keeping himself several feet ahead of Cabrera as he faced the exit. Rico could hear the echoes of screams and cheers but only one word stood out in his conscious mind.

"Run!" someone shouted in his ear.

The almost anti-gravity effect of Cabrera's slow motion collapsed and, in a brief fraction of a second, Bates dashed out of the classroom with Cabrera darting after him into the hallway. A rush of students chased Cabrera into the hallway like the scattering of leaves being magnetically yanked in the direction of a fatal hurricane wind. Rico impartially watched the whirlwind dash in front him, leaving only Mike and him behind.

"This will end badly," Mike mused out loud.

"For who?" Rico asked, wondering if Cabrera would have the stamina to catch Bates.

"Good point," Mike agreed and sat down, apparently unmoved by the volatile events. He reached under his desk and picked up a novel to read.

Rico watched Mike's detached behavior in disbelief. But then he thought about himself and how he had been able to resist the attraction of the circus heading out the door. Rico, bemused and disappointed, felt that Bates's enrollment in the school would soon end with the possible dismissal of the class's new English teacher. So, reluctantly following Mike's lead, Rico sat down and began to read an Alistair MacLean thriller about an impossible mission against impossible odds. Later in the day, Bates had been removed from the campus and Cabrera retained his employment until the end of the school year when he reenlisted in the Marines. Whether the decision to reenlist came from the Archdiocese or had been initiated by him, Cabrera strived to teach Latin and English Literature with some veneer of professionalism and stability. Later in the month, he would be given the task of supervising the post-Gaudeamus event in the neighboring cemetery.

Each year, every freshman learned to dread and fear one of the most anticipated three events of the year. The first celebration was Gaudeamus, which meant "let us rejoice" in Latin; then the Christmas party; followed by the three-day retreat in January, which ended with a four-reel movie in the auditorium. For the most part, the freshmen served as the victims, since Gaudeamus, replacing the usual Halloween on October 31, functioned as the platform for their initiation into the seminary. Without too much surprise, the seniors coordinated the skits the freshmen performed on stage, which would humiliate and disparage the freshmen in front of the rest of the faculty and student body. Rico's performance had been borrowed from a popular *Cheech and Chong* skit he heard on an LP. Juan and Rico listened to the record when it had been banned and repressed. They both liked a skit about two Native Americans on a trail, although they made small modifications to the original so that they could perform it in front of the student body. The skit opened with Rico as a chief and Juan as a brave. The chief stops the brave who almost steps on a pile of buffalo excrement:

"Oh," the chief exclaims, pointing to the stinking pile. "What's that?"

"Uh?" the brave responds. "Don't know."

"Looks like buffalo waste. Pick it up," the chief orders.

"What?" the brave objects.

"Pick it up," the chief orders again.

The brave picks up the shit and massages it.

"Ugh," he utters.

"What does it feel like?" the chief asks.

"Like buffalo waste," the brave unhappily concludes.

"Smell it," the chief orders.

"Uh?" the brave rejects the idea.

"Smell it," the chief shouts.

Cautiously, the brave holds it up to his nose and sniffs, rapidly wrenching his face away from the shit.

"What does it smell like?" the chief pursues with his inquiry.

"Buffalo waste," the brave assures him, attempting to drop the shit on its original pile.

"Taste it," the chief commands.

"No," the brave protests and tries to shake the shit off his hand.

The chief then pull out an obsidian knife and holds it up to the brave's neck.

"Taste it," he threatens.

Looking at the knife, the brave reluctantly moves the remaining shit to his lips and quickly touches it to his lips. Immediately, he spits it out and violently shakes the remaining shit from his fingers.

"What does it taste like?" the chief presses, still holding up the knife.

"Like buffalo waste," the brave assures him, continuing to spit out the foul taste.

"Good," the chief responds and puts away his knife. "Good thing we didn't step on it. Let's go."

The brave follows the chief off the stage but takes a distrustful look back at the pile of buffalo shit.

When they finished, the student body gave them a standing ovation. Some of the faculty snickered and the Monsignor seemed amused, although the allusion was lost on the staff. The mature students understood that Rico and Juan had just flashed their metaphorical middle finger at each faculty member. The other students just laughed at the skit's sophomoric humor. This year, as a sophomore, Rico did not have to perform onstage. Unfortunately for Rico, he had the undesirable task of coordinating "the Hunt for the D-Dorm Queer."

When the seminary's population fell in the late 1960s, the C and D dormitories had been abandoned in the second wing of the school. So, to frighten the lower classmen and to discourage them from wandering into the empty dormitories, the seniors began to tell the story of a headless monk who haunted the D dormitory. How the decapitated ghost had been transformed into the D-Dorm Queer escaped any rational explanation. But the myth persisted and, after the ritual of Guadeamus concluded, the sophomores would gather the freshmen in groups and order them to climb the neighboring fence and enter the cemetery. Among the dark canyons of the mausoleums and the shadows of the oak trees blanketing the tombstones, the freshmen charged the cemetery to frighten the D-Dorm Queer back into his D-Dorm habitat. The D-Dorm Queer had only a few hours before midnight to return to his gravesite or he would be doomed to roam the vacant dormitory for the next year.

"I have to what?" a plump, acne-faced freshman protested.

"Run through the cemetery and scare the Queer back here," Rico explained for the twentieth time. "He's got to return."

"Why?" the paralyzed freshman demanded to know.

"What the fuck," Rico tried to think of an excuse. "He's our mascot, you shithead. What would a seminary be without something of the supernatural floating around?"

"I'm scared," the freshmen protested.

"You're goin' to be more scared when I kick your ass!" Rico threatened him. "You pussy."

In the dark shadows, glimpses of young freshmen could be seen darting through the bare spaces of the marbled mausoleum blocks with their bronze-laden epitaphs. Out on the cemetery fields, the scurrying freshmen hid and ran, looking like frightened bats circling in confusion and desperation. According to plan, Rico prodded and coerced the freshmen to move in a single direction in the north section of the cemetery near the orange groves and avocado trees, where only fragments of light reached the dark crevices of eerie oak trees and lopsided burial plots. Several empty sarcophagi, white concrete vessels where coffins would be interred, lay near dug-out plots covered with velvet cloth. Among these hidden and cryptic scenes, the seniors lay in wait to pounce upon, frighten, and terrify the freshmen before abandoning them among their imaginary nightmares and horrors. Watching the freshmen cry, squeal, and scream elicited weeks of laughter and storytelling that would be used for repeated entertainment during the long, dreary nights of late winter. Nearby, standing next to one of these sarcophagi, Rico could make out the shape of the plump acne-faced freshman he had accosted near the mausoleum.

"Shithead," Rico called to him. "You see the queer?"

"What?" the freshmen jumped, staggering closer to the sarcophagus.

From within a sarcophagus, a hairy, fat senior sprang out wearing Tim Curry's costume from the *Rocky Horror* film. Dressed as a transvestite, he added to the grotesque and outrageous. He wore a large, afro-wig and long, blood-red fingernails. Dead-white makeup pasted his face and a nearby lamp lent a counterfeit luminescence to a darkened area around the gravesite. The senior's red lipstick and bloodied make-up appeared almost black in the low light.

"I'm the D-Dorm Queer," the senior shouted, holding up a long, plastic penis with two plastic testicles attached to the base. "And I am going to fuck you up the ass, you faggot!"

The freshman instantly leaped into the air and shouted in a high-pitched voice that reached a fever pitch before descending into a lower octaves of groans and unintelligible utterance.

"Oh, God," he mumbled continuously. "Oh, God."

"There is no fucking God, you faggot," the senior responded, climbing out of the sarcophagus in large, glossy red, spike heels. "Bend over! Ha. Ha."

He took the plastic penis and pretended to ram it in and out of the freshman's anus. Waving it in front of the freshman's face, he held the penis in an erect position. On cue, the freshmen bent over and, instead of engaging in any sexual foreplay, vomited violently. Nearly simultaneously, a loud sound of defecation followed.

"Did you just shit in your pants?" the senior stopped suddenly and waved the penis in front of him like a censer at a Catholic mass. He seemed to be warding off a malicious spirit. "You're a fucking faggot, shitting in your pants!"

The freshman collapsed on the ground and began to cry. Surrounding the freshman and escalating into a chorus of guffaws, costumed seniors stepped out of their hiding places and began to jeer at and ridicule the soiled freshman. Various vampires, Frankenstein monsters, werewolves, and mummies moved towards and away from the freshman in delight. Soon after, other freshmen began to mock their classmate.

"Got the Hershey squirts?" a classmate hooted and fell back on a sarcophagus, laughing and taunting his classmate.

Rico and the sophomores joined in the riotous behavior until the freshman's humiliating state sank into their conscious. Their victim lay on the grass, trembling and crying in stuttered fits.

"You okay, dude?" Rico asked, nudging the freshman's shoulder for a response.

"Get up!" a vampire ordered, not allowing him any quarter. He pushed the crying freshman with his foot.

The transvestite rubbed the plastic penis across the freshman's neck. "Let's go. The fun's over."

As if a military command had been given, the seniors moved in unison towards the cemetery fence, looking like a monster-movie crew walking towards the commissary between shots. The sophomores joined them and some of the freshmen followed. A few helped the fecal-stained freshman stand. He moved with careful steps, still sniffling and mumbling intelligibly. The transvestite looked back at him when he reached the cemetery fence and mockingly held up the plastic penis like a baton.

"Good job," he congratulated everyone in sight. "The D-Dorm Queer is back for another year."

A hollow cheer went up and the monster crew began to leap over the fence. First, they climbed up one by one and then the other students joined them en masse. Rico remained behind and watched the muddled freshman approach the fence with two seemingly frightened and intimidated friends.

"God," the freshman continued to repeat as they neared.

In the distance, Rico caught a glimpse of the pale sarcophagi against a monochromatic background. He then turned to look at the freshman for a second before leaping over the fence, too.

"God help me," Rico heard the trembling freshman's voice whimper from behind.

Phase 5

Father Clement again sat in an imperial posture that reeked of stoic detachment. The transition from a virtual story to another virtual phase caused the participants to mentally stumble and hesitate through a dim fog of awareness. Being aware of the transition's lethargy, Clement, or the computer, waited until the participants reached full cognition, even though their motor skills slightly lagged behind their mental resurgence.

"I need a fucking Excedrin," Juan demanded, holding his head while resting it on the table.

"Get me one too," Rico muttered, feeling as if his tongue had swollen to twice its size. "This is becoming really annoying and uncomfortable. Can't you do anything to buffer the transition, Bill?"

Bill also painfully rubbed his forehead and tried several times to speak, but uttered only unintelligible sounds. The third attempt was successful.

"I'll slow down the transition buffer next time," Bill promised.

"It seems to be more difficult each time," Mike also observed, rubbing his eyes and tilting his head back.

"It will continue to be tough," Bill admitted, speaking through his hands, which were cupped over his face. "There's a degradation of memory as we transition from story to story, and I am using compressions to maintain the cohesiveness of our psyches."

"What kind of degradation?" Rico felt a pulse of panic race through his virtual body. "Don't tell me we are fucking dying too!"

"No," Bill denied emphatically and pulled his hands from his face, revealing a pale, bloodshot visage to his classmates. "There are too many anomalies in the human mind. Complexities and contradictions which the computer's algorithms must compensate for. So I use compressions to speed up the process and delay. Otherwise, too much of my technology would waste its effort reinventing the wheel."

"Duplicating patterns," Rico understood.

"Yes," Bill responded proudly. "But there is a side effect, as you can tell."

"But you said degradation," Rico countered. "That word has some fucking unpleasant connotations."

"You like that word," Mike expressed his displeasure at Rico's language.

Rico ignored him and stared at Bill.

"Bad choice of words, *degradation*," Bill ignored Mike and answered Rico. "I should have said a weakening. My mistake."

"Right," Rico sarcastically, doubting Bill's clarification.

Bill never misspoke in the past but Rico understood that Bill was reticent to admit the true meaning of his explanation. The whole experience through phase transitions seemed to have reached some critical juncture on a technological level. Privately, Rico wondered how long the experiment could continue before there would be real damage to their memories or cognitive states, since the computer continued to tap into the depths of the unconscious, extracting unfathomable, long-forgotten and buried memory resources. It could disturb other natural cerebral areas in the process—if the concept of nature still existed within a computer.

"I forgot all about that Gaudeamus trip," Juan recalled the recent story.

"That was unforgiving," Mike concluded. "We always seem to be leaving these experiences in the negative."

"God," Clement pronounced with clear authority. "Where was God?"

"God is a joker," Juan concluded, "on Halloween."

"There is no God," Rico sputtered. "You heard the senior. That's why no one helped the poor fucker."

Clement half-rose to object, as if he were a real priest, and then he sat back with a small smile of contentment, hinting at some private amusement.

"You could have helped him," Mike reminded Rico of his involvement. "You're God's hand in this manner. You could have showed some compassion."

"What compassion?" Rico snapped. "Can't you see it was a joke and the little dude just got scared? But that is what your God does. Right?"

"What do you mean?" Mike brushed away the insinuation.

"You know," Rico answered with a surly smile.

"Explain!" Clement commanded.

Rico held up his middle finger and waved off Clement.

"That's not part of the agreement, Rico," Bill reminded his friend. "We are here to have a discussion."

Rico looked over at Juan, who shrugged as if to say Rico had to make up his own mind. He sighed and leaned a little forward to address Mike.

"Your God," Rico spoke in a measured tone, "first off, doesn't exist. But that is not the point." He waited to see Mike's reaction but his poker face revealed nothing. "Your fucking cannibalistic God feeds off fear. Fear of retribution. Fear of condemnation. Fear of abandonment. An all-good merciful God doesn't fit this bill. I love clichés. And, for the *pièce de résistance*, if you really want fear, he will throw you into a pit where you can burn for all eternity. Don't forget, He's a jealous God. What a goof! A God who is omniscient and creates people he knows he will condemn to eternal torture. Real nice! That is the God you want me to worship? Fucking right?"

"You know God works in mysterious ways," Juan commented in a solemn tone, mockingly blessing himself.

Both he and Rico chortled before Rico pointed to Clement.

"You are condemned for being a cocksucker," Rico passed a mocking judgment on Clement.

The avatar remained unmoved, and Mike momentarily closed his eyes as if calculating his next move.

"This is like the old days," Bill observed, appearing to be pleased at their histrionics. "You two liked taking shots at people and getting a laugh out of it."

"Yeah," Rico agreed and tapped Juan on the arm. "Come on. Where is this merciful God? Why does he allow for death and disease on his innocents? Why can't he stop the Devil? Is he impotent against another rival god? Mike...let me ask you a serious question?"

Mike, opening his eyes, nodded an affirmative.

"What makes your God any less ridiculous than the other pagan gods?" Rico demanded to know, "or the gods of the Hindu or Muslim faith? How can three persons live in one godhead? Is the Christian God a jealous rival to Shiva, Vishnu, and Brahma?"

"I can't prove that God exists," Mike said simply. "There is a preponderance of evidence that supports God's existence."

Pretending to be stunned, Rico tried to mouth a response and then changed his mind after looking at Juan who simply shrugged. Bill appeared intrigued and Clement remained aloof and withdrawn.

"But you can't prove the negative either," Mike completed his statement.

"Oh," Rico rejected his argument. "That is a 'cop out' as we said back in school. You with your education should know better. You can't..."

"Disprove a negative," Mike coolly finished his thoughts. "But you can't."

"The onus is on you to prove the affirmative," Rico reminded him of the simple proof in philosophy. "You can say you have a Lilliputian in your pocket and I can ask you to prove it. And if you can't prove it, it doesn't exist. Believe all you want but you gotta prove it. Show me!"

"I can't prove it," Mike repeated. "But I know it does exist."

"Then pull the little guy out of your pocket," Rico challenged him. "Or the God? Where is your God who has caused so much misery and violence in the universe and this planet? I am still waiting."

"God allows misery and suffering so we may come closer to Him," Mike explained. "He gives us these burdens to draw us closer to Him. That is why He sent His Son, so that we are not alone in our suffering. Anyway, let me ask you something. Can something come from nothing?"

"Good question," Rico accepted, holding up his hand. "I'll tell you."

"Go ahead," Clement's avatar suddenly became animated.

"There was never a nothing," Rico spoke confidently. "There was something. Always."

"That something is God," Mike added as a direct counterpoint, pointing his finger up at an unseen divinity.

"Go on," Rico pushed for him to continue.

"Before time there was something," Mike expanded his commentary. "It's common sense that something had to exist to make the universe."

"How can that make sense?" Rico disagreed, turning around to give Juan a confident smile. "Nothing exists before time. So without time, how can anything exist? It's a contradiction in terms. But physicists now have evidence that something physical existed before our universe. Why can it not always exist? De facto!"

"Not on a spiritual plane," Mike became agitated and shifted his position in his chair. "God exists outside of time. He is perfect. Omnipotent, omniscient, and…"

"I know," Rico interrupted. "And omnibenevolent. Does God know what He's going to do tomorrow? If so, could He do something else? If God knows what will happen, and does something else, He's not omniscient. If He knows and can't change it, He's not omnipotent." Rico looked at Bill. "Can I have a few minutes to explain?"

Bill appeared uneasy, and Rico read his body language to mean "no."

"I want to answer this so-called metaphysical truth," Rico protested. "He can't get away with this."

A small earthquake rattled the cafeteria and everyone grabbed the table. Rico felt like diving for cover but stopped himself once he realized the futility of any evasive action.

"No," Clement terminated the debate. "It's ended."

"We can talk about God's nature another time," Bill nervously concurred with the avatar.

"That's the point," Rico tried to communicate. "How can you discuss a deity's nature when it's a fantasy?"

Rico looked around and felt uneasy at the continued tremors. He knew Bill had been covering up some vital fact about their status and the operations of the program. Or, he thought, Bill played a Machiavellian role and ended his diatribe against Mike's archaic views. The fact remained that Rico wished to speak to his daughter. He needed to remind Bill.

"It's all right," Bill assured everyone and stood up. His body language had a commanding effect on everyone.

"Bill?" Rico tried to plead. "I told you I have to do some things. Another story can wait."

Bill waved him off.

"I think we know that Rico began to lose his religious faith at the cemetery," Bill surmised. "And I am sure more spirited debates will come." He paused and smiled. "No pun intended."

Rico smiled at the feeble joke but Mike appeared peeved. Pushing the sessions forward, Bill continued to stall Rico's ability to talk to his daughter.

"We need time," Rico tried to intervene. "Time to reflect! Time to converse! Right, Bill? I need to talk with you."

Bill raised his finger to his lips and the environment began to melt away into a new virtual realm.

"Let's proceed," Clement commanded. "*Vamos con Dios.*"

"No," Rico objected loudly. "*Vamos con ordenador.*"

Chapter 8

Suffer the little children to come unto me.
– Jesus

A rush of teenage boys scrambled from the refectory to the dormitories to prepare for their first day of the January three-day retreat. As a treat to all the seminarians, they were permitted to sleep one hour later, and they consumed a generous breakfast of eggs and pancakes before experiencing a unique spiritual journey. For most of the students, the retreat provided an escape and an adventure away from the drudgery of academics and the boredom of routine. Although they filled their days with spiritual reflections and activities, the events allowed them to socialize and play. Their recreation period had been extended and the evening events concluded with large meals and celebrations. On the third day of the retreat, a four-reel movie played in the auditorium.

In the days before the Internet and video recorders, full-length movies, shown in a school auditorium, offered a unique luxury for the semi-impoverished seminarian living on charity from his parish's coffers. No one knew the title of the movie and its anticipation added to the festive mood. Leaving the dormitories in a bustle, the students rushed briskly to the chapel where the retreat would begin. Only the juniors and seniors directed the retreats. Since it was his first retreat, Mike's enthusiasm reached a crescendo. He looked forward to bonding more closely with the Lord, and he found the excitement that surrounded him a little odd for a retreat. Most students seemed to be heading to a rock concert instead of a religious retreat.

"Twat are we doing later?" Louis spoke in coded obscene language outside the chapel.

"Football or basketball," Rico laughed.

"Twat?" Juan mocked Louis.

"Can't you think of anything but pussy?" Rico teased his classmate and laughed again.

"Twat did you say?" Louis repeated the joke and laughed. "I can't. Can you?"

"No, you faggot," Rico blurted out and tried to punch Louis in the chest.

Rico missed but Louis managed to slap Juan in the chest instead.

"Ouch, you fucker!" Juan rubbed his chest.

"Twat was that?" Louis almost shouted.

Leaping up in the air, Louis ran ahead of his classmates and into the quad area before entering the church.

"He'll probably jack off in the back," Juan made a prediction.

Rico laughed and a few of the other neighboring seminarians chuckled at Louis's brazenness. Late in the evening, he urinated out the dormitory window, hitting an occasional seminarian below. Other times, before the morning bell, he would pretend to experience an explosive orgasm under his bed sheets. In the chapel, everyone would listen to one or two of Louis's fake coughs, hiding a vulgar word sandwiched between indecipherable phonemes. Mike patiently observed the tomfoolery and experienced an involuntary smile at Louis's antics, until he told himself that the behavior was unacceptable. Rico noticed the brief humor on Mike's face before it vanished.

"He's funny," Rico challenged him. "You've got to admit it."

"You guys are really crude," Mike chastised them and walked ahead.

Juan and Rico laughed at Mike who ignored their taunts.

"Twat did you say?" Juan asked as he entered the chapel.

"Twat do you mean by crude?" Rico added, and they laughed until the Spiritual Director met them inside.

"Please be seated," he gravely ordered.

They sat unwillingly, showing false humility, but the brimming excitement and thrill of being out of school continued to electrify them. Most seminarians felt the same but Mike, who sat respectfully behind Juan and Rico, waited anxiously for the opening homily. Although he had been in the school for four months, Mike had not made any friends except for a casual acquaintanceship with John who sat alone in the front pew. A priest entered the chapel from the side sanctuary. With a welcoming smile, the tall, handsome red-haired priest, sporting a casual shirt and black slacks, beamed like one of Raphael's cherished cherubs at the congregation of miscreant teenagers and future Catholic priests.

As soon as he appeared, everyone recognized Father Larry and applauded. He had given a one-day retreat earlier in the year and often made appearances as the head celebrant for Friday masses. His popularity did not derive only from his youth, which naturally helped since most priests on campus were over 50 years of age, but from his affable personality and liberal perspective. Unlike the other priests who drove conservative Buicks and Oldsmobiles, Father Larry drove a pristine 1965 red Corvette and occasionally sported a Harley motorcycle.

"Hi, guys," Father Larry greeted the audience.

The students cheered and whistled en masse and Father Larry waved his arms as if he were leading a pep rally. For several moments, he soaked up their adulations and the students enjoyed the fanfare.

"You gotta think he gets some serious pussy on the side," Rico almost shouted into Juan's ear. "The 'Vette helps too."

"No shit," Juan agreed.

Mike heard similar comments about sex and cars and wondered again why his classmates wanted to be priests or even why they attended a seminary.

"Okay," he held up his hands.

Looking over at the Spiritual Director who openly showed his contempt at the students' behavior, Father Larry continued to smile but motioned everyone to calm down. He raised his finger to his lips, even though his smile seemed to grow with every fragmented cheer and whistle that whimpered away in broken and reluctant decibels. Mike passively watched but felt that he bore witness to an inherent goodness or divine grace. God touched Father Larry in a special way, enabling him to reach a new generation of priests during this socially revolutionary period. He slowly felt spiritually drawn to the man while feeling a calm peacefulness blanket his soul. Father Larry continued to raise his arms to quiet the students before he stepped away from the podium holding the microphone in one hand while pulling the cord with his other hand. Tapping the microphone a couple of times, he spoke into it with a clear, cheerful voice that instantly changed pitch.

"When you die," Father Larry began, "and meet Our Father," he paused to look straight ahead at apparently no one, "which Beatitude would describe you? Jesus gave us many Beatitudes. Which one calls you blessed?"

The smiles and smirks disappeared from the congregation's faces as fast as the warming smile of relief grew on the Spiritual Director's face.

"Do you know the Beatitudes?" he challenged him. "I'll give a dollar to the person who knows."

Many hands intermittently shot up but the priest focused on one hand.

The hand shot up from a thin, undersized freshman wearing a buttoned black cardigan one pew in front of the priest. Acknowledging the enthusiastic student's volunteering hand, Father Larry pointed his microphone directly at the freshmen as if he had extended a regal staff. The freshmen shyly stood up and cleared his voice.

"What's your name?" Father Larry asked, retracting the microphone in time so it caught his voice. He then stepped forward and held it to the freshman's mouth.

"Pedro," the freshmen almost stuttered.

"Go ahead," Father Larry encouraged him. "Please."

"Well," Pedro thought for a moment and named the Beatitudes in almost one breath. "Blessed are the poor in spirit, those who mourn, the meek, those who hunger and thirst for justice, the merciful, the pure of heart, the peacemakers, and those who suffer persecution."

Father Larry lifted the microphone in triumph and turned around, applauding Pedro with the microphone in his hands. The students joined him and everyone applauded. A few whistled and cheered. Surprisingly, the Spiritual Director showed the most pleasure as he held up his right thumb.

"Good job," the priest congratulated him, handing him the dollar that all the seminarians envied to possess. On campus, the dollar bought the precious few items sold in the archaic vending machines in the recreational room. "And which one is the most important."

"Are they all important?" Pedro questioned in a squeaky, subdued voice since he had no access to the microphone.

"Yes," Father Larry agreed still smiling, "which one does God value most?"

Pedro remained silent and everyone fell silent too. Mike felt the urge to answer the question since it was very obvious to him. The urge to raise his hand overwhelmed him but he resisted. Father Larry looked around and his eyes made contact with Mike who froze when the priest's eyes locked on him.

"I think you know?" Father Larry invited him.

Mike nervously stood up and felt his legs slightly tremble. His confidence evaporated and he began to doubt his resolve.

"Don't worry," the priest joked. "Everyone is staring at you."

The congregation nervously laughed and the joke caused Father Siemens to smile too. But his smile and the students' smiles melted away in an instant.

"It's the last," Mike uttered nervously. He then raised his voice as if to make an announcement. "Blessed are those who are persecuted for the sake of righteousness, for theirs is the Kingdom of Heaven."

"The Kingdom of Heaven," Father Larry repeated with approval and began to applaud.

This time the congregation applauded with less aplomb, Mike sat down with controlled dignity and a small feeling of accomplishment and pride— despite the subtle rejection. But from the sanctuary, Father Siemens nodded his approval at Mike for everyone else to see.

"Very good," Father Larry made eye contact with Mike one more time and then addressed the whole audience. "The Kingdom of Heaven will be gained through suffering and maybe death. All of you must understand that being priests, you will suffer much for the Lord. Are you prepared to enter the Kingdom of Heaven and to accept the pain and suffering the Lord will send you?"

Father Larry paused, and Rico could feel the jovial mood of the chapel being sucked right out of the quad.

"My dick is already suffering," Rico whispered to Juan.

"Shhh," Mike tried to silence him.

"You don't have to go far," the priest added. "The Kingdom of Heaven is already here. Our Lord told us."

The congregation waited in silence for the famous dénouement – the theme for the retreat season.

"What's the point?" Juan demanded in a whisper.

"I bet you we have to suffer," Rico quipped.

Both snickered and they caught Father Larry's attention. He smiled directly at them.

"How do you expect to suffer?" the priest asked Rico and Juan, but everyone knew the question was for them to answer. "Like eating at the cafeteria each day?"

Father Larry's facetious tone made everyone snicker nervously. Siemens seemed slightly uneasy about the direction of Father Larry's comment but he managed to maintain a plastic grin on his face.

"Yes," Father Larry continued in a light-hearted tone. "Some Christians died but God doesn't want us all to die. I know you all make sacrifices. The cafeteria," He repeated and the congregation snickered again. "The long hours in study hall? The long hours at prayer? Sometimes the lack of sleep?"

As Father Larry addressed each sacrifice, he held up his free left thumb and pivoted in a small circle so he could face each seminarian in a 360-degree arc.

"And girls?" Father Larry nodded enthusiastically. "Right? That social life all of your friends are having at those other schools."

A surge of reciprocal enthusiasm shot through the student body for the mention of girls released a pulse of hormones. Father Siemens's careful contentment evaporated.

"Except for him," Rico commented cynically, pointing a finger at Mike.

"No shit," Juan agreed.

"Sh-h-h!" Mike expressed his disdain for their sophomoric behavior.

Many of the student body had girlfriends on the side, although it had been prohibited from the first day they entered the seminary. Rico turned around to face him.

"Don't you get your dick up, Mike?" Rico blurted out.

Mike suddenly blushed, and Rico immediately turned around to see a grinning Juan.

"But," Father Larry called for everyone's attention, holding up his index finger instead of his thumb. "Is this really suffering for the Lord? These next three days, you must ask yourself, 'How I can genuinely suffer for the Lord? What can I give to God that helps me pay the price that Christ paid on the cross for us?' How much do you truly love the Lord to offer Him your honest pain and suffering? What will you give up? Remember, the Lord will make you suffer for Him but he wants to know what you can offer freely."

He paused and continued to turn around, trying to make direct eye contact with each seminarian.

"Do you love our Lord," Father Larry inquired, "and His Blessed Mother?"

He stopped moving and returned to the podium, letting the microphone dangle from his side. Reaching the podium, he nimbly tossed the microphone up and it almost magically slid into its holder with a screeching click. An admiring sound of awe murmured through the church as Father Larry carefully looked down to read a passage from the scriptures in front of him.

"For God so loved the world," the priest began to read, 'that He gave His only Son, that whoever believes in Him should not perish but have eternal life."

Father Larry then looked up with moistened eyes and spoke in a soft, but strong tone.

"Do you want to have eternal life?" he asked rhetorically. "Offer yourself to the Lord these three days. Make the commitment. May God Bless you. If you're lucky and attentive, you can win more dollars."

A burst of applause and cheers exploded and Father Siemens made no effort to hide his discomfort. Rico thought that the Spiritual Director probably resented the popularity of the visiting priest more than the fact that he offered a bribe to the impoverished seminarians. Throughout the retreat, Father Larry would command a dominant popularity among the priests and staff until movie night. Except for several brief, unannounced visits to the seminary office, the seminarians would never see Father Larry again.

As the seminarians stood up to leave, Father Siemens stood and motioned for them to sit down. A rumble of disappointment pulsed through the congregation. Despite the expression of unpopularity, Father Siemens managed to smile victoriously.

"Thank you, Father Larry," Siemens said in a saccharine tone. He then turned to address the student body. "If I can donate a five-dollar bill, would anyone volunteer to write the life of Jesus before the deadline?"

The allusion to the major religion class assignment invited a wary laughter and hiss from the student body that clearly communicated the seminarians' dislike of the project in Father Siemens's class. During the first semester, before the Christmas break, every sophomore had been required to summarize the four gospels into one twenty-page report containing the major events and sayings attributed to Jesus. Most students never completed the assignment on time, or they completed it incorrectly. Father Siemens still waited for the reports from half of Rico's class. Rico received an average grade and Juan never submitted the assignment, almost earning a failing grade for religion.

"Please go to your assigned break-out classes," Father Larry added, looking at his watch.

The student body quickly rose from their pews and poured out of the chapel in all directions. Most exited into the quads and small groups walked through the main nave.

"He said my report was very thorough," Mike reminded Rico and Juan of his success.

"Can I copy it?" Juan asked.

Rico laughed at the joke and Mike mouthed a sarcastic "No."

"Why are you guys here?" he asked them seriously.

"Do we have a choice?" Juan quipped.

"No," Mike's tone revealed some frustration. "Why did you enter the seminary? You don't seem to want to be priests."

"Actually," Rico began to joke, avoiding the question. "I came for the waters, for my health."

"Waters?" Mike expressed his confusion. "There are no waters here."

"I was seriously misinformed, I guess," Rico ended the joke.

"You got that from *Casablanca,*" Juan laughed.

Mike stood up and gave them an angry glare as he quickly stepped out of the chapel. He walked through a channel of students rushing to their break-out classes for the first part of the retreat. Looking at his schedule, he walked to Room 3 in the main transept behind the chapel. As with all break-out classes, the retreat course had a mixture of classmen from the student body. Mike, as in the other classes, would be one of two sophomores. There would be one senior, two juniors, two sophomores, and two to three freshmen.

Feeling relieved, Mike pleasantly scanned the room and saw no other sophomores. When he walked into the room, a few of the students had already been seated in a circle of desks. In the front of the circle, an unknown Brother from a local church stood behind a folding chair in front of the classroom. He was dressed as a priest wearing a Roman collar. Appearing to be over fifty years of age, the Brother seemed very fit and athletic. He body communicated health and his face showed satisfaction. Seeing Mike, the Brother pushed his brown-dyed hair to the side and motioned for Mike to sit close by, next to a junior and freshmen. Mike did not personally know any of the students since he was new to the school but he recognized their faces.

"I'm Brother Jacob," the athletic religious identified himself. "We are still waiting for a couple of the Lord's sheep to arrive. Shall I send out a shepherd?"

After finishing his allusion to a famous Biblical parable, the remaining students, who were not sophomores, shyly entered the rooms and greeted the Brother in a low apologetic tone. Their arrival caused Mike to have a deeper sense of relief at not having his classmates participate in the break-out class, especially Louis, Rico and Juan. He hoped these present students would show more dedication and reverence than his more pagan classmates. The Brother's affable expression remained steady and welcoming.

"Good," the Brother began. "How is everybody?"

Everyone mumbled a "good" or "okay," forcing a smile on his face. Mike smiled pleasantly but he felt anxious about participating in his first three-day retreat.

"I bet it felt great to get some extra sleep," the Brother tried to lighten the atmosphere. "And a better breakfast."

The students reacted with a happy smile and small laugh.

"We're so lucky Father Larry could join us," he added. "You know he is in great demand?"

The students nodded in approval and smiled at the Brother.

"So Father Larry reminded us that we must all suffer for the Lord," the Brother repeated the opening theme. "But these three days, we will discover that suffering is something beneficial for our souls."

He looked at every nervous seminarian who privately began to contemplate his future suffering. Mike felt that the cross he must bear would be the ire of ridicule throughout his life.

"Remember," the Brother continued with his lecture. "Every Good Friday comes before Easter. Always before Easter."

He paused again and looked around.

"How do you expect to avoid suffering for Him?" the Brother pressed. "He who hung on a cross, humiliated and degraded by the very creatures He created. But you know you have to have humor to be a great saint?"

The Brother waited to let the paradox sink in.

"Yes," he confirmed their silent doubt. "Without humor we can't suffer well and make it meaningful. I remember a story about St. Theresa of Avila. She reformed the Carmelite Order and suffered from physical problems. One day she was travelling during a storm through the countryside of Spain, suffering from painful migraines and racked with physical pain. Her wagon hit a rut in the road and she was thrown into a ditch full of mud and ice water. Looking up at the sky, she yelled, 'Lord, if this how You treat your friends it is no wonder You have so few of them.'"

The small group burst out laughing and the Brother also sniggered a little.

"This is one example of how humor carries our pain," the Brother picked up the pace. "Padre Pio, the Italian monk with the stigmata for 30 years, suffered greatly. A party was given in his honor and a parishioner said, 'Oh bless you, Padre, and all the good that you do! May God grant you another hundred years!' Padre Pio looked at him and said, 'What did I ever do to you?'"

Again the small group laughed and the Brother sniggered some more. He then walked over to the podium where a basket sat. Reaching inside the basket, he pulled out several colored strips of paper. Behind the Brother, Mike noticed a stack of poster boards and markers.

"I am going to pass out these strips of paper," the Brother told them as he began to hand them out to each student. "You will keep the quote to yourself until I tell you what to do."

Mike received a yellow slip of paper and read the following quote, "Now the Pharisees, who were lovers of money, also heard these things, and they derided Him. Luke 16:14." He read it several times and looked up at the Brother who intensely watched each student read his own quotation.

"Now," he instructed the students. "Read your quote to the class."

The Brother pointed to a shy, undersized freshman who momentarily stared in disbelief but found the courage to read his slip of paper.

"Okay," he nervously began and cleared his throat. The Brother patiently smiled as everyone waited. "It says 'For in that He Himself has suffered being tempted, He was able to aid those who are tempted.'"

"And where is it from?" the Brother pointed out an absent reference.

The freshman's eyes rapidly scanned the slip of paper and remained obviously befuddled with the failing effort.

The Brother leaned forward and pointed out the reference under the quote.

"Oh," the freshman mumbled. "It says Hebrews 2:18."

"Hebrews, chapter two, verse eighteen," the Brother patiently corrected him.

The other students laughed softly as the Brother kindly smiled at the freshman as if he were a misbehaving dog who had soiled the kitchen floor.

"Next," he pointed to Mike who sat next to the freshman.

Mike read his quote and waited.

"Good," the Brother looked satisfied that Mike did not botch the quote and its citation. "Go on."

Every student routinely read his slip of paper that recalled Christ's sufferings during different states and moments in the Gospels. When the last student finished reading his slip of paper, he looked up and waited.

"Good," the Brother expressed his approval. "Now I want you to write a response on the back of the paper. How does this quote relate to your life? What has happened in your life so that you can offer up this particular moment of suffering as penance for your sins?"

Several students seemed confused and the Brother immediately anticipated their questions.

"Our friend here," the Brother pointed out the freshman again, who smiled nervously and fidgeted in his chair, "mentions the time when Jesus was tempted. How does temptation affect you in your life? How will you address temptation when it comes? What will you call upon from your spiritual arsenal to fight the Devil when he tempts you? Clear?"

No one responded and the Brother opened his mouth to continue, but the freshman interrupted him.

"What's an arsenal, Brother?" he asked in a meek tone.

"It holds all kinds of weapons," the Brother blurted out. "Begin."

Some chuckles could be heard, and the other students began to reflect and write on the reverse side of the slip of paper.

Mike felt sorry for the freshman but he quickly dismissed his sympathies, focusing on the task at hand. He soon remembered how he had been derided since elementary school for his religiosity and serious focus. Although he believed the derision would end when he entered the seminary, the Elysian Fields of adolescent Catholic faith, he unfortunately discovered to his dismay that his classmates expressed more contempt for his beliefs than those who attended regular Catholic schools or even public schools. The recent encounter with Rico and Juan just added to his frustration.

"Young man," the Brother addressed Mike after five minutes of waiting, leaning forward to read the tag on his shirt, "would you like to help me?"

Mike looked up and felt a wave of panic blanket his heart, fearing he would have to read his response. He sadly realized that he had made his response extremely personal.

"Yes," Mike consented with some trepidation.

"No. It's easy," the Brother sensed his anxiety. "Come with me."

Mike followed the Brother to the back of the class and took hold of the varied colored construction paper he handed to him.

"Distribute these to each student," he told him.

Relieved, Mike smiled weakly and happily handed out the medium-sized paper, which slightly curled when each sheet was pulled out of the bundle. Looking skeptically at the paper, the freshman accepted it and struggled to hold it out in front of himself since his arms were too short.

"Place it on the floor," the Brother watched his struggle.

He then passed out several colored markers to each student after Mike made a complete round. Mike picked out a light-blue construction paper and several dark markers. All of the students then sat on the floor next to the paper, poised to create something to display in the classroom.

"Now," the Brother spoke with a careful, measured tone. "I want you to visualize your pain and struggle. Write the quote on the construction paper. You can write it as a title or as anything you like. Then, draw a picture, or several pictures, that depict your struggle. Represent your pain and suffering using images and not words. Do you understand?"

A junior then eyed the freshman who seemed a little perplexed by the instructions as he toyed with the markers. He quietly spoke to him and the Brother seemed satisfied with the fraternal exchange. Mike took his paper and markers to the corner of the room and almost out of every other seminarian's sight. He set out to write the quote in black in the right-hand corner of the paper. Staring at the quote for a while, Mike began to feel a growing sense of frustration. After looking around, he noticed that several of the other students had become seriously involved in their project, energetically drawing images and characters alongside colorful illustrations. The Brother took an active interest in each student's efforts, communicating his approval with a nod, a smile, a positive facial gesture, or a simple thumbs-up. After viewing most of the papers, he looked at Mike's endeavor and paused, expressing a momentary show of concern. Subduing his frown, he waited for Mike to complete his project as it began to take shape. Smiling, the Brother left Mike to view another student's work.

Mike decided to use abstract representations and color to represent his interpretation of the quote and its impact on his life. Writing down phrases and fragmented sentences in a nonsymmetrical order throughout the paper, Mike lightly colored over his words, careful not to obscure their legibility. Many of the phrases emphasized repressed anger or frustration about times when he felt injured or insulted, such as:

"You fag!"

"What the hell's your problem?"

"Jesus freak!"

"Mama's boy!"

"Is it Jesus yet?"

"Cum and follow me!"

After deciding the appropriate colors he should use to symbolically represent each quote, Mike added another quote of his own.

"Blessed are they that suffer persecution for justice' sake, for theirs is the kingdom of heaven."

Mike followed the other students who began to tear tape off a roller and place their construction paper up on the classroom's walls and blackboards. Except for Mike's presentation, all of the sheets of colored paper contained images and characterizations in both sophisticated and simple forms. Many illustrated violent depictions of martyrs or caricatures of Jesus being tortured, along with suffering Christian missionaries in far-flung lands. Only Mike's poster showed a stark contrast in style, with an absence of any imagery. The Brother made another round and again silently looked at each poster, omitting any comments or facial expression. He maintained a stoic expression until he reached Mike's poster. A brief expression of surprise crossed his face, but it vanished as quickly as it had appeared. He looked over at Mike with calm composure and then stepped back to study Mike's poster further.

"Okay," he announced, turning his back on Mike. "Let's begin. Each one of you, please tell us about your poster."

Purposively leaving Mike for last, the Brother covered a swath of adolescent angst that turned into an orgy of confessions. He randomly pointed to a student who again read his quote. Each seminarian read his poster and its corresponding allusions with the grave reflection of a penitent who had unjustly suffered some malevolent recrimination. As any good confessor, the Brother patiently listened and encouraged the seminarian to find resolve in the comfort of God's love and forgiveness. The freshman made the penultimate presentation.

"Well," he nervously pointed out, "I have many temptations. I hope Jesus can help me control my temptation."

When the Brother turned around to take a careful look at the freshman's poster, a seminarian, directly in the freshman's sight, made a crude, masturbatory motion with his hand. Mike watched him with annoyance as the other seminarians laughed. The Brother quickly turned around, causing them to retreat into silence.

"Go on," he encouraged the seminarian.

"Okay," the freshmen continued. "I wrote the quote in the middle and had the pictures connect like a wheel." He made a circular motion with his hand over the poster. "I followed my temptations from childhood. You can see me taking a cookie here. Here you can see me crossing the street without permission. And here you can see me cheating on a test. Here I am lying to my Mom. Here," he paused, "I am looking at a *Playboy*."

The room erupted into a hilarious roar of laughter. The Brother even smiled and allowed the laughter to diffuse itself. Waiting several minutes, the Brother raised his hand to calm the seminarians.

"I'm glad you only wrote the title on that magazine," the Brother pointed amusedly at the picture of Playboy bunny ears.

Blushing, the freshmen took a closer look at the picture and shrugged. He then looked up at the Brother and awkwardly smiled. Some seminarians continued to make crude remarks and gestures when the Brother was not looking in their direction. Then the Brother turned to Mike and nodded for him to begin.

Mike stood up and the laughter vanished. Suddenly, everyone in the room seemed either bored or curious.

"You did something different," the Brother interrupted Mike before he could begin.

"Yes," Mike responded, annoyed. "I wanted to keep this textual and almost abstract."

"I see," the Brother responded with interest. "Can you explain how each of these quotes impacted you in your temptation?"

"They all pushed me to almost reject my faith," Mike stated boldly. "But I am determined, Brother."

"Determined?" questioned the Brother, taking a more somber stance on the subject.

"Not to lose my faith," Mike clarified. "My faith in my vocation."

Mike waited for the Brother to comment and then began explaining his poster.

"I simply quoted what others have told me about my faith and beliefs," Mike spoke frankly and began to read each quote out loud. "Some seminarians even said these things to me."

"Really!" the Brother responded, curious. "That's odd."

"Many students don't belong in a seminary," Mike clarified his opinion. "I suggest that they look into their conscience and reflect on the reasons for their enrollment. I also want to ask the faculty and Bishop…"

"Thank you," the Brother interrupted Mike, looking at his watch before speaking again. Most of the students seemed uneasy and the Brother attempted to rectify the hostile atmosphere Mike had produced. "Good job, everyone. We'll use these as springboards for the rest of the retreat. I am impressed with your honesty and humility. Great blessings will come from this experience. Let's take a moment to pray."

He made the sign of the cross and everyone followed.

"Father in Heaven," the Brother prayed. "Send your grace and love, and may Your Holy Spirit descend on us this day so that we may be able to carry our cross like your Son. And may we carry it with good spirits and love for our fellow men. Amen."

"Amen" everyone repeated, closing the prayer with another sign of the cross. The Brother then waved them off to their next destination. A few seminarians began to collect their posters but he halted their actions.

"Leave them here," he instructed. "We will be using them these three days. Thank you."

Mike left the room, taking a casual look at the other posters, and before he stepped out the Brother addressed him.

"Michael," he spoke as Mike turned around. "Courage. Follow your calling and pray. God will guide you."

"Thank you," Mike answered, sincerely feeling some small swelling of relief and exhilaration.

When Mike stepped out into the hallway, his surroundings seemed brighter and more cheerful. He felt suddenly tuned-in to the spirit of God's presence emanating all around him. The next two days of spiritual experiences carried him on a hammock of divine love, rocking his soul in God's bosom as he described the religious effects to himself. Receiving communion deposited a fresh emotional ecstasy, and afterward, tears of joy clouded his eyes. After spending several torturous months in an institution such as the seminary that should have promoted hope, faith and love but failed to deliver on its commitment, Mike felt rewarded and at peace with his choice. He had feared leaving the seminary for another school and he further dreaded the possibility of attending a regular Catholic high school that served as a spiritual whited sepulcher for "cafeteria Catholics." The best part of his current spiritual journey was spent with like-minded individuals who wished to serve God with the same zealous zeal. On the third day of the retreat, during morning prayers, Mike's feelings of elation and tranquility began to wane.

"What's on tonight?" a student behind his pew demanded to know.

"Can't tell you," another student refused.

"Hey," the first student insisted. "It's no big deal."

"Okay," the second student easily capitulated. "I heard they got *Kelly's Heroes.*"

"Bitching," the first student cheered.

"Hey," the older student protested. "Shut the fuck up. I only heard."

"That's cool," the first student retreated into silence.

The thought of spending three days in communion with God and to end it on a sour note annoyed Mike, and his doubts began to rise again. When the other seminarians left for breakfast, Mike continued to pray, searching for the repose he had felt earlier in the morning. His two-day odyssey of bliss might turn into a shipwreck with the sirens of vulgarity screaming and scratching at the periphery of his conscious. As he knelt and prayed, Mike began to wonder if God had begun to test his resolve with a new temptation. Keeping this new possibility in his mind, Mike watched his annoyance linger and then fall away as he accepted his new cross.

"Lord," Mike whispered out loud. "As you said on Calvary, 'Thy will be done.'"

He blessed himself and decided to fast instead of attending breakfast. Later in the day, his negative premonitions began to diminish, although the rumors about the movie further circulated and the excitement began to mount. Mike felt he could not weather the sophomoric content of the movie and he even asked the Spiritual Director to be excused from attending the showing. Later, in fact, he decided to fast for the whole day, until the hunger fought for his attention against his spiritual aspirations. After seeing his Spiritual Director and making a confession, he returned to his empty dorm and lay on his bed, again meditating on his spiritual experiences these last three days. Although God seemed to refuse any further consolations, Mike decided to accept this second disappointment as a sign of God's test. He happily embraced his disappointment, which he now believed would one day be transformed into joy. Feeling as if he had finally grasped the meaning of Jesus' suffering and the joy it would return, Mike felt a warmth pass over his body like a thick blanket that then seeped into his body and consciousness. For a moment, he felt as if this mysterious warmth had lifted him up and suspended him in a bath of joy and love. God, Mike believed, had descended on him and embraced him with His eternal love.

"Oh God," he cried, as streaming tears covered his cheeks, moistening the sheets next to his head. "I love you, Jesus."

As soon as the warmth filled him and lifted him up, it began to seep slowly away, gradually escaping his body.

"No, Lord," Mike protested and the tears of sadness swelled.

A deep feeling of abandonment sank into his mind and he held up his arm as if to grasp some invisible person.

"Please!" Mike implored.

The warmth finally evaporated and left him cold. Not wanting to remain alone in the dormitory, Mike made a supreme effort to lift himself out of his bed. He decided he needed to speak to his Spiritual Director or even to the Brother who directed his retreat. His encounter with God could not be ignored and he needed to understand this epiphany. Taking the north exit facing the basketball courts, Mike wished to avoid the students milling around in heightened excitement over the movie's showing in an hour. Once outside on the side road, Mike heard a loud popping sound and saw some students in the far darkened corner of the D dormitory gathered around a small dark mound. As he approached, the amorphous brown mound instantly transformed into a four-footed animal. Then it changed into a mutilated gopher missing part of its mandible.

"We stuck a firecracker in its mouth," an unknown seminarian proudly announced to Mike.

The gopher painfully wobbled from side to side and tried to balance itself in position that prevented its head from making any contacted with the asphalt. A small squeaking noise could be heard as another student poured a clear liquid over the animal. From where he stood, Mike thought he smelled alcohol. The gopher then winced and began to hobble in a circle, stop, and hobble again, trying to escape his unseen torturers.

"Light it," someone in the dark ordered.

Another seminarian withdrew a lighter and struck the flint. Then, taking the lighter and lowering the small flame to the gopher's tail, the seminarian lit the animal afire. In the dark, the grey animal instantly turned into an orange ball of crackling flames. It made several attempts to leap up but then quickly succumbed to the fire that singed and scorched its flesh. After a few violent jerks, the animal remained still and the dark smoke of burning flesh wafted in Mike's direction. Appalled, Mike covered his nose as another unknown seminarian leaped up in his direction. The sadistic scene caused Mike to experience an unconscious paralysis.

"We tried to stick one up his ass," the seminarian said gleefully. "But it wouldn't fit. Shit that was cool."

"He suffered for his sins," another seminarian, holding the lighter, quipped and then laughed.

Mike's unspoken repugnance paralyzed him. He wanted to run. An unexplained urgency propelled him to escape on his original path to his Spiritual Director, but he instead entered the chapel. Pressing down a feeling of nausea, he fell at the feet of the Madonna on the right side of the chapel. For a long hour, Mike prayed for the gopher, knowing that the animal would never enjoy the rewards of paradise for its suffering. He could not make himself forgive the seminarians who tortured the animal. He could not forgive them because there would be no divine retribution or justice for the victimized gopher. But Mike still prayed for a long time to an echoing silence. He prayed to a God who rejected animal souls in heaven, ending the retreat in desperate supplication. Someone, later in the evening, entered the chapel to tell him that the movie had ended.

Phase 6

The return from a deep virtual reality to a shallow one passed smoothly. Again, Clement remained impassive and the others remained aware and conscious, maintaining a moment of paralysis before being able to speak. At first, unintelligible sounds escaped their mouths, then Juan succeeded first in speaking.

"Shit," he spat out and shook his head. "Can't any of us watch something fun or enjoyable? I remember hearing about that sadistic shit. There's too much drama in these reruns of our life. By the way, do you guys still watch reruns on television on the outside? I hear everyone goes on the computer for stuff."

His three companions continued to make unintelligible sounds as Juan patiently waited.

"Cat got your tongue?" he poked fun at them. "Or is it the quantum chips? Hey, what happened to those retards that killed the gopher? Later in life?"

Bill's mouth opened first and he spoke clearly.

"I think some went to jail," Bill recalled vaguely, speaking with a thick, cumbersome tongue. "At least one did. A real sociopath."

"Yeah," Rico conceded, making an effort to respond. "One of those asswipes ended up torturing and killing his ex. Bill...I want to remind you."

Bill gestured a *later* hand signal to Rico, who impatiently remained quiet.

"The other entered the holy orders," Mike added sadly. "But he was defrocked for taking church funds and having an affair with the Bishop."

"See!" Rico derided. "Your prayers did them some real good. No kidding? Banging an old Bishop?"

"Are we picking up where we left off?" Mike asked Bill.

Bill began to respond but Juan interrupted him.

"Go for it!" he exclaimed.

Juan almost leaped up and expressed a sophomoric glee for his friend's belligerent tone. Despite the fact of having lived as long as his friends in virtual reality, Juan had never had real life experiences and the emotional benefits of physically aging into his nineties. Bill half stood up in his chair and Rico waved him off. Looking at Clement, who sat immobilized, Rico took his silence as a cue to continue with the debate.

"Why didn't God save your fuzzy friend?" Rico challenged. "Don't get me wrong! What those guys did was fucked up."

"I am glad we can agree on something," Mike concurred, offering Rico a passive smile.

Rico politely bowed his head and returned the smile.

"God doesn't interfere with free will," Mike stated emphatically. "They made a decision, which shaped their character and destiny."

"Any psychologist would agree with that," Rico conceded Mike his point. "But free will? What if they had a mental disease—which they seemed to later in life."

"It was a spiritual weakness," Mike insisted. "Their whole life continued on a path of sin and evil."

"That's the fucking problem with people like you who have faith and religion," Rico began to set up his argument. "Everything is a self-evident truth. You approach life with a holistic solution to its problems."

"What do you mean exactly?" Bill jumped into the conversation, showing genuine interest in the debate for the first time.

Juan leaned back and watched curiously as Mike demonstrated some uneasiness.

"Okay," Taking a deep breath, Rico accepted the task. "Mike, did you know you are a skeptic? Like me? Even a nonbeliever?"

"Excuse me?" Mike appeared momentarily befuddled until he realized Rico's ploy. "I won't let you have this one. I know where it's going."

"Of course you do. But it's true," Rico assured Juan and Bill who seemed almost amused. "He has rejected God to be a Christian."

"God?" Bill seemed befuddled for the first time. "How?"

"All gods are ridiculous and absurd," Rico added. "Except the Judeo-Christian God?"

"Of course," Mike acknowledged. "Those gods are pagan and don't offer the Truth."

"Truth?" Rico repeated.

"Here comes Pontius Pilate," Juan warned.

"In a way, the old governor had a point," Rico concurred. "Your gods, and your faith, don't function on truth."

"The faithful support revealed Truth," Mike defended himself. "The truth of our Lord is He died on the cross to save us."

"I am talking about real truth too," Rico clarified. "The truth of empirical evidence."

"We're covering the same old ground," Bill objected. "This argument is in a stalemate."

"Let me," Rico held up his hand, seeking permission. "You see. Your revealed truth answers life's problems. It allows you to suspend critical thinking. See, an insane man is insane because his delusions are not believed by anyone. But in religion, any Faithful's delusion is believed because others believe it. So, mass delusions are supported because the majority supports them. Therefore, in their eyes it is not insanity. But like I said earlier, every religion thinks that the other's religious beliefs are delusions. I take it one step further. To its conclusion, I, being a skeptic, believe that all of you are delusional. If you think about it, how can one religion's delusion be more delusional than another? Have you ever really sat down and asked yourself if it's all a delusion?"

"You speak of delusions and you sit in a virtual word?" Mike mused.

"Ironic," Rico agreed. "But this virtual word has a semblance of the real. It's based on math and scientific proofs and technological applications."

"You must remember," Mike spoke softly. "I can't prove God doesn't exist. He doesn't need the support of the scientific community to prove his existence. I have one proof that transcends this world and all of its material empiricism."

"Okay," Rico conceded. "I can guess but you tell me anyway."

"Love," Mike dropped the word like a soft raindrop. "I feel His love and it sustains me."

"Why does it sustain you?" Rico followed up.

Clement made a subtle, curious move towards Mike that caught Bill's and Juan's attention. Rico felt his movement, as did Mike, but both men instinctively ignored the avatar.

"Because," Mike spoke in measured, careful speech that seemed to count each phoneme. "I am treasured."

"Treasured?" Rico asked for clarification.

"Simply," Mike pronounced his words leisurely. "I am not alone. Someone always loves me. I am special and remembered…"

"*For you formed my inward parts; you knitted me together in my mother's womb. I praise you, for I am fearfully and wonderfully made. Wonderful are your works; my soul knows it very well. My frame was not hidden from you, when I was being made in secret, intricately woven in the depths of the earth. Your eyes saw my unformed substance; in your book were written, every one of them, the days that were formed for me, when as yet there was none of them. How precious to me are your thoughts, O God! How vast is the sum of them!*" Rico interrupted, quoting a Biblical passage.

"Excellent," Clement complimented Rico.

Not listening or looking at the avatar, everyone stared at Rico and remained silent until Rico broke it.

"Psalm 139," Rico added. "I memorized it because when I was a freshman I once needed to feel special and loved. That is the great comfort of religion. Skeptics can't give that assurance. That security. That special love. Skeptics only give cold hard facts. Numbers and solutions. No solace.

We failed on that account. Maybe our brave new world will offer a better and more humanistic form of consolation."

"Then why do you not believe?" Clement asked.

"How ironic," Rico mused at Clement's question. "Because a lie is a lie. There is no comfort in a lie."

"Why is it a lie?" Bill asked.

"Listen," Rico held the cup of his hand to his ear. "Don't you hear the silence? When billions pray, there is only the echo of silence. The silence never speaks. The silence is deafening."

Rico pressed his question on Mike.

"Didn't the silence crush you back then?" Rico repeated. "What did you do after the day of the gopher?"

"I prayed and prayed," Mike spoke flatly. "Love isn't a feeling. It's a relationship."

"With an absentee landowner," Rico concluded.

"So what do you live for when you have nothing?" Mike inquired in a calm philosophical tone.

"Many things," Rico asserted. "My family first. But let me begin… "

"But don't you want to be loved by the divine?" Clement interrupted, asking Rico. "Cherished by someone?"

"Not by a non-entity," Rico quipped, expressing sudden surprise. "What the hell would a computer know about the divine? Good programming, Bill."

Rico gave Bill a thumbs-up and Clement just stared at him.

"Oh, no!" Juan reacted to the shifting walls and background.

"We have to make another journey," Bill inserted. "Time is running out."

"Bill!" Rico shouted, sinking into another layer of reality. "What about my daughter?"

Before Juan, Rico, or Mike could object, Clement nodded and the environment began its predictable liquefaction into a second layer of virtual reality. Rico traveled into another virtual recreation, stymied for several moments. He caught a glimpse of flashing images projecting worldwide street riots, triage centers in large parking lots, mass graves and shrouded piles of bodies, and then an imposing flashing red light. A brief image of Rico's daughter materialized as she shouted orders to a medical team. Rico could not hear her but he shouted her name. She continued to speak, not hearing his voice either. Then the environment suddenly became dark and silent.

Chapter 9

The greatest loss is what dies inside us while we live.
– Norman Cousins

Attending the seminary, most of the students received little relief from the mind-numbing routine of a schedule that predictably propelled them through predictable days. Only the fanatical dodged the boredom. Throughout the day, students escaped the numbing routine during specific slots in their common schedule. These moments of reprieve had ironically their own hypnotic effect, pressuring students to gobble every second of perceived freedom. In the morning, the twenty minutes between breakfast and first period offered the students an opportunity to complete last-minute homework or to defecate yesterday's meal. A tight schedule persisted until 3:00 pm when every student changed for a two-hour recreation that offered only an artificial resemblance to free time. Each student followed a prescribed protocol to participate in a preselected intra-mural team or to volunteer for some meager and anemic inter-mural team, competing against a small, exclusive private school no self-respecting public high school would consider competing against in the city leagues.

Since early morning breakfast, the only private moment, before bedtime, conveniently arrived after dinner and before study hall. The one-hour gap had unintentionally been created when the original seminary founders drew up the seminary schedule. The Bishop had directed that the students say the rosary in the cafeteria immediately following dinner. Unpredictably, the praying of the rosary had to be shifted to its current pre-dinner schedule due to the first Rector's plight with irritable bowel syndrome. Since the Rector's episode with the porcelain god, he permanently decided, receiving the blessing of the faculty and a compassionate nod from the Bishop, that the rosary would be prayed before dinner. Thus, a tradition began.

This fortunate turn of events gave the seminarians a miraculous gap between the mundane task of study hall and the monotonous repetition of the rosary beads. Some students opted to study but most escaped to the entrails of the recreation room below the D dormitory where Gaudeamus ghosts retreated after midnight, according to the traditional legend. After dinner, the heightened spirits of sugar-deprived adolescents haunted the subterranean hallways. The recreation room had once housed the sport shower rooms when a burgeoning population competed with more outside schools. Near the vacant shower room and restrooms, a barbershop had been enclosed, along with a laundry room.

For a decade, one of the student's fathers volunteered his barber skills. The barbershop contained all the traditional chairs and accoutrements of the profession, and they remained stored and abandoned when the barber stopped offering free haircuts. Death played a role in the barber's retirement. Since its heyday, the barbershop remained closed, along with the laundry room, and no one could access the room except for the staff and students who resided on weekends. Soon afterward, in the tradition of the seminary, rumors and myths evolved around the recreation room and its sealed rooms.

During rosary, Rico asked Juan to meet him at the end of the recreation room near the barbershop.

"Hail Mary, full of grace..." echoed in the background as they whispered to one another.

"What if the seniors show up?" Juan objected, knowing how the current senior class jealously guarded its space around the mythical senior lounge.

Last year, the senior class opened its door and allowed lower classmen to wonder in to watch TV on their new 25-inch color RCA. Juan's brother and his classmates rarely closed their doors. Presently, the student body had been relegated to the main recreation room where they squinted at an old monochrome Emerson TV that had been donated a decade before. Only two channels worked on the set.

"Scoot over to the barber shop," Rico recommended. "Tony will be there."

The mention of Tony made Juan a little nervous. He understood why they were meeting but he felt that Tony would be an annoyance.

"I hope he doesn't smoke before we go," Juan reminded Rico of his objections. "He does that shit too much."

Rico began to explain his decision but Father Siemens loudly cleared his throat disapprovingly, catching Juan and Rico in conversation. They returned to their rosary beads after exchanging a glance and continued to pretend to pray until the end of the rosary when the students walked to the cafeteria for dinner. Both Rico and Juan looked for Tony but he had been absent during the rosary, too. They asked others about his whereabouts, but no one knew. They quietly ate their dinner until the closing prayer and official dismissal.

Afterward, pushing their way through the recreation room, they met in front of the barbershop. As usual, the recreation room had been filled.

Roaring laughter and the sound of bells preceded the galloping students who descended the stairwell. On the south side of the room, two donated pinball machines clanged and whistled in front of a long line of waiting competitors. Behind the machines stood two parallel pool tables where pairs of students played against one another. Behind the pool tables, the cork-inlaid walls supported the billiard cue sticks and triangles. Rico and Juan had to pass through the suffocating coagulation of students who only observed the pinball players and rolling pool balls. Despite the machines and games, the conversations and mocking insults had more entertainment value. Once they passed the pool tables, the recreation room narrowed into a hallway that concealed the bathrooms and shower rooms, along with a snack room that served candy, potato chips, ice cream, and soda. A junior ran the busy snack shop and Rico and Juan found themselves pushing their way through another suffocating crowd of famished, sugar-deprived students.

Passing through the small hallway, they entered the back of the recreation room where more students, mostly freshmen, slapped ping pong balls on worn, faded green table tops. One pair of students played on a table without a net. Behind the ping pong table, a small group of freshmen watched a game show on the small monochrome TV. Most of the upper classmen had given up on TV since the time slot showed few shows of interest. The freshmen intensely stared at the TV set as if to expel the reality of losing their only tenuous connection to the outside world. The rest of the student body gave up on the farce but the seniors enjoyed watching a color TV as a statement of privilege. Taking a casual assessment of their surroundings, Rico and Juan walked past the freshmen, who ignored them, and into the small alcove at the end of the recreation room where the seniors entered their secluded lounge.

The only entrance to the recreation room faced the south side, which led to a stairwell to the faculty's private elevator at the end of the chapel hallway. At the other end of the recreation room, near the senior lounge and barber shop, the north entrance remained inaccessible. Although it was locked from the outside, it could be opened and accessed from the inside. Rico and Juan had planned to leave the recreation room through the north exit and exit through the fire door, walking up the stairwell that opened onto the field. In the dim alcove, Juan and Rico remained out of sight and almost alone. The seniors had already sequestered themselves behind two steel doors that were slightly ajar. Unlike most other days, they roamed into the recreation room in pairs or alone. Today, they huddle en masse, avoiding contact with the other students.

"What's going on in there?" Rico asked Juan since Juan had more contact with the upperclassmen.

"I don't know," Juan quickly answered, which meant that Juan might know but he was prohibited from saying.

"Does it matter?" Rico asked the most important question.

"No," Juan emphatically declined. "Waste of time."

"Yeah," Rico agreed.

"We going to the club?" Juan asked further.

"I think we should," Rico confirmed. "But I wanted to meet Tony here."

"He might be at the club?" Juan surmised.

Backtracking through the recreation room, Rico and Juan walked up the stairwell and through to the end of the far hallway, at the end of the building, where they then entered the library. Some students meandered in the library, preparing ahead of study hall for their next-day classes. Rico and Juan walked through the library after greeting the monitor, a junior, and then straight to the back laboratory doors.

"Not there," the monitor called out.

Rico and Juan froze in their steps.

"What?" Rico asked.

"Father Prada cancelled the club today."

"Shit!" Juan exclaimed.

"No deer penis," the monitor joked.

Rico and Juan laughed as some muffled giggles rippled through the library. Prada mentored the Hunting Club and many students looked forward to the display of guns. Prada actually taught the club like a class and, at the end of the semester, the hunting club offered a certification class that would legally license the student to hunt.

"He was going to bring a Colt .45," Juan spoke disappointedly, remembering how he had dreamed about handling an automatic pistol and aiming through its iron sights.

"You see Tony?" Rico asked.

"Uh," the monitor thought. "Yeah. He left before you guys got here. I don't know where he went."

"This is fucking crazy," Rico concluded and left the library with Juan.

They returned to a recreation hallway that seemed to have absorbed more than twice the number of students since they'd last left. Rico and Juan had to almost push everyone aside until they reached the senior lounge. The seniors remained sequestered but hoots and laughs penetrated through the doors and could be heard in the hallway. For some strange reason, the priests and staff avoided the recreation hallway during the free hour, as if the area became verboten to adults. The clergy rarely violated the unspoken taboo of appearing during the one-hour break. If they had appeared, they would not have approved of the general behavior. A couple of students slapped the old TV as the picture displayed a snowy background. Another student twisted the rabbit-ear antenna, momentarily causing the snowy display to clear. When he released the wires, the same fuzzy picture appeared.

"What a piece of shit!" Someone yelled.

Beaming, Tony stood in front of the lounge doors, wearing a windbreaker. Rico could smell nicotine on his clothes and breath. He could also smell another pungent odor.

"You smoke?" Juan asked the obvious.

"Shit, yeah," Tony admitted. "Let's go get some."

Juan led the way up the north exit, which led to the D Dormitory that the legendary queer ghost was said to inhabit. An eerie green nightlight lit the way to the outside quad that faced the A and B dormitories. Once outside, the sting of the cold February air greeted them. Rico instinctively zipped up his jacked and observed the condensation of air escape his breath. He then turned to hold the door before it closed, placing a matchbook over the brass lock pins. Carefully, Rico let the door slip back into its frame.

"Now we can go back inside," Rico explained.

"Old tricks still work," Tony agreed. "Always does."

"Dude. It's cold," Juan complained.

"Let's go," Tony urged.

They instantly understood Tony's allusion and where they needed to walk. A thin, moist fog hovered over the track and football field outside the dormitories. A stream of distant amber light cut an irregular gap in the fog as it peppered the students' windbreakers with fine beads of water. The polyester layer seemed to attract more of the moisture that gravitated into clumps on the flat surfaces, only to run off in quick spurts down their sleeves and front lapels. Using the dim environment to their advantage, they walked stealthily under an electrical tower that supported the Department of Water and Power's electrical cables above haphazard, uncultivated sugar canes clumped together at its foundation. The towers stood several hundred feet high and looked like steel stick men from a distance as parallel girders extended outward like maniacal arms in both directions. The cables transmitted the electricity coming from the mountain generators to a routing station where the rest of the electricity would be distributed to the city below. Pausing to see if anyone walked about, they unconsciously listened to the humming sound of the electrical cables above that crackled and sparked with irregular frequency. The fog seemed to wrap itself in the ghostly reflection of light, irritating the electrical surge that moved through the raw, exposed cables. Rico looked up and watched the cables oscillate under the constant temperate pulse of the dissipating electrical current that moved in steady and descending streams of energy.

"How much voltage?" Juan asked abruptly.

"Huh?" Tony returned to his senses for a moment.

"The voltage," Juan added impatiently, pointing up. "In the cables."

"Fuck if I know," Tony dismissed the query.

"I think several thousand volts," Rico surmised. "Maybe tens of thousands. All that juice has got to run the houses and factories in the valley."

"Yeah," Juan nodded in agreement. "That juice will cook you inside out."

"Yeah," Rico responded in an animated tone. "I heard someone died here screwing around with the cables."

"My brothers told me." Juan confirmed the rumor. "Over ten years ago. This kid got a toy plane for Christmas and he flew it up to the cable. The contact electrocuted him."

"What a fucking dumbshit," Tony snickered. "Shit. That must have been nasty."

"Like I said," Juan repeated. "It cooked him inside out. Kind of like a microwave."

"My neighbor has one," Rico recalled, seeing a microwave in action for the first time. "I've seen it cook."

"Shit," Tony exclaimed again. "Did he die fast?"

"No," Juan said sadly. "He lingered for a couple of days."

"That's cold shit," Tony commented sadly.

They remained quiet for a while under the crackling sounds of the electrified cables. A cold, malevolent shiver spiked through Rico's spine.

"This is freaking me out," Rico observed, staring up at the cables. "Let's go."

The other two boys silently agreed and they moved away from the wilting, brown sugar canes toward the handball courts. Crossing the service road, they saw distant car headlights moving across the bend near the cafeteria.

"Shit," Juan almost shouted. "Run!"

Dashing over the service road, they dived into a bunch of hedges away from the tennis court, far from their ultimate destination. For a short while, the headlights sent a straight beam that seemed to immediately dissolve in the thick soup of fog. Soon after, the headlights dimmed and then went slowly dark somewhere near the cafeteria. The murky afterglow of the headlights melted behind the foggy blanket that ebbed across the seminary quad.

"Food service," Tony concluded.

They accepted his assumption and followed Tony out from the hedges, across the cracked, green concrete of the tennis courts, and toward the gray, monolithic handball courts built like ancient ziggurats. As they approached, the court slowly revealed itself, exposing the pock-marked cinder blocks that seemed to be precariously stacked on one another. Moving to the eastern rim of the court, they avoided being seen by any casual observer or visitor to the campus.

"What the hell are we doing here?" Rico asked impatiently, knowing the answer he would receive.

"Smoking, you dumb fuck," Tony quipped, removing some cigarettes from his pocket.

"I don't do pot," Rico objected and began to walk away.

"Wait!" Juan almost shouted.

"It's really tobacco," Tony assured him. "Don't go chickenshit."

Rico felt flush and his antagonism began to escalate against Tony who often crossed the line between a joke and an insult.

"Don't worry, buddy," Tony assured Rico. "You won't get cancer."

Juan laughed and then giggled as he took a cigarette. Tony lit his cigarette first and then passed the match to Juan who quickly lit his own cigarette. Rico watched them smoke for a while and they all silently stood around in the thick smoke, huddled against the wall to avoid the cold, moist breeze that blew down from the north hillsides.

"So who do we fight today?" Rico alluded to their occasional fantasy war games.

"You can be the target," Tony suggested after looking over at Juan. "Last time I got attacked."

"And you almost turned it into a real fight," Juan reminded Tony of his indiscretions.

They sometimes played a war game using fallen acorns as weapons. The enemy would get a jump-start and try to ambush his two opponents, hitting them with as many acorns as possible. The last time they played, Tony took the role of the enemy soldier. When his ambush failed, he succumbed to the raining acorns. Not being able to muster an effective counterattack, Tony pushed Rico hard against a tree and raised his fists, threatening to start a fight.

"You assholes play too hard sometimes!" Tony objected to their excessive attack.

"That's the point," Rico retorted. "It's a game."

"You can be the enemy then," Tony challenged.

"No problem," Rico responded, catching a glimpse of Juan's sardonic smirk.

He immediately understood that they would break the rules and turn the tables on Tony when the opportunity presented itself. Rico watched them smoke, feeling the tug of temptation to ask for a drag. Preparing to open his mouth, he noticed that the light from the mysterious vehicle appeared again through the heavy veil of fog. Making a U-turn, the vehicle moved back to the service road and toward the tennis court.

"It's not a truck," Rico watched the lights approach and a silhouette appear. "It's a car."

"What?" Juan asked, confused.

"Shit," Tony realized the consequences of the approaching car.

They ducked down behind the concrete barrier although any passing driver would never have noticed them hiding in the courtyard. The fog's thick blanket gave them cover, but their guilt and fear instinctively pushed them back.

"We gotta go back that way," Tony pointed out the recreation door. "We'll get busted if we go through the front entrance."

"In fifteen minutes," Juan made note after looking at his watch. "Brother will take roll in study hall."

"I know" Rico murmured.

Study hall could not be avoided and their absence could cost them a serious detention. At the same moment, Rico wondered how Tony was able to miss the rosary with impunity.

They waited for the car to park in front of the swimming pool. The lights shut off and then the driver and passenger doors creaked open. Two dark silhouettes climbed out of the car and began to walk toward the Stations of the Cross, behind the D dormitory.

"They look like priests," Juan observed, noting their completely black apparel under a hissing sodium lamp.

"I don't recognize the car," Tony commented. "Looks like an Oldsmobile."

"Maybe Buick," Juan surmised.

"But it's not a Monte Carlo," Rico noted.

The two happily agreed since the Monte Carlo would belong to the Monsignor. Any car but a Monte Carlo or a Gran Torino, owned by the Dean, implied a visitor.

"Visiting priests," Rico guessed. "Or seminarians from St. John's."

Tony and Juan felt relieved, hoping that a pair of major seminarians had entered the campus grounds. Most of the major seminarians enjoyed visiting their old school and they would ignore seeing Rico and his friends scurrying back to the recreation hall. An unspoken bond of "us-versus-them" perpetuated the seminarian student body until ordination day. But they still would not take the chance of being seen. The visitors could still be priests or other religious visitors.

"Wait till they get behind the dorm," Rico advised.

"What the fuck are they doing there?" Tony asked rhetorically.

"Who gives a shit?" Rico retorted. "Dump the cigarettes."

Tony and Juan doused the still smoldering cigarettes in the wet grass and pressed them into the soil. Rico watched the two visitors walk behind the dormitories and then waited a few seconds.

"Let's go," Rico ordered, determining that they would not soon return.

Tony and Juan looked up and peered ahead, satisfying themselves that the visitors had disappeared. Tapping Rico on the shoulder, they followed him as they ran in the same direction as they had arrived, taking the exact path across the service road and through the sugar canes. Waiting a few more moments, the echoing hum from the electrified cable drowned out all other sounds, encroaching on their consciousness and creating an almost manic impulse to dart out into the open field. With great effort, they instinctively repressed the fear and waited several more moments.

"I can't wait," Juan blurted.

"Let's go," Tony began to slowly lean forward to run.

Rico felt the escalating urge to run too. Ignoring his better judgment, he took the initiative and leapt away from the sugar canes, scampering fifty yards for the recreation room door. The electrical hum nipped at him from behind, sending a pulse of panic through his body. Rico failed to notice his friends in hot pursuit. He ran with so much explosive energy that he had forgotten to breathe. When he reached the door, his diaphragm forced air into his lungs and Rico, stunned, stood trembling as a large gulp of fresh air rushed into his lungs.

"Fucking door," Juan pulled at the handle.

"Shit," Tony grabbed the handle and pulled it with Juan. "Someone fucking locked it!"

"How the fuck?" Rico questioned, returning his attention to his immediate surroundings.

He looked on the ground and saw the matchbook cover on the floor.

"Someone followed us," Rico surmised. "Or we got fucked."

"Shit," Tony looked around to see if anyone was present. "Let's get the fuck out of here."

"Wait," Rico warned him.

In the distance, the sound of muffled speech and shuffling feet approached. Ignoring Rico's plea to remain still, Tony leapt out of the small alcove in front of the door and made an irrational dash for the front entrance of the school, almost a quarter of a mile away from their location.

"Come here, young man," a surly voice commanded Tony, who stopped dead in his tracks and walked meekly back to the alcove.

Halfway upon his return, Tony paused as he watched the two visitors confront Rico and Juan who futilely continued to give the door a try.

"What are you boys up to?" the voice demanded.

Rico recognized the voice immediately and soon recognized the Monsignor's silhouette beginning to assume definition once it had penetrated the fog's boundary. Preceding the Monsignor, a red, glowing ember materialized into a cigarette. The Monsignor pulled the cigarette out of his mouth and dropped it on the grass, crushing the tobacco underfoot.

"Don't tell me you were contemplating on saying the rosary," the Monsignor cut off Rico's attempt to respond.

Rico looked at the other priest who wore the rank of a Monsignor on his cassock. Red Cardinal borderlines on the edge of the cassock extended from head to foot. Around his waist, a red cummerbund tightly tugged itself below his protruding waistline. The visitor seemed to be slightly younger than the seminary's Rector. His hair was less gray and his brown eyes sat back in two dark orbits on his face. He had a thin nose and straight-edged lips, which hinted at some distant mischief. Although the Rector seemed miffed and embarrassed at the encounter, the visitor appeared amused and even entertained.

"Speak up!" commanded the Rector.

"It was him," Tony announced, pointing an accusatory finger at Juan. "He wanted to step out."

"Why?" the Rector demanded, losing patience.

"I think we should continue inside," the visitor remarked.

The Rector looked apologetically at his guest and then seemed to compose himself.

"Monsignor Vega is pastor at St. Brendan," he introduced the visitor.

"I hope to see you soon," the visitor smiled. "I am visiting for a couple of days. Tomorrow I will say mass."

"Thank you, Monsignor," the Rector spoke and pulled out his keys.

The visitor gave them a half-salute and walked back around the D dormitory towards the car ports.

"You boys really embarrassed me," the Rector declared angrily. "He is making a visit for the Cardinal. What is he to think?"

Once the Rector had unlocked the door, he paused as he looked down and saw the matchbook cover.

"Smoking," he concluded. "I can even smell it on you."

"I told you," Tony repeated desperately. "They suggested it. I didn't want to."

"Be quiet!" the Rector barked, picking up the matchbook cover.

"They did it," Tony protested. "They made me do it. It's not my fault, Monsignor."

Without looking at his friends, Tony turned away and hung his head with a manufactured contriteness.

"Bullshit," Juan cursed, to the Monsignor's astonishment.

Phase 7

Rico awoke in a hazy cubicle filled with opaque walls through which he could see transparent buildings. All appeared to be represented on a large monitor screen until he reached out and moved about the scenery. Although the buildings, overpasses, houses, shopping malls, and streets appeared to be intact, emptiness dominated and overshadowed the edifices. No vehicles moved and none hovered above, where they once scrambled haphazardly on their routine chores and to their destinations. He searched through the emptiness and then instantaneously saw thick piles of human bodies strewn everywhere. Death and rot occupied the recent emptiness below with an apocalyptic horror. The bodies were nameless and unrecognizable. Descending through virtual space to the streets below, Rico stepped over them with horror until he stumbled and fell over a body. Looking down, he stared into the familiar face of a deceased young woman. Her face sent shivers of foreboding through his body. He instinctively screamed and violently tried to embrace the woman, who was unable to rise or to speak. She then vanished from his grasp, as did every other deceased human body in his surroundings. The virtual emptiness returned, only to suck the buildings into its virtual vacuum. At that moment, Rico realized that he had no home to return to.

Chapter 10

*Grown-ups…are a strange breed! Their brains weigh close to three pounds,
and that's not three pounds of cheery delight!*
– The Tick

The end of Rico's sophomore year followed the tradition of a long-anticipated event. The famous pool party occurred on one of those late spring days when a hint of summer gently caressed the seminary's grassy fields. The smell of jasmine lingered in the air, and the perfect balance between the intemperate winter and the dry heat left the students free to wear t-shirts. In the distant hills, the runoff from the snow and the winter's rainfall produced green hills and colorful patches of flowers. The stern, brown and gray San Bernardino Mountains enjoyed a little of nature's cosmetic tinges before the dry, desert heat would wither the fragile tentacles of life and replace them with sage and dead brown weeds. A long, empty afternoon greeted the seminarians after a better-than-average lunch filled their bellies. An inexplicable happiness and excitement packed the cafeteria for the seminarians' instincts waved off the cold, dreary, winter days, and winter's companion of short dismal hours filled with predictable routine and soulless activities. For some unknown reason, the cook, Alfonse, served tuna sandwiches for lunch. Fish remained a rarity on the menu except for Lent when it appeared on everyone's plate each Friday.

Normally, fish sticks and tartar sauce sent the seminarians home on Friday but today was a Thursday. On the Catholic calendar, Thursday fish never fell on the plate of any penitent seminarian. But tuna fish sandwiches offered the promise of a different day. The first bite into the sandwich arrived with welcome and relish. Then, after the second bite, Rico could not refrain from eating more. Each bite only increased his appetite. It could not be satiated. Other students enjoyed the abundant availability of the sandwiches, but for Rico, each sandwich dissolved into a powerful memory only to be recaptured with the next bite. Masticating tuna provided Rico an assured comfort between the preface of hungry appetite and the epilogue of unsatisfied hunger.

"Easy, dude," Bill warned his classmate. "You're gonna barf on that shit."

"I love it," Rico admitted without shame, taking the leftovers off the serving plate and moving them to his dish. "I never knew I could love tuna so much."

"Let us pray," a disembodied voice commanded from the elevated platform.

All the students instinctively stood up and completed the sign of the cross while a Brother recited a simple *Glory Be*. Rico muttered the words and defensively held a sandwich at his side. When the prayer ended, the students dashed to the exit on their way to the tennis courts, basketball courts, handball courts and swimming pool. Near the swimming pool, a barbeque would be held later in the afternoon, to the delight of both faculty and student body.

"You know that shit has a lot of mercury in it," Bill anxiously pointed out.

"Okay," Rico grabbed his final sandwich and followed Juan and Bill outside the cafeteria.

They stopped in the parking lot, waiting for Rico to gulp down the last portion of the sandwich.

"So where we going first?" Bill questioned.

Juan and Rico laughed at the bits of tuna that trickled out of Rico's mouth, providing them with instant humor. Their laughter erupted into perpetual hoots and chortles.

"It's the mercury," Juan repeated Bill's warning.

They briefly looked at one another and began to laugh again. Rico managed to swallow his last bite of tuna.

"We're going to the pool," Rico spat out the words along with additional tuna.

Turning around, they noticed that some of the students had already exited the dormitories and had begun to walk toward the tennis and handball courts. As the service road led them toward the rear entrance of the dormitories, Rico could hear the laughing, shouting, cursing, and yelling of scores of students streaming out of the first- and second-story windows. One student from the second floor saw Rico and his friends walk by and decided to turn around and moon them. A few moments later, some other students joined in, and a chorus of black, brown, and pink rear ends flashed their vertical smiles in Rico's direction. Some pubic tufts of hair added a distinct mustache to the inverted face.

"Some fucking hairy asses," Juan commented with annoyance.

Rico made an obscene gesture and turned around to kiss his palm and point to his ass.

"Kiss my ass, you faggots!" Rico yelled.

Juan's happy disposition soon returned. Unlike Juan, Bill broke out into a hearty laugh while the derrières quickly vanished from sight.

"This is great!" he shouted as remembered their destination.

"Let's hurry before everyone pisses in the pool," Bill reminded his friends.

"Shit!" Rico exclaimed and made one final obscene gesture before sprinting off.

Bill quickly followed Rico, and Juan trailed behind them. All of the dormitory students returned indoors and their boisterous shouting and laughing began again. Deciding to pick up the pace, Juan managed to jog ahead and pass Bill. Soon, Juan and Bill joined Rico and took half-hearted jogs and spurts along the service road before cutting across the grass. They reached the dormitory exit door only to be greeted with an onrush of students wearing their gym clothes. Others sported their boxy bathing shorts, carrying ragged towels over their shoulders. Some of the pool-bound students halted to wrap their towels into tight bundles tapered at the end. Their rat-tailed towels soon served as weapons to sting the exposed legs, bellies, and arms of their opponents and victims. The snapping sounds of cotton mingled with the yelps and screams that broke out when the recoiling towels made contact with someone's skin.

"Shit, that hurt!" Juan shouted and jumped away from a random attack. "Wait till I get you at the pool."

"The fuckers better not hit me later," Rico warned his friend as they pushed through a thinning line of departing students.

"I'm the best! Don't forget," Juan proclaimed and held up an imaginary rat tail, imitating a violent striking movement towards Rico's leg. "Blam!"

"Show me how to make one," Bill asked.

"Blam!" Juan smiled and leaped in the air.

He pushed himself ahead of Rico and scampered into the dormitory.

"I would like to learn how he makes them," Bill repeated to Rico.

"His rat tails get torn up," Rico reminded Bill. "Do you have towels to waste?"

"It's just cool," Bill ignored the consequences of destroying his towel.

"I don't give a shit," Rico repeated his warning. "As long as he doesn't hit me with it."

"He'll go after Tony," Bill remembered the last time they went to the pool.

Rico tried to ignore Bill's allusion to a fight that had broken out between Juan and Tony.

"Fuck him," Juan shouted from ahead. "He's been a dillweed."

"Why they fight?" Bill demanded to know. "Is it because of the Monsignor?"

"No," Rico answered. "Tony paid for that."

"Then what?" Bill insisted.

Rico stopped to face Bill directly, speaking in a calm and audible voice.

"Called him a faggot," Rico declared.

"So?" Bill responded skeptically.

Rico ignored the question and continued walking towards the dormitory. More students quickly exited the dormitory and Rico found an almost empty dormitory when he entered.

"Everyone is almost gone," Juan announced excitedly, wearing his bathing suit already.

Rico walked to his bed and found two comic books on his bed covers.

"Who in the hell took these out?" he asked no particular person.

Bill walked over and picked up the comic books. The books had been recent editions but had been read avidly. Torn covers and dog-eared pages marked the comic scenes where seminarians pursued the pages in desperate need to escape into fantasy.

"I love Rex Reed," Bill confessed and began to read a copy of the Fantastic Four.

"You like Mr. Fantastic?" Rico skeptically queried. "That's interesting."

"Yeah," Bill murmured, beginning to read the pages. "You think his ability to stretch like a rubber band is a metaphor."

"Yes," Rico realized the meaning of his allusion although he never thought about it. "His intelligence."

"He's the real power among the four," Bill explained. "His intelligence leads and molds them."

"And the other three represent other metaphors?" Rico continued the line of thought.

"Carl Jung's archetypes of the human mind," Bill spoke, while continuing to read. "Remember how it was explained in class?"

"Who's Carl Jung?" Juan asked curiously, forgetting about the lesson in their religion class.

"A psychologist," Bill stated abruptly. "Didn't you pay attention last week in religion?"

Juan ignored the questions and turned away.

"I've got to read more about him," Rico sincerely promised. "I just thought they were all for fun."

"They are for fun," Bill almost finished the comic book. "But they are more."

"I want to read it after you," Juan demanded. Bill put down the comic book to look up at Juan. "Check this out."

He delicately and meticulously wrapped a towel into a rat tail. Bill curiously watched as Juan undid the towel and wrapped it again to his satisfaction. Lifting it up at the large end, Juan admired his instrument of pain and then grabbed the tapered end with his free hand.

"Wow," Bill expressed his admiration.

"Blam!" Juan snapped the rat tail.

The snapping towel sent a reverberating cracking sound throughout the nearly empty dormitory. Since the dormitory had been almost abandoned, the snapping towel created a boomerang Doppler Effect, causing a high-decibel shriek to echo and fade for a long second. Bill instinctively stepped back. A few seconds later, a broad smile broke on his face.

"Wow!" he almost shouted.

Juan held up the rat tail and showed its tattered tip dangling as loose shreds.

"You see," Rico confirmed the inherent hazards of using a rat tail. "It fucks up your towel."

"It's beautiful," Bill said joyfully, dismissing Rico's conclusions. "Who cares?"

Juan smiled and unfurled the rat tail. He then folded it in half and threw it on his shoulder.

"I'll see you in the pool," he shouted and leaped up, dashing out of the dormitory.

Bill watched him leave and then turned to Rico who had completely undressed.

"Let's hurry," Rico reminded him, searching for his bathing suit. "We can watch Juan get into a fight soon."

An unrecognizable voice laughed from the next dorm. Juan's reputation as an instigator was renowned.

Catching himself in a daydream, Bill shook off his daydream of snapping towels and moved hurriedly to his cubicle. He dressed in less time than it took for Rico to find his bathing suit. When Rico had finished changing, he saw Bill exit the dormitory, gripping a long, thick, green-and-white-striped towel. A moment later Rico followed Bill, carrying his yellow towel. They escaped down the hallway of the "D Dorm Queer" and through the labyrinth where the many ghosts and goblins occupied the dark corners of the seminary's buildings. Out in the bright daylight, the empty service road invited them to join the rowdy, riotous company of students. Splashing water and screams of delight could be heard erupting from within the gray cinderblock walls. When Bill and Rico crossed halfway over the service road, Juan darted his head out of the pool's entrance gate, beaming with euphoric joy.

"Come in. Hurry!" Juan yelled. "The water is warm. Hoo!"

"I want to see the rat-tail fight," Bill told a smiling Rico.

Rico did not relish the thought of intervening between Juan and some victim of his rat-tail skirmish. Juan had a strategic and tactical advantage over anyone who could possibly challenge him, and he also had a sadistic streak, enjoying the effective pain his rat tail could administer. Anyone on the receiving end of Juan's rat tail often immediately surrendered after a painful welt began to grow. Rico could only remember two students who stood a second hit until discretion became the better part of their valor. Anticipating the screams of one or two freshman fools, already standing up to Juan on the grass area, Rico instead witnessed the scene of a pool filled with shouting and laughing students. One third played volleyball on the grass area. Another third played water polo in the pool. And the remaining third dived into the water from the side of the pool or waited in line to dive off the short board.

Taking a quick assessment of those who participated in the controlled chaos of the pool events, Rico soon found Juan dropping his rat tail and begin bouncing off the diving board. He prepared himself to dive-bomb into the pool as he sprang up and embraced his legs, pulling his knees up to his chin. Contact with the water caused a small vacuum to wrap itself around Juan, and a plume of water exploded in a 360-degree direction. The wave rippled up to the sides of the pool causing a player to lose the water polo ball. It bobbed uncontrollably in a see-sawing motion. The player had a difficult time grabbing the ball until Father Siemens lifted it out of the water. The effect created the illusion of some water adhering itself to the surface of the ball and stretching itself out, only to snap quickly away.

"No wonder Juan is dive-bombing," Bill concluded. "Siemens is here."

"Yeah," Rico answered, relieved to see Juan's rat tail lying against the wall's cinderblocks.

Rico looked across from the volleyball game and saw several students lounging and sunbathing on the bleachers. He then looked back to the pool and saw Father Siemens pass the ball to a student near the floating goalpost. Big John floated in front of the goalpost as he allowed his girth to supplement his lack of athletic skills. Despite a player's effort, he could not get past John to score a goal. Even a team-tag could not reach over or around the impassive John. Rico watched the absurdity with genuine pleasure and he began to laugh at the players and John. A sudden lurch pushed him over the side of the pool and he could not stop himself from falling into the water. The shock of the cool water immediately sent him up to the surface. Breaking through the surface, Rico saw a dripping, wet Juan holding his belly and laughing, pointing his finger at him.

"Hoo!" he shouted.

From behind Juan, Bill sneaked up and began to push Juan towards the pool's edge. Juan tried to resist and held Bill off. Then, Bill grimaced and gave Juan a forceful lurch forward. Juan resisted against on the pool's edge, trying to balance himself, but eventually, gravity won the battle. With tangled legs and flailing arms, Juan fell into the water close to Rico's side. He looked up to see Bill smiling devilishly at both of them. His mischievous face predictably disappeared when another student pushed the unsuspecting Bill into the water, too. Without attempting a dive-bomb, Bill's hefty body caused an instant wave as he sank beneath the water.

"Way to go!" Juan shouted to one of his victorious brothers, who gleefully returned to his volleyball game.

Bill then shot out of the water, ecstatic with a special and momentous discovery.

"Zack is here!" he shouted.

"Turkey legs!" Juan exclaimed.

"Get those turkey legs!" Rico commanded.

The three friends made a beeline toward a freshman bobbing in the middle of the pool, between the divers and the water polo players. Father Siemens observed the escapade with amusement, dismissing it as a simple expression of fun. Most often, the pool activities transformed from an organized competition and game into a free-for-all adventure. The staff remained aloof unless the threat of injury appeared. Rico and his friend had targeted an overweight, pink-skinned and red-headed, misshapen boy. His densely freckled skin seemed to concentrate across his cheeks and nose. Diving under the water, several feet before reaching Zack, each student made a grabbing motion towards Zack's leg. The refracting water created a distorted view of his celluloid flesh, which had earned him the name Turkey Legs.

As Zack helplessly watched Rico and his friends move toward him like hungry sharks, he attempted to push away closer to the pool's edge. With extreme effort, he moved like a doomed character in a nightmare. The pursuit was predetermined and inevitable. The victim, despite the best intentions and effort, faced certain and unmerciful capture. With each painful push against the surface of the coarse cement at the bottom of the pool, Zack's pursuers closed the distance. A silent scream burst forth as Rico and Bill each grabbed his legs. Juan leaped out of the water and pushed down on Zack's head as Rico and Bill pulled his legs apart. Zack's natural buoyancy worked against their efforts until Juan's counterweight tipped the balance. In slow motion, Zack tilted to the left and sank like a crushed buoy. His shoulder hit the water first and his head followed. Juan leaped on the opposite shoulder, forcing Zack's body to submerge. Across from Juan, Rico and Bill surfaced, struggling to pull Zack's legs out of the water. The struggle was brief and Juan descended with Zack into the water as Rico and Bill pulled his legs above the surface, holding Zack's grossly fat and amorphous thighs like two hard-won trophies.

"Turkey legs!" they shouted, followed by a chorus of screaming, cheering classmates.

Father Siemens momentarily stopped playing to raise his hand up in victory.

"Turkey legs!" everyone repetitively shouted.

A moment later, Juan shot out of the water, and Rico and Bill lost their prize. Zack's legs flapped alone against the surface of the water. His head soon broke through the surface and a large geyser of spit sprayed out of his mouth towards Bill. The spit mingled with the students' splashing water. Catching his breath, Zack heaved himself up and fell with useless defeat back into the water. Soon, other students joined the free-for-all and Zack shot up and crashed once again into the water. Despite their hedonistic efforts, they failed to completely submerge him the second time.

"He's too fat," Bill pointed out. "You gotta know the technique."

"Turkey legs!" Juan shouted victoriously.

Zack gleefully bobbed on the surface of the water, brushing the water away from his face. After several blinks, he spoke to Rico.

"I like your comic books," Zack commented, still allowing spittle to escape his lips.

"What?" Rico reacted incredulously. "You read them without asking me?"

"Yeah," Zack confirmed, wide-eyed and happy. "Can we trade?"

"Trade?" Rico questioned. "How many do you have to trade?"

"Let me show you," Zack offered, allowing more water to dribble out. "I brought them to school when I saw yours last week."

"Sure," Rico agreed half-heartily. He wondered if Zack truly possessed some good books.

"Okay!" Zack spoke enthusiastically, spurting out one final stream of water.

He then unrepentantly floated toward the aluminum ladder at the edge of the deep end. Gripping the edge with his pudgy hands, Zack made a herculean effort to climb up the ladder. The chlorinated, blue-green water seemed to stick to his body and slowly slough off his skin in long streams. When he completed his ascension, the last layers of water behaved like gravity, pulling down his bathing suit and revealing the deep crevice of his vertical smile.

"Hah!" Juan shouted and leaped out of the water.

Zack lifted his suit as a chorus of laughs and whistles screeched out in all directions.

"Turkey legs!" A multitude of voices could be heard. All the shouts and laughs escorted Zack's jiggling, sun-burned body off the pool deck.

"Go, Turkey Legs!" more students repeated the chant. Even Siemens joined the sophomoric chorus.

Rico followed Zack out of the pool and across the pool deck, toward the exit.

"I'm coming," Bill announced from behind, shaking the water off his body like a dog.

Rico took a look behind him to see Bill scampering across the rough concrete, avoiding the dry, hot spots that soaked up the intense California sun. They all exited the pool gate area at the same time a volleyball whizzed by Bill's head. Waving at the surrounding area near his head, Bill stooped instinctively to avoid any additional unseen, errant balls that may pass his way. Outside the pool area, the onset of searing pain, on their bare, pink soles reminded the three seminarians of the foolishness of walking onto the service road without shoes or sandals. They leapt about like trotting horses, hoping to outrun the sizzling asphalt and reach the grass before singeing the soft, pink skin under their feet. When they stepped on the grass, each seminarian stamped his feet to reduce the scalding heat that seemed to soldier viciously into their soles and heels.

"Shit! It's hot," Zack complained as he searched for cooler spots on the grass.

Rico and Bill automatically put their sandals on while Zack continued to leap about.

"Hot!" he repeated and leapt about the grass.

"It's your skin," Bill observed. "It's all pink. You have no calluses."

"What?" Zack asked and took notice of Rico and Bill's sandals.

He cautiously put his sandals on his feet, hesitating first to test his skin's sensitivity. Bill laughed.

"You're skin's too soft, Turkey Legs," Rico commented with a laugh.

Ignoring Rico, Zack put on his other sandal after rubbing his soles and toes.

"Let's go, Zack," Rico called out and walked towards the dormitory's entrance. "Spiderman is going to call you chicken shit!"

Bill guffawed and followed Rico. Taking a couple of wary steps, Zack joined his companions. He walked with a slight limp all the way to the dormitory. Once inside, the natural cool air greeted them, in sharp contrast to the oppressive cauldron of the California sun. Originally, the architects used thick concrete wall materials as insulation for the winter cold and summer heat. The effect simulated a wine vault buried two stories below the ground.

"That feels good," Rico expressed their contentment.

"Ah," Zack exclaimed and took off his sandals. He began to fan his feet. "The tiles are cool too."

"Can we stay here for a while?" Bill spoke nervously.

"We can't," Rico reminded them of the rules about returning to the dormitories during recreation time. "I don't care to do detention with the juniors for a week."

"He'll make us clean the toilets," Bill observed.

"If we're lucky," Rico quipped.

"Let's go then," Zack protested and made a movement towards the exit.

"Got cold feet?" Bill joked.

Rico and Bill laughed before Rico grabbed Zack's arm and pulled him back.

"Hey," he reminded Zack. "We can tell him we needed to change. Remember we're wet."

"Oh, yeah," Zack acknowledged, looking down at his perspiring belly. "I want to play handball next."

"Good," Rico answered, rolling his eyes in Bill's direction.

Bill smirked, giving Rico his feral smile. He then walked quickly through the lower exit and into the freshmen dormitory. When he entered, he paused for a moment.

"It stinks in here," Bill stopped to cover his nose.

"Freshmen," Rico took a careful breath. The smell of athletes' feet and moldy material choked out the cool, refreshing air of the outside transept. "You guys really reek."

"It smells okay to me," Zack dismissed their criticism. "Sometimes it's worse."

Bill's smirk evaporated and he blinked twice before following Zack to his bed. Rico made a feeble effort to cover his nose. When they reached Zack's bed, towards the end of the dormitory, the smell seemed to increase.

"Don't tell me the smell is coming from your bed," Rico protested, masking half of his face in his hands. Bill pulled his t-shirt on and pulled up the collar to cover his nose. "Jesus!"

"No," Zack denied, showing some offense at the snub. "It's his." Zack pointed to the bed next to him.

Rico and Bill looked to the left of Zack and saw a stained, beige cover haphazardly stretched across a disheveled bed.

"Calvin never changes his sheets," Zack pointed out and sat on his bed. "I kind of got used to it."

"Shit," Rico cursed and walked over towards the bed.

Pulling the cover off, Rico exposed yellow, stained sheets that had been crumpled into a flat position. The pillow case seemed to be encrusted in a deep, yellow and milky stain.

"The seniors like to pull it off and spit on the pillow," Zack expressed with voyeuristic pleasure. "It's gross but he doesn't care." Looking around, before whispering, Zack added, "Some say the seniors jacked-off on it."

A sudden surge of disgust and impatience surged through Rico.

"So? Show us," Rico demanded and hovered next to a reclining Zack.

"What?" Zack seemed dazed for a moment. "Oh."

Slightly blushing from embarrassment, Zack awkwardly stood up and opened his closet. He fumbled through the bottom portion, extracting a cardboard box. His belly lightly hung over the box as he dropped it on the bed.

"Check it out," he invited Rico and Bill.

Rico moved first and lifted up a stack of comic books with various titles. Gripping a handful of comics, he handed a miscellaneous stack to Bill, who sat down on the bed. Rico joined him and they perused the comics for several long, silent minutes. Occasionally, Rico and Bill would systematically reach into the box and pull out more comics, again repeating the process. Halfway through the examination, Rico uttered his first comment.

"How long did you have these?" Rico asked.

"Since I was a kid," Zack announced proudly.

"Look," Bill held up a comic. "It's the Hulk versus the Fantastic Four."

"They've gotta be a least ten years old," Rico observed. "You got every hero."

"There's a bunch of *Spidies* in order," Zack demonstrated as he pulled another stack from the bottom of the pile in the box. "The Green Goblin kills Gwen in one of them."

Without a word, Rico snatched the comic Zack held and read the cover of the Spiderman 121 edition. The cover showed Gwen, Spiderman's girlfriend, falling off a bridge to her death as Spiderman desperately tries to rescue her.

"This is fantastic!" Rico held up the Spiderman like a talisman. He then reverently touched the other books and began to count them. "They're all in order."

"I told you," Zack proudly confirmed. "And I got more at home."

Bill and Rico stopped to look up at him.

"How many?" Bill asked with a trembling voice.

"Maybe hundreds," Zack mused trying to create a mental image of the comics he possessed at home. "They all fit in about five boxes."

"Look," Bill almost shouted and held up a Fantastic Four comic. "*Galactus and the Silver Surfer.* It's the first battle between them. I love how the Watcher sends the Torch back into time. Wow!"

Rico felt a surge of happiness and wonder at the treasure of comics. He knew instinctively that the comics would be highly valued but he did not care if rereading them lessened their value. Possessing and reading the classics of Marvel comics superseded any joy he could imagine, short of having sex with a voluptuous young woman.

"This is really incredible," Rico admitted and carefully opened one of the Spiderman editions.

Sitting beside Bill, Rico watched his friend lose himself in the Silver Surfer edition. Completely engrossed in the adventurous escape, Bill's feral smile stretched aggressively, reading over the pages as every word and animation absorbed his imagination.

"Zack," Rico stood up and gave a disgusted glance at Calvin's bed. He then identified another bed across from Calvin's area that appeared cleaner.

Walking over to the bed, he sat down and reposed himself on the bed, lifting up the unknown freshman's pillow as a support against the steel cabinet behind the short post. "I am going to read every one of these before spiritual reading tonight."

"Me too. I'm taking some to the chapel," Bill declared, looking up at Rico like a satiated wolf.

Feeling a strong symbiotic affinity with Bill's motivations, Rico nodded approvingly.

"Yeah," Rico agreed. "It's better than that boring shit they make us read."

"That library is boring," Zack concurred with Rico, alluding to the seminary's spiritual library and mandated readings. He stood up and pulled out another box. "These are yours, too."

He proudly plopped the box on the bed next to Bill. Rico leaped up and dashed across the narrow aisle to join Bill who had already begun to extract more comics.

"These are D.C. comics," Bill noticed immediately.

Rico eyed a Green Lantern comic and joyfully held it up.

"I think I'll be up all night," Rico predicted.

"We can read in the luggage closet," Bill reminded Rico of the place where students hid in the evening to cram for examinations.

"No one will be there," Rico observed, since the students had recently completed their midterms. "All night!"

"Great way to begin the weekend," Bill spoke enthusiastically, dropping the D.C. comics and returning to his Silver Surfer. "Zack! This is great!"

"Yeah," Rico uttered and took some Green Lantern editions to the bed where his Spiderman editions sat.

"I'll bring all of them next week," Zack promised.

For the first time in a long time, Zack felt welcomed and needed among his peers. He began to inspect some of his stacks and pulled out a particularly childish-looking comic book cover.

"I got some Archie's," Zack proclaimed, holding up the comic.

Rico looked up and instantly dismissed the book as childish. Then, he changed his mind.

"I'll give it to my brother and sister," Rico accepted the offer.

Satisfied with the acceptance, Zack happily sat down and began to read the Archie comic book. They all sat for a long while before a creaking door and heavy footsteps took them away from the world of Jugheads, Green Goblins, and alien monsters.

"Gentlemen," a familiar and odious voice drew them away from their childhood Elysian Fields.

They all looked up with desperate dread.

"You're supposed to be outside," Father Siemens reminded them, standing in a pair of green flip-flops. He wore an orange shirt and green shorts, and a red-striped towel hung over his wet shoulders.

"We were going to change," Rico improvised quickly, putting down his comic books. "Then we got caught up."

Rico gestured at the comic books on the two beds. Siemens walked over to the beds and made a cursory examination of the comic books.

"These are very immature," he spoke in an amused tone as if he had caught them playing with toy soldiers. "Please find a more mature activity. One that has real spiritual value."

"But comic books have meaning," Bill objected. "There are ideas and complexity. Some of the vocabulary is elevated, Father."

Bill held up a Fantastic Four magazine and turned to a particular passage.

"Here, Father," he pointed out a scene with Mr. Fantastic talking to the Thing. "He is discussing Einstein's theory of relativity. And he also uses words like 'dissipate.'"

Siemens barely looked at the comic book before smiling broadly.

"Please put them away," he ordered in a kind but firm voice. "I don't want to be seeing them."

Zack quickly began to retrieve and re-pack the comic books.

"I'll look for you outside," Siemens reminded them. "In ten minutes. Where will you be going?"

"Basketball," Rico volunteered since he had no choice and wanted to preserve the comic books for later. He was happy that Siemens did not confiscate them. "We have a new ball."

"Good," Siemens approved. "I may referee. Bye, gentlemen."

He then gave them a beaming smile and walked outside, in the direction of his room near the dormitory section. When he left, Zack had just finished packing the comics back into the boxes. He lifted the boxes and began to place them in his closet.

"I have to take these home," Zack said sadly.

Bill leaped up and confronted Zack. Bill's reaction shocked Rico for he had never seen him express any violent or impetuous feelings.

"I'll kill you, Zack," Bill warned him. "We'll split them and take them to our homes. If you want them back, we'll return them at the end of the year."

Bill looked at Rico, who nodded in agreement.

"Okay," Zack timidly conceded. "But don't get me into trouble."

Bill immediately grabbed and lifted up a box and Rico took another.

"Zack," Rico commanded. "Bring the rest to our dorm on Sunday. Don't worry. Siemens won't see them. We'll hide them in the luggage room."

Zack smiled, expressing pride and mischievous glee at being a participant in some incorrigible act of defiance.

"Thanks so much, Zack," Bill told him and offered him his warm, feral smile.

Zack puffed up and watched them carry the boxes away.

"I'll bring them," he promised as Rico and Bill took the back stairwell, away from Siemens' room and prying eyes.

Later in the evening, they clandestinely hid in the luggage closet and read most of comic books until the morning bell. Bill could not stop smiling and giggling with joy as he turned each page over, attentively following the scientific exploits of Mr. Fantastic' s battle with the enemies of humanity. He fell asleep clasping his heroes to his chest.

Phase 8

"We're not going home!" Rico shouted. "The whole world is fucking dying."

"Like us," Mike added.

Mike's stoic response shocked Rico, who almost suspected that Mike knew about the holocaust on the planet. He scowled and attempted to speak before Bill interrupted him.

"You don't understand. I had no reason to believe this disease would progress so rapidly," Bill defended himself. "I initially wanted to send you back."

"But there is nowhere to go," Juan finished his thought after having seen Rico's experience in his virtual mind.

Rico slammed the table and shouted in Bill's direction.

"You and Juan can't go," Rico spoke what no one wished to say. "But Mike and I have some semblance of a life. Even if it's short!"

Mike nodded and pursed his lips.

"I agree with Rico," Mike said surprisingly. "It is unethical to have kept us here. We should meet our end in a natural manner."

"But you don't understand," Bill repeated. "I had to remove your bodies from the threat."

"Remove," Rico contemplated. A cold feeling gripped his chest. "That has an ominous ring to it."

"We are removed from the pathogen," the avatar spoke. "At this moment, our ship is orbiting the planet in a geo-synchronous orbit above North America. We are at an altitude of…"

"Shut the fuck up!" Rico rose and struck Clements with a plate.

The plate had no effect on the avatar except for interrupting his lecture.

"That is why there were so many interruptions and earthquakes?" Juan concluded out loud what everyone was thinking privately.

Bill nodded in agreement.

"Your violence is irrelevant," Clement commented, offering a congenial smile.

"Do you feel better?" Bill sarcastically asked Rico. "We can't be harmed."

Rico threw the plate down and remained standing.

"You don't get it," Rico pled, as tears began to well up in his eyes. "My daughter? I saw her in the interim. She is dying or dead. This plague killed a beautiful woman who wanted to save humanity."

Mike patted him on the shoulder for comfort.

"It's not your fault," Bill stood up to comfort Rico. Rico held his arm up and Bill sat down. "She could not fight this pathogen. No one has any immunity to it. Its source is ancient and some scientists think it may be extra-terrestrial."

"There is a probability of three-percent survival," Clement added factually.

"Bill," Rico spoke with a carefully measured tone. "You don't get it. I didn't have a chance to say goodbye. You just showed me the aftereffects."

"Bill," Mike added. "You took away our choice. Your intentions were good but the result is . . . well, shitty."

Juan remained sullen and silent throughout the exchange.

"I wanted to spare you," Bill tried to justify himself. He extended his arms as if to plead and then dropped them to his side. "I just…"

Bill failed to finish his words as tears too began to quietly run down his cheeks.

"Spare me?" Rico contested. "I'm caught in a virtual world. Circling the Earth in a silicon circuit. And my family is gone."

"We're all gone," Juan surmised.

"And our souls?" Mike inquired philosophically, as if expecting an answer from the avatar.

"It's a carbon circuit," Bill dismissed the possibility.

The avatar appeared to bow in agreement.

"That's the problem of being old school," Rico quipped sarcastically. "You are a bastard."

Rico let his words sit and observed an almost stoic Bill whose composure imitated Clement's self-possession, except for the drying tears.

"I want you to land this device," Rico demanded, approaching Bill with another plate in hand.

Rico looked at Mike, who appeared undecided. Then, he looked over at Juan, whose eyes were downcast. Unlike Mike and Rico, he had no body to return to since the accident in his youth.

"I can't," Bill simply stated.

"Why the fuck not?" Rico raised his voice, holding up the plate. "Don't tell me it's the pathogen. I don't care. I prefer dying as a human being."

"That's the point," Bill note sadly.

"Oh Lord," Mike suddenly had an epiphany. "You didn't?"

Bill looked apologetically at Mike, who for the first time showed genuine anger.

"You violated our freedom," Mike castigated Bill. "Our very humanity. This is intolerable."

Mike stood up and thought about storming off until he realized where he was standing.

"Freedom?" Rico tried to let the word sink into his consciousness.

Juan lifted his eyes up and spoke sympathetically to Rico.

"We are staying here," Juan confessed. "In this machine and in orbit around the Earth. Begin to deal with it. There is no one home and nowhere to return. We're dead!"

Rico remained silent, absorbing the information. The plate dropped from his grip.

"Our bodies?" Rico concluded. "Terminated?"

"We've been disembodied," Mike spoke the obvious, which no one could openly admit.

"You killed us?" Rico accused Bill.

"No," Bill rejected the accusation. "You live and have centuries and millennia to live."

"You know, Bill," Rico stated in a cold, malevolent tone. "If I could personally kill your body I would do it in an instant."

Without communicating his intent, Rico instantly grabbed a serving knife. In one swift motion, he took the knife and plunged it into Bill's chest cavity. But instead of killing Bill, Rico slipped through a large crevice and into a dark chasm. Falling through pitch-darkness, he landed upright in a gladiatorial arena built on wood pylons. Looking up, he faced his opponent, Mr. Fantastic. Mr. Fantastic stretched into an elongated, twisted height, scores of feet above Rico and out of the arena center. Rico looked down to see his bumpy, orange-encrusted skin. Knowing he had morphed into the comic character of the Thing, Rico instinctively tore away several of the pylons and hurled them at Bill, whose rubbery abdomen gracefully folded and curled itself, evading the flying projectiles. The battle came to a standstill until Rico decided to catch up to Bill's distant height and turn himself into the Human Torch.

Bill responded and confronted Rico's avatar with the persona of Spiderman, and the arena disappeared into the concrete cliffs of Manhattan's business districts. Rico pursued Bill's web-slinging escape. He threw balls of fire that barely missed Bill, only singeing the web fabric that held Bill in balance over the city streets. Neither won the battle, though it continued for virtual hours as the alternating comic characters and scenes from their past adolescent readings played out. They never spoke but fought to a final standstill with Bill using Mr. Fantastic's coil-like arms in a tight grip around Rico's character, the Thing.

Goddamn you!" Rico managed to curse at his classmate.

The irresistible force and the immovable object remained in a bellicose grip of an eternal instant. Then, they once more found themselves in a new virtual reality, far from their anger, resentment, and bitterness.

PART III

The visitors spent weeks and months deciphering the drives and programs to translate the information. With slow, meticulous calculations, they divided the programs into their basic components and then into *their* basic components of binary numbers. Unlike the other human programs built on synthetic composite material, much of the unintelligible material contained an organic program, so the level of complexity increased a million times. Then, one alien programmer decided to examine the structure of human DNA. Comparing the organic organization of three of the four bases of DNA, adenine (abbreviated A), cytosine (C), guanine (G) and thymine (T), the breakthrough translation uncovered the Rosetta stone of this unique human program.

Whoever had assembled and recorded the program used a ternary sequence employing both quantum and nucleic acid technology. Since their arrival, the aliens discovered that the whole human race never benefited from this ingenious program. But the unknown human programmer who spent his remaining days in orbit around the Earth employed an anonymous satellite lost in unrecorded time. To the surprise of the aliens, the human inventor had surpassed even their ability to recreate reality in a virtual world. So they watched the recorded events unfold, and they learned.

Phase 9

On a grassy hillock somewhere near the coastline of San Louis Obispo, Rico stood under a singular oak tree that shaded a simple, unmarked bronze plaque, holding a small bunch of flowers collected from the weeds and miscellaneous plants throughout the nearby valley. Rich floral colors and hues created a potpourri of nature's random collage of imperfect beauty. Looking down from the flowers held to his face, Rico stared at the plaque. On top of the plaque rested a tattered, white, stuffed bunny with faded pink ears, missing eyes, and a slight yellow patina ingrained in its polyester fur. Lying on the plaque like a chalk-lined crime victim, the bunny's arms and legs pointed in different directions as its tattered face stared up at the tree's dark canopy. Rico reached down toward the plaque and lifted the bunny into an upright position. Sadly, the bunny slowly slumped to the side into a chaotic posture with its ears folded back behind its head.

Crouching further down, he used the flowers to prop up the bunny, arranging the flowers and the face of the bunny in the direction of the open, grassy fields below. The bunny and flowers remained immobile until a distant Pacific breeze unexpectedly slapped the bunny back and separated some flowers from the bunch. A few flowers floated out on the current of air and toward the surrounding fields, disappearing among their brethren before vanishing forever from Rico's vision. Even if Rico could follow the flowers' path, the welling of his tears obscured his view. He could watch no more.

Chapter 11

Do every act of your life as if it were your last.
– Marcus Aurelius

Music occupied Mike's life and provided spiritual nutrition, mental relief, and physical escape. Whenever he needed to find shelter from the crass verbal abuses of his classmates and the empty distractions they heaped upon themselves, Mike climbed up the back stairs, ducked behind a narrow door next to the Dean of Students' Office and entered the choir loft where he seated himself behind the chapel's pipe organ. Here, alone in presence of the musical instrument of peace and harmony, Mike prepared himself to be immersed in the same notes that the ancient Pythagoras measured with the perfection of mathematics, while listening to the harmonious sound of the blacksmiths' hammers against ancient iron anvils.

Recreating the historical event in his mind, Mike could imagine hearing the harmony of the spheres, reproduced in the bellowing rhythms of the pipes, that carried him to the private shelter he cherished in his mind—the perfect seminary where he would be permitted to cultivate his love of God and his relationship with the Almighty. Choosing one of Bach's cantatas, Mike took a moment to offer a prayer. He then played the first, eerie and deep-reaching notes with a suave dexterity that effortlessly carried his fingers and soul through the chords, elevating his thoughts to the sublime possibilities of a unity with perfection. The cantata carried him away from the immediate present and shielded him from all earthly imperfections.

"Mike!" Tapping him on the shoulder, a distant voice called to him.

Mike's ephemeral world vanished. The cantata instantly collapsed and dissolved away. Sadly, Mike remained alone and isolated in the choir loft.

"Yes," Mike responded apprehensively, afraid to return to his surroundings.

He ignored the voice and began to play the cantata. The keys and pumping sounds of the organ picked up their pace as Mike waited for the unknown visitor to leave him. With all his efforts, he only played mechanically. The music barred him from again entering into its comforting solitude.

"Mike," the same voice called to him with brawny authority.

He again then felt a hand lay itself on his shoulder.

Mike instantly stopped playing and jerked back out of his bench seat, standing up to face his interloper.

Turning around, he saw Father Siemens smile, holding his hand up and his palm facing forward.

"I assure you," the priest spoke calmly. "I come in peace."

Mike staggered back and sat down. His mind raced through the hundred different thoughts and his heart pounded with the force of hundreds of organ pipes, thumping rapidly in his chest wall.

"Son," Siemens felt suddenly concerned for his welfare. "Are you all right?"

Mike's mind slowly returned to the present moment and he realized where he sat and what piece of music had been played in the church. He then recognized the priest, relinquishing the pleasure the music had momentarily donated to his soul.

"I was playing Bach," Mike stated in a half-apologetic voice. "I needed the music."

Siemens observed him for a moment, expecting some sort of confession.

"It helps me, Father," Mike added confidently.

He suddenly felt a wave of resentment surge through his body. Siemens had interrupted his communion with God, and he had again lost the refuge he sought in the very place that should have sustained his yearning vocation. As he looked up at the priest, an immediate feeling of shame gushed through his mind and heart.

"I'm sorry to interrupt," Siemens apologized as he looked up at the organ, admiring the pipes and how their near-vertical height barely avoided touching the ceiling.

Mike followed the priest's gaze and, with the priest, admired the aesthetically stacked grid of short and long pipes.

Making contact with Mike's eyes, Siemens broke the long silence.

"Your music is inspirational," Siemens complimented him.

Mike continued to stare absentmindedly at the pipes before hearing Siemen's words.

"Father?" he sheepishly asked him to repeat himself. "You what?"

"I admire the cantata," Siemens again complimented him.

Mike expressed surprise that the priest understood the type of music he had played.

"I love Bach," Mike blurted out.

"Yes," Siemens concurred. "Bach wrote this music for the churches in his time. It contains some of his best works. You know almost a third of his cantatas are lost?"

"Lost?" Mike asked in amazement, not able to imagine how anyone could misplace such magnificent music.

"The music sheets were thrown away," the priest clarified, "As packaging paper for fish or keeping out the winter drafts. Farmers used them for plugging holes in their barn walls."

Mike thought about what Siemens had said and began to laugh.

"You're joking, Father," Mike dismissed the assertion with a large toothy smile that stretched like a yawning mule.

"I wish," Siemens smiled in return. "But it tells us how close we are to the precipice of chaos."

He held up the first finger and thumb of his right hand, dramatizing the short distance between civilization and barbaric bedlam.

"It did happen?" Mike incredulously accepted his word. He promised himself to look up the information. "Such philistines. What a sad waste."

Mike momentarily mused about the lost cantatas and how their musical genius helped some poor farmer keep out the cold December draft over two hundred years ago.

"But some of the music is saved," Siemens reminded him with a warm grin.

Mike thought about his meaning and then understood.

"God has saved it," Mike concluded Siemens's allusion.

"Yes," the priest agreed. "He may reveal it to us through other works or when we meet Him after this life. But it is still there in His mind because He gave us Bach and the music. It is all a gift."

Siemens then laughed lightly to himself.

"What?" Mike asked, wondering what the private joke was in Siemens's mind.

"I think it is cosmically ironic how God used Bach's papers to plug holes," Siemens explained himself, trying to repress another outburst. "He is telling us to pay attention to Him and not to the artist. He wants us to keep in mind the essentials in life."

"You shall worship no other god," Mike paraphrased the first commandment.

"Exactly," the priest agreed. "We need to be constantly reminded of the true and holy source of our genius and joys."

Mike reflected on the reality of paradise containing billion of works of art from millions of artists of different disciplines. Like some type of Dewey Decimal System, Mike could peruse millions of folders in the afterlife and uncover great music that had been forgotten. He wondered about the great lost works of Bach that could be heard and enjoyed again. Then, he played with the thought of listening to music Bach never wrote. Could this genius also be a manifestation of God in a different light? Mike continued to extend this line of thinking and imagined that every person and great work functioned like a chink or cut on a giant diamond, reflecting a band of light in every angle. The refraction of light represented each person who remained a reflection on the precious Divine Jewel.

"We are all reflections of God's beauty," Mike revealed his thoughts out loud.

Siemens looked at him and raised his hand to gently touch his shoulder as if to give a blessing.

"There are many metaphors," Siemens accepted Mike's analogy. "But there is only one God."

"I understand," Mike responded, watching some of the chapel's light reflect off the organ's brass and chrome pipes.

"You see, Mike," Siemens began to lecture. "The church has always supported music for its ability to inspire."

Mike looked away from the pipes and turned his attention to Siemens.

"The church has always believed that music is useful if it reminds us of divine beauty," Siemens added to his thoughts. "You found that special grace."

Mike listened but remained silent, remembering how Bach's music lifted him and carried him to a realm away from the mundane, corrupt life of the seminary. It filled him with a special joy that had always been inexplicable.

"I think I have, Father," Mike blissfully agreed.

"Music like this," Siemens enthused, "and Gregorian chant, my favorite, support the soul's yearning for God's love. The popular music the students listen to is a perversion. It distracts the soul and tempts it."

Mike's face blushed as he thought about a confrontation he had had in the dorm over a song.

"What happened?" Siemens encouraged him to speak.

Mike stumbled for the right words and the correct chronology of story, but his emotions obscured his ability to recreate the tale.

"Start from the beginning," Siemens gently prodded him.

"One day," Mike paused, waiting for the words to float up to his vocal chords, "I was reading in the dorm and someone played a rock song."

Siemens watched him with a nonjudgmental smile but remained silent.

"Then," Mike measured his words, "a student turned up the radio when it played a group called The Ohio Players."

"Who?" Siemens questioned, not able to find any reference to the funk and R&B band.

"They are very popular," Mike pointed out, dismissing any further description. "They were singing a song called *Fire*. It was about . . . "

Mike could not finish his final word while facing Siemens.

"Sex," Siemens finished his thought.

"Using the metaphor," Mike clarified. "Fire. It was embarrassing."

"And what happened next?" Siemens continued to prod, knowing that Mike omitted the worse personal transgression.

"Well," Mike mumbled before blurting out his next sentence. "I told them it was sinful. We should listen to something else as seminarians."

Siemens again waited patiently.

"They laughed," Mike confessed awkwardly. A rush of anger again gripped him. "Then they told me to 'fuck off.'"

"Ah," the priest's tone implied sympathy and disapproval.

"They always humiliated me," Mike babbled, feeling an overwhelming need to cry.

He held back his welling tears and averted his eyes from Siemens.

"We have many who don't belong here," Siemens confessed sadly.

Mike's watery eyes focused on Siemens's face, displaying his disbelief at hearing Siemens's admission of failure.

"You see, Mike," Siemens continued without missing a beat, "we have a strict policy for admittance at the seminary. Character references and an interview are necessary before any boy is accepted. These requirements hold more value than grades or test scores. But as with anything else, mistakes happen, you know?"

Siemens's words stopped cold and he averted his eyes from Mike, who watched him look up and take a deep breath. When the priest turned around, his face expressed deep sorrow and misgivings.

"You know, Mike," Siemens struggled to find the words he needed. He then decided to use the only words he had available. His words expressed cold, hard facts.

"We can't over-discipline or expel the boys that humiliate you or criticize you," the priest blatantly told him.

"Why?" Mike demanded beseechingly to know the reasons. "Why?"

"Well," Siemens muttered awkwardly, "it has to do with logistics. You understand."

Mike quickly grasped Siemens's allusions and the revelation stabbed his ideological being in the heart.

"You can't, Father," Mike objected. "You have to do something. You have to cut the sick branches to save the vine. Christ told us."

"Yes," Siemens agreed with an ironic smile. "But Christ did not tell us how to pay the bills."

Mike looked down and thought about the implications of Siemens's words. The priest spoke first before he could continue his critique.

"It all has to do with funding," Siemens continued in a sheepish tone.

"You mean money?" Mike clarified the metaphor. "The seminary keeps these vipers? These sinners who affront God during mass and adoration? Who blaspheme Him whenever they have the chance? They are inherently agnostics and atheists! They are not even Christians. And you let them continue to study for the sacred priesthood?"

The last words sharply stabbed Siemens, who could not find reason to defend any of the administration's or the Cardinal's actions. He could only say the obvious.

"And then the Church closes these doors and we lose a few good men for the many who fail or will fail," Siemens counterargued. "They will not go to the major college or theology. You will. We keep this place open for you, Mike. And for the others like you. Do you understand?"

"No," Mike sadly admitted. "I don't think my suffering excuses the school's relativism. Actually, Father, it threatens my vocation when I am battered every day."

"That is why I am reaching out and talking to you, Mike," Siemens justified their conversations and his reasoning.

Mike dropped his head and let his mind wander for a while until Siemens tapped his hand.

"It's okay," Siemens tried to assure him. "God may be testing your vocation. You need to believe in Him and trust him. Pray for strength."

Mike nodded agreeably.

"Go ahead," the priest gently ordered him. "Continue to play."

Siemens stood up with open arms, towering above the student, and he waited for Mike, who paused for a moment and then stood up. Leaning forward, Siemens reached out and gave Mike a deep hug.

"You're a good man, Mike," Siemens told him in a tight embrace.

The embrace slowly became uncomfortable to Mike and, although Siemens sensed it, he held onto Mike for several long seconds. Mike tried to diplomatically break away as he gently but firmly pushed his body away. Siemens slowly and regretfully released his grip. Taking a small step back, Siemens raised his hand and began to bless Mike.

"In the name of the Father," he called out.

Mike quickly kneeled and looked up at the stout priest, who offered a beneficent remedy to Mike's spiritual doubts and emotional anguish.

"And the Son," the priest continued. "And the Holy Ghost."

"Amen," Mike ended the blessing emphatically.

Siemens motioned for him to stand. When Mike pushed himself up, Siemens made a motion to leave the choir loft.

"Come see me after night prayers," Siemens told him. "I have something that may help."

"Okay, Father," Mike agreed, still feeling a sting of apprehension.

Siemens smiled and turned around, nimbly leaving the choir loft.

The encounter with Siemens caused Mike to have a mixed reaction. He felt strange about Siemens's embrace but the priest had earned the reputation of being a cleric who showed warm, physical affection. Mike's background made the gesture uncomfortable, since his family had always been reserved about showing public feelings. As for the later visitation, Siemens's words whetted his appetite and inspired his curiosity enough to suppress any doubts about visiting the priest after evening prayers.

Turning his attention away from Siemens's visit, Mike began to play the organ again. The music, carrying him off to his mental and emotional retreat, blocked out his surroundings until another person abruptly interrupted his music.

"Mike," a familiar voice called to him once again, distracting him from his playing.

He then felt a hand shaking his shoulder.

"What?" Mike demanded to know, experiencing a surge of irritation.

"We have to go to evening prayers," John reminded him of the time.

Mike looked down at his Timex and then up at his friend.

"Okay." He slowly stood up, extracted a recessed wooden overlay, and carefully placed the oak cover over the keys of the organ.

"The music is beautiful," John complimented him,

Mike acknowledged the compliment with a wide smile. John, the only semblance of a friend he had at the seminary, had never been very close but had become Mike's friend through default. No one befriended John at the seminary, which made him an outcast like Mike. But, unlike Mike, his pariah status had more to do with his physique and not his personality. John, since his freshman year, had become morbidly obese and his mixed ethnicity—his mother was a Swede and his father was African-American—added more fodder to the cruel taunts the Christian seminarians leveled at him. Like Mike, John desired to be a priest with all his heart. Despite his sincerity and effort, his classmates tested his resolve and tried to humiliate him whenever possible. Insults like "wide load" and "Oreo cookies" plagued him from morning prayers to lights out. Yet, unlike Mike, John showed an affable demeanor and never responded in the negative. Although the taunts and insults never diminished, most students had some sympathy for John; whereas, Mike received disdain from everyone else, except for John. For Mike, it had always been ironic that John liked him but he never truly reciprocated the friendship since the first Youth Day over one year ago.

"Thank you," Mike responded automatically.

John looked admiringly at the organ for a few seconds.

"I would love to learn how to play," he instinctively asked Mike after many past and failed attempts to solicit lessons.

Mike ignored him and decided to leave.

"Let's go," he ordered his acquaintance.

Releasing a heavy sigh, John reluctantly followed Mike to the door of the stairway.

They walked down below to the main chapel where students began to file into their assigned pews. John sat apart, on Mary's side, from Mike, on St. Joseph's side, this year. A junior from their class read a pre-assigned excerpt from a seminary prayer book whose authorship dated back to the Reformation era. Normally, priests from the staff would preside and offer a blessing at the end of the day. No priest sat behind the seminarian's podium, which did not seem to disappoint anyone in the audience.

"Let us pray," the seminarian began, making the sign of the cross.

Everyone mimicked his motions. Looking around, Mike saw some seminarians opening their books. Some others read from other books while a few seminarians continued to study from a textbook.

"Turn to page 56 of the regular calendar," the seminarian instructed the audience.

Those students who opened their prayer books began to read a Psalm out loud, followed by several silent moments of meditation. Mike's mind wandered and he chastised himself for not paying attention to the sequence of prayers. His mind continued the trail back to his conversation with Siemens. Although Mike welcomed and even pursued spiritual consultations, he continued to be anxious about seeing Siemens. He knew he could not refuse and felt that some of his private feelings and thoughts should remain with himself.

"Mike," a familiar voice again drew him away from his thoughts.

John stood by his pew and pointed to the departing students. The prayer had ended.

"You okay?" John asked.

Mike smiled and stood up.

"Thanks," Mike made an effort to smile.

He walked ahead of John and followed the line of boys dragging themselves to the dormitory. Some small cliques had become entangled in heated conversations about an impending examination or homework assignment. But, for the most part, the students drifted in somnambulistic fashion, desperately awaiting a solid eight hours of sleep. For those students who had a test the next day, they would be "cramming" for hours in the luggage room or under their sheets. Mike, lost in his thoughts, wandered aimlessly through the hallways, towing John nearby.

"Mike?" John interrupted him for the third time as Mike made the wrong turn into another dormitory. "The dorm is here."

Mike silently stood in front of Siemens's room in the middle of the hallway across from the restrooms and the shower rooms. A stairway to the upstairs dormitories stood on the left. The architects had designed the hallways as the transepts between the A and B wings of the dormitories.

"Father Siemens wants to see me," Mike explained in a monotone voice.

"Oh," John muttered, standing awkwardly for a moment before deciding to walk alone to his dorm. Priests often consulted seminarians after night prayers—a common practice.

Mike watched him and then paused to stare at the door. Changing his mind, he began to follow John to the hallway. He would tell Siemens that he had been tired and went to bed. When he turned around and began to walk away, he heard a click and the creak of Siemens's door opening. An effusion of yellow light filled the hallway and eclipsed the anemic incandescent light hanging from the cracked alabaster ceiling.

"Sir," Siemens called out. "Come in, Mike."

Mike froze in his place and briefly caught John's dreadful stare through the dormitory door window as if John could read Mike's apprehension.

"Come in," Siemens repeated in a tone one octave higher.

Mike slowly turned around and gave the priest a wide, painful smile. Siemens stood outside the doorway still wearing his priestly garb, except for his collar, which had been unbuttoned and hung out of its shirt-clip.

"I am glad you're here," Siemens professed as Mike walked reluctantly into the room.

Upon first entering the room, Mike noticed that the room barely offered enough space for one person. A single bed that resembled a cot rested at the foot of an imitation wood divider that separated the bedroom from the foyer. To the right of the bedroom, a narrow door led to the restroom. The door opened to a dark interior.

"Sit down, Mike," Siemens motioned for Mike to sit in a padded desk chair made of red oak.

Mike nervously sat on the crotchet-covered green pad and noticed the deep-set lounge chair in front of him. Siemens sank into a yellow and brown fabric chair. A long brass lamp hung strategically over the chair, where he would comfortably read his books. Books! The word reverberated in his mind for Siemens's room had been almost decorated with books from wall to wall. Every inch of space against the walls of the cramped room housed shelves of books. The books looked antique and well used. Their brown and red binders blended with the maroon shag rug under Mike's feet. In one small area of a shelf next to Siemens, a small phonograph and radio had been cuddled between two volumes of European medieval history.

"I obviously like books," Siemens commented and chuckled at his understatement.

Mike instinctively stood up and began to peruse the titles. He noticed that the books were actually old. Most of them had been printed decades and centuries ago. In one corner, close to Siemens's phonograph, a collection of music books containing yellowed scores had been crammed between brittle leather covers.

"There's a Gregorian sheet in that one," Siemens pointed out, standing up to gently wedge the book out of its place.

Flakes of leather and decomposing parchment shook loose from the book and momentarily hovered in the stale, still air of the room before sprinkling onto the shag rug below. Siemens cautiously opened the leather binder and extracted a thin vellum sheet which held a richly decorated score of simple notes on a skeleton scale. Extending his hand, Siemens gave the manuscript to Mike, who opened his two palms to reverently receive it.

"It has no real collectible value. A sixteenth-century copy," Siemens explained. "But my grandfather inherited it. Its value is its beauty and spiritual tradition."

Mike stared at the notes and began to play the music in his head. He recreated the process of some unidentified monk in an obscure, cold, dimly lit hall composing a sanctified tune he heard in his head, to be played for the Abbot during vespers.

"Do you like it?" Siemens asked against the background of Mike's daydream.

Mike heard Siemens's voice but failed to digest the words. He could only hear the notes play out in his mind as he sat behind a large pipe organ, overlooking a congregation of friars and monks, while trumpeting the tunes through the arched canyons of a long, narrow, stone nave.

"I see you like it," Siemens sought Mike's approval despite his apparent absorption.

Without an invitation, Siemens slowly extended his hand and touched Mike's shoulder. The tactile sensation registered slowly on Mike and then abruptly terminated his long, utopian daydream about an undocumented medieval event. Siemens's hand then moved slowly from his upper shoulder and began to circle his shoulder blade. The priest towered above Mike and appeared to display more physical presence and charisma than when Mike had first entered the room.

"Father?" Mike inquired nervously, letting the parchment fall to his side.

Looking up, Siemens seemed to be perspiring and a nervous twitch tried to break out into a smile.

"You and I have some kindred sensitivity," Siemens explained faultily, "like the sublime pleasure of this music. Mike, few people appreciate its beauty. It is so old yet young and refreshing."

He then lifted his hand and moved it to his side.

"Please sit down and relax," Siemens offered his favorite chair.

Mike looked in the direction of his extended hand and froze. He could not will himself to move although he did want to move. With an unyielding grasp, Siemens gripped Mike's shoulder and began to gently but firmly direct the seminarian to his chair.

"Please, Mike," Siemens pleaded in an almost high-pitched tone. "You'll see. I promise."

A feeling a nausea twisted in Mike's stomach and he felt light-headed as he almost staggered toward the chair. Siemens's grip seemed to claw under his skin and press into his bone. The sudden clutch caused Mike to shudder and he felt his legs give out as a gush of vomit rose up his esophagus, only to be forced down. Suddenly, a loud knocking could be heard on Siemens's door. The priest released his grip and left Mike to hover uneasily over the chair. Mike steadied himself with one hand, holding the armrest as Siemens turned the lock and opened his door. John, panting and agitated, stood anxiously at the door.

"Father!" he shouted briefly, catching a glimpse of Mike pushing himself off the armrest and straightening his posture. "I need help."

"Help?" Siemens responded doubtfully. "What happened?"

Siemens display an expression of irritation that clearly told John that he better have some clear and verifiable reason for his interruption.

"My sugar," John blurted out. "I took my blood test."

Siemens looked at John, not comprehending, and then an expression of both frustration and concern swept across his face. John held up a type of litmus paper and his bandaged finger.

"It's too high," John continued to explain. "I need my insulin shots. You have the needle."

Siemens tried to object and then remembered he had followed the Rector's orders to lock away all the hypodermic needles. Normally, he handed them out to diabetic students during a routine schedule with the nurse. He never thought their storage would foreshadow a true emergency. John had been very careful with his medication and the school nurse, Sister Rose, administered the shots during the day. The priest never took an interest in John's medical condition and did not know what crisis now faced him.

"I'm feeling really sick, Father!" John almost cried.

Gathering his wits, Mike walked to the door and slowly felt the ebb of vomit retreat back into his guts.

"Help me, Mike," John pled.

Siemens noticed Mike for the first time since John had entered the room. Mike glanced at the priest and then took a hard look at John, who seemed pale even for his swarthy appearance. A light sheen of sweat gathered in a small fine spray across his forehead and cheeks. John's illness caused Mike's nausea to return.

"He looks really sick," Mike commented to Siemens. "We need to get him his medicine."

In the hallway, a growing crowd of spectator seminarians in their boxer shorts and pajamas, milling and staring at John, leered apprehensively at the groaning diabetic.

"Oh," John moaned and leaned against the door post.

"Wait, sirs," Siemens commanded and disappeared into his room.

His disappearance allowed Mike to step out of the room and stand next to his friend. A few seminarians asked John how he felt and some others began to comfort him. John continued to lean on the doorpost and hold onto Mike's forearm. An instant later, Siemens opened the door and stepped out of his room wearing his Roman garb.

"Escort John to the infirmary," Siemens ordered Mike. "I'll return with the medicine." He paused and then looked at John. "What do I bring?"

John did not hear his question until Siemens repeated it.

"What do I bring, John?" he spoke in an agitated voice.

John had lost himself in some wayward thoughts until he forced his memory to rise to the surface.

"A vial and a syringe," he almost whispered.

"Go. Hurry!" Siemens ordered Mike. He then spoke to the other seniors. "The rest of you return to your dorms."

Mike instantly departed to retrieve John's medicine. When he reached John's bed, cellophane wrappers and crumbs lay scattered on top of his dresser and on the floor next to his bed. After frantically searching from the top to the bottom drawers, Mike found John's diabetes kit and an empty bag of Oreo cookies in the bottom drawer. Feeling a welling force of tears rise, Mike grabbed the kit and raced off to the infirmary.

Phase 10

When the hyper-virtual world faded from view, Mike sat at the cafeteria table, placing his bowed head in the palms of his hands. Juan compassionately watched him in long silence, which he broke with a pat on Mike's back.

"You okay?" Juan asked.

"John was a saint," Mike muttered, loud enough for everyone to hear.

"Too bad he died," Juan said forlornly. "Heart attack, I remember."

"The diabetes killed him," Mike recalled. "All for me."

He did not wait for a response. Nudging his head slowly up, Mike stood stoically upright, leaving the cafeteria table and walking out the door before anyone could further comment or before he might openly break down.

"I didn't know," Juan angrily commented when Mike's virtual body dissolved into the outside parameters of the program where another illusion welcomed him. "John was really a good kid."

"I didn't know either," Bill remarked to himself.

"Siemens was kind of strange," Juan reflected, "I always thought."

"John paid a price for his sacrifice," Bill added to his remark.

"It's costing us all too much," Rico spoke accusingly to Bill.

Bill remained silent, keeping his eyes averted from Juan and Rico. Occasionally, his threw a glance at the avatar, which remained still and lifeless.

"The world is dead and we sit here," Rico felt his anger deflate into self-pity and desperation, creating a mental masturbation without a past or future. "Stop it now and let us mourn or at least die, too."

"Mourn," Bill repeated. "For whom?"

"Good grammar," Juan quipped and produced a low nervous laugh.

"At least for us," Rico pled, holding out his hand. "Please, Bill."

Bill's head drooped and he continued to avert his eyes.

"I can't stop the program till we answer the questions left unanswered. You know that already," Bill spoke in a clear, almost staccato, tone. "It must progress to senior year."

"What questions?" Rico demanded, spitting out some of his frustration. "There are no more questions."

"It is predetermined," the avatar interrupted, mouthing the response through the slit of his mouth.

Rico stared at Clement and accusingly pointed his finger at the avatar.

"You know it is preprogrammed like a safe," Bill used an old analogy. "You can only open it during business hours."

"We're not machines," Rico jibed.

"You are now." Bill reminded him. "Only your essence. Only your memory operates here. These are the last vestiges of your humanity."

Rico stood up and then sat down, conceding with a nod. Bill reached out to comfort him but Rico evaded his friend.

"I don't feel like a memory," Rico confronted him. "I feel like me."

"Is that all I have ever been?" Juan mused sadly.

"No," Rico disagreed. "I want a funeral, Bill, for my daughter." Rico reached over and grasped Juan's shoulder. "Juan, I want you there with me."

Juan looked down and nodded in agreement.

"Also Mike," Rico requested. Bill tried to respond but Rico cut him off. "Not you. I want a real funeral. Mike can officiate if he wants to."

The avatar looked questioningly down at Bill, who continued to look down at his lap.

"I'd be honored," Mike's voice spoke from an unseen venue. "She deserves the honor. This is what makes us human. Our loved ones, our friends, and our family."

Mike returned. Bill looked up to see him standing next to Rico and compassionately patting his shoulder. His eyes made contact with the priest and he blinked approvingly. Mike lowered his eyes, accepting the responsibility of closure for Rico's daughter, and he then began to slowly walk away again.

"That was what John taught me," Mike declared, as his body began to dematerialize. "He taught me how to care. That is partly why I became a priest. I wanted to care."

Rico turned around to face Mike before he vanished.

"We need to put some closure to the world and to ourselves," Mike suggested with a fading voice.

Rico looked back at Bill, who continued to avert his eyes. Then, their surroundings began to change.

"An answer," the avatar pondered wisely, "to one important question."

Mike stood in a simple black suit and black shirt beside a white-draped, oak coffin with silver handles in the seminary chapel's altar entrance. Next to him stood Rico and across from the two men stood a solemn Bill and Juan.

Taking out a small, brown leather-bound book, Mike opened the antiquated missal and began to read.

Happy the man, and happy he alone,
He who can call today his own:
He who, secure within, can say,
Tomorrow do thy worst, for I have lived today.
Be fair or foul or rain or shine
The joys I have possessed, in spite of fate, are mine.
Not Heaven itself upon the past has power,
But what has been, has been, and I have had my hour.

Mike made a sign of the cross and Juan followed his motions. Bill kept his head down and Rico stared forward at some unknown object.

"I did not know her but she was a true servant of humanity," Mike praised her. "Her type has given of herself and has saved millions for millennia. She as others served as our beacons of love. She was like John."

Mike then looked at Rico and motioned to Rico with his missal. Rico cleared his throat and moved up the altar steps to face his three classmates.

"Thank you," Rico expressed his gratitude and Mike gave him a warm but sad smile. "John should be honored too."

Taking another look at his friends, Rico began to speak again with great, weighty effort. "To paraphrase another great writer, I come here not praise my daughter but to mourn her. Her actions speak for themselves to a population who will not remain to appreciate them or treasure them. Only a small band of humans…"

Rico stopped to look graciously at Mike before he continued.

"Souls," he corrected himself.

Mike's expressions remained friendly and attentive.

"…remember my daughter and the whole of humanity. We are to mourn for the loss of humanity and the remaining cliques of humanity who may survive. But if we have anything we can learn from great humanitarians like my daughter, we can learn to cherish the moments we have remaining and to love. She and John will not be forgotten."

He then stepped down and his classmates approached their bereaved friend and together hugged Rico. When they finished, they left him alone with the coffin. Rico stood for a moment and waited for his friends to leave. As planned earlier, Rico dropped his head. A white marble mausoleum designed as a chapel appeared behind him, and he stood alone on a semi-grassy knoll on a field in central California overlooking the blue-green Pacific Ocean. Seagulls and the distant crashing waves offered some companionship to the rich silence that embraced the scene. Rico knelt at a diminutive iron-gridded door that covered a marble plaque with a poem by Edgar Allen Poe inscribed on it:

For the moon never beams without bringing me dreams
Of the beautiful Annabel Lee;
And the stars never rise but I feel the bright eyes
Of the beautiful Annabel Lee;
And so, all the night-tide, I lie down by the side
Of my darling- my darling- my life and my bride,
In the sepulcher there by the sea,
In her tomb by the sounding sea.

Rico touched the inscription and cried for a long time.

Chapter 12

The papa say "Oy, if I get that boy
I'm gonna stick him in the house of detention."
I'm on my way, I don't know where I'm goin',
I'm on my way, I'm takin' my time, but I don't know where.
– Paul Simon

Many weekend retreats offered volunteer seminarians an excursion to the Sisters of Charity convent homes among the elevated groves of Mission Hills. After spending long hours entertaining and indoctrinating eighth-grade Catholic elementary students to consider the priestly vocation and relinquish all secondary-school temptations and pleasures, the upperclassmen accepted the Sisters' offer to visit the vast acreage of the property that was filled with native oak trees and rows of citrus trees that protruded like leafy toothpicks in the rolling knolls and hills shielding the convent from the creeping population of the suburbanite San Fernando Valley. Looking east and west of the Valley, one could see small pockets of the original land grants dating back to the old Rey de España donations in the 18th century, which had been inherited and bought after California became a republic and then a state during the Gold Rush.

The Sisters' property once had been owned by the old mission and then it passed to ranch hands after the Civil War. Soon after the First World War, the church bought the land for a fraction of its potential inflated value in the 1970s and leased it to the Sisters in perpetuity. Today, suburbia encircled the convent with hills of cloned tract homes and strings of asphalt roads.

"We are going after Sunday mass," Juan celebrated, after morning prayers in the dorm.

Juan retrieved a long canvas case from his closet and carefully placed it on the bed.

"You brought it?" Rico asked excitedly.

Juan admired the case and smiled broadly.

"Did you bring me something to use?" Rico pressed, wanting to extract the contents of the case.

Juan gently prevented him from touching the case as he passed his hands over the case's surface, almost stroking it and expecting it to purr with delight.

"This is my baby," Juan affirmed. "Check this out, dude."

Juan returned to his closet and pulled out a brown, leather satchel with two long buckled straps that resembled the old courier bags tied to the side of a vintage dispatch motorcycle.

"This is it," Juan announced, carefully pulling out the contents like a curator in an old museum.

Rico glided toward the satchel and saw two rubber-sealed glasses and leather goggles and two pairs of black, thin, rabbit-skin gloves.

"Where did you get this stuff?" Rico demanded, taking the gloves and goggles into his possession.

He turned to the canvas bag for a moment but then consoled himself with the items in his hand.

"My neighbor," Juan revealed proudly. "The old dude was a World War I vet and a dispatcher at Amiens."

Rico marveled at the fact that he held a piece of history. Letting the leather straps run through his fingers and over his palms, he tapped the thick glass.

"How strong?" Rico asked, trying out a pair of gloves.

"He said it caused more blindness," Juan spat out and laughed, mimicking the toothless gums of the vet. "Only good for dust."

"Wow," Rico admired the goggles and held them on the bridge of his nose with his gloved hands.

Looking through the glass and peering about the dorm, his vision was discolored by a slight yellow sheen.

"Needs cleaning," Rico concluded, slightly losing his admiration for the historical artifacts.

He then glanced down to see Juan sitting next to his canvas bag.

"These are not what you said you'd bring," Rico said irritably, shaking the goggles and dropping them onto the satchel.

Juan seemed to ignore his friend's protest, retreating into a world far removed from the ordinary routine and obligations of any seminarian. Gently pulling the rust-speckled zipper back, he reached into the canvas bag and extracted a black pump BB rifle with a 20-power scope mounted on the upper chamber. The walnut stock had been waxed to shiny perfection, revealing wavy lines of grain at varying degrees and depth. Staring at the scope with jealous awe, Rico leaned forward to obtain a better view. Juan, catching his friend's admiration of the rifle, held up a finger of pause with his free hand and carefully let the rifle rest on top of the canvas bag. He then reached into the bag and extracted an equally crafted RWS BB pistol. The pistol had a smaller scope mounted to its slide, but its stock showed a slightly different craftsmanship than the rifle. Unlike the rifle, the bottom of the pistol stock had a handrest carved out to provide balance and accuracy to the seven-inch barrel. Juan effortlessly handed the pistol to Rico's sweaty, greedy hands, opened in supplication as if he awaited the Holy Eucharist at his First Communion.

"It can fire a BB or pellet up to seven hundred feet per second," Juan added, as Rico grasped the gun and awkwardly fumbled the stock so it would balance itself. "You can hold it with one or two hands."

Rico switched the pistol from a one-hand position to a two-hand position, aiming at a distant, imaginary target.

"The one hand is enough," Juan commented. "The gun has no recoil."

"Bitching!" Rico exclaimed, jerking his hand up in the air as if he had actually fired a Dirty Harry 44-magnum revolver.

Both Juan and Rico pretended to shoot at imaginary squirrels on Sister Flora's property in the afternoon.

"We're so fucking lucky," Rico almost squealed, rehearsing his stalking ability and the trajectory of his BB pellet striking and killing a squirrel.

"Maybe we get a rabbit," Juan mused. "My brothers told me they once bagged a rabbit."

Juan's brothers represented lifelong seminarians that occupied the seminary through generations and produced no priests.

"Really?" Rico reacted with wonder. He remembered how his mother once cooked a rabbit in hot, boiling salsa and how delicious it tasted, coming apart in succulent shreds on his pile of linguini.

"The Sisters will cook it," Juan assured him.

Rico's mind switched from salsa to Mexican food, for the Sisters were mostly from Guadalajara and had often prepared delicacies on the weekend. Their food was a welcome respite from the bland, processed food offered during weekdays.

"Taco rabbit," Juan mused, thinking Rico's exact thought. "Burritos Conejos."

They both laughed out loud and Rico momentarily fell to the side before leaping up and taking another imaginary shot.

"Burritos Conejos," he repeated and laughed.

"Rancheros de Conejos," another familiar voice chimed in.

Startled, both Juan and Rico looked over to the opposite side of the dorm and saw Bill smiling his Cheshire grin at both of his classmates.

"Bill," Rico saluted him, holding up his pistol.

Juan also held up his rifle to be admired, then looked down the target, pointing it at an imaginary rabbit.

"Cool," Bill complimented their weapons. He then stood up and made an announcement. "Want to see a real gun?"

"What?" Rico questioned, not doubting Bill's subtle boast.

Bill had a reputation of producing and creating amazing products, both on paper and in reality. His abilities astounded everyone and all doubters soon became believers when they saw Bill's final products. In the computer lab, Bill accepted his teacher's outrageous challenge, as a joke, to build a faster calculator and over the weekend Bill returned to school with a motherboard, transistor chips, and LED display that calculated beyond the simple four functions of the school calculator that had been valued at several thousands of dollars during the 1960s. Bill's calculator could also do square roots and log calculations three times as fast. He submitted it as his final project – an easy A grade, he thought. At the end of the semester, the priest failed him on a technicality. Bill did not follow instructions when he built the calculator. His invention had been off-topic. An inconvenient technicality and a lesson Bill learned very well. No one fooled him again.

"Look here," he invited his friends.

Juan and Rico peered cautiously towards their friend whose smile seemed to wrap itself around his upper cheekbones, revealing two yellowed crenate rows of teeth.

"Inside," Bill opened his thin-gauge steel closet doors and extracted a rifle with the markings of a science fiction weapon.

"What the hell is that?" Juan could not contain his shock.

"Shitttt, mannnn!" Rico spoke, allowing the air in his lungs to whistle through his two front teeth.

They took a long hard look at the rifle but it did not look like a conventional rifle. Using black plastic and elongated compression tubes that encapsulated the fore-end and barrel, Bill reshaped and added various devices to enhance the function of the rifle. Behind the trigger guard he attached a black aluminum drum that resembled the magazine storage of a Thompson machine gun.

"How does it work?" Juan demanded to know. He tried to touch the rifle but Bill slightly recoiled when he leaned forward. "I don't have VD."

"No," Bill said, losing his smile and adjusting his seating position on his bed. "The drum contains five hundred BBs."

Like a good sales pitch he let the number sink into their consciousness.

"The tubes here," he pointed to the fore-end on both sides, "rapidly feed CO_2 to the chamber so all I have to do is hold the trigger."

Pointing the rifle in another direction, Bill squeezed the trigger, and a sharp squealing sound of rapidly compressed air whistled through the firing chamber. Bill repeated the action and waited.

"Where're the BBs?" Rico asked the obvious.

Bill's smile returned.

"You want five hundred BBs ricocheting all over the dorm?"

"Oh, shit," Juan shouted and danced in a circle. "The fucking seniors challenged us to a BB fight."

"Yeah," Rico realizing the potential of Bill's rifle. He pointed to it. "That thing will kick ass. We won't tell them until the ambush. Then we show them!"

Rico yanked the rifle from Bill's hands and pointed at a nondescript target at the end of the dormitory

"Pow! Pow," Rico imitated the rapid fire of the CO_2 semi-automatic.

He then fired the rifle in the same manner that Bill had done earlier. Squealing again, the CO_2 cartridges seemed to hiss like an angry rattlesnake.

"Oh, shit," Juan kept repeating and dancing. "This is bitching!"

"Wow," Rico expressed his admiration, holding the rifle up like a battle trophy.

Juan reached for the rifle and Rico instinctively pulled it away before having second thoughts and handing it to him.

"No," Bill commanded loudly.

He stood up and retrieved his rifle, examining it for any mishandling.

"This is complicated," Bill muttered with suppressed frustration, mildly berating Juan and Rico.

He then retrieved additional CO_2 cartridges and carefully replenished the rifle's containers on top of the bed.

"This is fucking unbelievable!" Juan expressed his admiration. "I can't wait to nail those fuckers."

Rico jiggled his head in agreement and Bill looked up with secret glee, finishing the cartridge replenishment.

"When are we leaving?" Bill almost whispered.

"After Mass," Juan assured them. "The Sisters are making lunch. Then, we can go hunting. I'll drive us there."

"Cool," Rico uttered as he fantasized about the afternoon.

After the Mass, they would drive in Juan's new Vega to the ranch house and the Sisters would escort them to the salon where a five-course meal would be served. The tortillas would be hand-rolled, and the meat would all be packed with delicious spices and secret ingredients. Rico looked forward to dipping the freshly fried blue corn tortilla chips in a rich, spicy cilantro sauce.

"What the fuck is that?" a familiar voice shouted from behind them.

Almost jumping, the three friends instantly reacted with dread when they recognized Tony's voice. He stood behind them holding an old Daisy Ryder that had been refinished but still failed to hide its primitive origins.

"That's bitchin," Tony called out, pointing at Bill's rifle with his Daisy.

Throwing the rifle on a bed, Tony leaped to Bill's area and slightly pushed Rico and Juan to the side. He then grabbed the gun and held it up and wielded it like Excalibur in King Arthur's hands.

"That's no fucking broadsword," Juan warned him.

Ignoring Juan, Tony made two more swipes and pointed the rifle at the ceiling light. He then pulled the trigger, followed by a squealing rush of pulsating air.

"Goddam it," Bill yelled, ripping the rifle out of Tony's hand.

Taken aback, Tony stared incredulously at Bill and fumed for long silent seconds.

"I just finished compressing the cartridges," Bill explained, trying to calm down.

He ignored Tony, retrieved more CO_2, and began the process of pressurizing the rifle.

"What the fuck is wrong with you?" Tony cursed and made a threatening move towards Bill's bed.

Rico intercepted and blocked Tony, who gave him a slight, threatening shove.

"What the fuck is your problem, dude?" Rico countered Tony's anger.

"You play too much, Tony," Juan called him out. "You don't know when to stop."

Glaring at Juan, Tony gave him the middle finger.

"Shut up, faggot," Tony insulted Juan, who only smiled at his puerile behavior.

"Your mother," Juan returned the middle finger and laughed in Tony's face.

Taking a wild swing at Juan, Tony tried to punch him, but Juan's reflexes allowed him to move almost a foot away before Tony's fist swiped through the air, making contact with nothing.

"Fuck off," Rico stood between the two and pushed Tony's shoulder back. "What the hell is wrong with you?"

Juan continued to look Tony as he moved back, holding both middle fingers up in an antagonizing and posturing move.

"That faggot wants some," Tony pointed an accusatory finger at Juan and then held up his fist.

"Hey," Rico warned Tony. "You grabbed the rifle. Bill would have shown it to you."

"Really?" Tony doubted Rico's sincerity. "When do you guys share anything?"

Rico felt bad and Juan expressed some remorse by dropping his taunting fingers.

"You don't have to be an ass," Rico retorted, still fuming from the confrontation.

"Screw you guys," Tony stormed off, leaving his Daisy rifle behind.

"What's his problem?" Bill asked naively.

Rico repressed a welling feeling of sarcasm when he noticed the expression of disbelief on Bill's face.

"He's very competitive," Rico surmised.

Juan laughed scornfully at Tony.

"Not competitive," Juan disagreed humorlessly, "fucking crazy."

Bill looked over in Tony's direction and appeared for a long moment to be lost in thought. He then turned to his rifle and made some further adjustments before placing the weapon back in its case.

"Let's go fix our stuff," Juan advised Rico. "We have to go to Mass."

"Yeah," Rico concurred after looking at his watch.

Bill put the rifle back into his closet and then returned to his bed with a book. Rico watched him as he and Juan cleaned and stored their guns.

"Are we really going to have a BB fight?" Rico pressed the question, beginning to have some doubts about the skirmish.

He then looked at the goggles and stretched the straps until Juan took them out of his hands and stuffed them in a bag.

"My brother told me it was planned," Juan assured him. "He's a senior."

Rico looked at Bill and then back at Juan, who finished placing his rifle in a bag.

"They'll go apeshit when they see that gun," Rico jerked his thumb in Bill's direction.

"Tony will probably tell them," Bill warned them both.

Rico and Juan look at Bill and visibly showed their hostility about the possibility of being betrayed.

"Oh. Shit!" Juan cursed. "My brother will take it away from me and shove it up my ass!"

Juan's brothers had all preceded him in the seminary and he was the last of several brothers to graduate after a long history of familial escapades and roguish behavior. Many had been suspended over the years but none had been expelled. The family had a guardian angel among one of the Prelates of the Archdiocese.

"If you're lucky," Rico concluded.

The seniors had a fearful reputation for being vengeful and rascally. They did not like to lose any contest and often would cheat to win. Juan confirmed the rumors to Rico in secret. Fortunately for Juan and his two classmates, his brother and the senior class never discovered the secret of Bill's rifle. Tony remained silent. When they finished putting their rifles away, the students walked over to the chapel and completed their last obligations as retreat hosts.

Sitting in the chapel with their designated eighth-grade novitiates, they patiently waited for the Mass to conclude as their minds drifted off to the hills and fields of the Mission Sisters, where large orange groves grew and rabbits darted in and out of the sagebrush and lush green grasses. Rico's heart basked in the excitement of imagining how he and his friends would wait on a small knoll behind a gnarly lemon tree and rain down a hailstorm of BBs on the seniors once the skirmish had officially started. His thoughts evaporated when someone stuck his finger into his right shoulder blade during the reading of the Gospel. Before he could answer, Rico heard a loud whisper challenging him.

"Hey," a familiar voice taunted him. "Ready to get your ass kicked?"

Rico recognized Juan's brother Marty and he slightly turned his head to see him smirk out of the corner of his eye.

"Stay cool," Marty told him. "Better wear your goggles."

He heard a distant snicker, and when he turned around, he only saw several eighth-graders who gave him a wry and confused look. Marty had disappeared. Rico ignored them and returned to his daydreaming, envisioning a swarm of unexpected BBs stinging Marty and his friends from head to foot. Rico's thoughts quickly returned to the present when he noticed Juan smiling at him with vengeful glee from the other side of the aisle.

"Then Jesus asked them, "When I sent you without purse, bag or sandals, did you lack anything?" "Nothing," they answered. He said to them, "But now if you have a purse, take it, and also a bag; and if you don't have a sword, sell your cloak and buy one. It is written: 'And he was numbered with the transgressors' and I tell you that this must be fulfilled in me. Yes, what is written about me is reaching its fulfillment." The disciples said, "See, Lord, here are two swords." "That is enough," he replied.

A moment later, the students and guests sat down and began to listen to the homily. The priest during the retreat, Father Tom, had been a guest speaker. He did not generate too much enthusiasm nor did he invite any derision during the two-and-a-half days of prayer, play, and reflections.

"So?" he began the homily, stepping down from the podium and greeting the students at the bottom of the nave. "What does this strange passage say? How does it apply to us today?"

Rico looked up and saw Siemens and the Monsignor express their consternation at some students who joked in the back of the congregation where parents and guests sat. When Rico turned around, the view pleased him for the disrupting noise came from both parents and eighth-graders, who had enjoyed a private joke and laughed out loud. Father Tom patiently smiled and waited for a second like an indulgent schoolmaster.

"This is a difficult passage for us," he began to explain, deciding to ignore them. "It is also a bewildering one for young people and old."

The priest then took a moment to stare down the disruptive parents who had retreated into their parental façade of thoughtful gravity.

"So, can someone take a stab?" the priest held up his arm, imitating a slashing sword.

Everyone in the congregation laughed.

"What was the sword used for later?" the priest continued to inquire. "Mmm?"

An eighth-grader meekly raised his hand, and Father Tom motioned for him to speak. The young student, wearing a wrinkled navy-blue tie and white shirt, stood up nervously.

"Uh," he began, fumbling for the right words. "To cut a servant's ear so Christ could cure him."

"To cure him," the priest repeated. "God allows harm and injury to show us the greater good. Christ healed the servant and He died for us all the next day. And what was the result? He saved the world. He saved the world!"

Father Tom let his words sink in.

"Remember," he emphasized the word. "Remember. No matter what ill falls upon us or others, there is a greater good waiting for us. Our faith tells us so. We may not see it, but it is there. That is God's test. Are we ready to wait for the greater good?"

He pointed at the eighth-grader who had spoken, watching him slightly squirm. Father Tom then randomly pointed his index finger at others, one at a time.

"And you?" he pointed his finger at Juan. "Are you ready to show God your trust and faith in Him? May God bless you."

He made the sign of the cross and the congregation followed him with the blessing. Then, when he turned around to ascend the altar steps, a timid applause began, augmenting into a loud standing ovation and cheers. Siemens almost glared threateningly at the students until he remembered seeing the parents and guests applauding in the chapel. The Monsignor pouted and looked down at his feet. Rico took advantage of the moment and stuck his middle finger at Juan.

"Are you ready?" he mouthed Father Tom's words and then mimicked the firing of a trigger with his other hand.

Juan smiled and held up his thumb, repeating Rico's flashing trigger finger. When the Mass ended, Juan, Bill and Rico met in the front of the chapel to escort the visiting eighth-graders to their dorms in the C and D buildings and their parents to their cars. Without waiting further, Juan ran to the students' parking lot and started up the Vega. Following predetermined protocols, Rico and Bill raced in the opposite direction to retrieve their rifles. They grabbed their cases and sacks and made a dash out of their dormitory, almost running into Father Siemens.

"*Caballeros!*" he shouted at them, towering above them. "Where are you going?"

Looking down at their cases, he quickly summed up their destination.

"I hope you're careful at the Sisters' place?" he demanded with clear authority. "I told Sister that the shooting could be a problem."

"We wear goggles, Father," Bill assured him.

Siemens studied Bill for a moment and he tepidly expressed some satisfaction with Bill's answer. Bill's reputation was impeccable, and although he was not a model of religiosity Bill did demonstrate the attributes of the ideal student who never caused the administration any concern or grief. If on the other hand Rico made a response, even if the response had all the sincerity and logic an adolescent could muster, Siemens would probably have confiscated the rifles. Rico felt grateful that he remained silent and he kept his eyes averted from Siemens's stare, afraid that the priest would discern his feelings of triumph.

"OK, *caballeros*," he mocked them. "Be back before Adoration. I told the Sisters. And clean up after dinner."

"Thank you, Father," they both responded simultaneously and moved with quick purpose to Juan's Vega parked outside.

After turning the corner, Rico noticed that Siemens had disappeared from sight.

"Let's fucking go!" Rico urged Bill with a light punch on the arm.

They then made a quick romp and reached the front entrance in less than half the time it would have taken them during normal school hours. No one stood on the steps except for some meandering visitors and parents. Most of the seminarians had abandoned the school grounds. They quickly identified Juan's yellow Vega. He had opened the hatchback of the car and stuck his face outside the passenger side window. The smoky engine chugged loudly.

"Get inside!" Juan shouted at them. "Everyone got the fuck out of here already!"

The remaining parents overheard Juan and stopped speaking in shocked disbelief to stare at the seminarians. Bill waved to the parents and Rico pushed him into the passenger's side while climbing into the tight rear seat. Juan then gunned the asphyxiated two-barrel carburetor and peeled out of the driveway, leaving several shocked students and parents staring after them.

"I think we left them with a bad impression of us," Bill commented, offering his friends his wide, toothy smile.

"Fuck yeah," Juan said proudly as the car leaped with jolting squeaks over the cracked concrete speed bumps.

"Shit," Rico shouted, almost hitting his head on the ceiling.

Juan and Bill laughed as they took Mission Boulevard to San Fernando Road on a long winding freeway that looped north and east above the common streets of the East Valley. Looking out their windows, they enjoyed the remaining hints of distant snow in the San Bernardino Mountains and the green patches that decorated the granite gray appearance of the mountains' sides. Summer remained further off, so the smog from the lower valley had not crept up north to overshadow the bold, blue sky. Within fifteen minutes, they reached the exit that took them farther north under the shadows of the rising mountaintops.

"Man, this will be cool," Juan commented, dreaming about Bill's rifle.

"So, are we ready to go?" Rico asked Bill.

Bill nodded in the affirmative.

"My brother is already waiting up there in the bushes," Juan explained. "We'll park outside and go to the south. Then we can ambush them."

"Don't they know that?" Rico suddenly became alarmed at the plan.

Juan's brother and classmates had used the property long before them. They often took excursions to the property on random weekends to drink. Some rumors circulated that the seniors would meet girls there from a local high school.

"No way, Jose," Juan responded to the objection. He laughed. "I heard my brother talk to his friends. They talked about hitting us when we arrive not far from the house. They think we will just park the car and walk straight into the groves."

Rico still had his doubts but the presence of the goggles and Bill's rifle offered him some solace.

"How many shots will that thing fire?" Rico pressed Bill.

Staring out of the window as the scenery changed from post-war tract homes to empty lots and patches of unattended orange groves, Bill seemed to ignore Rico for a moment, and then he turned to look into Rico's eyes with malicious intent.

"Enough," Bill answered with his wide grin and toothy smile. "I estimate at least a thousand."

"Shit!" Rico exclaimed, wondering if he should fear Bill more than the seniors. "Check that they have their goggles on before you shoot."

"Ha!" Juan screamed. "We're gonna burn them."

"Yeah," Bill responded with glee and took his smile to the window and the approaching knolls that introduced the Sisters' property.

They entered the Sisters' property and Juan turned off the engine, letting it coast on the property until it came to a stop. Getting out of the car, they together pushed the small car under the shadow of a large lemon tree. Then, Juan carefully pushed his key into the hatchback lock and twisted it with a small "pop."

"It's so quiet," Rico commented on the eerie silence. "Who would have thought a lock could make so much noise?"

"Shut up," Juan reminded him of the need to be stealthy.

The creaking doorsprings made an unusual squeal as the hatch slowly lifted up to reveal their armaments. Rico and Juan restrained themselves from jumping forward and grabbing Bill's case. The automatic rifle had secretly whetted their appetite to the point where they became almost physically ill with anticipation. Bill stooped to reach for the case and lifted it, slowly pulling the case out of the hatchback.

"Hey?" he paused to ask a grave question. "Who's going to fire the gun?"

Rico and Juan then looked at each other with envy. Wanting to scream "Me!" they barely held back. Any loud noise would have risked their position.

"Who?" Bill called them out of their stalemate.

"Juan," Rico interrupted Juan. "He knows where his brothers and friends will hide out. I'll back him up."

Rico grasped and pulled Juan's rifle out of the hatchback. Bill then gently handed his rifle to Juan. When Rico opened Juan's rifle case, he turned to his friend.

"I'd better get a shot after you," he said with a small chuckle.

Juan's eyes lit up and he nodded " yes," looking down at Bill's case. He felt as if he held the fabled Excalibur, and both Rico and Bill waited to witness the extraction of the sword from the stone. Removing the release and unzipping the case, Juan reached into the case and fumbled around. He then plunged his arm deep into the case.

"What the fuck?" he felt like shouting.

Bill angrily snatched the case away, almost pulling Juan's arm with it.

"What the fuck?" Juan repeated his consternation.

"It's gone," Bill concluded.

"Really?" Rico looked into the open, empty rifle case.

"Goddamn it!" Juan leaped up in the air and slammed his foot down. "Now we'll get our ass kicked."

"Who took it?" Rico thought out loud. Before he could answer, Bill's skeptical eyes confirmed the distant dread he felt welling up in his consciousness. "No."

"No. What?" Juan demanded to be included. Then, the realization of the thief struck him, too. "You're shitting me?"

"That asshole," Rico confirmed their worse fear.

"Tony will fuck everything up to look like Superman," Juan predicted the worst-case scenario. "We better run up the hill."

"Put on the goggles," Bill reminded his friends. "There will be copper-coated BBs everywhere."

"What a dickhead," Juan cursed Tony as he secured his goggles. "I want to shove this up his ass."

Juan held up his rifle as Rico retrieved the pistol.

"I want to grab Bill's gun and empty a clip up his ass," Rico grumbled, gesturing with the pistol in an upward motion.

"We gotta go," Bill pressed his friends.

"Let's go this way," Juan pointed to a new direction, leading his friends away from the rendezvous point where the ambush had been planned. "We gotta grab it from him."

They stealthily moved in a wide circular path on the outskirts of the citrus groves. Rows of orange, grapefruit, and lemon trees covered the property next to narrow irrigation canals that twisted through the lumbering knolls. Their path forced them to jump over the canals instead of paralleling them in long, casual turns beside the mountain. Bill, being less athletic than his friends, fought back the feelings of nausea and cramping calves as he pushed himself up the steep grade.

"I'm too tired," Bill pulled back and stopped.

Rico and Juan moved a couple more yards and noticed that their principal ordnance man has deserted them.

"Come on," Juan urged him. "We're close."

"I can't," Bill refused, taking several long breaths. "Give me a few minutes."

"Come on, Bill," Rico took a step back towards his friend.

Bill held up his hand to ward him off.

"Go straight," Juan moved his hand in a direct motion, like a tomahawk throw. "We'll wait for you at the top."

Bill nodded and waved to them.

They raced ahead for about five minutes when a loud burst of disjointed high air pressure locked them in an irrational paralysis of fear.

"Shit," Juan spoke what they instinctively knew had occurred. "The asshole is already shooting."

"Let's go," Rico slapped Juan on the arm and dashed off, leaving his friend behind.

In an instant, Juan caught up to Rico and another burst of carbon dioxide ripped through the atmosphere, followed by indistinct angry shouts and cursing. Juan and Rico leaped over the last knoll and stumbled on a scene of seniors gathered around another senior who sat holding his face. Their BB rifles lay on the ground, dispersed about the dust and bushes. Juan's brother looked up at the sudden appearance of Rico first and then Juan.

"What the hell?" he yelled at them. Both students held their guns in their hands. "You shot him in the face. He didn't have his goggles on."

Rico saw that a thin stream of blood had begun to trickle out of one of the eyes of the collapsed senior.

"They shot me in the eye," the senior cried repeatedly. "Goddam it. They shot me in the eye."

Rico and Juan cautiously approached the injured senior, but Juan's brother intercepted Juan and grabbed him by the collar.

"What the fuck you thinking?" he shouted threateningly.

"He didn't shoot it," Juan yelled at his brother and pointed at the top of the ridge that overlooked the nuns' convent.

Everyone looked in Juan's direction and then up at the ridge. Tony stood for a brief moment staring at the angry crowd. Disappearing behind the maze of orange and lemon trees, he dropped Bill's rifle and darted into the groves. Bill then appeared and walked up to the rifle and picked it up.

"What the hell is that?" one of the seniors asked.

"My rifle," Bill admitted foolishly, examining its condition before removing the CO_2 container.

"Tony shot it," Juan came to Bill's defense. "Not Bill."

"He's in real trouble," Juan's brother told both Juan and Rico. He quickly turned around and walked over to his injured classmate. "We gotta get him to the hospital."

He carefully lifted the injured student to his feet as one of the nuns came out of the convent carrying some clothes and bandages. All the seniors walked in the direction of the convent, leaving their BB rifles on the ground. A few nuns joined the entourage of students.

"Damn him," Juan cursed as he and Rico walked up to Bill.

Bill fumbled for a moment with his rifle and the sound of a loud hiss told them that the CO_2 had been released.

"He had no right to take it," Bill condemned Tony.

"He's an ass," Rico added angrily. "Now we have to explain things."

"Yeah," Juan said sadly. "I'm going to burn that Tony."

Fortunately, when they returned to the seminary, Rico and Juan discovered that the senior had not lost his eye. The Rector interviewed all three of them, discussing only the facts. He confiscated Bill's rifle. Refusing to answer their questions about Tony's whereabouts, the Monsignor immediately sent them to the dorm. Some students told them that Tony had been called into the Rector's office earlier and then left with his parents before evening prayers. They did not see Tony for a week, but the next day Bill was called into the Rector's office and soon after a brief interview with the Monsignor, the staff voted to expel Bill. Tony returned with a suspension on his record and Bill was never seen again, along with his cutting-edge rifle that became an iconic myth for the rest of Rico and Juan's high school years. As for the Sisters' property, long seminary tradition ended without fanfare. As for the rabbits, they dodged the intemperance of adolescence only to face the imminent overpowering force of suburban development.

Phase 11

Finding himself again in the cafeteria, Rico reached over and tapped Bill, who seemed to be staring obliviously off into the distance, and then shook his arm.

"Hey," Rico shouted. "Come out of it!"

Bill continued to passively remain still like a catatonic patient in a mental ward.

"What the hell is wrong?" he demanded to know from the Clement.

The avatar turned his attention to Rico and spoke in a distant, detached tone.

"I have retrieved his memories," the priest announced. "But there are some lapses."

"Lapses?" Rico wanted a clarification.

Mike and Juan stared at Clement and then at Rico before Bill interrupted their impending questions.

"Lapses," Bill repeated groggily.

Everyone waited, feeling a sense of dread and anxiety.

"What do you mean?" Mike asked slowly.

"Lapses," Bill pronounced the word with more clarity. "Lapses."

He slowly began to move his arms and he then rubbed his face, taking a glass of virtual water and pouring it over his head.

"Really," Juan voiced the irony of Bill's action.

"It does have an effect on memories," Bill scientifically assured him. "I boosted the retrieval sequence."

"What happened to you?" Juan insisted, expressing his fear.

"The same thing that will happen to you," Bill told him. "Our memories are degrading."

Juan stood up and pounded his fist on the table.

"Just like the BB rifle," Juan reminded his friends. "His shit brings us no good."

"He kept your essence alive," Mike pointed out, coming to Bill's defense. "You would have long been dead."

Bill gave Mike a gratuitous smile while Juan sat down, seething at the rebuff.

"I am dead," Juan reminded everyone.

"We all are," Rico added. "What's going on?"

"We're in orbit," Bill began to explain carefully. "I didn't anticipate the effect of gamma and cosmic rays."

"No shit," Juan retorted sarcastically.

"Juan and I have been here longer," he continued to explain. "So I estimate we have faced more degradation. Solar flares add to the degeneration."

"Okay," Rico accepted the explanation. "How much real time to continue on this course?"

Bill remained silent and thought about the answer.

"Hypothetically," he answered with careful judgment. "We could have infinity."

Rico looked askance at Bill, who smiled mischievously.

"But maybe a few millennia would be more accurate," Bill corrected himself.

"4045," the Clement provided the estimate. "Complete amnesia would occur. The process can be reversed if we return to Earth."

"We can't," Bill contradicted the suggestion. "We don't have a reentry vehicle. Anyway, in half that time we will be imbecilic."

"Later we'll burn up!" Juan interrupted and threw his arms up. "Hey, Bill. What happened after you got expelled for popping that kid's eye?"

"He didn't do it," Rico answered irritably for Bill. "You were there. What's gotten into you?"

Bill raised his hand, motioning everyone to calm down.

"I was expelled as you know," Bill proceeded. "Then I went to the local high school. There I met the teacher who changed my life. He later invented the disk drive and I followed him to his new company after graduation. You know the rest."

"So they did you a favor," Juan spoke sarcastically. "Lucky for all of us."

"Are we lucky?" Rico agreed with Juan's negative allusion. "Do we have more of a chance here than down there?"

"Maybe we should have died there," Mike entered into the conversation. "This seemed so unnatural. It even feels sinful."

"Oh, shit," Rico suddenly became angry. "You're going to start some philosophical sophisms about natural and unnatural death. Didn't you think about all of this before Bill took you inside the machine?"

"Yes," Mike said. "But I thought my body would be alive and I could reenter it."

"And what about your soul?" Rico disagreed. "Your soul is here. Isn't it? Or are you realizing that you don't have a soul? Pretty cool to find out that your god doesn't exist and you can be alive without his help. You now need the help of an inanimate, godless machine. What a goof."

"That is a bit disrespectful," Mike responded with resentment.

"Only if it is malicious," Rico offered his explanation. "The facts are evident. We are dead and our memories are in a machine with our personalities intact. So where is the soul? You have an answer for that Bill?"

"Our memories are now fragile," Bill warned them. "We are running out of real time. Both Juan and I are in real trouble. So we better go to the next episode."

"I have to comment on what Juan said," Rico pressed Bill with his resentment. "Your career success caused me to miss my daughter's death."

"No one forced you to come on board," Bill reminded him. "We must continue!"

"Can't we take a break?" Rico demanded with strong resentment. "This is too stressful."

"That's not completely true," Juan retorted, looking at Bill who stared nervously in his direction. "Bill manipulated things to come into play."

"What?" Rico demanded to know the details.

Bill appeared surprised and glared at Juan. Rico tried to speak but Clement unexpectedly interrupted him.

"Let's begin," the avatar commanded.

"No way!" Rico protested. "Stop."

The setting began to dissolve into its next background and Rico could feel his virtual body disintegrate as his consciousness faded into a watery dream.

"I will promise you something," Bill faintly offered Rico as the final conscious moments of the cafeteria ended.

All became black and empty.

Chapter 13

Our remedies oft in ourselves do lie, which we ascribe to heaven.
— William Shakespeare, All's Well That Ends Well

Fear. Rico's greatest fear was surgery. In the summer of his sophomore year, he had been struck down with a fierce fire of pain. The pain erupted on the right side of his abdomen and radiated out to his lower body. It had occurred when he played basketball at a local park with some neighborhood friends on a hot, dry, California July day. His friends chose to play in the intermittent shade of some eucalyptus trees that swayed under the gentle influence of a dying Santa Ana wind. When the shade passed over the small group of players, the temperature would oscillate from 110 degrees Fahrenheit to 80 degrees Fahrenheit and back to 110 degrees, due to the bone-dry conditions of the landscape.

"I'll play guard," Rico volunteered, racing to the west corner of the court and waiting for his opponent to dribble down-court.

His opponent was a red-haired, freckled boy who had a difficult time passing a ball while dribbling. He needed to pause, aim, and pass the ball in three separate movements. Taking advantage of the boy's clumsy skills, Rico waited for the directed pass and slapped the ball out of his hand.

"Hey," the red-haired boy yelled in objection as if Rico had cheated.

His teammates joined him as he rapidly dribbled the ball to the basket, hoping to perform a fast break. Eying his teammate ahead of him, Rico made a slight leap and pushed the ball ahead of him and into the hands of a waiting teammate under the basket. The teammate gripped the ball, took a step, and single dribbled before making a perfect layup, scoring the first two points of the game.

"Hey," Rico mimicked the red-haired boy's squeaky objection and shared a high-five with his scoring teammate.

With a loud slap, Rico ran forward and tried to block the red-haired boy, who attempted to pass the ball to his teammate. The ball bounced past Rico, who made a futile attempt to swat it away. Then as if he had a second thought, Rico followed the ball and the sprinting red-haired player down the court, trying to intercept his opponents before they set up their attack under the basket.

"Shit," Rico shouted and clutched his side, halting his rush forward.

His team, lacking his presence down-court, lost their guard position, allowing their opponents to find an opening field to shoot a ball into the basket.

"Yeah," the proud red-haired boy shouted his victory in Rico's direction.

Looking at Rico at the middle court line the red-haired boy witnessed Rico wincing in pain, falling on the asphalt.

"You hurt?" he shouted to Rico.

Startled, the players all turned around to look at the pain-ridden Rico who failed to get up.

"Rico," a friend shouted. "You sprained the ankle again?"

Rico continued to writhe in pain and several of the players approached him apprehensively.

"You okay?" one player asked.

Rico gripped his right side and motioned towards the painful area with his left hand.

"It hurts too much to get up," he muttered with halting speech.

A player had the foresight to run off and call for help. One of the parents lived nearby, and when he told her she jumped in her car and rushed to the basketball court.

"Rico," the mother spoke to him as he barely managed to sit up. "I am going to take you to the doctor. Do you know your mother or father's phone number?'

Rico told her and the mother spoke to her son who stood a few feet away.

"Go home and call his dad," she told the boy. "I'll be at St. Joseph's in Burbank."

The boy nodded and the other students helped to lift Rico into a Volkswagen Squareback. The short walk became agonizing, but Rico limped along while the mother leaped to the driver's side.

"You come with me," she ordered the boys, who assisted her.

Plopping Rico down on the rear seat, the three boys piled in, with two in the rear and one in the front. Rico held onto his side as the seated position caused a pulsing pain to ripple on and off through his abdomen. The mother started the motor, then rumbled the car into motion and pulled out of the basketball court and across the rocky lawn, finally reaching the asphalt street. The jittery motion of the car, a combination of the stiff suspension and uneven surface, exacerbated Rico's pain. Adding to the discomfort of the ride, the open windows allowed rushing hot desert air into the car. A moan involuntarily erupted from his throat.

"Hang in there, son," the mother comforted him above the whine of the accelerating car. "I think you've got appendicitis."

"What?" Rico asked in disbelief.

"Your appendix," the mother shouted louder now that the car had reached 50 mph and hot air buffeted the interior of the car. "My older son had the same attack years back. He went and called your folks."

"Oh," Rico remarked, letting her explanation soak into his consciousness.

Appendicitis had been a commonly known illness among his peers but Rico never thought it could strike him. Another pulse of pain reminded him that the situation had become real despite his wishful desire to dismiss its presence.

"Ouch," he moaned, waiting for the next fluctuation, coming like a slow tide, to recede from his body. "How?"

"I don't know," the mother told him. "You'll be okay unless it bursts."

"Bursts?" Rico repeated.

"Breaks open," the mother told him. "Don't worry. We'll be in the hospital before that happens."

The car entered the on ramp of the 405 freeway and began a difficult accelerated climb as it struggled to merge with the traffic at 55 mph.

"Bursts," Rico repeated again, using the word in place of the word "ouch."

"I heard you can die?" one of the players commented to the mother.

The mother quickly scowled at him over her shoulder and sent him a meaningful expression of disapproval.

"Only if he stays this way for long time," the mother tried to reassure Rico. "Don't worry."

"It's cool," another player assured Rico. "My cousin had the same thing."

Rico stopped listening to them as the pain began to well up again. The thought of his appendix bursting led him to foresee the possibility of death as a realistic option. Death had never entered into his purview and, as with most teenagers, it had always seemed far off in the distant and vague future, like all other disagreeable realities such as old age and home mortgages.

"It hurts like shit," countered Rico, holding down the area above his appendix.

The mother looked askance into her rear mirror as everyone nervously smiled and snickered in the car. Despite feeling the urge to lecture Rico on the social turpitude of cursing, she did not need to repress her feelings for she could not keep herself from joining the other players with a smile. A few moments later, the VW veered off the 101 freeway and onto the off ramp, where the mother quickly guided the rumbling machine into the hospital's emergency room parking lot. The players instantly helped Rico out of the car and guided him slowly through the parking lot and then through the glass-tinted doors of the emergency room. Stopping in front of a small office cubicle, Rico made the supreme effort, despite another spike of pain, to sit in a fairly worn aluminum and fabric chair in front of the desk. Behind the desk, an over-age Hispanic attendant sat. She seemed preoccupied with a small stack of hospital forms. She looked up at Rico, the mother, and the other players who all squeezed into an area designed for only two people. In the background, behind the desk, Rico could see a small, tightly clothed nun observing him and his friends.

"What is the matter?" the attendant asked impatiently.

Rico tried to speak but could only elicit a moan.

"The boy has appendicitis," the mother blurted out.

"Are you a doctor?" the attendant asked sarcastically.

"I've seen this happen before," the mother retorted irritably. "Maybe he should see a doctor right away?"

Rico continued to moan and twist in his chair. The attendant extracted another form from under her desk and dropped it into the roller of a typewriter on her left side.

"I need name and address," the attendant began, keeping her eyes on the keys.

The mother began to provide the information as the attendant typed the information onto the form, gracefully gliding the carriage back and forth with every new addition of information.

"Insurance?" the attendant demanded, stopping her typing and looking up at the mother.

"I don't know," the mother paused. "I am not the parent."

"I can't accept him without parental permission," the attendant angrily blurted out.

The small outburst caused Rico's pain to again spike.

"Ouch!" he shouted.

The nun who stood in the background came forward and carefully eyed Rico before turning to the attendant.

"Please take the boy to the examination room," she firmly but gently commanded.

The attendant watched her and hesitantly stood up, following the order. Even though her body language told everyone that the nun had broken protocol, she walked out of the office and around to where Rico sat. He studied the nun through the veil of pain and could not place her, despite the familiar grey and white draping of her order. She belonged to his school's religious order of Sisters. Unlike the nuns at the seminary, she wore dark glasses and displayed a stern façade. Recognizing Rico, she broke out with a wide, friendly smile.

"You are a seminarian?" the nun asked. "One of our Sisters teaches at the seminary. I was there and I remember your face from when we were visiting."

Rico nodded happily, feeling some comfort at being recognized, although the recognition did nothing to alleviate the pain.

"His parents should be here soon," the mother explained to the nun.

"Don't worry," the nun assured her as the attendant motioned for Rico to stand up. "We will have the doctor look at…"

Her voice trailed off as she looked over at the typewriter.

"Rico," the nun read his name. "I'll call the Monsignor."

Rico nodded gratefully. He stood up and hobbled painfully, under his friends' support and guidance, to an evaluation room where they laid him on a gurney. The trip resurrected bad memories of his dislocated wrist a couple of years ago. Lying down only aggravated the pain, so Rico instinctively rolled to his good side and pressed on the area, feebly trying to ward off further attacks. Ironically, one of the nurses who had treated him in the past walked into the room. She was a plump, red-haired woman with deep acne scars and bright friendly eyes. Rico remembered her helping the attending doctor finish sealing the cast on his right arm.

"You look familiar," the nurse spoke to Rico after giving him a momentary glance. Her name tag read *Jeanine*. "You were here some time ago, I think.'

"You will soon have your name on one of these rooms," one of players joked.

The other players laughed, and for the first time the nurse noticed them and raised her clipboard, extending it in almost threatening manner.

"All of you must wait outside," she ordered and waved the clipboard at them.

The players smiled at Rico and sauntered away.

"We'll be outside," they told him. "You'll be okay."

One of the players sympathetically patted Rico's shoulder as he left. The nurse kept a careful eye on them until they left. Then, seeing the woman in the room, she smiled and addressed her.

"You can stay with your son," she spoke kindly to the woman.

"I am not his mother," the woman denied. "He was hurt and I drove him here. His parents have been contacted."

"Oh," she said, taken aback. Looking at Rico, she came to a quick decision. "Stay with him then."

The nurse walked over to Rico and looked down at him, focusing on the area where he held himself and where the pain radiated in his abdomen.

"So where does it hurt exactly?" she asked and gently motioned for Rico to roll over on his back. "Let me look."

Rico nervously turned over and winced from the pain. He pointed to the area of the pain.

"Here," he held his hand over his lower right side.

The nurse placed her hand over the area and then took a while to examine him.

"You need to change into a garment," she gently ordered and produced a blue-cotton hospital garment with an open back.

"Can you please wait outside," the nurse asked the mother.

"Sure," the mother agreed reluctantly. "Of course."

"Don't worry," the nurse assured her. "The doctor will be here very soon. He's in good hands."

The mother gave Rico a squeeze on the arm and smiled at him before leaving the room. Drawing the curtain around Rico, the nurse waited for him to change. Rico removed all of his clothes and draped himself in the garment, making a feeble attempt to close the back of the garment with a drawstring. The pain caused him to stop several moments before he continued to cautiously move again. Sensing that he had changed his clothes, the nurse withdrew the curtain and collected his belongings, placing them in a clear bag. She momentarily stepped out of the room, then returned a minute later and bypassed Rico, going directly to a glass cabinet and table in the corner of the room. She stood for a few minutes at a table and manipulated several objects on a tray, then came over to Rico with a vial and syringe. The appearance of the syringe slightly startled Rico but the nurse assured him with a wide smile.

"Don't worry honey," she tried to allay his fear. "This will make you feel better."

Plunging the syringe into the vial, she carefully turned it upside down and withdrew the plunger slowly, allowing the tranquilizing liquid to fill the syringe. Then, reversing her motions, she pulled out the syringe and gently pushed the plunger so some of the fluid ejected out.

"This will make you feel better," the nurse repeated her assurances. "Turn around."

Fearfully complying, Rico painfully turned around and exposed his buttocks to the nurse.

"I'll be quick," the nurse promised.

Using her free left hand, she made a quick probe of his left lower quarter, wiped it with a swab of alcohol and quickly injected the tranquilizer into Rico's flesh. The sharp action caused him to wince at the same time as the nurse slapped a Band-Aid on the wound.

"You'll feel better soon," she spoke confidently. "You can turn around now."

Returning the syringe to another tray, she ambled out of the room, dimming the lights slightly before leaving. Rico sat alone holding his painful side until the ache started to numb. He felt light-headed and the pain gradually retreated into the background of his consciousness as a distant dull ache. The mother entered and seeing him rest, she quietly left. He remained asleep when another hospital official walked into the emergency room pushing a gurney in front of him. The man seemed to be in his forties with slightly graying brown hair, heavy sideburns and a thin mustache above a scarred upper lip.

"I'm taking you for an X-ray," the man explained. "I'm the X-ray technician. We need to see what's wrong inside."

Smiling at Rico, he glided the gurney up to Rico's bed and helped him to slide onto the top of the soft foam mattress. After lifting up the two safety bars, he turned the gurney in the opposite direction and the fluid casters glided Rico towards the hallway.

"It's a short trip," he explained the Rico as he secured the bar.

The mother stood outside and waved to Rico, who barely noticed her as he was whisked away. Manipulating the gurney with dexterity and skill, the technician pushed Rico down the blindingly bright hallway of florescent lights and sterile walls. Gliding over the tan and black linoleum floors, Rico could only catch the view of an occasional solitary examination machine or an abandoned patient in a wheelchair. One sleeping, elderly patient lay on a gurney up against the yellowed molding of the wall that came to a stop by a wide doorway. Taking a wide turn, the technician deftly maneuvered the gurney into a dimly lit room. In the middle, a single steel-gray glass eye, marked with a black crosshair, dangled at the end of a stainless-steel neck of circular steel joints. Below the examining eye rested a long, aluminum table above a cylindrical steel post and gray metal base. A yellow incandescent light shone on the semi-reflective table. The technician manipulated the gurney close to the table and dropped the safety bar.

"Move onto the table," the technician explained to Rico as helped him to slide off the gurney.

With the pain killers masking the effects of his pain, Rico was able to slide onto the table as the technician used his arms like two spatulas to help direct him to the center of the table, right under the square X-ray panel. He then pushed the gurney slightly away and walked to a monolithic lead barrier with a small glass portal that oversaw the large X-ray area. From behind the barrier, the technician turned on a switch and the mechanical glass eye lit up, spotting a beam that cast the crosshair image across Rico's chest. The technician momentarily left the protection of the lead barrier and he walked over to Rico's examination table.

"Move a little to the left," he asked Rico, gently guiding him under the X-ray portal.

The crosshair on the glass plate cast a shadow directly over the area of Rico's pain. Unlike the present situation, the last time Rico knew the cause of his pain – the dislocation of his wrist. It was obvious. Now he remained ignorant and fearful. Anecdotally, appendicitis caused the pain but he still did not know for sure.

"Don't move," the technician ordered as he moved back to the lead barrier. "Hold your breath when I tell you."

The machine began to rumble and a fierce, intense, menacing beam of light shone over Rico's abdomen.

"Hold your breath!" the technician shouted over the rumbling noise.

In an instant, a high-pitched electrical noise whined through the machine like the archaic electrodes in a mad scientist's movie laboratory. The whining hissed for a split second until the glass eye's light dozed off, as if being euthanized.

"Okay," the technician announced, appearing once again from behind the barrier.

He approached Rico and gently rolled him to his side, despite Rico's brief shudder from the pain.

"Sorry," the technician apologized as he adjusted the glass crosshairs. "Don't move."

Lying on his side, Rico began to feel the pain send a throbbing stab through his system. Although the painkiller helped him, the drug now barely masked the pain that emanated from the area and his awkward posture aggravated his painful abdomen.

"Oh," Rico muttered under the overture of whining electrical circuits and the rumbling cathode tube. "Shit, it hurts!"

The technician could not hear him from behind the barrier. And if he did hear Rico, he would have pretended not to hear. A proper X-ray demanded precise positioning and absolute immobility.

"Hold it," he barked the order over the slow crescendo of noise that escaped the electronic build-up.

Pain undulated impatiently under Rico's skin while he made the supreme effort not to move. He did not want to repeat the wait in the same position. When the glass eye flashed and diminished again, the technician exited for the third time and repeated his routine, rotating Rico on his other side. Rico continued to endure the pain for what seemed an eternity. Any objective observer would have simply pointed out to Rico that the X-ray of his right and left side had all been taken within a span of five minutes. But pain and its effects suspended time and space, like a jealous wife catching her husband *in flagrante delicto* – pain's recriminations pounded away without mercy or promise of parole.

"All done," the technician said gleefully.

He leaped away from the barrier and skidded quickly to Rico's table, making a gentle effort to roll Rico onto his back. Despite his conscious effort to be careful, Rico needed to exhale painfully when his body twisted and wiggled itself onto the gurney.

"The doctor will see you in your room after he looks at the pictures," the technician explained in a sudden singsong intonation.

With careful attention, the technician helped Rico completely slide back on the gurney. Rico caught his last glimpse of the glass eye bidding him farewell when the gurney slid away toward the door. He made the same reverse trip to his interim room, and the hallway's inhabitants had not changed since his earlier arrival. The same machines and patients occupied the areas near the walls, where they formed brief interruptions to the smooth flow of gurneys that travelled to and from the emergency room and X-ray facilities.

"Here we are," the technician announced, maneuvering the gurney back to the same place in the emergency room cubby.

Once Rico returned to his hospital bed, he began to drift into a light, amnesiac sleep where he felt awake but detached from the current events. The mother walked in to observe him and then left to wait again in the lounge. Forgetting what had recently transpired, Rico's mind drifted to the basketball game before the pain had hit, and to other basketball games in his past. He remembered both successful shots and layups, including air balls and missed passes.

Drifting in and out of dream-glory games and tragic losses, Rico's mind turned to his parents who were working-class immigrants with little free time to engage or participate in his life. His father worked two jobs and his mother sewed at a local factory that sold generic fashion items to a label company. Then, in a spark of realization, Rico wondered where his parents had been for all of his stay in the emergency room. A small, seething feeling of resentment and anger against his parents, despite the knowledge of their demanding and underpaid existence, entered his consciousness. They remained AWOL. Slowly, Rico began to become aware again of his surroundings, for the pain made a sudden throb, throwing him back into the present moment. The pain medicine began to wear off. Expecting his parents to have arrived, Rico also expected his friends to stay. He looked up and saw no one in his room and a strong feeling of abandonment gripped him.

"You're not alone," a soft, hollow voice told Rico from the darkness.

Looking up, Rico saw no one.

"God is with you," the voice assured him. "He is testing you."

"Testing me?" Rico instinctively answered.

From the dark shadows where the syringe basin rested on the table, a short, middle-aged male nurse appeared like a boat coming out of the fog. At first, only a silhouette could be seen and then the particular details of the person. Finally, the edges and characteristic distinctions of his body materialized. The nurse wore dark, archaic-framed glasses, not worn in a decade, which contrasted against his white, albino features. Although he was not technically an albino, the very fair, nearly white-blond hair, gave the nurse a milky appearance as it complimented his pale and nearly gray skin.

Behind the thick, magnified glasses, the nurse's blue eyes floated like two ocean-rich Earths against a blank cosmic background.

"Yes," he assured Rico with a grimace. "He's testing you."

Rico tried to respond but a sharp pang interrupted his question.

"They are coming to operate on you," he revealed. "Your appendix is going to burst if they don't remove it. This could be potentially life threatening."

A cold dagger of fear and dread eclipsed the thumping pain of his bursting appendix.

"What?" Rico challenged the diagnosis. The thought of dying left him flabbergasted. "How?"

The nurse stepped momentarily back into the shadows and produced an IV bag decanter on a pole. The glass bottle clattered against the stainless pole as it rolled towards Rico's bed.

"Are you ready?" the nurse asked. "These trials are sent to everyone. Medical science helps but you must have faith. Your life is in someone else's hands."

Without an explanation of his next actions, the nurse took an alcohol-soaked cotton ball and rubbed it over a vein near Rico's right elbow. He reached over to the IV and found a needle, poking it into Rico's sterilized skin. Rico winced.

"Take a deep breath," the nurse advised him.

Rico felt the needle plunge into his vein. Observing the process from the side, he watched the blood from his vein being siphoned up the tube that led to the IV bottle. The nurse caught his attention and moved his free hand toward the bottle. Near the nipple of the bottle, two plastic tourniquets allowed the saline solution to enter Rico's vein. The nurse turned the valves to control the speed of the drip.

"This is a saline solution," the nurse explained.

Rico watched his blood retreat as the saline solution began to drip, forcing the blood back into his vein. Within a few moments, the plastic tube cleared. Satisfied with the progress of the IV, the nurse smiled and began to tape the outer area of the needle around Rico's arm so it would not inadvertently slip out.

"Now we don't have to inject you over and over," the nurse added reassuringly. "You won't be bothered again."

From the hallway outside, a loud conversation could be heard and several familiar voices joined in the exchange. The nurse looked up and then returned to the tray where he had found his needle and IV solution. After a brief clattering of instruments against the stainless steel tray, he returned to Rico's bed. The noise outside escalated for a minute and then subsided.

"Be strong and pray," the nurse finally consulted Rico. "The Lord is evaluating your faith. Pray fervently."

"Am I going to die?" Rico muttered feebly, feeling the need to cry washing over him.

"Only God knows," the nurse answered in a cavalier manner. "Pray. Surgery is a very tricky endeavor. Nothing is guaranteed. I'll pray for you. I promise."

He paused, making a silent prayer, then smiled at Rico and quickly stepped out. The lights remained subdued in the room and Rico again lay back on the bed, alone and abandoned. He did not hear the conversations outside, for his thoughts hovered over the image of his body lying in a coffin at a funeral home. He began to pray.

"Hail Mary…" he began but stopped.

Suddenly the idea of praying seemed futile. But he tried again.

"Hail Mary, full of grace," he continued to whisper, wondering if a real rosary would assist him with his concentration.

Suddenly, Rico became aware of the silence. A loud, empty silence greeted his prayers. No matter how he pleaded and prayed, the silence remained.

Then, his parents, the mother, and his friends entered the room with an elderly doctor. The lights returned.

Phase 12

When everyone returned to the cafeteria, the transition froze for a moment in a facsimile of suspended animation. Each avatar, except for Father Clement, remained frozen in virtual time and place, but Rico felt aware and consciousness nevertheless. As quickly as the suspension ensued it instantly passed away into the virtual room of the cafeteria. Everyone except for Rico seemed resigned to the revelation of the storyline—as if the movement between past experience and present virtual existence had become commonplace. Rico looked at Bill with annoyance after dismissing an attempt to vent his anger at the computer's avatar.

"Why, Bill?" Rico demanded to know.

"Why?" Bill responded confusingly. "We talked about this gathering and its purpose."

Rico exhaled loudly and then held his breath for a few seconds.

"No," Rico corrected him. "Let me clarify."

He waited before speaking again. Mike and Juan assumed similar expressions of perplexity, wondering if Rico and they had lost his mental balance.

"Why do I conclude each story in a hospital?" Rico blurted out in frustration. "I am caught in some cycle. My life is more diverse than a couple of stays in the hospital."

"How did the surgery result?" Mike asked sincerely.

"Fine," Rico answered abruptly. "I got better."

"Then it's a motif," Mike added in a casual tone. "An archetype."

"Archetype?" Rico questioned and thought on the subject.

"Yes," Mike confirmed. "You experienced a paradigm shift or a change in your life. Your life took a new direction after this surgery."

"And the last?" Rico referred to the experience of his broken arm.

"It was an important moment for Bill," Mike looked at Bill for confirmation.

"Yes," Bill agreed. "I consciously became aware of my calling when I helped you with your dislocated wrist."

"Okay. Calling?" Rico meditated sarcastically on this event. "Just a coincidence that I went to the hospital."

"I don't think this last one was a coincidence," Mike added didactically. "You had a major life change."

"Yeah, Rico," Juan agreed with a half-smile. "You took a new path."

Rico reflected on the event, and its importance slowly dawned upon him. As the realization formed in his mind, Father Clement became animated and leaned forward.

"God never answered," Rico sarcastically spoke out loud.

"You refused to listen," Mike retorted.

"How?" Rico decided to play along.

"How?" Mike repeated with disdain. "How do you miss the obvious? The joy of life? The rising feelings of love? The hope for tomorrow? These values and human exhilarations can't come from neurological synapses and physical receptors. There must be some spiritual overlay that endows us with these feelings, these ideas and these joys."

"Again," Rico reminded Mike in a calm voice. "By the way . . . nice rhetoric." Rico smiled and paused. Mike ignored him. "First, we are disembodied persons whose memories have been downloaded into a machine. So how are we still able to feel and think? Isn't it obvious that this is all mechanical? Otherwise, what Bill pulled off wouldn't work."

"But this does prove God's existence," Mike continued to explain his argument. "Since we have our memories, God has allowed us to have our souls. Until the machine ends those memories, our souls will be tied to this machine."

"So you are now saying that a computer has a soul?" Rico concluded, giving Bill and Juan and questioning look.

The avatar leaned back and smiled at some private joke.

"You are again being too literal," Mike dismissed Rico's conclusion. He then turned to Bill and Juan. "You are alive for so long because God allows it. But know we can see that we are being called away as our memories are failing."

"There's degeneration," Bill confirmed. "The computer can objectively hold the memories in digital form for an unlimited time. But as I said before, cosmic radiation and other factors are beginning to take their toll on the electrical pathways. The Heisenberg principle is also in effect. There are too many unpredictable elements on the quantum level for the computer to control and manipulate."

"My point," Mike pleasantly chimed into Bill's explanation. "It is all being held up by an outside force. The unseen power allows us to continue to enjoy our sentient ability. When the soul leaves, all the machine will have is fragments of us. It will be like photographs and video. Images without substance."

"That is what we are now," Rico disagreed. "Images without the substance of our bodies! The computer is maintaining a facsimile of our personalities. But the memories are the essence of our minds, not our souls."

"Then we are not alive?" Juan sadly concluded. "We are talking photographs and videos of ourselves?"

"No," Rico disagreed with trepidation. "We are obviously more. But what we are I am not sure. It can be only a reflection of what I once really was in life. A copy of whom I think is alive. If it thinks it is alive, then it is alive. My memories are doing this contorted dance in cyberspace. How would it know the difference, Bill?"

"I don't know," Bill admitted. "But we are talking to one another."

"Copies can't be alive," Mike informed them in a didactic tone. "More is involved here. You admit that there is a problem. I am trying to have you understand that a 'divine more' is operating in the background. There has to be a power beyond the natural."

"It is strange," Juan agreed. "I have my doubts. But Mike makes a point."

"And what is the evidence?" Rico challenged Mike and Juan. "You, the copy, are making an assumption—an inference about itself—and calling itself a soul. This is like a mirror within a mirror. How far back can you go? So when you don't have a clear answer, you have a God as a fallback. The very fact that we are here makes me believe that Bill's machine is more credible in keeping us alive than any god. I have faith in the avatar and Bill."

"Faith?" Mike questioned amusingly. "You used the word."

Rico spontaneously laughed out loud.

"You thought you had me?" Rico chortled. "My faith is not blind. It is based on the proven facts and evidence of engineering and mathematics. Physics is measurable."

"But you still don't know for sure?" Mike continued to challenge. "Do you, Rico?"

Rico paused and thought about Mike's question.

"No," Rico admitted. "I don't know. But I have more facts and probable evidence to go on."

Juan whistled upon hearing Rico's response, and Mike leaned back with a smug expression of victory.

"I don't know. That is the difference between me and you," Rico added. "I don't know and I look for answers. You have the answers before the questions arrive. That isn't knowledge or faith. That is a delusion."

"What?" Mike reacted bitterly.

"You heard me," Rico raised his voice. "You have a conviction, which is based on absolute certainty. There is no doubt in the face of any proof to the contrary."

"My beliefs are based on reason," Mike asserted.

"You're right," Rico countered. "Your reasons, or at least the Church's reason, yet it is not falsifiable because it can't be proven true. If you told me you could fly into the sun and return, it would be a delusion. Yet I can't prove it is not true and you can't prove it's true. But it is a delusion."

"Then how did this universe appear from nothing?" Mike questioned seriously. "Poof! Just like that with an origin."

"There was always something," Rico explained. "But why can't the universe be a god in itself? Why can't all of matter and energy be the uncaused cause of Aristotle and Thomas Aquinas? Isn't that enough?"

Mike remained silent and stared at Rico.

"Well?" Rico pushed for an answer.

Everyone slightly leaned forward, including the avatar, awaiting an answer.

"No," Mike answered slowly. "It's too cold and empty. Too impersonal for me. It is sterile."

Everyone remained silent, especially Rico, who expected a further clarification.

"But is that your true wish?" Mike put forward. "A belief in a cold, sterile and impersonal world?"

"If that is what it is," Rico sadly admitted. "I have no control to change what it is. At least I don't try to make it into what it is not."

"Maybe," Mike partially agreed with Rico's assessment of his own perspective. "But you always will have your doubts, never really knowing?"

"Yes. I don't really know," Rico admitted. He looked at each of them and nodded. "But I won't embrace a pat answer—an illusion that has no evidence. I won't give in to wishful thinking."

"I don't call it wishful thinking," Mike clarified. "I take a leap of faith and hope. Better to take the risk and hope and be right. And if I am wrong, I have nothing to lose. Maybe in the long run, that is what makes us truly human in this machine."

"I wonder what your soul would say," Rico mused, offering Mike a wide, friendly smile.

Mike reflected on his words and then began to laugh. For the first time they both laughed at each other's obstinacy.

"You two will die on a molehill," Juan warned Mike and Rico in good humor. "Especially if it is the last hill in existence."

"Sure," Rico nodded.

Mike agreed with Juan and nodded, too.

"At least we know of our limitations and faults," Mike admitted. "We aren't completely delusional yet."

His comment sparked another round of laughter between the two.

"Faults," the avatar spoke musingly. "We are here to find our faults and our limitations."

Once again, the lights dimmed and the scene began to evaporate. All senses melted away and all sounds began to flicker.

"Oh, shit!" Juan's expletive was the last sound heard before being transported to the next episode.

Chapter 14

I harbor for good and bad, I permit to speak at every hazard,
Nature without check with original energy.
– Walt Whitman, "Song of Myself"

When Juan re-animated, he sat uncomfortably behind an old, gray Underwood typewriter that the seminary had purchased over twenty years ago. All the seminarians sat in strict rows facing a large black and white QWERTY poster in front of a white, antiseptic wall. Loud clanking keys reverberated in the room, creating the impression of a busy office or editorial room before an impending deadline. In May the warm, dry winds brought an early heat wave, and the suffocating air lingered in the stale, stuffy room. Despite the open lattice windows, the temperature continued to slowly rise and smother the seminarians who, after being granted permission, happily removed their black ties. Juan, unlike most seminarians, lacked an affinity for typing on the heavy mechanical keys. Like Juan, the other students propped up their instruction manuals for QWERTY on a small easel. Following the manual and the soft, authoritative words of this instructor, Juan mentally planned the drill of pressing down on the heavy, resistant keys in strict combinations, with the goal of developing his motor skills. He fought hard to avoid looking at the keys, although the temptation perpetually presented itself. Today, in the afternoon class, he practiced the "fff-fjf-jfj-jjj" drills.

"Be sure your hands are on the home row keys. Use the proper finger for each letter and have your wrists flat and your thumbs on the space bar," the instructor reminded the seminarians as they began their drills.

Juan attempted to follow his instructions, but his eyes kept wandering toward the keys and away from the keyboarding manual. He had reached the end of the line and slammed the carriage back when a soft hand touched his shoulder.

"Accuracy is important," the instructor reminded him. "Speed is not important."

Juan looked up and smiled at the young Franciscan Brother who had recently taken his vows. The Brother had an athletic build hidden under his long, black cassock. He possessed a cherubic face with light-brown locks and blue eyes in a soft, pale, peach-fuzzed face. Looking up at the Brother's face, Juan could read in it a kind and patient man who appeared to be not much older than the students whom he taught in the stuffy room. Among the faculty staff, the Brother worked on a part-time basis and only offered typing classes. Occasionally, he would supervise study hall in the evening. Otherwise, outside the seminary, he worked with the juveniles in an outreach program for a local parish.

Rumors had spread that he hoped to land a teaching position the next school year. When the Brother pressed the Monsignor about a full-time teaching position, the Rector could only speculate. Recently, the Monsignor had been vexed that his seniors failed to submit typed research papers in his religion class, and instead they had opted to submit them in longhand. So he pressed the lower classmen and certain seniors to master their typewriting skills and to apply them for all essay assignments. The added demand to their academic studies caused Juan and his classmates, such as Rico, to sweat even more in the already stifling environment. Unlike the students, the Brother remained oddly cool and composed as he taught.

"The true measure of the typist or keyboardist is that he no longer thinks consciously 'I must press my fourth finger of my left hand without moving up or down.'" the Brother explained as if he were reading the typist's thoughts. "He doesn't truly think about it but his finger thinks first and responds automatically."

Juan again looked up at the kind man and smiled. The Brother gently tapped him on the shoulder again and walked away to supervise another student.

"Thank you, Brother," Juan muttered to himself, admiring the Brother's good will.

Continuing the drill, Juan began to feel frustrated. Rico, another failed typist struggling under the Rector's command, sat nearby and seemed to work effortlessly through the drills, occasionally stopping to check his answers. Juan made brief eye contact with Rico and then looked over at his work.

"Stop," the Brother ordered. "Count your words and circle your errors."

Everyone automatically counted their words and within a few seconds, a few shouted triumphantly at their results.

"Hey," one of the seminarians announced. "I got no errors."

"Have," the Brother corrected him. "Congratulations."

The jubilant seminarian ignored the grammatical admonishment and began to share a high-five with his friends. Juan noticed that most of the seminarians, including his friend Rico, seemed pleased with their results. Looking at his count, he realized he would have failed the drill if he had taken a test.

"Now," the Brother instructed. "Open the keyboard book to page 39. You have three minutes."

The Brother extracted a Longines stopwatch from his pocket as he waited for each seminarian to position himself to type. Juan bristled when he heard some unannounced screeching carriages and clanging bells reverberate in the room's close confines. With dread, Juan fixated on the Brother's stopwatch as the heat of the room began to swallow him in its suffocating presence. A small bead of sweat dangled on his forehead and then it dripped suddenly onto his return key. Trembling, Juan tried to remain poised, holding his fingers strategically in place over the circular metal keys.

"Begin," the Brother ordered.

Juan's mind jumped on command but his fingers froze after hitting the first three keystrokes. The Brother walked towards the window near the QWERTY poster and stood in the comfort of a lattice's shadow. His eyes surveyed the room with gentle, spiritual aloofness as if he were conducting a professional orchestra at La Scala. Juan's attention was mindlessly transfixed by the QWERTY poster. Rico looked at Juan's paralysis and became concerned. He momentarily stalled on the keyboard.

"Hey," Rico called to Juan without moving his head. "You okay?"

Juan did not hear him and he continued to stare forward. The Brother seemed to be oblivious to Juan's abstention from the work, looking at the seminarians who pounded hardest on the keys and then at his stopwatch. A sudden feeling of nausea and a very slight tightening of the chest took hold of Juan. He felt a fluctuating rush of warmth flow through his arms and legs, intersecting in his groin area.

"Rico," Juan called to his friend above the clang of the slamming keyboard strikes. "Rico!"

Barely hearing him, Rico slightly turned his head to better listen to his friend's plea.

"It's happening again," Juan spoke embarrassingly.

Juan's allusion to a past event caused an alarm bell to go off in Rico's head.

"Can you stop it?" Rico implored Juan and then abruptly looked up at the QWERTY board, avoiding eye contact with his friend.

The Brother then noticed Juan's distraction.

"I can't," Juan pled for help when the Brother glanced at his stopwatch.

The next feeling came as a volcanic rush. A long, streaming hot rush of heat and energy travelled through Juan's legs and abdomen, meeting in his lower groin before erupting through his penis. The sudden physical sensation paralyzed Juan as an explosion of semen spilled into his pants with thundering impulse. The flow pulsated strongly and slowly as it began to regress as fast as it erupted. The surprise explosion left him wet and angry without providing the complete satisfaction of a pleasurable orgasm.

"It happened!" Juan almost shouted but no one could hear amid the clanging and ringing metal sounds.

Rico stopped to stare perplexedly at his friend.

"Stop!" the Brother commanded above the din, and every typewriter went suddenly silent.

Juan looked at the Brother who reciprocated with a quizzical stare.

"I've gotta go," Juan announced to the Brother and waived a request for permission, rushing out of the typing room.

"When you gotta go," a seminarian sang.

"You gotta go," another seminarian chimed in.

Everyone laughed and even the Brother smiled, believing, like the other students that Juan needed to visit the restroom. Exchanging glances with the bemused Brother, Rico remained still and stupefied.

Phase 13

When the visitation ended, all four ex-seminarians returned alone to the cafeteria. Juan sat isolated at the head table on the platform with the over-sized crucifix hanging over his head. His three classmates were nowhere to be seen, only the avatar sat at the head of the table. The recent experience disturbed him, for no one but Rico knew of his personal weakness. Still, Rico never knew the true cause of the sudden, unpredictable orgasms that plagued him

"Where's everyone?" Juan challenged the avatar.

"They are here," the avatar confirmed.

"I don't see them," Juan looked around.

The avatar remained silent.

"I don't see them!" Juan shouted again.

The avatar continued to remain silent.

Juan looked again and saw the whole, empty cafeteria. Taking one final look at the avatar, he leaped off the platform and walked to the main entrance door. He pushed the aluminum release bar but the door remained lock. Frustrated, Juan turned on the avatar and shouted in his direction.

"What's going on?" Juan asked desperately. "Where's Bill? Rico? Mike?"

"Here," the avatar answered calmly.

"Here," Juan paused to reflect on the avatar's words. "Here but not here with me?"

"Correct," Father Clement conceded. "It is time to reflect."

"You mean accept," Juan corrected Clement. "You bastard!"

Before Clement had an opportunity to respond, the scenery began to morph into a small chapel where Juan sat in a pew facing the chapel altar. Looking around, he again saw no one. If he was being forced to reflect, Juan decided instead to sleep a virtual sleep. He defied the request. He finally accepted who he was. So he lay back on the pew and closed his eyes. His dreams soon took him to his childhood Christmas when he was most happy and free from any sexual distress or judgment.

PART IV

The visitors watched the program play and ran the storage information through their computers after a virtual translation buffer had been made. Despite the clear availability of the satellite's information, human culture and its history remained incomprehensible. All of Earth's science provided them few new scientific innovations except for the unique program left by the unknown human programmer named Bill. Human civilization had gone extinct and alien probes surveyed the surface, returning later to the orbital lab with samples and cultures. As a selected group of alien scientists researched the possibility of occupying Earth, another group of researchers made a startling and puzzling discovery. Their computer had been compromised, but it posed no threat. One specific program, about a reunion that centered on a primitive belief in a godhead, left a fragmented virus that contained more than a ternary program. The inherent code offered the possibility of resurrected human lives. Astonishingly, the unknown human programmer had ingeniously offered the aliens an unusual and unique option.

Phase 14

When Juan awoke, he discovered himself lying on the wet concrete walkway next to the pool in the early morning, soaked to the skin in his shorts and t-shirt. Raising his head, he saw the surface of the water lapping gently against the tiled aqua-green wall where the depth was measured against the interior side of the pool. An unseen breeze seemed to push the water against the upper edge of the pool. Across from Juan's point of view, three wooden lounge chairs rested in front of the aluminum bleachers where students once watched and cheered makeshift water polo games. The lounge chairs remained empty on the concrete as if they had been temporarily abandoned, waiting for their occupants to return and finish their sunbathing. Juan, lifting his head and shoulders and propping himself on his left side, noticed the opaque presence of Bill, Rico, and Mike resting on the reclined chairs. Blinking several times, he pushed himself up and threw his feet into the water, sitting directly in visual line with the bleachers. His feet splashed in the water and he took careful note of the view across from him. His classmates continued to remain opaque and motionless, slowly dissolving into the air. A distant laugh could be heard and then loud thunder clapped the area. Startlingly, a sudden revelation struck Juan in an instant.

"I am the cause," Juan announced in the vanishing virtual reality of Bill's dissolving vision.

Chapter 15

Dream on!
– Aerosmith

The fever began the week before graduation. Mike felt unusually lightheaded in his economics class. With strong will and determination, he repressed the physical symptoms, attributing the lightheadedness to his fasting. It then grew worse on the weekend when he had to unexpectedly stay at the seminary. For months, Mike had wished to purify himself for his first step toward the priesthood. But he could not find the peace he thought he needed to take the next major step toward his priestly vocation. This conflict began when he had privately met with the Rector. An acceptance letter reached the Rector, who called Mike into his office after evening prayers. The summons unsettled Mike, emotionally echoing a previous time when he had had an embarrassing encounter with Father Siemens.

"Mike," the Rector welcomed him from behind his desk.

Normally, the Rector would address seminarians by their surnames and the casual salutation shocked Mike.

"Congratulations," the Rector extended his hand.

Mike tepidly took the Rector's hand and shook it. Feeling the limpness in Mike's grip, the Rector extended his other hand and warmly shook Mike's hand again for what seemed a long time.

"I don't understand?" Mike questioned the Rector as he loosened his grip.

The Rector motioned with his hand for Mike to sit down. Mike skeptically sat down at the Rector's insistence, even though the Rector's amicable gesture confused him. As Mike sat slowly down in a dark, black leather chair with brass rivets along the seam of the chair and its armrest, the Rector continued to smile cordially at him. He then looked down at his black leather blotter and lifted up a folded sheet of onionskin paper. From Mike's perspective, the paper contained a letterhead and a small paragraph below the salutation. On the other side of the paper, Mike could see that the typewriter had left deep indentations in the thin, delicate sheet. Appraising the letter for a moment, the Rector's fingers appeared to almost blend into the paper as if it would melt away between the epidermis of his thumb and forefinger.

"Well," the Rector reflected and sank into his chair. His bright smile had begun to wane. "I called you here to congratulate you."

"You did, Father?" Mike's anxiety began to rise, especially after noticing the portrait of Christ's sacred heart hanging against the wall behind the Rector. A crown of thorns pierced the exposed bleeding heart of Christ for all to witness. "Why? I'm sorry."

"Oh?" the Rector looked directly at him with expectant eyes. "You don't know?"

"No?" Mike uttered automatically.

"Well," the Rector continued contentedly. "We received a letter from the major seminary. Your application was first accepted by the Bishop. We never had a Bishop send a letter of congratulations."

A weak smile cracked on the Rector's face as he handed the letter to Mike. Nervously accepting the letter, Mike read it and noted that His Excellency, the Bishop, had signed the letter, wishing Mike "the Love of Christ's guidance on your journey toward the priesthood."

"Father Siemens was to tell you," the Rector casually added, but then dismissed his explanation. "But never mind! You have the Bishop's blessing. A first among us."

Mike looked up to see the Rector's face beaming with joy, yet all he could see was Father Siemens's proximity as he once tried to touch him inappropriately.

"What do you have to say?" the Rector gently demanded an answer. His tone carried a hint of impatience and threat. "I must answer the Bishop soon since this letter has been addressed to me."

"Yes," Mike agreed, nodding his head and looking up at the beseeching Christ with the tortured and bleeding heart. "I am honored, Father."

The Rector grinned and stood up to once again offer his hand to Mike who shook it with more feeling.

"God bless you," the Rector told him and withdrew his hand. He then placed the letter in an embossed envelope and handed it to Mike.

Lifting his hand up, the Rector made the motion of blessing; Mike bowed his head.

"May the Lord guide you and bless you," the priest finished the sign of the cross.

"Thank you, Father," Mike said gratefully and took the letter in hand.

Leaving the Rector's office, Mike gently closed the door and stood momentarily alone in the hallway. A feeling of abandonment, like the empty, deserted hallway, gripped Mike with terror. His anguish caused him to almost crumple the letter, but an unexpected papercut stopped him.

"Oh," he mumbled out loud and looked at the sliver of blood that oozed from a thin red line on his palm. "My mother will be happy."

Mike tried to console himself about his mother's reception of the good news, especially since the woman often had a novena said for him and made long evening adorations in front of the communion host in the local parish chapel.

"My poor mother," Mike wondered if his mother felt his fear, too.

At first, Mike thought it had been fear that formed an impediment for his soul. He then realized that he suffered again from a bout of doubt. As often as he prayed and sought communion with God, he only heard silence. God seemed to retreat and ever so slightly evaporate from his consciousness as if He were playing a cruel joke. The experience reminded Mike of scenes from Dante's *Inferno* when a condemned soul sought to replenish his thirst in a pool of water, only to have the water retreat from his lips.

"Why, Lord?" Mike asked exasperatingly and repeatedly.

It was the week before his graduation rehearsal. His parents had to leave town to visit his grandmother and he stayed on campus for the weekend, receiving the dispensation to sleep alone in the dormitory for two evenings. Although he stayed alone, the Rector had made sure that Mike found some company among the Sisters in the refectory whom he assisted with the meals for the priests. Otherwise, Mike had the time to reflect and think on his own. But after the Saturday supper, Mike spent some time with Father Aubrey and watched a baseball game. Sports never appealed to Mike but the priest had a kind and gentle nature Mike admired and respected. So he could not refuse the invitation to watch the priest's favorite team.

"I love the Detroit Tigers," Father Aubrey admitted coyly, as if he had violated a code. "Maybe they can win?"

The priest sought his assurance even if it were a white lie.

"Maybe?" Mike agreed and sat back in an old, rusty, folding chair that Aubrey produced from a small storage room in the hallway of the staff quarter.

Satisfied, Aubrey smiled and accepted the tepid concurrence from his pupil. Mike knew baseball well but he watched it halfheartedly. The innings passed quickly and Detroit scored three runs before the sixth inning.

"We're winning!" the priest screeched and stood up, punching the empty air.

He then looked sheepish, expressing embarrassment at his behavior.

"You know," the priest spoke in a somber but proud tone. "The church in Detroit welcomed me as a priest when I first came to America. It was the city of my new home."

Aubrey smiled and unapologetically sat back in his chair, admiring his team. Mike felt a little sorry for him and also amused. But another feeling, more base and physical, began to sluggishly grip him. His lightheaded feeling occasionally passed but, sitting on the chair for an extended period, he felt a strong flush grip his cheeks and temples. The seventh inning arrived and the priest stood up when the organ played.

"The seventh-inning stretch," the priest announced and began to sing. "*Take me out to the ball park. Take me out the…*"

Noticing Mike's emergent malady, the priest's voice sudden fell silent.

"Mike," the priest touched his shoulder. "You don't look so good."

He placed his hand on Mike's forehead and took note of his temperature.

"You are burning up!" he said with alarm.

Mike nudged his head in agreement and leaned back in the chair.

"I should go to bed," Mike concluded. "Sorry, Father."

The priest hesitated and held his hand up to ask Mike to wait.

"I'll be back,' he promised and momentarily left the room.

Mike closed his eyes and felt a heavy dreariness descend on his eyelids, almost taking him into a deep slumber. He began to drift away under the command of the worsening fever, until a grip on the shoulder nudged him back to consciousness.

"Mike," the priest repeated his name. "Mike. Wake up."

Mike looked up at the priest and saw him extend him two white pills.

"Take these aspirins," the priest commanded. "Then go straight to the infirmary and sleep. I'll tell the Monsignor."

Mike reluctantly took the aspirins and stared at them. Then, as he brought them to his mouth, the priest almost shoved a small glass of water in his face.

"Drink," the priest continued to command. "Or it won't go down."

Mike swallowed the pills slowly and then took the glass of water and gulped it down, forcing the aspirins to plunge down his esophagus. Handing the empty glass to the priest, he clicked his tongue several times to remove the vague metallic taste of water from the mineral-clogged pipes. Looking at the TV, he saw that Detroit's opponent had loaded the bases.

"Here," the priest put down the glass and placed his arm under Mike's armpit. "Let me help you."

Mike temporarily let the priest prod him off the chair but, once he managed to teeter on his feet and gain his balance, Mike gently waved the priest away.

"I'll be all right, Father," Mike assured him.

He smiled at the old man and then staggered carefully toward the door. With his back turned to the priest, he could hear a sudden eruption of angst and disappointment blare out of the Aubrey's mouth.

"They got a grand slam!" the priest shouted and then began to stammer in an incomprehensible mixture of English and Polish. Mike tried to take a look back but the weighty burden of the fever made it too difficult. With some effort, he opened the door and stepped out of the priest's apartment. Once outside, Mike made the long sojourn to the infirmary almost fifty yards away. Normally, the walk would take a few minutes, yet he felt the weight of draining fatigue in his head slip like sand down into his gullet and torso, coming to rest in his thighs and calves. When the fatigue reached his feet, he froze, incapable of moving forward.

"God," he muttered, his eyes becoming teary from frustration and weariness. "I'm so sick."

So instead of lifting his foot, Mike instinctively shoved his foot forward and began to move like the ridiculous caricature of a skier sliding along a cross-country snow track. Reaching the stairs, he stumbled one foot at a time down the dark stairwell until he collapsed at the bottom. Lying for a moment at the bottom of the stairwell, Mike let himself drift off into a long nap. A black hole swallowed up his consciousness until he abruptly opened his eyes on the infirmary bed. He lay under the clean white sheets of his bed, and his clothes had been removed down to his undershorts. A film of perspiration caused the sheets and pillowcase to cling to his skin.

"You have a high fever," Father Siemens declared, removing a thermometer from Mike's armpit. "Take these."

Mike tried to focus and then saw Siemens standing next to Brother Pat, who held a glass of water and a pill.

"Penicillin," the Brother explained.

Mike lifted his head with effort. Noticing his struggle, Siemens placed his hand under Mike's neck for support. Mike let the Brother drop the pill onto his tongue and he took a sip of water, which passed over the penicillin that had lodged itself on the roof of his mouth. With almost supreme effort, Mike managed to swallow the pill. Siemens then allowed Mike to drop gently back onto the pillow.

"My friend will come and see you," Brother Pat promised. "Doctor Shoup."

Mike half listened to the Brother's words, which faintly registered in his mind.

"Doctor?" Mike asked skeptically.

"We called your parents and they are out of town," Siemens expressed his concern. "So we need to have the doctor see you."

"Thank you," Mike mumbled his gratitude, tasting the trace of penicillin in his mouth. "When is he coming?"

"Soon," the Brother assured him, offering Mike more water.

Mike took another sip from the Brother who used his free hand to lift his head up. Not noticing the departure of the clergy, Mike immediately drifted into a hallucinatory sleep that carried him from the chapel and the confessional. At times he listened to the music of Bach that emanated from his fingers and feet as he furiously pumped air into the apparatus, producing a glorious strand of classical sound that carried him into a state of bliss. As the music ascended through the choir loft and into the stratosphere above the chapel, Mike not only followed the tunes but he witnessed them. In an inexplicable event that defied any rational explanation, Mike could see the music as a visual event that nearly eclipsed the sonorous rapture it produced in his mind and heart.

"I did, Father," Mike confessed to his Spiritual Director in a confessional box. "I did see the music."

The unfamiliar priest remained silent and unengaged behind the thick, red velvet screen that separated him from the penitent.

"Father?" Mike pressed. "How can this be?"

The priest cleared his throat before he spoke.

"It is a miracle," the priest hastily concluded. "You must say three Hail…"

"No," Mike anxiously cut him off. "How can I see and not believe?"

The priest remained aloof.

"Do you hear me, Father?" Mike began to feel a sense of panic. "I can't hear God. There's only the music."

Again, the priest cleared this throat.

"God can speak to us in many ways," the priest responded with a pat cliché. "You must have the ears to listen better. Closer."

"But I can hear," Mike asserted, confused. "The music is beautiful but empty."

"If it comes from God," the priest speculated, "how can it be empty?"

"I need assurances," Mike tried to clarify. "Music can only carry me so far."

The priest once again fell silent.

"Father," Mike demanded. "Why don't you respond?"

The priest cleared his throat loudly.

"I have," the priest assured him in a low, muted whisper. "You don't listen."

The last words startled Mike who opened his fever-encrusted eyes to see Juan hovering above him.

"Mike?" Juan called to him as he shook his shoulder. "You're having a bad dream. We're back from the weekend."

Mike stared at Juan, not knowing if he was in a dream.

"You were here all day," Juan explained. "The Rector gave me permission to visit. Everyone asked for you in class."

"Class?" Mike inquired.

Juan thought for a moment and then continued.

"It's Monday," Juan explained. "We graduate on Thursday. The doctor's been here a couple of times. He says you have a bad fever. How do you feel?" Juan anxiously waited for his answer. "They tell me you hardly ate," Juan added. "You only slept. A doctor saw you."

Mike remained silent and Juan continued speaking, unable to govern his anxiety.

"Do you want some water?" he continued, spying a prescription bottle next to a tray. "You took some penicillin."

Mike listened silently, trying to understand how the last two days had elapsed.

"God doesn't answer," Mike mumbled. "But I hear the music."

They both remained silent. Before Juan could speak, Mike made a declaration.

"I'm so hot," he complained.

Juan poured Mike a glass of water from a dented steel pitcher on a nearby table. Mike accepted the drink and took several long, heavy gulps before tilting his head back onto the pillow. Looking around, Juan could not find any other student in the infirmary. It was once a dormitory that had been arbitrarily converted into a recovery center for sick students. The infirmary was empty except for the two rows of ten beds. Mike's bed rested near the communal sink area tiles with small, yellowing porcelain surrounding discolored chrome pedestals that supported the sinks. Above the sinks, a line of mirrors paralleled the wall, sandwiching a six-inch crevice between the mirrors and sinks where seminarians temporarily deposited their toiletries. Juan took the pitcher, emptied it, and filled it under the sink faucet with cool water. Walking away from the sink area, Juan discovered Mike resting in a bath of sunlight shining through the glass windows above him. A yellowed linen sheet covered him and, functioning as a hot house, increased the June heat to an uncomfortable temperature. Gazing up, Juan walked toward the horizontal blinds and adjusted them so that the intense sunshine bounced off the ceiling tiles.

"I fixed the blind," Juan told Mike, noticing some perspiration on his forehead. "You want some more water?"

"No," Mike shook his head.

Making a careful examination of his classmate, Juan noticed Mike's parched and cracked lips. He then picked up the medicine, examined it contents, and showed it to Mike.

"Did you take any of these?" Juan asked uneasily. "It's full."

Mike stared at the bottle and shook his head.

"I don't know," Mike answered.

"Where're your parents?" Juan pried further.

"Gone," Mike muttered as if he needed to push the words out of his cracked lips.

Extracting a pill from the bottle, Juan placed it between his fingers and poured another glass of cool water for his classmate.

"Take this," he insisted.

Mike wanted to object but he allowed Juan to force the pill through his lips. Then, Juan once again lifted his head and offered him some water. Mike took only a small gulp of water.

"OK," Mike spoke the word with more clarity.

Juan placed the glass of water on the tray near the bed and then sat on the bed, within close speaking distance of his friend.

"Mike," Juan confessed. "I really need to talk to someone. I can't talk to a priest."

Mike listened to him but he could only grasp the words as if they had been communicated from a distant loudspeaker in the middle of a boisterous football game.

"Can you understand?" Juan demanded, nudging Mike's arm.

Mike thought for a while as he processed Juan's words. He then nodded slowly.

"See," Juan began faltering. "I have these feeling. My brothers don't understand. I don't know what will happen after graduation."

Mike listened but he could not string Juan's words together.

"What?" Mike asked, confused.

Juan paused to study his friend and then a feeling of panic caught him. He tightly gripped Mike's forearm.

"Mike!" Juan raised his voice an octave. "I have to tell someone. No one wants to listen."

"Listen," Mike repeated. "God doesn't listen. I only hear the music."

Juan released Mike's forearm and stood up.

"You don't want to hear me either?" Juan spoke accusingly.

Mike lost contact with Juan as his mind wandered away. He suddenly slept again. A sudden, low, baritone voice bellowed in their direction, startling Juan enough to jump away from Mike's bed.

"What are you doing here, young man?" the Rector shouted at Juan.

Juan nervously looked up at the Rector, stunned and confused. The Rector faced him down. Behind the Rector, stood a thin, rakish man sporting a light-colored, checked sports jacket, dark trousers, and white patent-leather shoes with a brass buckle. He held a medical-style, black, alligator bag in his gnarled right hand. He wore light-framed spectacles and his salt-and-pepper hair had been greased back. Behind the spectacles, his light eyes expressed an avuncular tolerance. He was around sixty years of age. He was the doctor who had prescribed the penicillin to Mike.

"I am visiting," Juan stated the obvious, feeling a slight rush of resentment. "I was told I could visit. Siemens said so."

The Rector stared at him as the doctor smiled at Juan and ambled straight to Mike's bedside. He removed his stethoscope and began to examine his sick patient.

"Uh," the Rector tried to amend his reaction after forgetting what the Spiritual Director had told him. "He is ill and needs his rest."

Waving his hand aside, the Rector dismissed Juan. The gesticulation was for Juan to heed.

"Go back to recreation," he directed Juan.

Juan ignored the Rector and watched the doctor begin to take Mike's blood pressure.

"Will he be okay?" Juan asked the doctor.

The Rector approached Juan and positioned himself between the bed and Mike.

"He'll be fine," the doctor said, as he stopped pumping the blood pressure device.

The Rector looked surprised and cast a quick glance in his direction.

"Please," the Rector placed his hand on Juan's shoulder. "He's in good hands."

The doctor continued to look at Juan, smiling warmly and assuredly. Juan conceded and bowed his head. Taking one more look at Mike, Juan disappointedly walked away and exited the dormitory. The Rector's eyes followed Juan out and he then turned his attention to the doctor and student.

"How is he?" the Rector expressed his skepticism at the doctor's last comments.

The doctor momentarily ignored the Rector as he studied the blood pressure meter while using his stethoscope. When the air sack deflated, he carefully unwrapped the cuff and gently placed the apparatus in his black bag. Taking a brief look at Mike, the doctor began to read his pulse while placing a thermometer under Mike's armpit.

"This young man is out of the woods," he spoke absentmindedly. He then removed the thermometer and read the red line of mercury. "He's fortunate for now. The fever broke."

The doctor placed the thermometer in his bag and deftly removed the stethoscope from his neck.

"Have you reached his parents?" the doctor asked, standing up and picking up the penicillin bottle. "He is not taking all of them."

The Rector looked confusedly at the bottle and then tried to speak before the doctor interrupted him.

"Someone has to follow up every four to six hours," the doctor advised seriously.

As the doctor placed the bottle of pills down, the Rector nervously coughed.

"I," he began to stammer. "I…I will follow up. One of the Sisters can come here."

"The parents," the doctor again gently prodded, offering the Rector a conciliatory smile.

"Yes," the Rector remembered. "They have been made aware. I assured them Michael was improving. They should be in town in a day or so."

The doctor incredulously watched the Rector.

"They can't come now," the Rector clarified as if he served as the family's attorney. "The grandmother is suffering from cancer. It's in the last stages."

"Okay," the doctor reluctantly accepting the explanation and picking up his black bag. "I will be here tomorrow?"

"Yes," the Rector solemnly welcomed the follow-up visit. "Thank you, Doctor."

The Rector then extended his hand and the doctor shook it limply. Taking another look at his patient, the doctor instinctively touched Mike's foot. Mike made an involuntary moan and turned his head to the side.

"He may have bad dreams or hallucinations. The fever could return," the doctor warned. "But it will pass. Do you know if he sleepwalks?"

"Pardon?" the Rector had been taken aback, distrustfully staring at the doctor. "No?"

"It's a remote possibility," the doctor noted. "I've seen it. He's strong and should be on his feet in a couple of days. Make sure he drinks plenty of water."

"Thank you," the Rector impatiently repeated, stepping aside for the doctor to pass.

The doctor took one more look at Mike and then slid past the Rector, not waiting for an escort to the exit. His arm slightly swung the alligator bag like a groaning pendulum. The Rector followed a few measured feet behind the doctor's footsteps, staying clear of the swinging bag. Once they stepped out of the dormitory, Juan peered into the dormitory from the opposite entrance door. Slyly sliding into the sink area, he momentarily watched Mike before reaching the bed. Crouching down by his bedside, in order not to be immediately seen if the Rector should return with the doctor, Juan touched Mike's leg.

"Hey, Mike," he tried to wake his classmate.

Mike moved his head aside but made no expression of awareness.

"I gotta tell you," Juan pled for understanding. "I don't want to go on this night trip."

The word "trip" caused Mike to stir and he appeared to focus his blank eyes in Juan's direction. Juan took his apparent response as approval to continue.

"They want to go to the beach," Juan blurted in a loud whisper. "I don't want to go. If I'm caught, I can't face my parents and tell them I won't graduate. The Rector threatened all of us if we do anything stupid."

Juan stopped to observe Mike.

"I also have something else I need to talk about," Juan mentioned sheepishly. "I need to get it off my chest."

"Chest," Mike repeated incoherently, giving Juan a brief respite of hope.

The moment quickly passed as a distant opening door rattled under the heavy weight of a steel lattice. Juan looked up and saw the silhouette of one of the nuns from the cafeteria. Angry and frightened, he hopped in a low stance, like a toad, until reaching the door in the sink area. At the same moment, the nun entered the dormitory and sternly marched towards Mike's bed. Removing a thermometer from her sleeve, she shook it before forcing it into Mike's mouth. Then, unsuspectingly, she turned to look in Juan's direction. At the same moment, Juan disappeared into the hallway and left the building through the north dormitory, never to return. Hearing Juan's galloping footsteps, the nun followed them into the hallway but failed to catch any glimpse of Juan. Returning to Mike, she extracted the thermometer, holding it up against a sliver of leaking sunlight that managed to avoid the ceiling tiles.

"The doctor is right," the nun approved smugly, placing the thermometer back in its case. "We'll get you well for graduation."

"Chest," Mike repeated Juan's words.

The nun listened to him and she kindly placed her hands on his forehead. She then made a little prayer, repeating an *Ave Maria*.

"Rest," she spoke to him. "I will bring you food. The sisters made some pesto soup."

Checking the water in the pitcher, the nun decided to dump the water and replace it. She then departed the dormitory with alacrity.

"Chest," Mike spoke again.

The sunlight had begun to shrink when the nun returned later and took his temperature again. Satisfied, she managed to give him some water and medicine but Mike did not respond to any attempt to be fed. She put the soup bowl down and covered it on the bed stand beside him. Frustrated but not conquered, she stood up and made a pronouncement.

"We'll have you eat the comida," she willfully predicted.

Then, as in the late afternoon, the nun marched back to her retreat house. When Mike was alone, seminarians would peer intermittently through the infirmary's lattice windows, leaving once they saw Mike in his incapacitated state.

"Chest," Mike stammered and opened his eyes.

It was evening. After a long day, the urge to urinate forced Mike to stand up. Sleepwalking, he visited the restroom. Walking barefoot, he stumbled out of his bed and passed the sinks. His movement contained no conscious thought as he stood in front of a urinal and relieved himself.

"Chest," he thought repeatedly.

Although his primordial need to urinate motivated his body to leave the security of his bed, in his mind, Mike saw himself examining a steamer trunk that rattled and shook. Leather bindings wrapped themselves around the beachwood trunk that rested on four scuffed brass knobs that dotted every corner. The trunk displayed traveling stickers from many destinations. Something alive, in the trunk, fought to escape. Mike tugged at the old padlock, pulling and pulling to open it without success. Then, making one final effort, he pulled hard and the lock gave way. Astonished, he began to hear music. Unknown music that carried a familiar motif wafted through the air and captured his attention, filling him with delight and peace. An impulsive need to cry came upon him.

"God," he exclaimed as tears of joy flowed down his cheeks, dripping onto the tiled bathroom floor.

He had discovered unknown music. Bach's rediscovered music perforated his senses.

"God hears me," Mike rejoiced.

He wiped the tears and sat blissfully, observing the music leak like a syrupy fluid from the steamer as it dissipated into the air. With open arms, he embraced the baubles of notes that frolicked about him.

Mike murmured again. "Bach?"

He followed the trunk as it ascended in front of him and levitated toward the hallway corridor. Enchanted, Mike devoutly pursued the trunk through the abandoned corridor and then through the exit. At the time, the seminarians sat in the chapel for evening prayers. No one saw him. Once outside, the trunk moved effortlessly across the service road that wound around the outer C and D dorms. The night air held a faint hint of summer and the fragrance of jasmine filled the environment with pockets of aroma. Around the bend of the road, the gleam of small floodlights cut across the nearby cemetery and cast elongated shadows of the Italian pines against the dormitory's wall. In front of Mike, the trunk took a detour over the grassy area between the road and the pathway for the Stations of the Cross that ran parallel to the cemetery wall. Although it was early evening, the automatic sprinkler had earlier created a spongy grass surface where Mike's feet sank, leaving random broken blades of grass on his heels and pajama cuffs. At the end of the grassy area stood a stony grotto that housed a statue of Our Lady of Guadalupe. The mysterious trunk landed at the statue's feet. It continued to play long tracks of groundbreaking music.

"The trunk," Mike spoke forthrightly. "I hear Bach's music."

Mike had the instantaneous revelation that the music belonged to Bach even though no other human had ever enjoyed its lost notes.

"Blessed Mother," Mike exclaimed. "You sent me the master's lost music."

Feeling an eruption of joy, Mike began to cry and sing, humming and praying in concert with the music.

"It's so beautiful," Mike praised the Madonna, genuflecting in front of the trunk and grotto, and waving his arms in synchronous motion with the music.

In the distance, Juan sat in the passenger seat of the 1968 Chevelle that drove slowly across the service road on its way to meet illicitly with other classmates at Zuma beach. When Juan saw Mike, he thought about pointing him out to Rick, but he remained silent. Juan's silence would be a fatal decision as they drove off.

After a long while, the music carried over into Mike's dreams and he fell asleep on the wet grass. In his dreams, he saw himself rewriting the lost sheets of Bach's music. The sheets he handled in his dream had been used after the maestro's death to wrap fish and plug chinks in walls. Mike stayed in the same place until later in the evening. The nun had gone to give Mike his medicine and has discovered his empty bed.

The school began its search soon after the nun's report, but it took a half an hour to find Mike in the grotto area. As Mike dreamed a blissful vision, the Rector and several seminarians found him lying prostrate on the grass, soaking up the grass's soapy water.

"Wake him," the Rector sternly ordered, looking relieved at having found Mike.

"What?" Mike shouted angrily when the seminarians tugged his arms. He automatically opened his eyes and sat up. He then looked around in the darkness where the eerie shadows of trees and bushes continued to move from side to side in a small breeze. His fever had completely broken.

"Are you okay?" the Rector demanded.

Squinting at the Rector, Mike turned his head toward the grotto. The trunk was missing.

"Did you see it?" Mike began to panic. "Could you hear it?"

"Hear? What?" the Rector answered skeptically looking around. "Son. Your parents are on their way."

"Oh," Mike moaned, ignoring the news. "Father. My music is gone."

He then fell back onto the grass and peered anxiously at the doting Madonna, witnessing only her absolute silence.

Phase 15

Rico watched Mike stare stoically at the large crucifix of a bloody Jesus hanging over the avatar. Both Bill and Juan were absent.

"You lost the music?" Rico probed.

Mike spoke without turning his head.

"I was given the music," Mike explained reluctantly. "A temporary gift."

"Gift?" Rico questioned and looked at the humiliated Son of God above Clement. "So why was this gift taken?"

Mike turned to look accusingly at Rico.

"You think I was punished?" Mike challenged him.

Rico leaned back and counted to ten before giving Mike his answer. An escalating feeling of anxiety began to grip Mike.

"If I did," Rico carefully explained, "I would have to first believe that God existed and cared enough to torture you."

"Oh," Mike groaned, his anxiety mounting. "You think it's all in my head."

Rico wanted to answer affirmatively but he waited. Mike looked up at the crucifix for a moment and then back at Rico.

"I did receive the music," Mike insisted, glaring into Rico's eyes. "You see, I believe in it. I have faith still after the years of silence. You and your secularism can't accept the truth."

"I can't argue that you believe you heard Bach's lost music," Rico conceded. "But you can't prove the non-falsifiable."

"I don't want to have another endless and useless argument," Mike dismissed the debate. He looked away. "You cannot understand the sublime epiphany of listening to divine music. I won't give in. I am waiting for it to come again. Most likely God will give it back when I pass on...from this computer."

"Anything is possible," Rico mused hypothetically. Mike, doubtful of Rico's sincerity, turned to face him. "Technically, we are dead. And you did remember hearing the music again after so many years, right? Aren't we two virtual memories speaking to each other in a silicon chip?"

Mike thought about his words and then laughed. Rico joined him for a moment.

"When I see Bill," Mike opined, "I will tell him to end all this for me. I've had enough."

Rico listened and thought about his classmate's feelings on the issue.

"He actually might," Rico responded. "I think this is supposed to end. Maybe we are getting there."

Mike turned around, startled that Rico had come to such a conclusion.

"So let that argument go for now," Rico offered a truce. "I want to know about Juan."

"Juan?" Mike remembered his involvement in the last computer reenactment. "He played a strange role in my memories. He had some urgent need to speak to me."

"Yes," Rico agreed. "You also notice that Juan and Bill are gone?"

Mike looked around to see only the avatar and the crucifix. The rest of the cafeteria melded into an amorphous gray bank of mist.

"Juan is the lynchpin," Rico revealed his insight. "He tried to tell you something that you missed before his accident."

"He did try," Mike recalled, again looking around for Juan in the virtual cafeteria.

"Somehow," Rico continued as he looked up at the avatar. "We need to uncover the truth. Bill might know but can't say. And Juan definitely won't say. Who knows? They have been in this machine so long that their memories could have been corrupted. Orbiting in space and being exposed to radiation could exacerbate the situation. I have no answer."

Mike looked at the avatar, who suddenly appeared interested.

"Maybe Bill and Juan need us and our memories," Mike concurred. "We have to uncover this truth. But they can't ask us directly? Or maybe Juan just needs to remember? It could be that simple."

"They could just take it out of the memory drive," Rico surmised. "We are expendable in a sense."

"Maybe the memory is tied to an innate human truth that a computer can't extrapolate," Mike wondered, looking up at the crucifix.

"Truth," Rico ironically repeated. "I don't want us to seem as sophistic as Pontius Pilate."

Mike looked away from the crucifix and back at the Rico.

"You make a valid point," Mike agreed. "But the truth is more tied to our humanity than we are led to believe."

Mike once again made eye contact with Rico.

"I am surprised you didn't say God," Rico teased him.

Mike smiled as if to say he would have mentioned God if not for Rico.

"I think I know where this is headed," Rico confirmed. "Juan needs his truth. We really don't. That is why Bill has us here."

"Then," the avatar interrupted Rico.

Both men looked up at Clement's stern but compassionate expression.

"Let us begin to find the truth," the avatar announced.

"I don't look forward to this," Rico told Mike, "because I have an idea where it's going."

"Do you?" Mike managed to ask before the cafeteria dissolved, replaced by a California paradise.

Chapter 16

Let's go back to Zuma Beach.
– *Rolling Stones, "Some Girls"*

A few hours after evening prayers, Juan and Rico clandestinely drove out of the carport behind the grotto. Juan could see the silhouette of Mike on the lawn, but he did not tell Rico.

"Let's get the hell away," Juan demanded of his friend.

As in the past, when they reached the administration offices, they turned off the engine. The car needed to be set in neutral and pushed along the service road before reaching the main boulevard in front of the old mission. There, under the facsimile of Father Junípero Serra's arch, they started the engine of the 1968 Chevelle and eased onto the near-empty Mission Boulevard before accelerating toward the San Diego Freeway's south exit. Out of the darkness, from behind them, a 1964 Ford Falcon followed close by. Building momentum, the Chevelle darted up the gradual incline of the freeway entrance until it reached the acceptable speed of 65 mph. The Falcon chased them with little effort.

"Hey," Juan noticed the speedometer reaching 70 mph. "We don't need a ticket."

Rico looked up at his rear view mirror and then at the speedometer.

"Tom is closing," Rico explained with a smirk. "I gotta swap the engine in this car. A bigger V8 like a 350 would be cool! This car is a dog."

Juan looked around and saw that the Falcon rode on Rico's blind side. Its creamy yellow lights glowed weekly, barely casting a dim beam ahead.

"We talked earlier," Rico yielded as the Chevelle began to slow to 60 mph.

Looking at the Falcon again, Juan snickered nervously.

"Tom's car is fast," Juan spoke the obvious.

"If they challenge us," Rico spoke candidly. "We won't keep up."

"So we brought all of the supplies?" Juan asked, taking a peek behind the seat.

Rico slightly turned his head and then took a quick glance at Juan.

"We got all the supplies and more in the trunk," Rico admitted. "Tom has stuff, too."

Juan then noticed a Highway Patrol motorcycle deftly passing them, weaving from the far left to the right lane.

"The beer is in the trunk?' Juan asked nervously.

"Yeah," Rico assured him. "They have stuff too, like I said. Why in the hell are you so nervous?"

Juan looked at Rico and then straight ahead, watching the Highway Patrolman veer off the freeway and onto the exit.

"Is it your problem? The shit about the typing room?" Rico pressed. "About your weird dreams? Dude, they're just dreams."

"Nothing," Juan lied weakly. "Forget it."

Rico looked doubtfully at him and waited. Then he turned on the radio to AM 98, the top-40-hits station.

"It's The Real Don Steele," the DJ screamed through the two crackling and anemic dashboard speakers.

The radio began playing Jethro Tull's "Bungle in the Jungle."

"It's Mike," Juan sheepishly admitted.

"What about Mike?" Rico snapped back, his attention interrupted. "He's getting better, right? Or is he sick again?"

"He's been sick for a while," Juan reminded Rico. "But he's better."

Rico nodded and his body slightly moved with the music.

Let's bungle in the jungle
Well, that's all right by me
I'm a tiger when I want love
But I'm a snake if we disagree

"Didn't you notice?" Juan confronted Rico.

"Notice what?" Rico began to sound irritated.

I'll write on your tombstone, I thank you for dinner
This game that we animals play is a winner

"Shit," Juan said disgustedly.

He looked over to his right and saw his raucous classmates, Tom and Chris, waving their arms and holding up beer bottles.

"They're drinking," Juan pointed out. "Fucking idiots!"

Rico glanced at Juan who pointed to the Falcon. Rico did a casual double-take.

"Shit," Rico yelled, waving his hand at the Falcon and slamming his steering wheel.

"You're not paying attention," Juan clarified, sighing and leaning back in his seat.

Rico skeptically squinted at Juan and shook his head.

"Those guys will screw things up," Rico predicted. He raised the volume on the radio as if to drown out his prediction.

The song had ended and Juan reached out to lower the volume before a new one began.

"What the hell," Rico protested, reaching out to raise the volume again. "We're already kind of fucked. Leaving the seminary at night. Big no-no!"

Rico cynically laughed alone at the absurd irony of their situation. Beer would be the least of their problems.

"I am trying to tell you something," Juan pleaded.

Rico let go of the volume button and waited for Juan.

"You were saying something about Mike?" Rico broke the silence.

Juan began to talk but Rico interrupted him again.

"Dude! Relax!" Rico exclaimed.

He turned up the volume as another song began to play. Rico wanted to block out the seminary and its affairs. Juan resigned himself to the situation and leaned against the window, allowing his head to rest on the pane. The radio began to play Led Zeppelin's "Stairway to Heaven."

"Shit," Rico cursed angrily. "Such a fucking long song."

"I like it," Juan meekly protested, sliding back in his seat.

Rico reluctantly acquiesced to the inevitable and let the music continue to play over the paper-thin speakers.

There's a lady who's sure all that glitters is gold
And she's buying a stairway to heaven
When she gets there she knows, if the stores are all closed
With a word she can get what she came for
Ooh, ooh, and she's buying a stairway to heaven

"It's beautiful, man," Juan concluded, as he closed his eyes and silently began to lip sync to the music.

"Yeah," Rico reluctantly agreed, holding out hope that a more energizing song would soon follow the long ballad.

Within a few minutes of leaving the seminary, Rico and his companions in the Falcon reached the 405 Freeway interchange and veered northwest on the Ventura Freeway towards Kanan Dume Drive in Agoura Hills. Cutting across the San Fernando Valley, Rico's car ascended up the grade, overseeing the Balboa Recreation Parks area. From his vantage point, he witnessed the carpet of street and residential lights shining in every direction to the north and west where they ascended to the Santa Susana Rocky Peak Park. On the south side of the car, the lights climbed and clawed in a patchwork up the Santa Monica Mountains, where the rich and famous resided in comfortable segregation from the working class below. Directly in front of him, the lights melded into a beam as the traffic bottlenecked on its approach towards Calabasas.

"I love driving through the hills," Rico commented, trying to break the silence.

Juan remained silent as he stared out the window, looking north toward the Susana Pass.

"Hmm," he grunted.

Rico disappointedly glanced at him and continued to initiate conversation.

"You know some girls could come by," Rico announced in an optimistic and cheery tone.

Juan looked away from the pass and examined Rico's wide, youthful grin.

"Tom promised," Rico said doubtfully.

"Really? You believe that bullshitter?" Juan dismissed the idea and sank back into his long stare out the window.

"Right," Rico allowed his friend to retreat into himself.

He watched Juan turn his head away and decided not to engage him any further. Juan's homoerotic dreams had haunted him for months despite his private assertion that he was straight. Juan privately claimed that no one but Rico knew about his secret demons. As in the past, Rico buried the thoughts and tucked them away in his forgotten memory files. In the seminary, students quickly learned to ignore uncomfortable subjects. They were the masters of denial.

Rico then took a look in his mirror to see if the Falcon continued to follow him. Satisfied that his classmates remained close behind him, Rico drove directly west into the city of Calabasas. A large Cadillac dealership stood guard, looking down onto the freeway on a hill that oversaw the city limits. Once he passed the dealership, the city lights began to diminish. Few residents lived in the western hills. Slowly, the hills began to encroach upon the narrow band of concrete that snaked through the dry hills of sage and chaparral shrubs. In the autumn, the hills would succumb to California's fire season. Long ago the town of Calabasas had garnered fame as a major producer of pumpkins. None could be seen in the dark veil of night that refracted the lights of the speeding cars along gray ribbons of concrete. Faint lights dotted the landscape and grew in brilliance near exits where gas stations and small motels waited beneath the overpasses. Rico drove through the alien country that seemed to be a throwback to California's earlier history, before the building boom of World War II. Passing Calabasas, Rico soon entered the city of Agoura Hills, and the glow of residential and business lights quickly contracted into a landscape of shrubs and live oak. Ahead of his car, Rico saw the glimmering green freeway sign announcing the fast approach of Kanan Dume Road.

"Hey dude," Rico called Juan's attention. "We're almost there. You think they miss us back at school?"

He then laughed hard to himself and stuck his middle finger up against the windshield.

"Fuck 'em," Rico cursed, spying Juan who continued to stare outside his window. "Fuck 'em all! They go to bed and we party!"

Rico felt a rush of energy as the road sign approached and he exited off the Ventura Freeway. When he reached the bottom of the ramp, the Falcon came alongside and stopped. Tom opened his window and began to shout.

"Juan!" Rico yelled. "Open the window, man."

Juan looked hopelessly at Rico and then slowly rolled down his window.

"I know my way there," Tom assured Rico. "Follow me."

"Cool," Rico waved agreeably, barely hearing Tom's voice above the screeching radio.

"I hope I can keep up," he said to Juan, who just listened.

Tom rolled up his window and accelerated ahead of Rico toward the southern direction of Kanan Dume. Rico followed close behind, and the exit lights quickly dissolved into the darkness of the canyon a hundred yards off the exit. During the day, the scenic drive, one of the broadest roads through the Santa Monica hills, provided wide vistas of mountains and native landscapes. Occasionally, a hidden mansion belonging to a Hollywood celebrity or local politico would materialize through the haze of scrub and the concealing hillsides. When the Pacific coast revealed itself, after a broad sinuous slog that lasted less than half an hour, the panorama of the ocean suddenly peeped out from behind a mountainside, only to disappear and reappear several times, like a child concealing himself from playmates during a game of hide-and-seek.

Each ocean vista lingered until the mountains dissolved into low, rambling knolls and the ocean finally captured the whole horizon. Rico enjoyed the ride as a few distant and dim lights darted over the road and hillsides along the way. They travelled through three well-lit tunnels before descending to the shoreline in the late evening. When Rico first saw the darkly mirrored ocean surface, he felt a wave of relief after having driven safely along a highway known for its vehicular accidents. He also felt relieved that he had won the argument to take Kanan Dume instead of Mulholland or Malibu Drive, where death surely awaited drivers behind every twisted turn and scrappy-sage roadside shoulder.

"We're here," Rico announced, feeling a rush of excitement.

Juan muttered some intelligible response but Rico ignored him.

"We get on Pacific Coast and pass the dunes," Rico laid out the course. "Then we'll be at Zuma. We'll go a little past Zuma where there are no patrols. Tom knows where we can park the cars."

"Okay," Juan answered unenthusiastically.

Rico decided not to confront his friend but instead to wait until they reached the beach. He felt that Juan would lighten up when they began to roast snacks and drink. Tom had secretly confided to Rico that he would invite some girls. Rico doubted the story but he played along with Tom, not wishing to dampen the festivities with an argument. Looking at Juan, Rico surmised that one unsettled and discontent seminarian before graduation was enough in his book. Despite his friend's mood, Rico decided he would have a good time.

"Look," Rico pointed out the passing sign. "Zuma!"

Juan glanced to the left where the western shore stretched. A last-quarter moon illuminated the ocean and revealed low, breaking surf that moved in 45-degree angles, leveling out before washing over the sand.

"We missed the tide," Rico commented sadly. "But Tom brought boogie boards too. It should be fun."

Juan appeared to suddenly show some interest as he gazed at the long stretch of beach. Only an occasional, abandoned lifeguard station, perched on gray, wooden stilt, interrupted the scenery.

"Over there," Rico pointed at Tom's car when they reached the end of the public beach.

Turning his headlights off, Tom led Rico to a small, hidden, sandy road amid a cluster of large willow docks, yellow lupine bushes, sagebrush, and the succulent plants common in the area. Moving slowly through the misshapen groves, they parked their cars, hidden from sight of the road, on a carpet of pampas grass and ice plants.

"Shit! It's dark," Juan observed.

"It's always dark in the bushes," Rico retorted.

They both laughed at Rico's double entendre.

"Lighten up, Juan," Rico said pleasantly, noticing that Juan's sad disposition was slowly melting away.

Juan nodded in agreement and looked out the window before facing Rico.

"Let's go party," Juan declared and held out his hand for Rico to slap.

"Cool," Rico exclaimed sliding his palm over Juan's hand. "We gonna party before graduation. Fuck'em all."

Ahead of Rico, Tom and Chris stepped out of the car and opened the trunk, rummaging through several boxes. In the weak moonlight, Rico observed his friends unload some small boxes and a couple of folding chairs. In a rush to join them, Rico pushed opened his door hard, and it bounced back against a thick bush. With slow and steady effort, he again pushed the door open, barely able to slip out. Once outside, the door slammed shut and the bush pinned him against its metal frame.

"Shit," Rico complained as he swiped at the bushes and edged himself away from the driver's side of his car.

Juan sniggered and effortlessly stepped out of the car, walking toward his classmates.

"You smell that?" Juan warned Rico.

Rico paused to take a deep breath when he sensed a whiff of cheap beer and smoke blending among the scent of succulent plants.

"They're probably already drunk," Rico offhandedly commented, strutting right toward his classmates. He ignored the possibility of his friends smoking pot.

Juan followed Rico to the Falcon where Tom and Chris finished unpacking several boxes of beer, some blankets, folding chairs, and a small charcoal barbeque.

"We got wieners and burgers," Tom said proudly when he saw Rico and Juan emerge from behind the bushes.

Rico and Juan stopped to stare as Chris pulled out a cooler and opened the lid.

"Look," Chris called out. Frozen hot dogs and hamburgers had been packed inside a conglomeration of chipped ice and frozen cubes. "We got some chow, dude."

"Where?" Rico challenged him but then silently retracted his statement.

"Ha," Tom laughed, closing the trunk. "You know where."

"The cafeteria," Juan said what everyone already knew. They pilfered all their foodstuffs.

"Let's get to work," Tom invited everyone to follow him. "What did you guys bring?"

"You know," Rico smiled.

Everyone laughed, looking at Juan.

"Got the Mary Jane?" Chris snickered.

"I think you guys tried some already," Rico said in a sardonic tone.

Tom and Chris looked at one another and began to laugh. Juan forced a smile on his face but he did not feel comfortable. His brothers provided him with a lid of marijuana, but at the moment its presence in his pants made him feel uneasy.

"Here," Juan extracted the lid, pulling out a bag of dried stringy leaves from a pouch hidden in his pants.

"All Right," Tom approved. "I got some roaches."

"Cool," Chris concurred.

Without a word, Juan tossed the lid to Chris.

"Hey," Chris fumbled to catch the bag of pot. "Got it."

"Be careful, dude," Tom joked, giving Rico his keys.

He began to carry some of the items.

"Don't forget. Let me get some stuff," Rico told his friends and walked past Juan with his classmates.

Leaving Juan alone, Rico scraped against the bushes to open his trunk. Inside, he pulled out a couple of bottles of wine and his boogie boards, along with towels and small boxes of condiments and buns. Under his clothes, Rico, like his friends, wore his bathing suit, and would take his clothes off once they had settled on the beach. From past experience, they knew that the beach patrol and police would ignore the area, especially during late weekday evening and early morning hours. But the knowledge made him edgy as he looked around before placing his towels on the boogie boards. Satisfied that no legal authority had been hiding nearby, Rico made three jaunts to the Falcon, carrying boxes of items and the boogie boards over his head, so the surface finish would not be damaged. When he finally returned with the bottles of wine, Juan met him by the car, holding out an open can of beer with one hand while finishing a sip of beer with another.

"This shit is cheap," Juan warned Rico.

Rico carefully put down the wine and took the beer.

"Thanks," he expressed his gratitude, taking a quick gulp from the can. "Awful."

Juan laughed as Rico opened his mouth to expel the taste.

"Guess what?" Juan asked not waiting for an answer. "They tossed the beer and are *toking*."

"Chris couldn't wait?" Rico pictured his classmate's jubilation at extracting the homegrown weed.

"My brothers grew it," Juan reminded Rico.

"We better get some before it's gone," Rico half-heartedly joked and placed his can on top of the cooler. "Help me with this shit."

Juan placed his beer next to Rico's and bent over to unload the boxes.

"I really want to do this," Juan confessed, happily lifting the board onto his head. "It will be cool even with the small waves."

"Cool. Take the car keys," Rico handed him the car keys. "I gotta get more stuff. Help me with the other boards and lock it up."

Rico carried off the boxes ahead of Juan. Juan then locked both cars, picked up the boogie boards and walked out to the beach area. He noticed his companions holding a joint with one hand while trying to organize their possessions with another. The awkward failure of setting up the barbeque while getting stoned resembled the TV commercial of a gorilla trying to open a Samsonite suitcase.

"Where you going?" Chris mumbled almost inaudibly. He looked up and took his joint out of his mouth to exhale some smoke. "Good shit. Tell your brothers."

"Thanks," Juan answered half-heartedly, dropping the boogie board.

He then stripped down to his swimsuit and left his clothes in a small pile.

"The water will be fucking freezing!" Tom shouted loudly.

Juan picked up a board and, ignoring his classmates, walked towards the surf. The partial moon cast a dim hue on the water, revealing the sea's white-foamy scum lapping against the dark, wet sand. Stepping on the wet sand, Juan prepared himself for the impending shock.

"It's fucking cold!" Tom called out again and laughed.

The two classmates pointed at Juan and laughed, continuing their comical nonsense of attempting to set up the barbeque as they fumbled with their burning joints. Juan let the board fall onto the sea's low surf line.

"He's serious," Rico commented as Juan began to paddle against the waves.

"Yeah," Tom responded and nodded. "We can join him soon."

Finally setting up the barbeque, Chris howled and laughed off the suggestion.

"Yeah," Rico joked mockingly.

He then noticed the haphazard display of food and cooking utensils on the sand.

"What the fuck are you guys doing?" Rico challenged.

"Nothing," Chris admitted, taking the last drag from his joint. "I fixed it by myself."

They all laughed and Rico began to set up the cooking utensils. Looking out to the sea, he could see medium-sized waves slap the sand and lap at Juan's feet. Rico waved to his friend.

"Cold?" Rico shouted.

"Fuck yeah," Juan confirmed and turned around.

From behind him, Juan could hear his friends' laughter as he prepared himself to feel the shock of the cold Pacific waters. The current carried the frigid temperatures from Alaska before dissipating several hundred miles south of the Mexican border.

"Shit," Juan cursed to himself as he held up the board against the crash of incoming cold waves.

Letting the waves wash over the board, Juan leaped up on the new plateau of seawater and paddled farther out to sea. The sea suddenly became dark, and only the hazy luminescence of the scum provided him a reference point. Fortunately, the moon hung directly west and opposite the shoreline. Juan followed the moon, occasionally adjusting the board's elevation to shield him from another undulation. After a period of fifteen minutes, he had paddled enough of a distance to survey the sea and find the best position from which to aim his board in the direction of the shoreline. With his back against the moon, Juan could make out a faint orange glow on the shoreline that danced in its steel barbeque urn. He paddled gently in a parallel line with the shoreline, enjoying the immense dark silence that surrounded him. The cold sound of splashing water kept him company and drove out the lonely emptiness of the sea.

"Shit. He's far," Tom commented, with a prong in his hand, as he began to extract a hot dog from the licking flames.

All three classmates stared out to sea and saw the faint silhouette of Juan paddling on top of a white boogie board. The pale texture of the board resembled the silver streak of a darting fish against the sea's surface membrane. Several waves shrouded Juan until the next wave pushed him a little closer to the shoreline. Seeing a large wave angling from the north, his classmates watched him motion the board into a favorable position as the turbulent water raced ahead of him. In an instant, Juan's board caught a good wave and glided rapidly forward, riding high on top of it, before it collapsed and engulfed him in a flume of foam and bubbles.

"Shit," Chris shouted, "he wiped out!"

The classmates watched, waiting for Juan to reappear, not knowing if they should dive into the water to rescue their friend.

"You see him?" Chris asked.

Rico watched another wave throw the board ahead of a larger ripple.

"Where did he go?" Chris continued to speculate.

Rico observed the board flipping uncontrollably above and under the rush of turbulent water. As he watched, Rico instinctively began to undress and walk toward the waves.

"He's there," Tom pointed out Juan, south of the shoreline.

"Juan!" Rico called out to his friend who emerged out of a small crashing wave.

Juan staggered out of the water as smaller waves pushed against his back. He stopped wading through the water, looking both north and south of the shoreline.

"Over here!" Rico shouted, pointing to the board. It reappeared north of where he stood.

Juan made an effort to see where Rico had pointed and it took him a long while before spying the board. Waving a sign of gratitude to Rico, Juan dived back into the water and swam in a parallel line toward the boogie board. Lifting it out of the water when he reached it, Juan stood up and waded back to shore.

"Shit," Rico spoke when he stood a few feet away. "That was a wipeout."

Juan stopped walking and looked out to the sea.

"No big deal," he dismissed his friend's concern.

Rico walked toward Juan and handed him a towel, taking his boogie board in hand.

"You're lucky," Tom called to him, holding up a roasted wiener.

Juan smiled and began to towel himself off, rubbing his hair as he walked towards the small barbeque pit. In the distance, a rustle alerted the seminarians, who immediately turned their attention to the sagebrush. Within a few moments, a giggling squeal preceded the emergence of two teenaged girls. Both girls wore similar tie-dyed cotton t-shirts and a wrap over their bikinis. One of the girls had dirty blonde hair, green eyes, and an almost anemic figure. A pattern of squashed freckles lightly spread in patches over her arms and face. She carried an orange plastic beach bag slung over her shoulder. Her Hispanic companion had a full figure and swarthy complexion. Under her arms swung a red cloth purse that closed with a pull-string. They sheepishly waved at the seminarians and walked carefully toward them.

"Over here!" Tom called to them.

"I can't believe it," Rico exclaimed. "I thought it was bullshit."

Rico and Juan reached the barbeque before the girls did.

"I told you some girls were coming," Tom proudly reminded his friends. His voice then dropped a few decibels. "But only two came."

"Where did you meet them?" Rico asked, *sotto voce*.

"Parish Youth Day," Tom explained, waving to the girls. "I got their phone numbers and they have their own car."

Rico and Juan remained silent and nervously watched the girls approach the barbeque. The girls suddenly stopped several feet from the seminarians and smiled awkwardly.

"Hi," the brunette greeted them while her blonde companion continued to smile. "My name is Anna. This is Collette."

"Hi," Collette greeted the boys.

"Please sit down," Tom welcomed the girls and began to spread a blanket. "We are cooking some hot dogs and hamburgers. Help yourself."

The girls sat down facing the sea and also facing the seminarians, who stood in front of them. Tom motioned to his friends to sit down and Chris instantly began to turn over the wieners and hamburgers, looking for the best cooked one. Tom then sat alongside Chris and again motioned to Rico and Juan to join them. They waited for a moment and then Rico offered a forced smile as he sat next to his classmates. Juan stopped rubbing his hair and reluctantly sat down, making sure he remained just outside the circle.

"This is Rico," Chris introduced him. "My name is Chis and this is Tom, as you know."

The three boys smiled and said "Hi" automatically. Chris momentarily panicked, looking for Juan until he saw him with the towel wrapped around his shoulders.

"His name is Juan," Chris introduced his friend.

Collette saw the boogie board next to Rico and began to strike up a conversation.

"You ride it?" she asked Rico.

"Sometimes. Maybe later," Rico smiled shyly and looked over at Juan. "He's the rider tonight."

"Oh," Collette exclaimed impulsively. "I always wanted to try."

"It's damn cold," Tom noted, laughing to himself.

She looked affectionately at Juan, who showed some discomfort at the sudden attention. Chris noticed and chuckled.

"He wiped out a little while ago," Chris mentioned, as if Juan's adventure had been a private joke. "But he's real good at it when it works out."

Chris turned to his friend and gave him a wink, letting Juan know that the blonde liked him.

"Yeah," Collette stood up and walked towards Juan. "Can I?"

Without waiting for an answer, she picked up the board and held it in front of her.

"It's real cold out there," Juan warned, looking out to sea and then at his friends.

Chris again winked a sign of encouragement to Juan who looked past him and at Rico.

"I can take it," Collette said bravely, assuming a posture of defiance.

"Go on, Collette," Anna encouraged her friend.

Tom and Chris laughed and cheered Collette on.

"Okay," Collette nervously accepted the challenge, taking off her t-shirt and cotton wrap. A sudden pall of silence fell on the seminarians as they watched. "Will you show me?"

Juan looked at his friends, searching for an escape from his predicament, but no one seemed to have the will to interfere. Rico only seemed a little sympathetic to Juan's dilemma. Reluctantly, Juan gently took the board away from Collette and walked her to the nearby water.

"Hold up the board," Juan demonstrated as he pointed the tip towards the sea. "Take that small wave and paddle out. Let the wave push you back.

"Okay," Collette responded warmly, not looking at Juan.

He noticed that she stared nervously at the sea.

"Just go for the small waves close to us," Juan added. "It's easy."

Collette took a half-step forward and stopped.

"Can you swim?" Juan asked gently, doubtful about her commitment. "Want me to show you?"

"I can do it," Collette smiled, rejecting his help.

"Go, Collette!" Anna shouted from behind.

Collette turned around to wave at her friend and she then faced the sea. She took the board from Juan and began to walk into the water.

"Oh! Damn," she cursed when she felt the cold water lap against her ankles.

A small burst of laughter erupted from everyone except Juan. Collette instantly looked perturbed and then turned towards the sea. Momentarily looking to Juan for encouragement, she noticed his apprehensive expression. Without waiting for Juan's reassurance, Collette pointed the board into the water and let it fall on top of the water, pushing it in front of her as she waded out to the first small, breaking waves. The board seemed to leap out in front of her and she continued to half-swim and push out with her toes against the sand under the water's surface. Juan could easily see her in front of him as she formed a pale glow moving perpendicularly against the pulsating foam of white water. The black sea encapsulated her silhouette as she swam toward the dark, colorless horizon. Seeing an approaching wave, Collette maneuvered the board in hopes of catching the force of the water and riding it fifty feet back to the shoreline. Miscalculating the break of the wave, the water slammed the board and threw her up before dragging her forward toward the shoreline. The board sprung independently through the air and effortlessly rode the wave to the sand, seeming to tether Collette along. She soon skimmed onto the sand, coughing and spitting out sea water. Her hair clung to her face, neck, and shoulders like algae. Bits of sand were sprinkled in the tangle of hair. Anna and the seminarians immediately sprang forward to help Collette while Juan stood motionlessly aside, watching the drama of the rescue attempt.

"You okay?" Anna shouted, reaching Collette a split second before the seminarians.

Anna began to swipe the sand away from her hair.

"Yeah," Collette answered bitterly, still coughing sea water as Anna tried to remove the web of tangled hair from Collette's face.

"You okay?" Tom shouted.

Collette nodded, and Chris and Tom joined Anna, carefully removing some of the sand and bristles of seaweed that clung to her body. They enjoyed themselves despite the girls' irritation. Rico watched and then noticed the dirty board a few feet away. He looked at Juan's detached mood before picking up the board and carrying it to his friend.

"You got hit worse," Rico concluded, "but she suffered the most."

Rico laughed, as Juan remained aloof from the whole situation.

"Hey," Rico tried to call his friend's attention.

"I can't take this anymore!" Juan exclaimed.

Picking up his clothes, Juan stormed off, leaving Rico alone.

Watching his friend walk past the barbeque, Rico turned around to catch his classmates' attention before turning back to spot Juan's departure from the group.

"What's wrong?" Tom asked, as Anna finished helping Collette clean up.

Rico shrugged and carried the board with him, dropping it off at the camp site. He pursued Juan. In the distance, he could hear Collette asking Anna to go home.

"Juan!" Rico shouted after his friend. "Hold up!"

The sound of Rico's voice spurred Juan to pick up his pace, but Rico managed to run faster and grab his shoulder when they reached the sage bushes.

"What's up, dude?" Rico shouted as he turned his friend around.

"I want to go home," Juan demanded.

"Why?" Rico countered in a half-joking manner. "You don't like girls?"

Juan glared at Rico for a long second as he laughed, and then, Rico, in a flash of pain, found himself on the sand, nursing a bloodied mouth.

"Why'd you hit me?" Rico asked incredulously, tasting the salty blood in his mouth.

"You're an asshole," Juan told his friend. "I tried to tell you. About Mike and the problem."

"What?" Rico demanded to know. "I don't get it!"

"Fuck off!" Juan sprinted to Tom's car and entered the driver's side. "You don't want to."

Juan took out the keys Rico had given him earlier, opened the Falcon's door, and jumped inside.

"Come back! It's not yours!" Rico shouted as an exploding muffler drowned out his warning.

In a flash, Rico understood Juan's allusion and trepidations. A fear gripped him as Juan shifted the Falcon into reverse and pulled out of the covering of the sage bushes. Making a wicked left turn onto the highway, Juan peeled out, accelerating south toward one of the canyon roads.

"What's going on?" Rico heard Tom shout in his ear.

"Juan took the Falcon," Rico explained and stood up, forgetting about his bleeding mouth. He felt a small pang of guilt at not making an extra effort to try to understand his friend. "We gotta go after him."

"Shit!" Tom shouted, stamping the ground with his foot. He looked at Chris who had arrived with the girls. "We'll be back."

"Where're you going?" Chris demanded.

"After Juan," Tom shouted as he pushed Rico towards his Chevelle. "He's got my car."

Rico caught a glimpse of the two befuddled teenage girls before extracting his emergency key from his wallet.

"Let's go home," Collette told Anna.

"Girls," Chris apologized. "They'll be back. Everything will be fine. Let's go to the camp."

Rico witnessed the futility of Chris's promise as the girls ignored his desperate plea while they began to walk toward their car, hidden on the other side of the bushes.

"What's up?" Tom demanded to know as Rico opened his door. He then jumped in the Chevelle with Rico.

"He got mad at me," Rico half-lied.

Rico gunned his car and rushed onto the dark, vacant, coastal highway. Tom looked over at Rico's swollen lip before turning his attention to the highway ahead.

"What did you say?" Tom continued to ask, not looking at Rico.

"It's personal," Rico declined to explain. "Maybe another time? Juan is just mad about some personal stuff."

"We all got shit to deal with," Tom philosophized in a pedestrian manner. "Where is he going with my goddamn car?"

"Let's find out," Rico speculated. "He's probably going back to the seminary."

"Keep going straight," Tom recommended in disbelief. Incredulously, he kept repeating the same phrase over again. "He got my car."

Rico ignored Tom.

"Shit," Tom repeated.

Rico drove south, accelerating to 80 mph. He pushed the Chevelle to the limits of its three-gear transmission. Seeing the Falcon in the distance, he peered over the steering wheel.

"Over there!" Rico pointed out. "I see him."

Tom scrutinized the area ahead and could barely make out the Falcon's brake lights.

"He's turning onto Topanga," Rico detected, quickly slowing the car. "What do we do?"

"Drive to catch up so we can stop him," Tom demanded. "Talk to him! He's got my car!"

"Through that canyon?" Rico answered skeptically.

The Falcon jumped onto the narrow stretch of Topanga Canyon Boulevard, which immediately began to wind uphill through the Santa Monica Mountains. Unlike Kanan Dume, Topanga was a narrow road with poor lighting that masked the dark cliffs below the road's unguarded shoulders. To make matters worse, the early morning fog had begun to creep through the hillsides.

"This is crazy," Tom admitted, barely able to see the red brake lights of the Falcon as it braked intermittently through the twists and turns of the road. "I think his front lights are off."

Rico watched Tom's car slowly race ahead. His car lights projected a wide, yellow mist only several feet ahead of the hood line. They barely revealed the contours of the Falcon's trunk and bumper.

"I can't see," Tom spoke nervously.

The Chevelle made an abrupt turn on a curve, and the back end of the car momentarily fishtailed before Rico steered it back onto the road.

"Shit," Tom cursed. "You can't catch up."

Rico wanted to disagree but he could not, since the Falcon mechanically outclassed the old Chevelle. After a few minutes, the Falcon's brake lights vanished into the deep inky canyon of bushes and trees. They then flared brightly.

"Over there!" Tom shouted.

Rico saw the Falcon lift up in the air and disappear over an oak tree that grew out of the cliff below the canyon road.

"Where did it go?" Rico spoke to himself, not consciously intending to ask Tom.

Within a few moments, Rico passed the spot where the Falcon had disappeared. Both classmates looked left and right. Juan could not be found. Driving slowly forward several hundred yards, Rico made a difficult Y-turn on the tight canyon road and retraced his steps. Nothing could be seen except for shadows and slices of moonlight that speckled the foliage alongside the road.

"There," Tom pointed out the silhouette of a bush, half masked in the darkness and moonlight.

Rico backed up the Chevelle and pointed the headlights at the foliage after parking the car on the opposite side of the road. A decapitated bush, in front of the oak tree, overlooked the wide empty chasm below. On the road that led to the bush, two wide, perpendicular, black tire marks stretched out into oblivion.

"He went off," Tom stated the obvious.

They quickly jumped out of the car and crossed the road. The car's lights created a visible path into the hazy darkness. Then the lights gradually dissolved into the void below. Looking over the side of the road, they could see nothing. Occasionally, the Pacific breeze and the sound of insects broke the silence.

In the early morning hours, the rescue team found the Falcon pinned between two fragmented sandstone boulders atop an ancient volcanic intrusion. Sadly, Juan could not be evacuated until the late afternoon. By the time rescued arrived, Juan had lost too much time. He never made it to graduation.

Phase 16

When Rico awakened, he found himself in a lounge chair watching a 1975 Zenith television set. Instead of sitting in the cafeteria, he sat in an enclosed room with dark brown paneled walls and a rust-colored shag carpet. Rico remembered the room as the senior lounge, which held the weekly Senior Composure Club meeting, where seniors would just "hang out" and watch their favorite TV shows, while gorging themselves on Hershey bars and Coca-Cola. Most of the furniture was absent, along with the FM stereo system. Alongside Rico sat Mike, Juan, and Bill, also in front of the old TV set. Glancing at his classmates before standing up, Rico instinctively turned on the TV and watched Clement's face materialize as a disembodied head. He turned the channel knob several times and Clement's face on the TV screen would vanish only to return on the next channel.

"Too bad we don't have cable or the Internet," Rico quipped and sat back in his chair.

He remained silent, for he was afraid to speak further. The last episode had answered the unspoken question that initiated the whole virtual adventure Bill had created and directed.

"I am sorry," Mike apologized to Juan.

He stood up and walked toward Juan, who appeared reluctant to join his friend. Mike stood over Juan. Rico and Bill watched for his next move. Suddenly, Mike bent over and hugged a stoic Juan.

"It's okay," Mike spoke, as Juan remained physically intractable. "I should have listened."

Teary-eyed, Mike released his embrace and stood up. As he moved to his chair, Juan slowly stood up.

"Mike," Juan called him and coughed uncomfortably. "I love you. So I never told you."

Mike turned around, gazed at Juan, and hugged him again. This time, Juan responded warmly and they remained in a long, friendly embrace. Bill and Rico watched, flabbergasted, until the two classmates separated.

"It was a crush," Juan added, embarrassed.

"I understand," Mike assured him. "A hug is sometimes just a hug."

Juan laughed and Mike joined him. Rico and Bill stood up and all four friends had a group hug for a long while. When they separated, Clement bellowed from the TV set.

"So, gentlemen," he reminded them of their dilemma, "what shall we do now?"

"We?" Rico confronted the avatar. "You are not exactly a seminarian."

For the first time, Clement responded to Rico's taunt with a grinding scowl.

"You know Rico," Bill commented. "You always had a way with people."

Rico sniggered and fell back into his chair.

"He's right," Rico confirmed. "What do we do? Stay in an eternal fantasy until our memories wear out? You and Juan will go first, but Mike and I are next. It's the same in the end."

Bill sat in his chair too and looked at a stolid Clement. Mike and Juan continued to stand up facing their friends.

"We've come to a crossroad," Bill sadly observed. "So to speak."

"We've come to a cross-circuit," Rico made a feeble joke.

"Bad," Juan good-humoredly condemned the joke and sat down.

Mike remained standing and Rico looked up at his pensive friend.

"Mike," Rico entreated. "I am sure you have some theological issues with this dilemma? No?"

Mike continued to reflect as he looked at each of his classmates before speaking.

"We're maybe talking about suicide," Mike spoke uncomfortably. "For me it's a grave sin."

"'To be or not to be,'" Rico quoted Hamlet. "'That is the question.'"

"Try to understand me for a moment," Mike seriously pled. "This is important for me. If we turn off the program, we will kill ourselves. It may have mortal consequences for our souls."

"Souls?" Rico challenged him. "Are you kidding me? Bill, you can turn me off!"

"It's not so simple," Bill stated emphatically.

Rico looked at him for further explanation, but Mike interfered.

"I don't want to revisit your agnostic tendencies again," Mike tried to avoid another philosophical confrontation, although he showed some agitation. "But don't you see any value in religion? Don't you value anyone else's consciousness?"

Rico remained silent, staring into Mike's eyes. Gradually, a small smirk appeared on his face.

"The universe and creation is a thing of awe," Mike admitted. "Science has given us so much to understand and value. It has shown us a new beauty that was hidden and not understood. But there has to be a meaning to all of this beauty. A purpose?"

Rico stood up and touched Mike's shoulder.

"Sit down, Mike. I agree with you in an important way," Rico asked, gently assuring Mike that he would not break into a diatribe. "Listen carefully."

Mike sat down, still looking skeptical.

"Rico," Juan wanted to warn him.

Rico held up his hand to assure him, too.

"Despite past horrors and persecutions, religion can be beneficial," Rico began truthfully.

"But?" Juan probed for the exception to the argument.

Mike looked to Juan in agreement.

"Really," Rico spoke honestly. "You see, religion offers people hope without the dogma and fear. That is what we humanists fail to remember."

Rico paused and saw that Mike was confused but engaged. His words also surprised Bill and Juan.

"Genuinely," Rico continued. "Religion offers people a community and support. It has been a place of refuge and sometimes served as a tool for the search of political justice. As a humanist, I think we speak the essential truth of reality, but we don't address some of the essential needs of humanity—like religion. We need religion but not its godhead."

Mike watched Rico, who held up his hand, asking for his friend's continued indulgence.

"As humanists," Rico clarified. "We would need more than the criticism of religion. Although I know we are right, based on the scientific method, we to offer people more than facts and evidence. It's too dry. There has to be an alternative. But I see that humanists shouldn't reinvent the wheel. They should adapt and recycle what works best in religion and incorporate the essential needs religious people seek."

Mike sat agape and, sensing that Rico wished to say more, waited for him to finish.

"The reasons for religion are the heart of our humanity," Rico concluded. "I think of the beatitudes and what was written even if I may not believe the Son of God spoke them:

Blessed are:

The poor in spirit: for theirs is the peace;

Those who mourn: for they will be comforted;

The meek: for they shall inherit the earth;

Those who hunger and thirst for righteousness: for they will be satisfied;

The merciful: for they will be shown mercy;

The pure in heart: for they shall see goodness;

The peacemakers: for they shall be called children of humanity;

Those who are persecuted for the sake of righteousness: for theirs is their just reward.

All three classmates remained quiet and thoughtful. Mike nodded approvingly.

"You see," Rico apologized. "I made some changes. But the sentiment is the same. Humanists think you can be good without God. I think if a God existed, He would want us to be good without Him. Goodness, love, and respect are their own reward."

Mike stood up and clapped his hands once but hard.

"I wish some of my fellow clergy were as honorable as you are," Mike complimented his friend and hugged him. "But then, we are the last seminarians. So, we see eye to eye on this one."

"Right," Juan agreed, standing up to interrupt their brotherly embrace. "But that just begs the question. What do we do now?"

"I don't want to commit suicide," Mike said forcefully, breaking away from Rico. "Even a virtual suicide. It would still be a sin made with volition."

They then turned to Bill, who smiled widely.

"My idea," Bill offered, "is to put us asleep."

"Asleep," Mike answered doubtfully. "Not terminated."

"Interesting word," Bill contemplated. "No. Just in suspended animation. Asleep. But in time, our memories with degenerate and we will...die. But you won't be the cause of your own death. It will...for lack of a better term...come naturally."

Mike quietly thought about Bill's explanation.

"I can accept it," Mike confirmed. "At least it works for me...you can choose your own course. I don't want to be the direct cause of my own death."

They all looked to one another for an answer, but they immediately agreed with Mike.

"Why not?" Rico spoke for anyone. "Most likely everyone is dead on earth. Technically, we're already dead. It won't hurt. Time most likely will not be an issue."

Bill laughed agreeably.

"Until the orbit decays in a few thousand years," Bill admitted.

"What do we do in our dreams?" Juan asked. "Will it be like my long stay before Mike and Rico came?"

"I have a surprise," Bill told his friends, not directly answering Juan. "We'll begin with an iconic moment from your past. A good moment, I promise. Then you can choose your own path after that. And in the end, the computer will give you the special moment again. Sort of a fond farewell."

"Can we see each other?" Mike inquired. "Are the parameters open?"

"No," Bill denied. "It would squash anyone else's free choice. If one of us changed his mind, all would be trapped by that classmate's decision."

Bill walked over to the TV set and turned it off.

"Goodbye," Clement's voice signed off as his image vanished.

"As you see, I turned him off," Bill explained, facing his friends. "Only one program will remain intact."

"I kind of miss him," Juan quipped jokingly. "Adios, amigo!"

"Really?" Rico said suspiciously. "I don't miss being hit with a pointer."

They spontaneously laughed.

"Well," Bill spoke uneasily, "before we go…I must tell you that I am sorry, Rico."

Rico took a moment to digest his words.

"It's okay," Rico understood his allusion to his daughter, Veronica. "I just wanted to see her. At least one more time."

"I didn't anticipate that the disease would progress…" Bill apologized awkwardly. "I am so sorry."

Rico hugged him and tried to hold back his tears. He failed to do so.

"Goodbye," Mike said warmly to everyone. "We're in God's hands."

Mike hugged Bill and then Juan.

"Or the computer's?" Rico retorted when it was Mike's turn to hug him.

Amused, Mike gave Rico a very long embrace.

"Are we ready?" Bill asked the unavoidable question as Rico and Mike separated.

Rico walked over to Juan and silently hugged him.

"Yes," Juan affirmed when they broke contact.

"'What dreams may come when we have shuffled off this mortal coil,'" Rico recited for his friends.

"'Must give us pause,'" Juan added somberly.

Rico nodded cheerily at Juan. With strong, regretful feelings, they quietly and sadly looked at one another for the last time. The three seminarians then focused their attention on Bill, who walked to the light switch in the room. He affectionately smiled at them.

"Ready?" Bill announced with aplomb. "Lights Off!"

He turned off the switch and the room went completely dark.

Chapter 17

Stay with me,
My love I hope you'll always be
– *Genesis, "Follow You Follow Me"*

When Rico awoke, he stood alone on a knoll in front of California State University's Oviatt Library, overlooking the wandering students and the scenery beyond them, where the science building stood in the distance. Amid the crowd, one coed stood apart. Her svelte figure balanced on lacy, wedge sandals, the young, female student strode with determined attention to her unknown destination. She had pale skin and long, wispy black hair that moved in several directions as if it fought against the speed of her stride and the breeze at her back. Wearing tight-fitting jeans and a multi-colored blouse, she clutched a language textbook close to her small breasts. Her presence caught Rico off-guard, and after he watched for a long time she disappeared into the distant crowd. For the rest of his life, Rico played the moment over and over in his mind. He often fell asleep, dreaming of her on that warm spring morning in his youth. It was his freshman year in college and he fell in love with an unknown woman. The image perpetually remained in his consciousness until the program disintegrated in an orbital burnout. He first took her image with him when Bill's lights went out. It remained with him when his final memories vanished. He was the last seminarian.

PART V

Before landing on Earth, the alien travelers needed answers. The committee of specialists conferred at length and waited for the probes to return from Earth, confirming that no humans had survived. The virus that had killed the humans would not harm the aliens. Humans had made a simple but fateful decision, and the aliens had arrived too late to help.

For the alien travelers, the probes would answer two questions, and so they made their two decisions. The four conscious human programs would remain in orbit until their final decay, and the seminarians would be left with their dreams.. Being sentient themselves, they appreciated the delight and delusion of dreams and hopes. Yet none of the aliens spoke of their secret desire to contact the human programmer, Bill. He truly had humbled them with his advanced programing language. When the second answer came from the committee, the aliens prepared themselves to inherit the Earth. There, new dreams and hopes would await them.

Also by RM DAmato

In 2033, every senior citizen is offered a second chance and a second career. At 65, John Sinclair, a life-long teacher, faces two choices—a second career or permanent retirement and early death. The state will pay for his genetic rehabilitation, university education, and an extended life span of 160 years. It's guaranteed! All Sinclair has to do is to mentor his young apprentice, commit to a new career, and avoid any dealings with a daft and spiteful school janitor, Fernando Smith. Like all incredible offers, Sinclair's new career comes with a toxic price tag. The question is—is he willing to pay?

Random Musings of a Late Baby Boomer explores personal and seminal moments from the early 1960s until the present. Adapting free verse style and conversational tones, the poems meditate upon the universal and existential questions that produce the events that "rub" a life. *Random Musings* rouses the dormant mind and slinks alongside the periphery of space's cold, black abyss with a hot dog as a companion.